I Read It
in the
Wordless Book

I Read It in the Wordless Book

A Novel

Betty Smartt Carter

Betty Smartt Carter

Baker Books

A Division of Baker Book House Co
Grand Rapids, Michigan 49516

© 1996 by Betty Smartt Carter

Published by Baker Books
a division of Baker Book House Company
P.O. Box 6287, Grand Rapids, MI 49516-6287

Printed in the United States of America

Library of Congress Cataloging-in-Publication Data

Carter, Betty Smartt, 1965–
   I read it in the wordless book : a novel / Betty Smartt Carter.
     p. cm.
   ISBN 0-8010-5558-X
   I. Title
  PS3553.A773312 1996
  813′ .54—dc20   95-39834

To
my mother and my father
and to Jon

*B*esides the Rex Dykema Funeral Home, there was no place cooler on a hot day in Dutch Falls, Virginia, than our public library. The man in charge of the thermostat happened to be my father's old schoolmate, Arnie Hagedoorn. Most people knew that Mr. Hagedoorn had been born with defective sweat glands. Nearly everyone in town claimed to have seen him at one time or another turn redder than a vine-ripe tomato without so much as dampening his armpits. Fans of the Falls Christian High Flying Dutchmen liked to tell about the night he saved a tournament game in the final five minutes, coming off the bench to make three fast-break layups before he collapsed and nearly died on the court while the cheerleaders shouted,

> Arnie, Arnie, he's our man,
> If he can't do it, nobody can!

and,

> We don't perspire, we do not sweat,
> The Dutchmen are not beaten yet!

A few years later, when he failed to pass an air force physical, Mr. Hagedoorn went to the old high school track alone and tried to end his life running sprint laps. This time he wilted at the feet of Nancy Talsma, a senior pole vault champion who had come to practice for the state finals. Nancy Talsma sprinted to a phone and called for an ambulance. She held his hand all the way to the hospital. The next day he woke to see her thin face looking down into his.

"Why are you staring at me like that?" he asked.

"Just rest," Nancy said. "You're going to be fine."

After three weeks in the hospital, Mr. Hagedoorn learned that he would have to spend the rest of his life in temperatures of seventy-five degrees or less. As Dutch Falls was a hot piedmont town and as he had no place else to go, the doctors advised him to seek out a cool place of employment—a grocery store, a bank, a theater, or perhaps a library. Most of all he was to avoid humid places with poor ventilation. This came as a great blow, his mother, Arlie Bell, told my grandmother, because Mr. Hagedoorn had always dreamed of becoming the head basketball coach at Falls Christian, spending his days in a stuffy office overlooking the swimming pool.

Instead, he became director of the Betsy DeBoer Memorial Library. It was a large library for a small town, but still not big enough for a member of the Hagedoorn family. They were wealthy people with high aspirations, not one of whom had ever been a librarian. Now that Arnie Hagedoorn sat in the director's office, he behaved like a man who had sacrificed his dreams to be there. He raised fines and he lowered the thermostat. In the thickest humidity of the hottest summer afternoon, long after the public had surrendered to T-shirts and technicolor flip-flops, Mr. Hornstra zipped his Great Depression sweater up to his ears and gulped hot coffee. Mrs. Ernst, at the circulation desk, rubbed her skinny arms to drive away goose bumps. The teenage shelvers practiced blowing smoke rings in the frosty air of the remote basement. Even after a brief visit to the library, it felt good to step out into the heat again. The air rushed through your legs and over your neck, and then—you were back in a steamy Virginia afternoon, the Appomattox sun boiling away all of your impurities.

Only slightly less cool in summer than the public library was the F.R.C. of V., the First Reformed Church of Virginia. Mr. Hagedoorn served as our head deacon, an office that his family had held for generations. Each June he took a week off from work to make our Vacation Bible School the chilliest in the state. That suited us Dutch children, who knew to dress in wool and flannel, but it fell hard on the occasional visitors. When Vietnamese refugees straggled in, or poor farm kids from across the river, or the Baptist triplets whose parents packed them off to one Bible school after another all summer, we shuddered to see their smooth, bare flesh pressed against our cold, metal folding chairs. The most saintly children among us offered them undershirts and cardigans.

Mrs. Hagedoorn, the former Nancy Talsma, directed our Bible school assemblies in the main sanctuary. Each morning we pledged allegiance to the Christian flag and then sat down on chilly pews under the great chandeliers to watch her leaf through the Wordless Book.

"What does the black page stand for?" she would say. Her voice leapt like a pole-vaulter from the loudspeakers above the choir loft.

"SIN!"

"Wonderful, children. What about this red page?"

"THE BLOOD OF JESUS!"

"Wonderful. And the white page?"

"OUR NEW HEARTS!"

"Yes, our new hearts. Washed clean by Jesus' blood."

The green page stood for growth in Christ, and the gold page—shining so bright that you could see yourself in it when she passed the book around—stood for heaven. Heaven was the wonderful place that waited for us after death, where we imagined the dearly departed watching over our comings and goings like people staring into a fishpond.

"I don't know why you children come in those sweaters," Mr. Hagedoorn grumbled as we old-timers stripped them off on the way to the playground. The children who had worn shorts and tank tops ran into the sunshine and just stood, soaking heat back into their skin. Mrs. Hagedoorn gave out snacks on the blacktop—lime Kool-Aid and plain, flat cookies with a hole in the middle. Even in blistering weather her fingers were icy when she gave us our drinks. People said that it took all day to thaw her out after a night with Mr. Hagedoorn.

"How's your father, Carolyn?" she would say to me.

"Fine."

"I'm praying watchcare over him every day."

9

"Thank you, ma'am."

My father was a former army chaplain, still serving as an independent missionary and diplomat in Southeast Asia three years after the withdrawal of American troops from Vietnam. This was the bicentennial year, when we took school field trips to Jamestown and memorized all verses of "America the Beautiful" in junior choir practice—with an added verse made up by Mrs. Nyhof that went,

> America, which God has blessed,
> When will you call his name,
> And strive to know his purposes
> Which on your lives hold claim?
>
> America, America,
> Turn back to his decrees,
> And follow the commandments which
> Thou brought'st o'er foreign seas.

Dominie Grunstra frequently mentioned my father from the pulpit at the F.R.C. of V. He admonished us to pray for prisoners of war still in Communist dungeons and for "our very own war hero, David Grietkirk, winner of the Silver Star, a son of this church, who we all remember saved hundreds of innocent civilians from the hands of the Communists and set up a church for them right there in the jungles of Vietnam—a church that even today proclaims the full faith of the Reformation."

Most currently my father served the Lord in Guam, helping to organize religious services in the refugee camps among the Vietnamese, Cambodians, and Laotians. They were dark, withered people with sunken eyes, sharp cheekbones, and black hair. My grandmother hung their pictures on our refrigerator with vegetable magnets.

"These pictures should remind us of all our blessings," she said. "The people there don't even have homes. They've lost everything. Your father must be a great comfort to them."

I turned twelve the summer Mrs. Hagedoorn had her first baby and retired as our assembly leader. I saw her often at church and at the library, wearing her hair in a green peasant hanky, holding on nobly to her long, flat figure, like a stick of gum in a bell-bottom pantsuit. It was something to be admired, my grandma said, how she tucked that baby in between her kidneys and her spleen. Things became so tight by the middle of June that they rushed her away in an ambulance on the second day of Vacation Bible School, five weeks early, and removed the baby by cesarean. He spent his first days in an incubator at the Baptist hospital, which would surely be the warmest days of his life, some people said, outside the womb. His father stood up in front of our assembly while Dominie Grunstra gave the good news.

"Children, we have a new friend—little Arnold Jakob Hagedoorn Jr. Let's give a round of applause to his parents."

Twenty pews of children clapped and cheered for the Hagedoorns' fertility. Mr. Hagedoorn grinned widely and blushed to the color of his red hair and fiery sideburns. Naturally he didn't break into a sweat. The dominie poked a black-robed elbow into his ribs and shook his hand. Mrs. Betty Vander Weert struck up a verse of "For He's a Jolly Good Fellow" on the organ.

"Since Mrs. Hagedoorn can't be with us this week to lead our little assembly," said the dominie, "let me introduce a friend of our church and a good friend of our virtuoso piano player, Mr. Bob Ferring. She is a beautiful lady who loves God and loves children, too. A lovely, lovely lady. Her husband is studying to be a minister like me—oh, poor guy, don't you think? What a job. Hah. Hah. Tommy Vos, sit down back there. I see you doing that. This is Mrs.—" He looked at a card on the podium. "—Mrs. Jordan. Let's clap and give her a big Dutch Falls welcome. A lovely lady. She ain't a Dutch girl, but she sure is pretty."

I strained to see through shoulders and ponytails as this Mrs. Jordan climbed to the pulpit and stood between the two men. She was a black-haired woman in a short, tight-fitting red sundress and matching pumps. She bounced a little as we clapped and then paused just as still as a model on a dress pattern, one foot turned out slightly and raised at the heel. Mr. Hagedoorn inched close to her, clapping and smiling, and suddenly she smiled back and threw both of her naked brown arms around him for a quick hug and cheek press. He blushed. They made a good-looking pair, if only for a second. The whole auditorium fell into thunderous clapping and cheering, for what I wasn't sure, though I clapped along. Maybe we were clapping just for her, since she was beautiful and there was no denying it. Her hair shone under the chandeliers, full and wavy and brushed against her cheeks so that some of it caught the corners of her shining red lips.

"She's so pretty," whispered Annajane Ten Kate, who was my closest friend.

"Yes," I said. "I hope we can meet her."

The dominie hurried out of a side door in the choir loft. Mr. Hagedoorn rushed to the thermostat, fanning himself.

"Well, how's everybody?" asked Mrs. Jordan.

"FINE!" we all shouted.

"Well, good. Y'all like to sing?" She put her hands on her hips and stepped up close to the microphone.

"YES!"

"Well, good!" She giggled and shook her hair. She grabbed the mike from its stand and nodded at Bob Ferring, our virtuoso pianist. He attacked the keys.

> The Lord said, come on, Joshua,
> Oh yes, come on, Caleb,
> Oh yes, come on, children, and enter into my rest.
> And Joshua said, yes, I want to,
> Caleb said, yes, I want to,
> But the children said, we're afraid to,
> And he said, then you won't be blessed.

Her singing voice was big and throaty, not the tinny vibrato of our own church soloists. She bounced on each step and caressed the microphone like a little silver hamster. She told us to join in and we did, clapping, stomping our feet. The next song had pathos. On the last verse of the song her sheer scarf slid from her neck onto an older boy's lap in a pew down front. He waved it in the air like a trophy. She walked down from the stage and put her arm around Suzy Stam, a girl with a glass eye. Then she climbed up again and told the audience to join her for a foot-stompin' chorus. "Stand up, y'all! Get your blood flowing! Put some life in those dry bones!"

12

At the end of my pew sat Mrs. Ronald Steen, an elder's wife who had taught Vacation Bible School since my father's day. Her mouth was shut so tight that only her lower lip showed, angry blue like a varicose vein. Just behind her sat Mrs. Talsma, little Arnie Hagedoorn's grandmother, furiously cutting felt for a missionary flannelgraph story. She and Mrs. Steen exchanged a hot look. Both of them remained in their seats while we children stood up.

"Whoooo-weeee!" Mrs. Jordan kicked her feet and did a few tap steps on the wooden edge of the platform. We clapped. She winked. Finally the music stopped and she stood there above us, catching her breath and smiling.

I told Grandma about Mrs. Jordan that night. She didn't say much, settled as usual in her after-dinner rocking chair with a black ball of yarn in her lap like a cat. She watched the evening news and knitted me a pair of winter gloves simultaneously.

"She's so pretty, Oma," I said, "almost like a movie actress."

"What did you say her name was again, Carolyn?"

"Mrs. Jordan."

"That's not a Dutch name."

"Well, she isn't Dutch."

Grandma looked up sharply. "Who invited her into the pulpit?"

"The dominie."

"The dominie invited her, then. An English woman. Mrs. Jordan. Mrs. Who Jordan?"

"They didn't say her husband's name."

Grandma bent into the lamplight and squinted at her stitches. "Well, she's surely all right if Dominie Grunstra asked her to sing in church."

"She's a friend of Mr. Bob's."

"Mr. What?"

"Mr. Bob Ferring."

"You mean Bob Ferring? That piano player?"

I nodded. "I saw them talking afterward and she had her arm around him."

Grandma sniffed and began tearing out rows. "You don't need to be noticing things like that at your age. The Lord doesn't like gossips."

The church building felt strangely warm when I arrived the next morning for Bible school. I was only five minutes early, but the halls were empty. A side door stood open. The dominie's study light glowed in his window nearby. I went into the dark corridor, through the checkered tile halls to the coatroom, and then to the main vestibule and dark sanctuary. I sat on the fifth pew with my Bible on my lap, waiting for assembly.

"Carolyn?" I heard after a few minutes.

I turned around. Mrs. Ronald Steen was standing at the light switch.

"Come on out now," she said. "The other children are on the playground."

"But what about assembly?"

She lifted her nose a little. "There won't be an assembly today. Mr. Hagedoorn has gone to the hospital."

On the playground Dominie Grunstra came out to say that Mr. Hagedoorn had been called to his wife's side on account of an emergency. It wasn't the baby, thank the Lord. Little Arnie Jr. was thriving in his incubator, but the doctors had discovered something wrong with Mrs. Hagedoorn. We bowed our heads and prayed. Then Mrs. Ronald Steen served our lime Kool-Aid and flat cookies. We went on to our various classes and no more was said about assemblies that week. I forgot about Mrs. Jordan.

Grandma and I lived across the street from the library, on the eastern edge of downtown Dutch Falls. Dutch Falls was an old and well-planned town, built on a grid like that great northern city designed by Quakers. There were cities in the South, Grandma said, even in Virginia, that might as well have been planned by a bunch of crickets set loose on a drafting board. Roads led nowhere, or changed names multiple times, or disappeared into shady fields and trailer parks only to reappear on the other side. But in Dutch Falls, all roads kept their names from beginning to end. Little roads led to big roads, which led to even bigger roads, which led eventually back to the center of town. And everywhere arrows pointed the way, so that one never need ask directions from English people or strangers. It was a harmonious and orderly way to live. It was Dutch, my grandmother said.

The architecture of the town bore the Dutch stamp, too. Most of our houses were gambrel-roofed brick barns, with clay pantiles imported from Holland and wide porches shaded by latticework and ivy. Up and down our street, people had once sat on these open porches in the evening talking with their neighbors across narrow driveways. Nowadays we watched television indoors and played Rook, rarely socializing in such an informal way with our neighbors. But the Dutch women still glanced out the bedroom windows after dark in case other Dutch women had happened to leave their blinds up. Grandma liked to say that our back-alley neighbor, Mrs. Brinkerhoff, must have prescription glass in her windows because she always knew what the neighbors were doing—when they were washing dishes, when they were spanking their children, or when they were having a secret glass of beer.

Not that Mrs. Brinkerhoff would have needed prescription windows, or even eyeglasses, for that matter. Our houses were built so close together that with only a slight stretch we could shake hands through the windows. This in spite of the fact that there had always been and still was plenty of cheap, undeveloped land in Groot County—rolling meadows, green woods, fallow fields that had not yet given way to subdivisions and strip malls. Only the northwest edge of Dutch Falls—a place called River's Edge, where most of the English lived—was under construction.

Our cramped living in town was not a result of land shortage. It was a result of the Dutch sense of economy of land. What if we needed space for a hospital one day, or a new school, or a road, and all the land had been squandered on nothing more important than keeping our neighbors at a greater distance? And furthermore, why build a new house when you could live in an old one? More than a few old families still lived in the houses their immigrant ancestors had built just after the founding of the first colony—people with names like us: Sikkema, DeGroot, Van Dyke, Van Til, and Hagedoorn.

Our own house was of the newer variety in our neighborhood, only one hundred years old. And yet Grandma promoted an aura of antiquity. While the current fad in American home decor was wall-to-wall shag carpet, she took pride in our polished plank floors. She swept and mopped them each morning. Once a month we hung the faded blue rugs on the clothesline and beat them with brooms. Between beatings she vacuumed them to stiff perfection. The wainscotted walls were always whitewashed, always scrubbed and polished. Our fireplace gleamed with glazed blue tiles from the Netherlands, always clean. Low, teardrop archways separated the dining room from the parlor (we called it the living room), and the parlor from the foyer, and the foyer from the family room, which had once been a library. A dumbwaiter connected the kitchen to the cellar. A flight of stairs next to the first-floor bathroom led to a furnished basement. Another flight from the foyer curled up past the second floor to the third, where Grandma had made a bedroom out of our attic.

My bedroom was on the second floor. From my window I had a clear view of the library, of the Chinese restaurant to the left of it, and of the Ten Kate deli and bakery to the right and down two doors. The cooking at the Ten Kate bakery was all Dutch, from the pickled herring to the flaky *bankets*. Much of our Dutch cooking in Dutch Falls came from cookbooks written in English, but Sadie Ten Kate claimed that her recipes were family secrets, some dating back three or four hundred years.

I often went to the bakery after a morning at the library and stared into the donut cases until Annajane or her mother offered me something. I could always eat the ruined pastry for free, just because I was a friend of Annajane's. Mrs. Ten Kate constantly ruined things. She would apologize to her daughter: "I'm sorry, Anna dear, I meant to grease those pans. . . . I'll make a note to myself not to bake those so long next time. . . . Oh, what was I thinking to set the oven so high?! Would you mind cleaning up the mess, dear? Mommy has a sore back. . . ."

The baking would go more smoothly on Saturdays, when Annajane was home from school. She was only one year ahead of me, but already at thirteen she had an air of authority about her. People who met her guessed her age anywhere between fifteen and twenty-five. She would scoop up a stray toddler to scold him for running in church and visitors would say to her, "What a beautiful child you have!"

The largest buildings in Dutch Falls, other than the library and the courthouse, were churches. There was our First Reformed Church, its stone steeple always sharp and imposing against the sky. Further down on Church Street stood First Presbyterian, towering over tiny Trinity Lutheran and Mt. Sinai Baptist on the next block. Of all the churches in Dutch Falls, First Presbyterian was largest in building size and closest to us in doctrine. At one time it had rivaled First Reformed in Sunday worship attendance—even siphoning off some of the unsatisfied Dutch. But it was going liberal now; it had replaced its prayer chapel with a bowling alley for teenagers. Nobody doubted that First Reformed had the largest Sunday school and prayer meeting of any church in the county. Not only that, but our dominie preached the full and unadulterated counsels of Reformed theology—which sometimes meant preaching on the eighth chapter of Romans for a full year, illuminating the doctrines of predestination and grace and hell in hour-long meditations that left us dreaming of the roasts that slowly stewed for us at home. We could count on attracting all the Dutch church-goers in town, but we also drew in the English Reformed who were disgusted with their own churches. We were Dutch second, said the dominie, and Reformed first.

Make no mistake about it! The F.R.C. of V. was no sister to those great Dutch Reformed congregations up North! The dominie had visited Reformed churches in Michigan, New York, and New Jersey. The Dutch Yankees lived like us in a lot of ways, he said. They ate the food we ate, they kept their houses clean and went to church. They believed in covenantal baptism for their infants and in Christian education for their children. But it seemed to him that many of those unfortunate Christians had compromised their testimony in the world. Tobacco they allowed. Alcohol they condoned, if supposedly in moderation. There were rumors—rumors that we oughtn't to give credence to, but which concerned us, nevertheless—of dancing, card-playing, and questionable language right in the gymnasiums of their schools. What's more, they had watered down true Christianity with worldly philosophies. Norman Vincent Peale was no hero to our Dominie Grunstra.

"Beloved," Dominie Grunstra said, "what's the use in calling ourselves Reformed if we stain ourselves with the philosophies of the world? If we sit in the seat of the unrighteous? If we insist on drinking soda pop instead of milk?"

It was independence, the dominie said, which had saved the F.R.C. of V. from being corrupted by worldly philosophies. Our founder was no dominie at all but a wealthy farmer named Janz DeGroot, who gave up his fortune in Hackensack around 1720 and moved to Virginia in order to preach Dutch Calvinism to apathetic English. Since it was illegal in Virginia at that time to preach anything but Anglicanism, he kept his religious mission a secret, living as a simple farmer. He gathered family and friends from New York and New Jersey—his twelve sisters with their large families, his cousins, his uncles and aunts, his old schoolmates. With their help he established an independent, Reformed church on a farm southwest of Richmond, on the Appomattox River. He preached there by night in a clean, whitewashed barn spread with straw and sawdust, with hymnals piled in stacks against the walls. He preached in English for the sake of the English, but in spite of his best efforts, the English never came. For all his good intentions, Janz DeGroot never preached to anyone but the Dutch. And the Dutch listened, and over time they multiplied. God blessed their fields with rice and corn, their families with children. By 1776, the farm on the river was a thriving village. The barn became the inner hall of a sturdy, wood frame church, which would one day become the gymnasium behind a great stone fortress, which would one day bear the weight of a mighty steeple and electronic bells.

My grandmother told me that Arlie Bell Hagedoorn claimed that her son, Arnie, was a direct male descendant of Janz DeGroot.

"How can that be?" I asked. "They have a different last name."

"That's a question we don't ask," she said.

"Why not?"

"Because we don't want to shame our ancestors."

"Why does Mrs. Hagedoorn tell people if it's shameful?"

"I guess she's not as proud as we are."

Like the Hagedoorns, my family had been at the F.R.C. of V. for generations. My great-grandparents had been married in the old wood frame church, with the iron bell ringing in the steeple tower and horses waiting outside. Grandma said that I'd be married in the splendid stone sanctuary someday, if I chose to be. I wondered if Dominie Grunstra would still be alive then, and if he'd preach his famous "Song of

Solomon" message at my wedding. People who didn't even know the bride and groom would come to a wedding just to hear the dominie preach that sermon. At the height of his oratory he would cry out in an exultant voice about the "joys of marital oneness" and lean forward and say, "For I think you know to WHAT I refer—those of you who have known what it is to be blessed, as I have, with a bride as lovely as Solomon's." And everyone would turn and look at Mrs. Grunstra. She was at least sixty, and no beauty, but who would have questioned a man's adoration of his wife? The older people remembered how Mrs. Grunstra had chased hard after the dominie when he was just a young minister and she was a sixteen-year-old soprano at the peak of the choir loft. It was her Dutch cooking that caught him, she said. Specifically, her *hachee,* Dutch hash with veal, vinegar, and sugar. Her fried pies reeled him in like a thrashing fish.

After my church and my house, I loved the library best. It wasn't beautiful; it had no form or comeliness that could make you want to look on it, none at all. It was a modern, three-story, box-shaped, brick building with a wheelchair ramp instead of a porch. Still, it offered a teetering quietness in its upper regions and a good view of the city. I claimed the third-floor picture window as my own. I sat there most summer afternoons with a book in my hands, sometimes reading and sometimes looking down into the streets for people I knew. I had to be careful. If I laid my book aside for too long, I might feel a warm hand on my neck and turn quickly to see Arnie Hagedoorn standing behind me, a stern look on his red face. He preferred, he said, that things be used for their appropriate purpose. The library was not for loitering. That was not its appropriate purpose. Did I think it was the library's appropriate purpose? No, of course I didn't. Reading was its appropriate purpose. Reading—not relaxing or loitering. Wasn't it amazing that the U.S. government valued reading so much that it set aside massive appropriations each year just so that I, Carrie Grietkirk, could have a place to read? From now on I would try to demonstrate my appreciation by reading rather than loitering.

This was the first summer when I'd rarely seen Mr. Hagedoorn in the library at all. Maybe he lingered at home with Mrs. Hagedoorn and the baby, or maybe he occupied himself at the church. In any case, the library felt warmer without him, in more ways than one. The long-haired English boys loitered brazenly on the human sexuality aisle with no one to stand over their shoulders or peer at them through the shelves. The long-lasting window display on car repair manuals gave way to a needlepoint tribute to John Greenleaf Whittier. I thought the librarians seemed more relaxed, too. When I asked Mrs. Ernst if I could sharpen my pencil at the circulation desk, she didn't warn me sternly about not writing in the books. She hummed a hymn softly as she took my pencil and sharpened it.

"Your daddy's still overseas, isn't he, honey?" she said.

"Um, yes, ma'am."

"I bet you're anxious to see him, aren't you?"

"Yes."

"Well, I'm praying for him. We haven't forgotten our men in the service."

"He's no longer in the service, ma'am. He's a missionary now."

"You just keep hoping that he'll be home soon." She looked at me and her eyes turned a little sad. I thought that she might have lost someone in Vietnam, or maybe even in Korea or World War II. I had seen her wear a yellow ribbon on her long, graying ponytail. Maybe she just liked yellow.

At noon one day, as I sat at my window reading an encyclopedia article on how to build a battery, I started thinking that it was lunchtime and that maybe I would walk over to the Ten Kate bakery for donuts. I looked down through the maples into the shady street. My eyes searched out the big red sign: *Ten Kate Homestyle Dutch Pastries, Pies, and Sandwiches—Always Hot, Always Fresh.* Maybe Mrs. Ten Kate had set out potato cakes today, or *oliebolen,* or better yet chocolate glazed donuts with whipped cream and cherries. Maybe Annajane would sneak me three or even four. I stood up to go and glanced down in the direction of my house. Something white caught my attention. It was Grandma, standing in her white apron in the shade of our porch, waving up in my direction. She stopped for a second, squinted, wiped her face, and waved again. Sometimes a wave meant that we were having company for lunch. Get home quick! Right now! But this wasn't a company wave. She pointed up at the sky and then lifted her other hand and beckoned me sharply, mouthing something. I thought maybe she was telling me to come home because there was a tornado watch. She was terrified of bad weather.

"What?" I mouthed down at her.

"———home!" was all I could understand. I shrugged my shoulders, gathered my things, and went downstairs. She had crossed the street to meet me.

"Your father!" she cried, and stopped, with her hand over her mouth. Her lips trembled and twisted when she tried to speak again. We stood there silently for several seconds, until it slowly dawned on me what she must be trying to say. I had always known it would happen like this. My father had been killed in some kind of accident. We only had each other now. Behind her the traffic rushed by, cars full of people unconcerned about the news.

Grandma took me in her arms in front of the passing lunch traffic and squeezed me so hard that I gasped for breath when she let me go. "Oh, dear, Carolyn," she said finally, through her tears. "I can't believe it. Your father is coming home! He's coming home."

This wasn't what I had expected. She looked deeply into my face, probably hoping to see her own excitement there. I didn't know what to say or do, so I just hugged and kissed her.

2

*W*e didn't shrink from discussing death at the F.R.C. of V. We never winced at talk of disease or pestilence. These were matters for company dinner conversation, for the women's telephone prayer chain, and for Sunday evening sermons. When a visitor once complained that he had never heard such morbid sermons, the dominie answered the charge by launching us into a seven-week series on the mortality of man. He heaped Old Testament references upon us—the death of the firstborn sons in Egypt, the sacrifice of Jephthah's daughter, the suicide of Saul. He told us that a careful consideration of our own mortality would make us stronger in the face of death. Physical suffering, he said, helped us discern God's purposes and make those purposes our own. Disability allowed us to understand our absolute helplessness before God. And bereavement was as bittersweet as the ferment of sacramental wine. The tears wept over the stillborn child or the departed grandfather represented the distillation of God's good work that never ceased in us. One day we would rise up and conquer death even as our Lord had conquered it when he became the firstfruits of the dead.

Death had already visited our house. Grandma often talked about my mother's funeral. "Carolyn, your uncle sang and I just cried. Your mother was so beautiful, inside and out. A godly woman. She knew how to take care of herself. She looked like an angel."

I glanced Grandma over when she said this, white-haired and stooping, but still beautiful. She had once been tall. Her eyes were dense and blue, like the ocean at Virginia Beach. Grandma took pride in her looks. She thought about her own funeral, perhaps, hoping she would look as good, hoping people would say that she had known how to take care of herself. I glanced down at myself—short and curly haired, heavyset, knock-kneed.

"Where was I during the funeral, Oma?"

"At home with Aunt Betsy. You were just two months old, after all, Carolyn. We couldn't count on you to be quiet, could we?"

She wasn't as happy to tell me about the day my mother died, but she was willing when I asked. She told me how my mother's car had spun out and flipped over a guardrail on the icy Powhatan Bridge. She told me that I could have been in the car that day too, except that I had been suffering from terrible colic and Aunt Betsy had urged my mother to take some time alone to pray and read.

"I'll sit with the baby for a few hours," she had said. "You need a break."

For a long time, I thought Aunt Betsy had told my mother, "You need a brake." I wondered why my mother hadn't listened, or whether she hadn't heard as she rushed out the door and drove away in a dangerous automobile. I didn't know what colic was either, and confusing it with "cowlick," I imagined that my mother had been tormented by a lock of my curly hair that wouldn't sit down by itself or fall into place when she combed it. Only now that I was older and took my turn in the nursery at church once a quarter did I understand about small babies that screamed and wriggled out of your arms no matter what you did to comfort them. How easily I could imagine my mother racing away from such a monster, hurtling toward her own death.

Grandma's face grew dark and sad at the end of the story, and she said, "I always look for God's purpose in taking her. Someday I'll ask him myself. But at least he spared you, Carolyn. At least she left you home that day."

In my room hung a portrait of my mother, the kind with satin drapery pinched up in the background and a signature scrawled in gold at the bottom right corner. She leaned with one elbow on some piece of furniture covered with red velvet, smiling at someone she didn't even know, maybe on a day when she wasn't in the mood to smile. But she was frozen that way forever now, a pretty young woman with

23

tinted features—brown hair in a glossy, coiffed style that looked like an upside-down Bundt cake mold, large blue eyes, cheeks blushed to a high pink as if she'd just run up a long flight of steps. Grandma said that my mother's parents had divorced while she was young. My Grandmother Schuyler was dead now, and my grandfather had left town long ago in some forgotten shame. There was no one living in Dutch Falls who could remind us of my mother, not one soul who could keep her alive for us.

However long I stared at my mother's portrait, I could never make myself remember the face later, when I walked home from school or lay in bed in the dark. When I tried to compose the features, they faded. The blue eyes, the pink cheeks, the dark eyelashes—they melted in my mind like watercolors running together in a kitchen sink. Better that I didn't dwell on her anyway, my grandmother said.

My memory of my father was only a little better. He had been gone for seven years altogether. Two or three times over the last five years he had planned to visit us, but each time he had written saying how badly they needed him where he was, how badly he wished he could see us, but how it wasn't God's will just yet.

"That's all in the nature of a hero," Grandma said. "Remember Elijah in the Bible? Remember Paul? They put God's work first because that was their calling. And your father has a calling, too. He'll come home when God brings him."

She had filled the house with pictures of him. When my Uncle Jim once called us the "David Grietkirk Memorial Museum," she didn't laugh. She took the opportunity to tell me all about my father's childhood—how he'd learned to swim at an early age, how he'd always been obedient, how as an Eagle Scout he had rescued a child from a city sewer. Uncle Jim said she made him sound like Lassie.

"Never you mind," she said, looking past him to me. "You can be proud of your father, Carolyn; never mind what Jim says." She pointed to a picture over the television of my father graduating from high school. "The dominie let him preach his first sermon when he was no older than that," she said. "He was so smart, I hardly understood a word of it."

I had few memories of my father that were all my own—a soft voice, a walk through a field of dry grass that smelled like onions, a spanking over something to do with a cheese sandwich. That was it. But I had his letters. He wrote us from exotic places: Pakistan, Cambodia, Japan, Thailand, the Philippines. The envelopes were thin and blue and smelled like a man's hand. They had fancy stamps—the heads of kings and queens, the peaks of famous mountains, and exotic flowers—all tracked and scarred by the black tattoo of the posting machine. Grandma steamed the stamps off carefully to save them for my cousins, Shirley and Victoria, who had long since outgrown stamp collecting and would probably only sneer at them. She opened the envelopes, first turning them upside down to let the clippings fall out—jokes and anecdotes cut out of the *Stars and Stripes* and the *Military Faith Digest,* which my father still read faithfully. She read the jokes aloud and we laughed, though we didn't always understand. Finally, she read what he had written in his own hand on paper as thin as tissue. Usually it was brief and light:

Dearest Mama and Carolyn,

    Greetings from the Santiago Refugee Resettlement Camp in Manila. I met a lovely lady who reminds me of you, Mama. She's the new head nurse here, in charge of all the medical personnel at the camp. She just got off the plane from Milwaukee a month ago and already she has this place whipped into tip-top shape. I told her she reminded me of someone back home. She said, "Wait, Pastor, I hope you're not going to say I remind you of your mother. Boy, have I heard that one before!"

"Well, I hope he won't be bringing her home to meet me," said Grandma to that. "She sounds flippant."

My father always finished his letters by saying that he would come back as soon as he could, as soon as he felt God telling him that his work was done. He blew kisses to me and Grandma and sent hugs to everyone else. "See you soon," he said, "if God wills it. Pray every day that he will make his will known." Now that he was really coming home, I went into Grandma's room and found all of his letters in a big box under the bed. I read them. I put them away again in order. I wondered what it would be like to see him in the flesh.

I imagined that he was like my Uncle Jim. Jim lived in Charlottesville and came to visit often with Aunt Betsy and my cousins. He was six years older than my father, which put him in his mid-forties, but no one would have guessed his age at anything under fifty-five. He was a tall man with leathery skin and silver hair that always looked blow-dried. According to my cousin Shirley, he used a curling iron to straighten the waves on top. Always there was an air of righteous extravagance about him. Grandma lamented the fact that he could never do anything in moderation.

"When Jim was just a boy," she said, "he broke six bones in six different football games. Then he grew up and got married and became an Arminian and took that course in door-to-door evangelism. He went from house to house arguing with all those English, until poor Betsy complained that she never saw him. Then he took those singing lessons and decided he was going to be a crusade singer. He sang so loud I was embarrassed to sit with him in church."

Finally, she said, in the late 1960s, Uncle Jim took three courses by correspondence from Westminster Seminary in Philadelphia. And through the mail, he repented of his Arminianism and returned to the Calvinism of his youth. Any other Dutch family would have been glad to rescue an eldest son from the clutches of the free-willers, but Grandma had revivalist tendencies. She watched Billy Graham on television and even ordered his books by telephone at the commercials. She supported missionaries who were not Dutch, people she had only read about in Christian magazines.

"I don't like your attitude, Jim," she often said to my uncle. "You ought to have more moderation. We're all Reformed in this house, but you walk around with a tulip pinned to your collar."

T.U.L.I.P., of course, was the famous acronym for the five points of Calvinist theology. The "T" stood for the total depravity of man, the absolute inability of a human being to do anything absolutely right. Uncle Jim liked to tease Grandma. He told her that total depravity was his favorite doctrine, that her grandchildren were black with original sin, that they were nothing but vipers in diapers, that goodness had to be struck into them with a rod of mercy.

"Don't listen to him, Mother," Aunt Betsy said. "Jim doesn't mean anything; do you, Jim?"

"My mother knows me better than you, Betsy," Uncle Jim said. "After all, she lived with my father. Now he was a man without moderation. There were a lot of hard rules to follow in the old days. Isn't that true, Mother? I remember him saying to Josephine, 'No radio in this house, young lady. That's just another form of cinema, and you know who the cinema belongs to.'"

Grandma frowned. "Don't mock your father. He was a good man."

There were rules enough at Uncle Jim's house. Shirley and Victoria could not wear blue jeans. They could not say "gosh" or "gee" or "good grief," which were really casual substitutes for the name of God—blasphemy in the eyes of the Lord. They could not buy Donny Osmond records or Donny Osmond posters or lunchboxes, since any money spent on that stuff went to buy robes for the Mormon Tabernacle Choir. Television was forbidden on account of the three B's— beer commercials, bed scenes, and blasphemy. At our house, now that Grandpa was dead, we watched plenty of T.V., and when my cousins visited, they were happy to join in. Victoria and Shirley stretched on the floor in front of the television. Even Aunt Betsy watched with us over her needlepoint, until my uncle noticed.

"Dear, dear, isn't this terrible?" Aunt Betsy would say to her husband as he happened to pass through the family room when a pretty T.V. lady was pulling on her panty hose. "I can't understand how our country has sunk to this level."

"Why don't you turn it off, then? Turn it off, Victoria."

"Yes, Vicky, turn it off," Aunt Betsy would say weakly. "We can't have you all desensitized to evil, can we?"

"But Mama," Vicky would say, "Daddy—"

"No argument. Turn it off, Victoria."

Victoria was the oldest, the one who always obeyed. Shirley argued. "I hate you! I hate you! What right do you have?"

"Shirley!" Aunt Betsy would say in a voice full of dread. "The way you're talking to your father, I'm ashamed. Jim, tell her not to talk to you that way."

"Betsy, she's vexed in her spirit. What can I do about that? It's probably in her genes. She sounds just like my sister, Jo."

Grandma and I would sigh and look longingly at the television.

My father wrote again to say that he would be flying in on the afternoon of the bicentennial, only a few Sundays away. We had been planning to leave church and drive straight to colonial Williamsburg for the fireworks and parade, but now we would stay home and watch the fireworks here.

"At least it'll be cheaper than Williamsburg," said Grandma, who thought it unpatriotic for anyone to charge admission to enter the cradle of our nation. "And if people around here really want to celebrate freedom," she said, "then they ought to celebrate the return of a real American war hero." Her mind turned on this for a while. Then one night at dinner she announced, "I've told the dominie that I'm going to give your father a bicentennial welcome home party. That'll show those English how patriotic we Dutch are. I'll invite everyone, and I'll bring all my children home, for the first time in ten years!"

Of course she was thinking now about my Aunt Josephine. Aunt Jo lived in New York City. So long had she been away from home that I couldn't remember ever meeting her. I knew her only from a small picture hanging by itself on the guest bedroom wall, a snapshot of a plump, red-haired, frowning woman in a green polka-dot dress next to a boy of about eight. The boy was her son, Nathan, now a teenager. No one ever told me what had happened to Nathan's father, or why Aunt Jo never visited us and only called Grandma late at night. I heard Grandma on the phone sometimes, at least her loud crying and arguing. "Think what your father would say! Have you forgotten about God, Josephine? All right, all right, then think of your brother David. Risking his life for God every day. You should get out of that city and come home."

In our devotions after dinner each night Grandma prayed about Jo's steady man-friend, Roger—or maybe it was Robert—whose vices were certainly better known to God than us, but who surely smoked cigarettes and drank beer and probably did worse things, things not fit to be mentioned in public. If Jo married him, she would certainly be unequally yoked, as the Bible said, to a nonbeliever, not to mention an English, or worse. Grandma fretted over the situation, asking God to soften Jo's heart and to build walls between Nathan and the devil and bring him sound Christian influence.

Now, in these few weeks before my father's return, Grandma prayed that Jo would come back to Dutch Falls and bring Nathan with her, so that the family could be together again, so that there could be true Christian healing. One night in a long bout of anguished devotional prayer, she determined that she would call Jo on the phone and talk her into it. She asked for strength, patience, humility, and peace in the conversation. Then she went immediately after devotions to the phone. She dialed the number in New York. Before long she was arguing so loudly that I clearly heard her saying, "I don't want to hear about Roger's—or Robert's—plans, your brother has escaped the jaws of death and you're going to be here to celebrate."

In the end it didn't really matter that much about Jo, whether she came or not. What mattered was that HE would come—my father, at last. He would be there, in just days. Home. Ordinarily Grandma rested in the evenings. She knitted in front of game shows or played Solitaire next to the radio. Now she ran in circles around the house fluffing couch cushions and pruning healthy plants.

Just before bed, she put her feet up and turned down the sound on the television to tell me things about my father. "He's the most reasonable person you'd ever hope to meet," she said. "The only one in the family who could get along with your Uncle Jim and your Aunt Jo at the same time. He'll let you know what he thinks, all right, but he's not the kind to argue. You'll see that. I can't remember when I've had a quarrel with Davey, in fact. He's always been my good boy. So you be a good girl, Carolyn, and do everything your father says. Because he's a father you can trust.

"Your father will be home day after day after day after tomorrow," Grandma said. And then, "Your father will be home day after day after tomorrow." And then, "Your father will be home day after tomorrow—and I better call Louise and get over to the church this afternoon, because that fellowship hall is a mess and I want it clean, clean, clean!"

She took me to the Empire Square Shopping Center that morning, two days before he was to arrive, to buy a new dress and a pair of shoes. She bought me a pink jumper and got herself a blue-and-red-checked dress with a white belt and an American flag pin to wear at the neck. We had lunch at Dryfout's Cafeteria and then we went home and she changed into a baggy gingham dress and rubber-soled shoes.

"I'll be at the church all afternoon," she said, leaning forward toward the bathroom mirror with a bobby pin between her teeth. She was combing her white hair back into a tight bun, as tight as an onion. "If Aunt Jo calls, don't you talk to her yourself. Tell her I'll call her tonight. Tell her I want her to be here by tomorrow night."

"How can I tell her anything if I'm not allowed to talk to her?"

"Don't be smart; you know exactly what I mean. One sentence won't hurt a thing—'Grandma wants you here by tomorrow night.'"

"But what if she asks me a question? What do I say?"

"Just tell her you're a good girl and always do what your grandma says."

"But that would be lying."

"Oh, Carolyn, never you mind. Run over to the library if you want. Keep out of mischief."

Upstairs in the library, I watched Grandma walk down Beatenbough and turn the corner, taking the shortest route to Church Street. Paper rolls and streamers flew from a paper bag in her arms, scissors and glue bounced in the pockets of her apron. Grandma rarely drove anywhere, no matter how many things she had to carry. Next door to the church, Louise Van Dyke would back her old Nova out of her narrow driveway and creep into the church lot just a few feet away. Everywhere Louise went, she drove. Louise had been Grandma's friend for years.

The two of them would meet in the playground and pat the sweat off their faces with handkerchiefs. They would gesture at the flower beds wilting against the red brick walls in the afternoon heat. They would gesture at the sun. They would enter the building at the big yellow side door and let it shut slowly behind them. With their voices echoing in the stairwell, they would descend to the basement, to the wide room under the sanctuary with orange tile and long tables. We called this room the "fellowship hall," and it was the scene of wedding receptions on most summer weekend afternoons. Children came to eat cake with heavy white frosting and to throw rice as hard as they could, hard enough to sting flesh and make mascara run. The hall and the stairwell always smelled like coffee. Grandma must have worked hard to reserve such a fine place on a Sunday afternoon in early July.

I was thinking of wedding cake when I heard two sets of footsteps and a familiar voice on the other side of a row of school yearbooks.

"Well, hiya, Arnie! Could you direct me to the elevator?"

"Uh, the elevator? I sure can." Mr. Hagedoorn's voice was warmer than usual. "There you go, Mrs. Jordan, right there on the other side of those shelves. You have a good day now; come back and see us."

"Thanks, hon."

"Promise?"

"Sure."

I didn't recognize the woman's name at first, but I tensed up, prepared to smile as she came my way. She walked by me whistling and smiling, without even looking down at me or at my books spread out on the table. But I glanced up just long enough to recognize her as the beautiful woman from Bible school, the beautiful English woman who had actually danced in high heels and a short skirt in the dominie's pulpit. I started to speak and then the elevator swooped her away. Mr. Hagedoorn's footsteps went slowly off in the direction of the stairwell.

I had been reading for hours. I gathered up my books and left. It was a hazy afternoon with a hot breeze. On afternoons like this, sulfuric smog drifted west to us from Hopewell and Petersburg and sat stinking low in the air. The heat from the pavement steamed up around my ankles. I didn't want to go home yet. *Mary Poppins* was playing at the Valley Orbitron, and though I had seen it five times already, I had money in my pocket and I thought I could make the matinee again today, if I ran.

Of course, I was forbidden to see any movie, at any time, under any circumstances. Like most of the Dutch, Grandma strictly opposed most forms of public entertainment, bragging that she hadn't set foot in a theater since 1935. She said that moving pictures incited people to sins even worse than drinking. Sins worse than drinking? I asked her what sins. She said, "Well, it's all one and the same. If you go to the movies today, tomorrow you'll be doing worse." I had sinned grievously so many times. On this particular afternoon, before I had gone very far, someone beckoned to me a few yards down on the sidewalk.

A tan woman with bright lipstick. It was Mrs. Jordan again. Now she had noticed me, and she wanted to speak to me. I went over to her eagerly.

"What's your name, kiddo?" she said with a wide smile. She wore a yellow knit sundress and a short-brimmed yellow hat that framed her dark hair and eyes like a sparkling halo.

"Carolyn Grietkirk," I said. "I recognized you upstairs in the library, talking to Mr. Hagedoorn."

"Oh, Arnie? Isn't he a cutie? I love his freckles. Listen, kiddo, do you ever baby-sit?"

"Yes, ma'am."

"Would you by any chance be able to baby-sit for me this afternoon? I have an emergency and I have to run out. I just need someone to watch the kids for an hour or two."

"Yes, ma'am, I can do it." I was thinking that Grandma would be too busy to notice.

She patted me on the shoulder and put her arm around me, her brass bracelets clinking as we walked a block to a dirty yellow station wagon. Her four children were waiting there in the heat, all boys. The oldest, maybe a year or two younger than I, put his head out the window.

"Hey, hurry up. We're dying in here."

The baby began to cry. Mrs. Jordan smiled and made a face at him. "Oh, it's a hard life, isn't it, Floyd? Mama's such a pain in the neck, staying in that big library so long." She opened my door and then drifted around to the driver's side, stopping once to grin and wave at someone in the passing traffic. The car smelled like sour milk and french fries. Under my feet was a rolled-up disposable diaper. I kicked it under the seat.

"Mama!" cried one of the middle boys. He looked about seven.

Mrs. Jordan was still outside the car, bent over in her open door, searching around for something on the floor.

"Mama, Peter made my mole bleed."

"Shut up; I did not," said the oldest.

"Peter," said Mrs. Jordan, in a patient voice, "do you want to give your brother a melanoma? Do you want him to be sick and crippled?

Do you want to feed him through a tube every day of his life until he's old and change his stinky diapers and wash his dirty hair?"

"Yes," said Peter.

"No, you don't. Leave his moles alone."

"Mama," said Paul, "now he's pulling up my underwear."

"Boys!" yelled Mrs. Jordan, and she climbed into the car and swung the door shut with one graceful motion, like an astronaut climbing back into a space capsule. "Boys, hush for a minute. This is Carla."

"Carolyn," I said. "You can call me Carrie."

"Carrie, this is Paul." She pointed to the one with the bleeding mole, "and this is John. John and Paul are my twins—yes, I know they don't look a thing alike. And this is Peter, my oldest. And this is Floyd, my baby. He's not even a year old yet and he's got us all wrapped around his little finger. Just like his mother, has to be the center of attention. Peter, put Floyd back in his car seat. O.K., I've got my keys; let's go. Did you hear me, Peter? Leave Paul alone."

She started the car and we drove off in a hurry. She did not handle an automobile as Dutch women did, who considered driving to be a slow and careful art, like surgery or cake decorating. She revved the motor at red lights and peeled away when the lights turned green. She sped up beyond a sign that said "Deaf Child at Play" and slowed down in front of a truck that wanted to get by. While we rushed along and while the baby cried, I told her that everyone at Bible school hoped she would come back next year. She laughed and said she was glad we liked her. She'd had fun visiting our church and had made a lot of new friends. She liked Arnie Hagedoorn. She had never visited libraries before, but now she loved the library and came there as often as she could. She didn't read much. She just liked the place.

"I do too," I said. "It's my favorite place."

"Oh, your favorite place." She laughed. "Well, I myself wouldn't go that far. But I do think that Arnie Hagedoorn is something special."

We drove to the northwest edge of town, to the English neighborhood called River's Edge. It was one of the older neighborhoods just east of the Powhatan Bridge. On all sides of it the land was being cleared to make room for ranch-style houses, most of them clustered around a long, flat shopping center called Riverchase, which the

Dutch disapproved of just because it had such an extravagantly large parking lot. As you drove down the Powhatan highway you could look straight through charred and crumbled tree husks to the Appomattox River flowing by at a steady pace. On dry days you heard tree saws bleating from no direction in particular and from every direction, loud and obnoxious in your open windows. You smelled fresh, dying pine. But Mrs. Jordan stopped before we reached the construction and turned down a street that hadn't been brand-new in at least fifteen years. The trees had come back on this street, though not the hardwoods. Skinny pines bristled everywhere like needles in a pin cushion.

"Home again, home again, jiggety-jig!" she said. We pulled up the steep driveway of a pea-green split-level with bright red shutters. The older boys threw open their doors and ran for the house. Floyd started to cry in the back.

"Oh, no, not again," Mrs. Jordan moaned. "Look at the time. Would you mind getting him, Carla? I need to run right in and put my face on. Listen, I can't tell you how much I appreciate this."

I started to say that I had done plenty of baby-sitting in my life and that I came highly recommended from everyone, including Dominie and Mrs. Grunstra, but she was already out of the car and halfway up the drive. I struggled to get Floyd out of his car seat. He screamed and kicked as we walked up to the door by ourselves.

"Hello?" I called in the doorway. "Is it O.K. if I just walk in?" Because no one answered, I did.

"I'll be there in a minute, kiddo!" Mrs. Jordan's voice drifted down from somewhere above. I set Floyd on the floor and walked over to the foot of the front hall steps. I climbed to the third step and saw her waving from a door at the end of the upstairs hall. There were perfect circles of bright red rouge on her cheeks. "Why don't you go down and meet Frankenstein," she said. "How old are you, anyway?"

"I'm twelve," I said.

"Oh, my gosh, I thought you were at least thirteen. Well, don't tell Frankenstein. Down the hall, to the right, down the stairs. Be careful what you say."

I walked hesitantly down the hall into the kitchen, still not sure

34

what she was talking about. Who was Frankenstein? Behind me and upstairs the boys were yelling.

"FRANK!" Mrs. Jordan yelled. "FRANK-EN-STEIN!"

"What?" It was a soft, sad male voice from a room below.

"TALK TO THE BABY-SITTER! I'M SENDING HER DOWN!"

I turned to my right and walked down a short flight of steps into a large room with mustard-colored shag carpet. A couch hunched against one wall, covered in clear plastic. An upright piano stood in the corner nearest me, next to a bright patio window. I noticed a film of dust on the keys of the piano—did anyone ever play it? Did Mrs. Jordan? Across the room was an old television with an exposed metal prong where a channel dial had once been. Sitting on its wheeled stand, the T.V. looked like an elderly invalid, sunning itself in the window.

"Come on in," said that sad male voice. I turned and saw him in the corner, on the other side of the piano. Frankenstein. He sat on a hard kitchen chair with a large book open on his lap. How strange that I hadn't seen him at first. He was a handsome man. His shoulder-length hair and long beard looped down in dark strings like seaweed. His eyes were heavy and dark.

"Hi," I said.

"Hi," he replied.

I sat down on the couch. The plastic bunched around my legs. I moved slightly and it sucked at the backs of my knees.

"It's a hot one," he said. "You might rather sit on the floor."

"I'm fine, sir."

"I guess my wife wants me to take her to the movies."

"I don't know. She didn't tell me."

"That's what she wants, all right. It's hot and I hate the movies, but she wants me to take her to the movies."

"I guess so," I said.

"I have a ton of work to do. But you know what comes first around here."

"The movies?"

"You betcha."

I remembered then that he was in seminary. "My father's in the ministry," I said.

"Oh, he is? And where does he minister?"

"He's a missionary overseas. He was in Vietnam. He's coming home soon. I haven't seen him in seven years."

"Oh, really?" he said, sighing through his nose. "I was in Vietnam. A few years back. How old are you, anyway?"

I heard a noise behind me on the steps and turned. Mrs. Jordan entered the room in a silky orange skirt that flapped behind her ankles. The perfect circles of rouge on her cheeks had been shaped into perfect triangles. She wore a wide, white hat. "Carla will be fourteen," she said.

"When," he asked, "in six years?"

This offended me, and it must have offended her, too. She turned up her nose. "She's old enough, Frank. She's at least as old as that girl in *Taxi Driver*."

"I surrender." He threw up his hands and slapped his book shut.

"You better get ready," she said. "Movie starts in fifteen minutes."

"I better get ready, then." He slumped up the steps to the kitchen and around the corner. His feet creaked on the longer staircase. She rolled her eyes when he was gone.

"Thank God," she said. "I couldn't have lived another day without the movies."

"Couldn't you go alone?" I said.

"Are you kidding?" She looked incredulous. "By myself?"

"I do it all the time."

She shrugged her shoulders. "I would kill myself if I ever had to go to the movies alone. Even going with Frank is better than that."

"Yes, ma'am," I said.

"Come upstairs, Carla. Talk to me while I finish my makeup."

I followed her up and sat at the top of the steps, where I could just see the hem of her skirt around the door frame. She talked steadily about mascara, how she never washed it off, so it just caked up like layers of mud. After several minutes she stepped back and stared into me with her eyebrows raised and her mouth turned down. "How do I look? Is this eye shadow too crazy?"

"No," I said. It glittered rosy pink above the black rim of her eyeliner.

"I wish I could start over. But there's no time." She moved out of sight again and shouted, "Hurry, Frank! I don't want to miss the previews! Come on!"

I went back downstairs and sat alone in the kitchen. After a moment Ginger pounded down the steps in her hard shoes. "Frank!" she called. "I'm losing patience!" She groaned and walked straight out the front door, letting the screen slam behind her. Outside, the car door creaked open and crashed shut.

Mr. Jordan came downstairs at last, wearing wire-frame sunglasses that sat high on his nose. His hair was wetted down and combed flat against the sides of his face.

"Have a good time," I said. "See you later."

"Stay alive," he said. He ambled slowly outside. The engine revved. Metal scraped concrete as they pulled away.

The house was humid, an English house designed for air conditioning, but without air conditioning. The ceilings hung low and no breeze blew from porch to kitchen. Now that the Jordans had left, I wanted to put my head down and sleep. But I heard the children shouting and bumping the walls upstairs.

"Hey!" I called out. "Hey, be careful up there!" I went to the bottom of the steps and called, "What are you doing up there?"

The door across from the bathroom banged against its frame. A plaque reading "As for me and my house, we will serve the Lord" jumped off the wall and bounced when it landed. But no one answered.

"Anybody up there?" I shouted. "I said, anybody up there?"

The answer was muffled. "No, there ain't anybody up here! So just mind your own business!"

I waited for a moment, thinking, then I left them alone and searched for something to do. There was nothing to watch on television unless you liked westerns or wanted to know how to make a pantsuit. I looked through the kitchen cabinets for a snack but found only old magazines, matches, candy bar wrappers, tube socks, plastic curlers, dried-up magic markers, and playing cards. Behind some tomato-stained plastic dishes, back between some greasy pots that smelled like popcorn, stood a half-empty bottle of wine. So the Jordans were drinking people. We, the Grietkirks, were not drinking people, of course, though we often talked about drinking people. The issue had come up two nights ago, in connection with Aunt Jo and her man-friend.

"You don't think he would bring liquor to the party, do you?" Grandma had said to Uncle Jim on the phone, talking about how Roger, or Robert, would behave at my father's homecoming. "You never know what to expect from worldly people." Of course by "worldly people" she only meant English, or non-Dutch.

"Just let Jo try to bring liquor into that party," Uncle Jim had said. "That'll give me the opportunity I've been looking for all my life, the opportunity to turn her over my knee and let her have it."

Besides the wine in the Jordans' cabinet, I found a crushed cigarette carton in the back of the silverware drawer and rock and roll records under the stereo in the dining room. Cigarettes were taboo in our house, and most of our record albums had titles like "John and Roxella Van Icke Play Your Favorites on the Accordion" and "Crusade Giants." I kept searching until I discovered a box of family photographs and newspaper clippings in a banged-up buffet cabinet. I shook out the box and spread the photographs across the floor in perfect rows as if setting up for a game of Concentration. The children's school photos I cast aside. What did I care about a younger Peter, with ears like airplane wings and no teeth? I didn't like Peter, or any of the children. For my purposes I chose the oldest photos, the black and white snapshots of Mr. and Mrs. Jordan in their wedding clothes, running buoyantly toward the camera down an aisle of rice and flowers. I studied Mr. Jordan as a younger man, beardless and smiling. I studied Mrs. Jordan, young and fresh and brilliantly pretty, her tan skin glowing at the edges of her dress.

I made a separate pile of Polaroid snapshots from the same period—jagged palm trees, an orange-streaked sky over the back of a convertible, a white beach, a swimming pool. Mrs. Jordan appeared in each scene, smiling under heavy sunglasses and sometimes fidgeting with the strings of a lemon yellow bikini. I decided that these were honeymoon pictures and I shuffled deeply in the pile on the floor, looking for a motel room in the background, or even better, a shot of the motel bed itself. Something to prove that the unthinkable event had happened, as if I needed proof with four boys stomping around upstairs. I found nothing, just a new series of an overweight, short-haired, smiling Mrs. Jordan and a long-haired Mr. Jordan with a Bible under his arm. I pushed ahead and found several magazine photos and newspaper clippings of Mrs. Jordan smiling under thick, white face paint and heavy eyeliner streaked up like accent marks on her temples. Only her mouth did I recognize—her wide smile. I couldn't tell where these photos belonged chronologically, before the short hair and cigarettes or after.

"Richmond Girl Lands Role in Broadway Production," one of the newspaper headlines read. I scanned the column quickly:

> Ginger Davalotti, the Richmond beauty who enchanted local audiences two seasons ago in *Oklahoma* and *Showboat,* has won a small, but pivotal role in the long-running Broadway production of *The King and I.* Out of 2,500 girls who auditioned, Miss Davalotti was chosen, according to Broadway watcher Rebel Cartwright, for her stunning smile and unique vocal qualities.
>
> "A talent like hers is truly rare, leading one to make comparisons with the greatest stage actresses of our time, though only time will tell whether her extraordinary stage presence is enough to take her to the top," remarked Ms. Cartwright. Miss Davalotti could not be reached for comment, as she has been honeymooning with her new actor husband, Frank Jordan, in Florida.

The theater. She was an actress. I stared at the paper, letting the truth of it sink in, and then I heard a noise on the stairs. I dropped the clippings and scrambled to my feet. Peter came into the dining room. He scowled when he saw the pile of photographs on the floor.

"What's the matter?" I said.

He sprang forward and knocked me back off my knees. "Those belong to my mama!" he yelled. My ankle twisted under my tailbone. My head hit the corner of the buffet.

"Ow!" I said. "Get off me!"

He pinned me down by the arms. My leg was still twisted underneath me. I didn't have the leverage to push him off. "You're stealing!" he shouted. "You thief! You have to be punished."

"I'm not a thief," I said. "I was just looking at some old pictures."

"Don't you know that thieves will be persecuted?" He squeezed my arms, digging into the skin as hard as he could with his fingernails.

"I'm not stealing. You're crazy."

"I could break your arms."

"Please stop, Peter."

He put his face down almost to mine and blinked. He was considering. "Are you filled with the Spirit?" he said.

"Am I what?"

"Are you filled with the Holy Spirit? Do you speak in tongues?"

"No." I didn't understand what he was talking about.

"Do you promise to speak in tongues if I get off?"

"O.K., anything."

He rolled off me. I put my hand to my ankle. It was sore.

"So do it," he said. "Speak in tongues."

"I can't right now. My ankle hurts too much."

"Here. I'll heal your ankle." He touched his hand to my ankle and let out a long wolf howl. "Woowee—come out, you demon! Get out of that ankle! Let this woman get up and walk."

I struggled to stand up, and meanwhile Paul and John entered the room. They looked like their father, dull-faced and handsome. "I think Floyd swallowed a quarter," Paul said calmly. "He's all purple."

I forgot about my ankle then and bounded up the steps to look for the baby. The last time I had seen Floyd, he had been sitting at the foot of the steps while Mrs. Jordan put on her makeup upstairs. What could have happened to him in all this time? A one-year-old alone and forgotten? I searched bedrooms, under beds, and behind doors. I strained to open the bathroom door on the left, but the door jammed against an open drawer and I could only peek in at the empty brown bathtub, the toilet with its seat removed and leaning up against it, the mass of wet towels heaped on the floor among scattered, half-used makeup jars. There was no baby, no Floyd.

"Where is he?" I shouted down the steps. "Paul, John, where's the baby?"

There was no answer.

"Where's Floyd?" I asked again. "I can't find him!" The house heaved, creaked, relaxed into silence. A clock ticked somewhere. I was alone.

In his crib, maybe. I looked for his crib. It was a long search before I found it, shoved back in a large closet of the master bedroom at the end of the hall. And yes, he was in it, though you had to push winter coats and heavy dresses and suits in plastic out of the way to find him. The boys must have put him there. He did look dead on first glance. He looked crushed and deflated like an old basketball. But he was only asleep, hugging a large, purple, high-heeled boot to his chest. The ink from the leather had seeped into the sweaty creases under his chin. I sighed and sat down on the bed to recover my thoughts. This was the master bedroom, this was the Jordans' bed. A black lace night-gown lay across on the pillow, under a pair of hiking boots twisted up in the old green bedspread. On the nightstand was a little pink book with a lock on it—a diary. I wondered what was in it, but I did the godly thing and put it aside without looking.

The other boys didn't come back and I didn't look for them. While Floyd still slept, I went downstairs and fell asleep on the couch in the family room. Outside, the afternoon had turned dark and wet. The windows rattled with the thunder of a brief storm.

Then suddenly, the front door slammed again and I sat up with a start. I didn't know how long I'd been sleeping. I heard someone run up the steps and close an upstairs door. Mr. Jordan came in, shaking his keys.

"The boys," I said sleepily. "They went out to play. I hope they didn't get wet."

"I'll take you home," he said in a bland way.

"I thought Mrs. Jordan would take me home," I said. He shook his head. I was disappointed. I wanted to ask her about the theater, whether she had met any movie stars and why she had left Broadway. Instead, he drove me home and I sat alone in the backseat like a child, too scared to speak to him. I pointed directions over his shoulder. When we reached my house I didn't have the courage to ask for any money. He didn't offer any. He waved and nodded as I went in. Maybe I wouldn't be asked back.

41

Suppertime had passed, but the kitchen was clean and dark. I found Grandma upstairs in the bedroom next to mine. She had unpacked all of my father's old things and now stood in the middle of his childhood room, looking around.

"Sorry I was gone so long," I said. "I wasn't even here in case Aunt Jo called."

"Well, that's all right. It's about bedtime, isn't it?"

"We haven't even had supper yet, Grandma."

"What? Supper? No, we haven't, have we? Help me sort out your father's books, Carrie. I have a lot to do before tomorrow."

I picked up one book—*Harper's Bible Concordance*. My father was a Christian man and a dominie, but what else did I know about him?

*T*he plane arrived on the Fourth of July as scheduled, on a windy, rainy Sunday afternoon. Uncle Jim and Aunt Betsy had driven in the day before with my cousins. Wherever I turned, Shirley and Victoria were there, buffing their nails in the bathroom or braiding their hair in the stairway mirror or having their party dresses adjusted in the living room by Aunt Betsy, on her knees with straight pins in her teeth. They slept in a narrow room just above mine and made scattered clicking noises on their floor half the night. Were they tap-dancing? Playing Parcheesi? Uncle Jim, Aunt Betsy, and baby Zachary slept down the hall from me, on the other side of the bathroom. Only my father's bedroom, next to mine, sat empty and alert, groaning like creation under flowers and starched sheets, under new dust ruffles and old pictures dusted and rehung. After seven years of spinster missionaries and great-aunts, it would have to be reformed to the tastes of a man.

At breakfast on Independence morning, Grandma announced that it was Uncle Jim's job to meet my father at the airport in Richmond. He was to act natural all the way back to the church basement, where the surprise party guests would be waiting with flags to wave and confetti to throw.

"Mama, that's a job for you or Betsy," he said. "You know I get to talking and tell everything I know."

"That's why I want you to tell Davey you have to stop at the church to drop off some things for the missionary clothes closet."

"Can't do it," he said through his nose as he drank coffee. "It's a sin to lie. Can't do it."

"It's not always a sin to lie," said Grandma. "Remember the Egyptian midwives who lied to save the baby Moses. God blessed them."

Uncle Jim looked thoughtful, as though he was flipping through the Book of Exodus in his mind, landing his large, gray index finger on the passage, and studying it carefully.

"Aha!" Grandma said. "You don't have an answer."

"I need to look it up."

"Aha! He needs to look it up!"

In the end she had her way. She heaped the backseat of his station wagon with old clothes from our attic. Everything wearable had long since gone to the church or the Salvation Army. Only the dregs remained—patched-up trousers, threadbare boxers, a school jersey, a few rugby-style shirts with brown rings on the collar and stains in the armpits—all rank with mothballs and dust. Before the rest of us left for church, Uncle Jim left for the airport, sneezing three times into his sleeve before he had even backed out of the driveway. Firecrackers snapped and popped in the air a few houses down. Aunt Betsy held baby Zachary and waved good-bye to her husband. She looked relieved, as though she had just solved a big problem.

"Oh, my," she said. "I hope he doesn't get into a terrible mood waiting at the airport."

"Well," said Grandma, "if he does, then I know Davey will get him right out of it. Let's just pray that they have safety on the highway." And she went inside to get her purse and a big box of kitchen supplies. She and Aunt Betsy were about to leave with the baby for church. They were setting off a full hour before Sunday school, as there was a lot of cooking still to be done. In a short time they would be up to their elbows in almond paste and pickled herring.

After they left, with many warnings to us to be on time and looking our prettiest in our new dresses, Victoria and Shirley put on tight jeans and clogs and said that we would skip Sunday school and go to the parade downtown before morning worship. Victoria announced it in a cool way, like a simple change of plans. I wondered where their jeans had come from and how they had hidden them. I was already wearing the pink jumper that Grandma had bought for me at the Empire Square.

"But I'm dressed for church," I said. "I don't want to change."

Shirley looked me up and down and rolled her eyes. "Just wear your stupid dress then." She folded her homemade lace-fringed dress with its patriotic Holly Hobby pattern on the apron and pushed it deep in her purse. She folded Victoria's too and pushed it down nearly as deep. Together we went in our raincoats to Founder's Square.

The parade tapered off just when we arrived, breaking up early as the churches rang their bells. Still, the streets were crowded with Dutch and English. I looked out over so many blond heads burnished gold in the rain, so many high foreheads and beak-like noses streaked with silvery raindrops. We picked up free flags from a young boy running by, one of the few Black children on the street. We raced to pick up candy that the beauty queens and Girl Scouts threw to us from the tops of the floats. As the last of the high school bands blasted by us, a news crew from Richmond parked nearby in a white van. A pair of men got out, one in dingy blue jeans with a camera on his shoulder, the other in a suit and trench coat, unraveling a microphone cord.

"Come on," said Shirley. "I bet you we can get on T.V."

Victoria swished along slowly after us. Shirley tugged her by the hand, shouting, "Hurry up, Vicky, come on!" The three of us ran in front of the camera shouting, "Hooray hooray! Hooray for the red, white, and blue!"

"What are your names?" asked the man with the microphone. He thrust it at Victoria, the oldest and prettiest of us.

"Vicky," she said with a slight smile, her eyes shooting away and then sweeping back, large and cloudy blue.

"Vicky," he said in a fruity voice. "Aren't you a pretty girl? How old are you?"

"Sixteen," she said.

"Ooh la la, sweet sixteen. And who's this little girl in the pretty pink dress?" I thought he was speaking to Shirley, because she was also pretty in a plump way. But he stepped past her and held the mike down to me.

"I'm Carrie Grietkirk," I said.

45

"Well, little Carrie, are you excited that it's the Fourth of July?"

"It's kind of rainy," I said.

He chuckled rhythmically. His Adam's apple jumped up and down like a mallet on a bass drum. "Tell me, Carrie, what does the bicentennial of our country mean to you?"

I looked straight at the camera and said in a strong voice, as Grandma would have wanted me to, "It means the freedom to worship God as I please, the freedom to go to church and believe that Jesus has died for my sins and that I should trust him as my Savior."

"O.K., Carrie. Are you going to church this morning?"

"Yes, sir."

He looked at his watch. "Better hurry. You're a little late, aren't you?"

"Yes, sir."

"All right! You kids are just super. Have a great bicentennial." He patted Victoria's cheek and crouched off quickly toward a group of older girls.

I felt disappointed as we walked over to the church. I should have said more. I should have told him that we were Dutch, from the First Reformed Church of Virginia, and that my father was a war hero, returning to America today. Grandma would have wanted me to tell him everything.

"You hogged the microphone, Carrie," said Shirley, angrily. "I didn't even get to say anything."

"I'm sorry," I said.

She would not forgive me easily. She walked faster, close to Victoria. I tripped behind them on the wet sidewalk all the way to church. Above us the sky dipped down in the middle like a tarp. White fog hung on the borders of the First Reformed parking lot, which lay before us like a box of jewels as we came down the last hill toward Church Street. The wet cars glowed in one sharp ray of sunshine.

"We can't go straight in the front," said Victoria. "We have to change our clothes."

"Well, I'm going straight in," I said. "I'm already dressed and I don't want to get in trouble."

"Listen to Grandma's little baby," said Shirley. "She always does what Grandma says."

46

"Shut up!" I said.

They clomped off to a playground door while I ascended the main steps to the vestibule of the sanctuary, several minutes late. The congregation was on its feet, roaring out "The God of Abr'am Praise." Our church had been singing hymns for only about three years now. Before that it had always been the Psalms, clear and beautiful and unsurprising. There had been no shocks in the Psalter, no blessings supernal or burdens rolled away or fountains filled with blood. The elderly Dutch women still longed for the old brown book, even wept for it. But Grandma, who liked the new red hymnbook, said it proved that things could change, even in Dutch Falls.

I slipped into the back and sat down on a metal folding chair with a bulletin in my hands. Someone handed me an open hymnal. It tipped and glided in my hands. I took control of it at last and joined in. English music, patriotic music, was what we sang today; it was bicentennial Sunday. My grandmother sat up in the choir loft waiting for her solo.

> I am a pilgrim
> Far from home.
> Though I am weak,
> My Lord is strong.
> I shall not fear,
> When he is near,
> I shall go on,
> I shall go on.

I saw her face, just a tiny pink circle from this distance, and I could feel her eyes move over the crowd, searching for us nervously. She must be thinking about the party later, about my father. The offertory came and she sang with shaky gusto. Then the dominie stepped up to pray.

"Before we go before the throne of grace," said Dominie Grunstra in a cheery voice, "let me remind everyone of the party following the service for David Grietkirk, a son of this church. David is a true war hero. He returns to us today after seven years of service in the Far East, first as a chaplain with the United States Army and then as a mis-

47

sionary, preaching to the poor and the sick and the unchurched there overseas. You all remember what he did for the innocent people of Vietnam, how the faith of the Reformation is being declared there today on account of him. I won't tell you that my wife remembers changing his diapers in the nursery here. I'll just tell you that lunch will be served at a reasonable hour. So please stay and celebrate our nation's birth with the Grietkirk family. Let us be seated so that we may bow in prayer."

The dominie began to pray as the congregation heaved back into their seats. The wood groaned. The metal squeaked and popped. "Lord," he said, "this is indeed a lovely morning in the life of thy people. Thou has blessed us in every way, with a marvelous country, with freedom and prosperity. With heroes like Davey Grietkirk. Yes, we owe everything to thee. Thy generosity o'erwhelms us. It is too high; we cannot attain unto it. We thank thee, Lord, this morning for thy house, for this beautiful church, which we inherited from our fathers and mothers as a token of thy love for us and our love for thee. Lord, we love it so, and yet we pray that we will not make idols out of things made by human hands but that we will glorify the creator and maker of all things. This church is thine, Father, and we are thy people called by thy name with a peculiar calling."

The dominie did not stop there. He gave us a long prayer and then a long sermon followed by a long communion. My thoughts attained mostly to things outside the sanctuary—such as Ginger Jordan, her handsome husband, Frank, and their career on the stage, and also the movies I had seen and would like to see. My fantasy life was rich in church. Was I not forever trying to pay attention and meditate on God, as the dominie said I should? I sincerely was. But how did one meditate on God? Sometimes I thought of the dominie in the high pulpit as Moses descending mightily from the mountain with stony tablets, looking out over rows of dull and recalcitrant heads, so many stupid Israelites. But perhaps all the others here were meditating on God and concentrating on the sermon. Maybe I was the only dreamer in the sanctuary.

When church was over, the party began. The congregation filed down to the fellowship hall yawning and stretching, straining the stairs. I stayed back, but Shirley and Victoria found me and pushed me into the stairwell ahead of them.

"Is my father here yet?" I asked. "I don't want to go down yet."

"Grow up," said Shirley. But then she caught sight of Billy De Ruiter and left me and Victoria alone. Billy De Ruiter was Victoria's old flame from elementary school, when the whole family had lived in Dutch Falls and Uncle Jim hadn't even started law school in Charlottesville. Now Billy was a boy with bony, bowed legs and a sketchy moustache. His orange hair stood up straight like a paintbrush. Victoria no longer cared for him at all, but Shirley pined for him whenever she visited. My grandmother disapproved of the entire De Ruiter family for reasons that I did not know.

I stood in a corner of the room and watched the congregation slowly file in. It was a big holiday crowd, including people who didn't always make it to church. There were farmers and textile workers and housewives who had known each other since grade school. They greeted each other with few words at first and lined up at the refreshment table. They filled their cups with strawberry lemon punch and positioned themselves around the hall on wooden folding chairs. The room was quiet at first since they were all dazed and sleepy from the long service, and only gradually did the noise level grow. The women started at whispers and gained volume like a slow-boiling pot. The men began with "yeps" and "nopes" and soberly worked up to complex sentences, getting louder until they broke out in booms of thick laughter from the corners.

Everyone remembered that the point of this gathering was not to socialize but to greet a returning war hero. We Dutch were always mindful of our purpose in any situation. But we were hungry, too, and it seemed unfair that we should wait for the hero's arrival before starting into the *gehaktballen* and gouda cheese. Some of the men began to call out for food, until their wives halfheartedly silenced them. Where was David Grietkirk? Still on his way, the dominie said. The crowd stared up at the windows, looking out into a noon rain. They turned and talked to each other and then stared again. One bowl after another of punch was drained and refilled. The fellowship hall overflowed and leaked from the gills, and still no sight of my father. Some-

49

one had made "Welcome Home, David" signs, which began to drop to the floor like withered leaves. The assembly lost its volume and returned to whispers.

I looked around and counted the faces I recognized. Mr. Hagedoorn was there, Mr. and Mrs. Ten Kate and Annajane, Dominie Grunstra and his wife, and the Ronald Steens. Mr. Klein sat in a corner alone, my father's old Sunday school teacher who had been a widower for seven years now. Mr. Van Zandt, band director at the high school, paced the room with his saxophone slung over his shoulder. He was a stooped man with a hooked nose and heavy cheeks. His big arms hung from his thin shoulders practically to his knees. When he held up his hands to give direction, it was hard to see how he supported the weight of his bulging, veiny fingers. Now he was giving frequent signals to the other instruments—a trumpet, a trombone, a piccolo, a drum—all wielded by the teenage Drechsel children, who were said to have committed themselves, every one, to music ministry someday on the mission field. I don't know if my father even knew the Riebersmas, a family at church who always sat in deck chairs at church functions (even in the sanctuary) because of back injuries. Anyway, they were present. Mrs. Riebersma sat in her deck chair near the refreshment table, hovering like a cat over the peanut butter fudge. There were about fifty others, including a small army of young single women and a group of bosomy matrons with blond hair like helmets. Everyone looked around aimlessly now, bleary-eyed and hungry. An hour or more had gone by. The women had stopped chortling together. The men grumbled.

I wished then for Grandma. All this time, she had been in the kitchen. I heard her voice above the clatter of tea cups. "Please notice, ladies, that I am reusing the coffee filters." Once she waved to me from the door and told me to be good and stay nearby. But now, as the ladies in white aprons marched in and out with trays of sandwiches and silverware, I wished that Grandma would leave the kitchen and stand with me in the hall. I felt responsible, because my father hadn't come and people were impatient. The rain had picked up outside. I watched it from a north window. The church stood in a warm, windy mist. The sky curdled above us. Someone had heard on the radio that the entire state of Virginia was under a tornado watch.

"Grandma?" I called at the kitchen door. She came into the hall, holding her hands out because they were dripping with soapy water.

"What do you need, dear? Grandma's busy washing dishes."

"Can't you come out here for a little while? I'm bored."

"Bored, Carrie?!" she said incredulously. "Why don't you play with Annajane, or one of your cousins?"

"I don't know where they are."

"What do you mean you don't know where they are?"

"I think they're outside."

"Outside! In this terrible weather?" She dried her hands and was ready to go after them when suddenly someone shouted, "Hey, they're here, they're here!"

"Who's here?" asked Grandma nervously. "Davey?" She held her hands up to her cheeks. "My Davey? I have to comb my hair. Carrie, comb your hair."

She rushed back into the kitchen. The crowd rose up and swarmed around the high windows, looking through the downpour into the parking lot. Their voices swelled together again. Lightning flashed on the cool tile. I drew away from the kitchen to a metal pole at the center of the room. The crowd rushed forward, flinging their signs high. The double doors burst open. There was a sudden shout of "Welcome home, Dave!" and then a group of old men roared out the Falls Christian High fight song:

> Three cheers for the Flying Dutchman,
> Three cheers for the man in white,
> For he always overcomes his foes
> When he fights for truth and right!

The doors crashed shut. The crowd roared, drowning out the thunder and the chinking of china. They surged around the doors, the tallest of the men bobbing up and down like horses, the women straining to see over the shoulders of the men. I could see nothing at all. I hiked up my jumper, wrapped my legs around the pole, and pulled up a few inches. The metal rang under my hands. The single women and the matrons had formed a phalanx at the back of the crowd, bristling with smiles.

"Let the man through!" my uncle boomed from somewhere deep in the crowd. His was a commanding voice; the crowd obeyed. Someone pushed from the nucleus and the crowd of single women stretched thin. The great blob of Dutch flesh grew and burst. It spewed out a tight group of four or five big men, close friends of the family, and at the center was my uncle, big and rain-soaked and smiling. Next to my uncle with an arm around his shoulders was a thin man in a blue suit, smiling under a heavy moustache, carrying the old clothes from our attic, coming forth from the crowd like Lazarus. He blinked and looked around. This man, I thought, is my father.

"Well, hello, soldier!" shouted the dominie, fighting his way from what was now the back of the crowd. His white hair, which had come loose from his forehead during the sermon, was in his eyes. "What do you have to say for yourself?"

My father shouted in a clear, high voice, "Dominie, you need any clothes?" He held up an old Falls Christian High jersey, full of holes and stains and wet from the rain, and draped it carefully over my uncle's head. It had come from our attic. My uncle stood still with his hands on his hips and let the crowd have its laugh. They barked and hooted. The crowd broke up and talked in small groups now. Each little circle laughed as it pressed toward the man at the front to shake his hand or hug him. The matrons threw their arms around him and kissed him, one after another. The relatives approached him dutifully. The red-nosed farmers pumped his hand. And he, my father, smiling brightly, looked from face to face. His eyes darted back and forth. His eyelids clicked up and down.

"Speech, speech!" called the dominie.

"No speeches," said my father. "Not until you all get your lunch. And anyway I have to find my best girl. Where's my mama? Where is she?"

"He always was a mama's boy!" shouted Uncle Jim. And then with a shout he threw the jersey over my father's head and grabbed him hard around the shoulders. "Let's take this boy to his mama—somebody help me. Come on—" He looked around and turned to the

52

dominie. "Come on, dominie, get him by the feet." The dominie nodded, perhaps reluctantly. He was a big man, built like a furnace, but he had a bad back. Everyone knew that. However, this was a special occasion. A couple of elders came to help. They slung my father up in the air on the count of three and carried him over their shoulders, without resistance, to the door of the kitchen.

"Mama!" called Jim. "Where are you? We got your boy here!"

"Help!" called my father, and everyone laughed.

"We got him!" said Jim. "Delivering him C.O.D. You got the cash, we got the cargo."

My grandmother did not come out.

"Why don't we put him down now, Jim," said the dominie. "I think your mother's a little shy."

"Which end first?" said Jim.

"Feet first!" shouted my father through the jersey.

"Put his dogs down then," said Uncle Jim, slapping his hand. He and the dominie set him up straight and pulled the jersey off. My father rubbed his short hair straight and looked around the kitchen and then beyond it. "Well, where is she? Where'd she get to?"

Everyone glanced around, to each side and behind their backs. Cameras flashed. We would be caught this way, smiling with our faces turned away, our eyes darting sideways. My father leaned over to hear my uncle whisper something to him. It was an opportunity to compare them, ear against ear, arm against arm. Uncle Jim had the height advantage, but my father had the straight back and trim waist. His features were boyish and fine. My father was a handsome man. It should not have surprised me. I had seen the pictures in every room of our house. I had listened to Grandma's stories about the girls who chased him home in their cars from his basketball games, blowing their horns. Maybe those girls were now the matrons, some of them still worshipful.

My uncle tapped my father on the shoulder and then stepped away, leaving him there in the doorway by himself. At first my father stood still, his eyes wide open and his mouth closed, his arms against his sides. No one moved or sang. And then the crowd began clapping in rhythm, calling out "Da-vey, Da-vey." He opened his arms and shut

53

his eyes, like a man about to leap from an airplane. A leap of faith would surely bring my grandmother out of the kitchen. Yes, out she came like a breath of wind. She had been standing around a corner, or behind a door, waiting to surprise him, waiting for my uncle to fall back so that the moment might be only hers and her younger son's, free of all jokes and hamming. She fell against my father's chest. The crowd clapped and cheered.

"And where's that daughter of his?" shouted Uncle Jim. "Where's that little snidget?"

"Yes, where is Carolyn?" my grandmother wondered. She lifted her head from my father's shoulder and looked around for me. Her gray hair had come out of its combs and lay across her shoulders like a little girl's. "She's just like her grandma, I'm afraid—shy. Where is that child?"

I was like Grandma? Apparently I was. My father had been gone for all these years and now I would rather hide from him than go to him immediately. Before they had found me among all the people, I slipped quietly away and went into the stairwell. This stairwell was always empty and dark. It was quiet. I stood on my tiptoes and looked through the glass window on the door.

"I bet she's with my two troublemakers," said Uncle Jim. I could hear him and see him. His face was red from all the exercise. "I bet she's with Victoria and Shirley. I'll find those characters." He started to walk in my direction.

"No!" I thought. "Not you! Don't you come!" Now I felt that I would rather leave than have Uncle Jim after me. I put my hand on the door and even started to push it open, but suddenly the will left me and I turned and ran as fast as I could, away from my uncle, up the stairs into a dark hallway. I kept running, hoping Uncle Jim wouldn't follow; but, remembering how stubborn he always was, I knew he would come. When my shoes clicked too loudly on the waxed tile, I flung them off. I ran past the children's chapel and library into the darkest, quietest corner of the building. Here was an empty restroom. Of course he wouldn't dare to enter a room with "Women" printed on the door. I rushed in and flung myself on the old brown couch beside the sink. The rain beat on the roof above me. The wind was rattling the brown

54

windows—I had forgotten about the rain and the wind. They didn't worry me, though. The air smelled like chewing gum and scented toilet paper. I grabbed a couch cushion and breathed into it, waiting.

I had been in this bathroom so many times before. Girls played hooky here on Sunday mornings. The older girls brushed mascara into clumps on their lashes while the younger ones crawled under the stall doors in their pert smocked plaid dresses and stood on the toilets to look over the top.

Now I listened only to the rain, and I thought how my uncle must be searching everywhere for me. He was storming around, shouting my name. He was opening doors wide, looking into empty depths, shining light into every corner, preparing strong words that I could understand. He bragged that he knew how to talk to children on their own level, in metaphors. "God is very disappointed today, Carolyn. You're trying to color a black spot right on the map he's laid out for your life."

A long time went by and I didn't hear him. Maybe he had given up. But then I heard quick, light footsteps in the hall, not a man's footsteps, unless Uncle Jim was walking on tiptoe. Was my grandmother after me now? I could have run into a stall, but what good would that have done? The door swung open.

"There she is," said Annajane. "I knew it." Annajane was small and gray in the dim light of the hall. Behind her came my cousin Shirley. They hit the light switch and the long, lemony bulb flickered on over our heads like dull lightning. It popped and then buzzed steadily. Annajane watched it, her hand still on the switch. She was not gray anymore. Her hair looked waxy gold in the light. With her face tilted up, her serious blue eyes and flushed cheeks shone. She was a pretty girl; everyone said so.

"Go away," I said. "I want to be alone."

"No way," said Shirley simply. She shuffled into the room ahead of Annajane and flung herself on the couch. "Grandma sent us looking for you. What are you doing in here? Don't you want to come down and see your daddy? Are you too shy?" she said in a nasty, sing-song voice.

Was I shy or wasn't I? Sometimes I was and sometimes I wasn't.

Sometimes I wanted to stand up in front of hundreds of people and scream, "I'm here! I'm me!" and sometimes I wanted to run and hide in a remote bathroom when my uncle called my name. This was the truth, and I could have confessed it to Annajane, but it was better not to expose your deepest thoughts in front of Shirley. "Just leave me alone," I said. "Y'all just go away." I got up and went into a stall. Shirley launched into a Sunday school song and got it all wrong.

> I may never shoot in the infantry,
> Fly o'er the enemy,
> Shoot in the artillery.
> I may never fly o'er the cavalry,
> But I'm in the Lord's army!

"My hair!" she gasped suddenly. "Why didn't you all tell me it looks like a rat's nest! That stupid parade got my hair all wet. It'll take me hours to get it right!"

When I came out of the stall she was tossing her bangs with a plastic fork in front of the mirror, dousing them with hairspray until they fanned out stiffly in the air and glistened with clusters of droplets like tiny stalactites.

"Come on, Carrie," said Annajane gently, coaxingly. She put her arm around my shoulder. "We'll go with you. There's nothing to worry about."

"Yeah, come on," said Shirley. "My daddy's going to kill me if I don't bring you downstairs. He looked all over for me and told me to. Anyway, Grandma's all worried because there's that tornado watch and you're not supposed to be upstairs in a tornado watch. So come on down."

We switched off the lights and left the bathroom. Shirley led the way out. We weaved a strange path through the building, crossing through the empty vestibule, climbing up and down the balcony staircases with our hands on the white carved rails, treading over the black-and-white-checked floors and plush blue sanctuary carpet. The empty church was a boundless frontier, a vast, unconquered territory. You had only to lay your claim to it and it was yours, at least until a door

56

slammed somewhere and a deacon appeared. You could write your initials on a bathroom wall or climb through a window into the inner courtyard and collect a pocketful of pink pebbles. You could take a handful of water from the baptismal font and rub it into your face, or tear up a bulletin and sprinkle it from the balcony into the nave. You could put on the organ shoes and pump the pedals, tear across the sanctuary to the piano and bang out simple chords, climb to the heights of the pulpit and sing at the top of your voice into a microphone, race on your hands and knees under fifty rows of pews and write your name in the bright red registration books.

I recovered my shoes in the hallway. When we reached the long corridor of the south staircase and found that Victoria was talking to a boy there, we charged down the steps giggling. Victoria screamed. The boy, who was thin and handsome, told us to get lost. Shirley lagged behind, and Billy De Ruiter appeared from underneath the staircase, smirking. Annajane pulled the door open to the fellowship hall. I stepped forward, almost running straight into Grandma.

"Were you looking for me?" I asked, out of breath. Annajane abandoned me suddenly. She went across the room to her mother and father, and kept her back to me.

"Where have you been?" Grandma balled her face up tight like a fist. "I've been looking all over for you."

"I'm sorry. I just had to go to the bathroom."

"Carolyn, what am I going to do with you? Don't you realize how you've embarrassed me?"

I felt myself trembling. I couldn't answer.

She went on, in a tight whisper. "What kind of welcome is this to give your father, your dear father, who has come all this way to see you? What can possibly be in your mind?"

"I haven't done anything wrong. I did the same as you did, Grandma. I was afraid to come out, because—"

"Stop it. I'm so nervous and bothered right now—you just can't imagine!"

"Sorry, Grandma."

She had pulled me over to a corner of the room, her cold hands tight around my arms. "And your Aunt Jo has called to tell me that she got on the road this morning and turned back after an hour. After one hour of driving she went back to New York! Your Uncle Jim is mad as a hornet. Well, we'll all have to make the best of an imperfect situation. I wouldn't want your father to suffer over this the slightest bit."

"No, ma'am."

She raked at my hair and gave me a push in the direction where she was now anxiously looking. My father was at the refreshment table. He stood with his back to me and I studied him as I slowly approached. Few people who see their fathers clearly for the first time after so many years see them from the rear. He had broad shoulders, in spite of his thinness. His legs were bowed, just slightly, so that his pants touched the backs of his knees. He was talking to Mrs. Riebersma. I came close and stood behind him.

"Do they serve it raw there, chaplain?" Mrs. Riebersma was saying over the roar of voices.

"Yes, ma'am, they certainly do. And if you're really courageous, you can eat it while it's still alive."

"Oh, my!"

"Just don't ask it to roll over or shake hands or anything."

"Oh, chaplain, you're pulling my leg!"

"Funny, that's just what the last one I ate said to me."

"Oh, yuck!" She stuffed a cheese puff in her mouth.

I came closer. "Excuse me?" I said quietly.

"Um, I think someone wants to talk to you," said Mrs. Riebersma, acknowledging me with a fat smile and a nod. She pointed around him and politely ducked away. He turned. His friendly eyes dropped down in my direction.

"Excuse me for interrupting," I said. "Welcome back."

"Oh, thank you." He looked at me blankly. Who was I? This plump, knock-kneed, brown-haired girl. Did I belong to a friend? Should he know me?

"I'm Carolyn."

His eyes widened. "Carolyn!" he shouted. "Carolyn? Well, I'll be doggone; is that you?" He hesitated for a second, fumbled with his plate of crackers and dip, spilled the crackers against his chest, pushed them back on his plate, put the plate down on the table, and wiped

58

his fingers on his pants. A shiny brown clump of fig preserves slid down one of his front pockets, dropped, and stuck to his shoe. "I'm making a mess of my—oh, forget it. Come here." He bent down and grabbed me awkwardly around the arms. He was warm. "What kind of father am I anyway, not knowing my own daughter? But look at you, just look at you! You're nothing like your pictures. I think Grandma's been sending me pictures of the wrong girl. You're just so—"

I thought he wanted to say that I was fat. Grandma had only sent him my flattering pictures. "Good to have you home," I said.

He laughed and looked at the people around us. "Now don't say anything you might regret later. Hey, can you believe it? I'm finally home."

"Yes."

He smiled and looked around again. But the party guests all politely ignored us, allowing us the kind of public privacy that families sometimes want on occasions like this. We spread clam dip on crackers and stood next to each other without talking, looking out at the loose congregation of people as father and daughter. Grandma waved from across the room, approvingly. At last Aunt Betsy came up and congratulated my father. Baby Zachary squirmed in her arms.

"So I see you found the prodigal?" She looked tired.

"The prodigal found me, Betsy," said Father. "Can you believe this kid? She's almost grown up."

"We think she looks like you."

He looked me over. "Well, she has got my curly hair, poor kid."

"And your eyes."

"Certainly."

I put my hand up to my face. His eyes? I had my father's eyes?

"Hey, soldier boy," said Arnie Hagedoorn, walking up unexpectedly from the other direction, "good to have you home."

I shrank away. They shared a manly hug, the kind that looks painful. "Arnie!" said my father. "Good to see you, man. Great to see you. How you been?"

"Fine, man."

"Is it true what I hear?" asked my father. "Is it true that old Arnie is now a—librarian?"

"Yep." Mr. Hagedoorn coughed again and hung his head, smiling.

"I never thought of you as the librarian type."

"That's my fate," said Mr. Hagedoorn. How could he look at my father the war hero without thinking of his own failed career in the military, his dashed dreams of coaching varsity basketball with an office above the swimming pool? "Hey look, I've changed a lot since high school. Got married. I'm head deacon at church."

"No kidding?! Just like your dad!"

"Arnie married Nancy Talsma," said Aunt Betsy. "You remember, Mrs. Dykhouse's niece, the star pole-vaulter? You know, Davey, the skinny girl. And he's just become a father."

"I'll be doggone," said my father. "Married to Nancy Talsma. I'd never have believed it. I'd never have thought, not in a million years. Boy or girl, Arnie?"

"Arnie Jr.," said Mr. Hagedoorn. "Just what we prayed for. He's going to be a point guard, like you. No sissy stuff for this kid."

"Congratulations," said my father. "The next Flying Dutchman. The fervent prayer of a righteous man accomplisheth much." He squeezed Arnie's shoulder. "So how's Nancy doing? Is she here?"

There was an awkward pause. Mr. Hagedoorn put his hands in his pockets. "Oh, she's doing great, Davey. You'll have to stop by and see her and the baby. She'll be thrilled. She prays for you all the time."

"Nancy's a real prayer warrior," said Aunt Betsy.

"That doesn't surprise me at all," said my father. "You'd have to be a prayer warrior to hook a lady-killer like Arnie, here. You should have known this guy in high school. He had women lined up. I remember my sister Jo—"

"Davey," my grandmother broke in. She had just come up behind us. "The Schippers have arrived. Do you remember Sheila? She used to baby-sit you and Jo."

"Oh, sure, O.K. See you in a little while, Carolyn—Carrie. Arnie, let's get together for lunch. That is amazing—old Arnie, a librarian." He pinched my chin and moved away with Grandma to another part of the room. Mr. Hagedoorn watched him for a second.

"So where is Nancy?" asked Aunt Betsy.

"Resting," he said. The corners of his mouth twitched. "Will you excuse me? There's someone I want to talk to."

Zachary started to cry. I took him from my aunt and held him on my knee, feeding him pecan sandies and wiping the confectioners' sugar from his wet mouth.

The party lasted about two hours. As the crowd slowly began to disperse, Mr. Van Zandt struck up a song with the Drechsels:

> Arise and shout, the battle is done,
> Awake and sing, the world has been won.
> Now put down your swords, ye saints of the Lord,
> And call his name blessed who calls you a son.

"Why don't you take Davey home in our car? He's going to collapse in a few minutes, and we don't need you here anymore. Betsy can do the cleaning up."

"What about the weather?" warned Grandma. "What about the tornado watch?"

"The wind's not blowing anymore," said Uncle Jim, impatiently. He hated Grandma's worries about the weather. "It's fine. Go home."

"Louise has offered Davey a ride home," said Grandma. "I'll send him on with Carrie."

"Now, Mama, I want you to get yourself home and rest."

"I will not be able to rest until this church is in order again, so just let me go about my business. Send Davey home with Louise. Carolyn, too. You make sure they go, Jim."

After more tears and kissing, my uncle at last pressed us into Louise's big car, which smelled like cats. Uncle Jim had lied, because the wind was still swift, though the sky had lightened. The thunder had stopped. Maybe the big clouds would blow off toward the ocean or to New York by tomorrow morning, the way they sometimes did. Then Grandma would be at ease again, the sky would be blue again. Father sat in front with Louise's purse on his lap. I sat in the back with his duffel bag and trunk.

"Good to have you home, Davey," Louise said as we creaked slowly out of the parking lot. "I feel like it was just yesterday that I stood next to your mama and waved good-bye to you."

"It's good to be home," my father said. "Did you ever hear the one about the soldier who buried five hundred dollars in his backyard before he left for Vietnam?"

"No, I don't believe so."

"When he got home he said to his wife, 'Darlin', get me the shovel, I got to dig up my five hundred dollars.' And she said, 'O.K., honey, but it's sure going to take you a long time to dig a tunnel over to Sears Roebuck.'"

"Shee hee!" laughed Louise. "We missed you around here. I miss your sense of humor."

"I missed being around here."

"Like I tell your mama, you've always been a favorite of mine. I just wish you'd cast your eye on one of my daughters. There's still time, you know, with the youngest—Valerie. You remember Valerie? Your mama's favorite." She winked. My father grinned. We had pulled up into our driveway. He got out and opened my door for me, grabbed his bags, and poked his head back in.

"How could I marry your daughter, Louise, when it's you I love?"

"Oh, Davey Grietkirk—get on with you! You going to be at the fireworks out at the high school tonight?"

"Maybe so, if I get some sleep first."

"Hope to see you." She drove away, waving wildly. Father shook his head. His smile was gone.

We went into the house together and opened the living room and kitchen windows to let in the early evening air. The curtains in the kitchen flapped too hard and knocked a cut-glass slipper from the window ledge into the sink. It didn't break, but Father closed the window and sighed. I helped him carry his trunk to his bedroom and his duffel bag to the laundry room. Then I watched him as he looked around from room to room, parted curtains, opened closet doors, peered into drawers, smelled the air. He sat down in a La-Z-Boy chair that my grandmother had kept off limits just for him for seven years.

"Do you want something to eat?" I asked. "I could get something for you."

"No, thank you. I'm stuffed."

"Can I watch T.V.?"

"Whatever you want, Carolyn." His eyes closed. His jaw relaxed. He began to snore gently. I turned on the television and sat down in my chair, only half watching. I kept glancing over, staring at my father. He slept soundly with his head lolled to one side and his lips open and moist. As he slept and I sat thinking, a gentler, cooler breeze pushed into the room.

After a long time, I heard troubled voices at the front door. I heard the door open, and Grandma speaking in the foyer to Uncle Jim.

"It's that boyfriend of hers," she was saying. "He's the source of this whole headache."

"You shouldn't have bothered asking her to come," said Jim.

"I know exactly why she didn't come. It's because of Davey's testimony for the Lord. Her spirit is under conviction. She knows her brother will drive a wedge between her and the world."

"A wedge? You're always thinking of reasons for what Jo does, Mama. Why don't you learn? It's in her genes."

"Genes. Shooh. No one in my family ever behaved like Josephine."

I heard more voices, clattering, and shoes thumping off in the foyer. Then they all came into the family room where Father and I were sitting—Uncle Jim, Grandma, Aunt Betsy, baby Zachary, Shirley, and Victoria.

"Oh, look at that," said Aunt Betsy, smiling down at my father. "He looks just like a sleeping baby. Mother," she said to Grandma, "how does it feel to have your baby home?"

Uncle Jim snorted and whacked the sleeper over the head. "Come on, baby. Get up and get ready to see some fireworks."

*O*ver the next four days my father and I barely crossed paths. Early each morning he left with Uncle Jim to go trout fishing in Prince George County. Not until late afternoon did they shuffle back onto our porch with their poles, sunburned and dirty. They'd sit and talk alone there with the sky in their eyes until it was time to wash for supper. They were quiet at the dinner table. When they fell asleep in their chairs later by the television, Grandma fussed around them as if they were still boys. "Hush, all of you; don't wake your daddies."

My cousins hardly left the house. Victoria remained pretty and aloof, doing nothing much to help or hurt anyone. She spent her days in the bathroom, softening rough skin, cleansing dirty pores, buffing away inequities. At suppertime she emerged rosy and steaming.

"Vicky washed her hair four times today," said Shirley. It was Monday night. My father had been home a full day.

"No, I didn't," said Victoria.

"Everyone knows you did. I counted. Just admit it."

"If I had washed my hair four times, would it already look so dirty? It's so greasy already. It looks like I rubbed oleo right in it."

"From now on," said Uncle Jim, "it's one shower a day. One, Vicky. Understand?"

"Oh, Daddy," said Victoria, "one shower isn't enough in the summer. I just walk outside and I get so dirty, it's disgusting."

And Grandma said, "Jim, speak kindly to my first grandbaby. I can't see that she's been anything but a jewel this whole visit."

Victoria smiled prettily and let Grandma kiss her.

Baby Zachary had developed a leaky nose and red eyelids. It was all the sugar he had eaten at the party, said Aunt Betsy, whose own eyes were red. They were both going back on the Healthy Life Diet, printed in the *Healthy Life, Holy Life Cookbook*, which Aunt Betsy had brought along in her big macrame handbag. She worked all day Tuesday in the kitchen with Grandma, making things that did not contain yeast, eggs, sugar, wheat, oats, rye, corn, lecithin, milk products including whey, and all other types of animal fat.

"You entertain Shirley," Grandma said to me. "Aunt Betsy and I are making healthy *oliebollen.*"

"Healthy donuts?" I asked, wondering how it was possible.

"It's your aunt's recipe. We make a dough out of rice and almonds and carrots, soak it in apple juice for half an hour, shape it into rings, and then fry the rings in vegetable shortening." She looked at me, shook her head, and rolled her eyes. Aunt Betsy faced the other way, working at the counter as Zachary played around her heels. With her chin against her chest, she looked like a plump child, her freckled neck showing over her collar.

"Find Shirley," said Grandma. "Entertain Shirley."

I found Shirley watching reruns of *Love, American Style* on an old black-and-white T.V. in Grandma's room. "Do you want to go to the library?" I asked.

"No, that's boring."

"Do you want to go outside?"

"No."

"Do you want to play in the basement?"

"It smells like dirty socks down there."

"What do you want to do?"

"I just want to wash my hair. I'm waiting for Victoria to get out of the bathroom."

So I spent that day, and most of my cousins' visit, by myself. I went to the library, worked in the garden, and sat in the living room with Zachary in the evening, picking up snatches of the men's conversation as it drifted in the window from the porch. My father's voice was high and soft, my uncle's low and resonant. People said my uncle could have been the next George Beverly Shea if Aunt Betsy hadn't held him back by telling him not to sing so loud at church. It was hard to imagine anyone holding back Uncle Jim. It would be like holding back a bulldozer. Your only hope would be changing the mind of the driver, which Uncle Jim would tell you was God, or else planting yourself in front of the treads. And Jim was as likely as not to run you over.

"What are your employment plans?" he asked my father one evening while they were sitting on the porch. I saw his face through the curtains. He sipped coffee with his eyes half shut and stuck out his lips as he swallowed.

"Don't have any yet, Jimbo," said my father. I couldn't see him from where I sat, but his voice came through clearly. "Guess I'll try to get a pulpit."

"You guess?" asked Uncle Jim. "Don't you know?"

"I'll go as the Lord leads, but he doesn't always tell me where he's leading."

"Seems to me a man ought to have a calling. Even I have a calling."

"You have a lucrative skill, Jim. That makes it easier."

Uncle Jim was a real estate lawyer. Grandma said he pulled in a salary three times what Grandpa had ever made, but he kept his family on such a tight budget that Aunt Betsy had to divide all their paper products in half—napkins, for instance, and toilet tissue. You never got more than half a paper towel at Uncle Jim's house.

"Proclaiming the gospel is a skill," said Uncle Jim.

"Man," said my father, "preaching's not really the part I'm good at. You know that. You were always saying I preach over people's heads."

"I never said that," said Uncle Jim.

"Yes, you did."

"What are you good at if not the preaching?"

"Golf," said my father.

"How do you like that," said my uncle with a laugh. "You're a mess, aren't you?"

"Yep."

"And to think I've always envied your calling so much. And you don't even have one."

"Jimbo, did you ever hear the one about the man who got up in the middle of a sermon and started to walk out the door?"

"Nope."

"Preacher said, 'Where you going?' The man said, 'I'm going to get a haircut and a shave.' Preacher said, 'Why didn't you get a haircut and a shave before you came to church this morning?' The man said, 'Before I came to church this morning I didn't need a haircut and a shave.'"

My uncle laughed heartily. At the end of his laugh he said in a softer voice, narrowing his eyes across the porch the way Shirley sometimes did, "Brother, if you have problems finding something, maybe I can pull some strings. I have a lot of friends up in Baltimore. I bet I could put you in a pulpit tomorrow with the right phone call."

There was a long silence. Cars swished by and the porch swing swayed and creaked. Something from the *Healthy Life, Holy Life Cookbook* hissed on a pan in the kitchen.

"That's O.K.," said my father. "I've got time to look. I need the break anyway, Jim, but thanks."

Uncle Jim patted his legs, looked around, and seemed at a loss. Finally he leaned forward and said, "To change the subject, Davey, will you explain something to me?"

"What's that?"

"Explain to me about Vietnam. You know the kind of thing I'm talking about, why we just gave up on the war. I don't get it. You know, I never heard Daddy complain about World War II. There's a fellow at my church, a psychologist, who says the problem with this whole current generation right now is that it wasn't raised properly. These kids never learned respect for God, or parents, or country, or anything. All they know how to do is complain."

"Well, I don't know," said my father. "I haven't been around. I don't know."

"I believe it's true. There's a lot of complaining and whining. At least I don't hear you whining."

"What would I have to whine about?"

"You tell me, war hero. You must have seen a lot of action."

"I didn't see that much."

"Tell me about the Silver Star, Davey. About saving those people and all."

"Oh, boy. No—sorry. No stories."

"Well, that's a pretty weird attitude to take with your own brother."

"Didn't Mama get the letter from my C.O.?"

"I mean the details. You know what I mean."

"I don't even like to remember the details."

"I'm not sensitive. I would have been over there in Vietnam myself if the time had been right."

"I know you're not sensitive, Jim." Father laughed out loud at the idea.

Uncle Jim sniffed. "So did it really happen or what? Was this just another one of Mama's Eagle Scout stories?"

"I'll only tell you one thing, Jim. I didn't do anything in Vietnam worth mentioning. Anything that happened, God did it all."

"Well, if it was so good, why'd you bother to come home, then?"

"I finally came to my senses. Don't you think seven years is a long time to be away from your family?"

"Sure, I guess it is. But then I've never left my family." Uncle Jim settled back down again and stared at his feet. "Can't see why you're so reluctant to talk about the medal. I'd think it would make a very inspirational story, something you could use in a sermon."

My father was quiet after that.

The following day was Friday, and Uncle Jim finally took his family home after lunch. Father looked sober as we turned from the porch, where we'd been waving at their station wagon for the last twenty minutes, to go inside.

"Davey, you look so tired," Grandma said. "You haven't had much rest."

"You're tired too, Mama. Company wears you out."

"I am tired. I want to go lie down and never get up."

We went inside and Grandma turned on the fans. It was going to be another hot afternoon, with another rainstorm around dinnertime to break the heat. Father and I sat down in the same family room chairs we'd occupied after his party, him in the La-Z-Boy and me in the red leather swivel chair that Shirley always said was tacky. Grandma mumbled something about her nap, but instead she went immediately to her sewing table and began measuring out satin for Victoria's birthday dress.

"Lie down, Mama," said my father. "Lie down and rest your weary old bones."

"Oh, you're a nut," said Grandma. "I'm not all that old. When my mother was this age she was still working a full day in the fields."

Father laughed and pushed backward in his chair. The footrest snapped up and clicked. "Well, I imagine Carolyn has been a help to you these last few years—cooking and taking care of the house and so forth. That's how it is, right, Carolyn?"

I watched him warily. He stroked his moustache. I thought he must be joking, but he didn't laugh.

Grandma was setting up her ironing board. "Truthfully," she said, "I don't expect Carrie to work like a grown woman. After all, she is a child."

"She's not a child, Mama. She'll be a teenager before you know it."

"It hasn't happened yet."

"But it will happen," said my father, looking over at me. "Won't it, Carolyn? Grandma can't do it all by herself. We're all going to pitch in from now on. That means me, that means you."

Grandma waved her hand in the air. "Never mind any of that. I'm just thankful to have a man in the house again, somebody to cook for. Of course, if you plan to get married again sometime, Davey, my dear, that would be fine with me. Just let me meet the girl first, so I can warn her what she's in for." She winked at him. I thought she would laugh lightly, as she sometimes did, but instead she looked away and sang softly to herself.

"Valerie, Valera, Valerie—Valera Hah hah hah . . ."

I turned on the television. Father hid himself in a newspaper. "Carolyn," he said after a minute, putting his paper aside.

I turned to him. "Yes?"

"Why don't you go out and play with your friends for a while? I have to talk to Grandma."

"Right now? But I want to watch this."

69

"You've been watching television all morning. All you kids watch the tube too much. Go out and get some fresh air."

"Can I have a quarter for donuts at Annajane's?" I asked Grandma.

"But we still have donuts in the refrigerator," said Grandma.

"I want real ones."

Grandma paused, then nodded sympathetically. She started to look in her purse, but Father cleared his throat and sat up in his chair.

"Carolyn," he said, "that's a waste of money. Get a donut out of the refrigerator and go and just stand in the sunshine for a few minutes like I ask."

"But it's so hot," I said.

"Do as your father asks, Carrie," said Grandma. "You don't want to be like your cousin Shirley, do you, provoking your father to wrath? Maybe you could go up to the library. Carolyn just loves the library, Davey. She spends all day there."

"She doesn't have to spend all day there today," said my father. "Just an hour or so."

"Well, fine then," agreed Grandma. "Did you hear that, Carrie? Didn't I tell you your father is the most reasonable one in this family?"

I went out and closed the front door hard behind me. The sky was a broad, bold titanium white that bleached the sidewalks and glimmered on the asphalt. It sought out corners and shady places and invaded them like hot mist. I jumped off the porch right into the rose beds and kicked through freshly mowed grass and clumps of uprooted onion weed to the street. As hot as it was, I didn't want to go to the library today. I wasn't sure where I did want to go, but I wanted to be alone in the heat and sulk.

All at once my mood changed. Right there on the sidewalk across the street from my house, near the library flagpole, I saw a crisp, green bill. I walked over and picked it up. It was a two-dollar bill, better than a bicentennial silver dollar. It was good luck finding one, if you didn't happen to believe in predestination—or if you believed, as my father had said to Uncle Jim just yesterday, that luck was something God invented to irritate Calvinists. Here lay a beautiful two-dollar bill, kept in mint condition until this moment according to the sovereign plan of God. It rested before me on the sidewalk, as plain as day. Why

70

someone else hadn't picked it up I didn't know. It was hot to my touch. I stuffed it into my pocket without looking around and headed off for the movies. Two dollars—exactly the price of a matinee ticket at the Valley Orbitron.

It was nearly time for the first matinee. I turned from Beatenbough onto Bridge Avenue, cut across Church Street through an alley, and ran as fast as I could down to DeGroot, then over to Founder's Square, nearly knocking over a man coming under an arbor of crepe myrtles in front of his house. "Sorry!" I shouted. "I got to get there by noon."

"I hope you make it on time," the man called after me. "God bless you!" The theater was another two blocks. I wheezed for the last fifty yards to the ticket counter and shoved my money into the slot under the glass, holding out my hand for my ticket. On the other side of the glass sat Bernie Grunstra, the dominie's younger brother, smiling. The dominie himself was opposed to theater of any kind, as he thought we all should be, but Bernie worked at the Valley Orbitron six days a week and appeared to have perfect peace about it.

"Here's my money," I said. "A ticket for the matinee, please."

He took the two-dollar bill and stared at it. I didn't know Bernie very well. He came to church only for weddings and funerals. When we happened to meet on the street, Grandma would pull me quickly in another direction, saying that he was a troubled man, that it was a tragedy for the dominie and Mrs. Grunstra to have such a person in their family, always dragging their name into the mud.

"Well, Miss Grietkirk," Bernie Grunstra said in a jolly, nasal voice without looking at me, "how is your grandma?"

"Fine," I said.

"Never see her anymore."

"She doesn't get out in the heat much," I said truthfully.

"And how's your Aunt Jo—she ever get home? I remember her well. We were pretty close at one time."

"She doesn't get home much."

"And now what's this you're trying to give me here? A two-dollar bill? Are you trying to kid me?"

"I found it," I said.

"Oh, you found it. Congratulations." He had a big nose and a wart on his upper lip. When he smiled, the wart turned from pink to white. He scratched it. "Very nice."

"It was right there on the sidewalk by the library."

"Very nice. Very nice." He nodded but handed it back.

"No, I want you to take it," I said. "I want a matinee ticket."

"Sorry, but I can't let you in," he said with a strange giggle. "I'm sold out."

I glanced behind me at the five or six men who were now waiting in line. They looked like farmers to me, in their overalls and caps. Their faces were tan and stiff, like hardened bread dough. Only one wore a suit. He stared off in another direction behind him, showing me just the edge of his dark cheekbone. I didn't recognize any of them; they weren't men who had ever attended our church regularly.

"Then why don't you close your window?" I said.

Bernie shrugged his shoulders.

"What about them?" I pointed to the men in line. "Are you going to let them in?"

"Look, run on home," said Bernie, smiling in a wiggly way. His wart turned white again.

"I just want to see *Mary Poppins* one more time," I said. "I can stand up at the back."

"It ain't *Mary Poppins* today. It's something else. Reservations only allowed. I only let in people who can speak French, because it's in French. See, all these fellows speak French. Don't you, fellows?"

The men nodded and looked at their feet.

"Believe me," said Bernie, "they didn't come to see *Mary Poppins*."

"Well, I'll see whatever it is," I said. "Just let me stand at the back."

"Nope, because you wouldn't like it anyway. There are no kids in it. No Herbie, the Love Bug. No doggies."

The faces behind me cracked for a moment in rough laughter and then hardened again.

"Oh, please!" I said.

"Take your money and buy yourself some candy. Now get!"

"Hey, let her in," said a long-haired young man just walking up to the back of the line. He was short and heavyset, with hairy arms and small, sweaty feet in sandals. He wore pink-rimmed sunglasses. "I'll sit with her," he said.

"No, I don't think so," said Bernie Grunstra firmly. "Little girl—get out of people's way and go play."

"No," I said.

"I'm getting just about riled enough to call your grandmother—" Bernie picked up the phone on the ticket counter and stared me down as he started dialing. I backed away.

"That's not fair," I said.

The man with the sunglasses stepped out of line, too. "Hey, babe," he whispered at me, grinning. "You can come in. I'll hold the side door open for you."

"O.K.," I said quietly. "Thanks." I nodded and watched him buy his ticket and go in. What luck, I thought, what fortune.

The theater was a blister-red building in the middle of the bright sidewalk. I walked casually around it, staying in the shade of some shaggy birch trees until I reached the side door. The door was steel gray and had no handle from the outside. I looked around warily, my hands sweating in my shorts pockets, my eyes watering in the humidity. A large car flew by me on the road and a white-haired lady frowned from the passenger's side. "Hi," I mouthed, though I didn't recognize her, and she waved. I hoped she wasn't Dutch. Finally, with a loud click, the door opened. A hairy hand waved out.

"Hurry up! Get in, quick!"

I rushed in, with the man tugging me by the wrist. As the door closed I glanced up at him. He looked younger without his sunglasses, maybe only nineteen or twenty. His eyes were milky gray around the irises.

"I'm Carrie," I said.

"Well, I'm Doug," he said. "Where do we sit?"

I started to say that I usually sat in the front row, but he was already dragging me by the wrist toward the back of the theater. He led me to a dark spot, four rows from the back in the middle of the row. There were only twenty or thirty people in the long, slanting auditorium. The air was heavy with smoke and Slim Jims.

"You want half a Slim Jim?" asked Doug, holding it out to me.

"No, thank you."

"You sure? They're good. I've already eaten three of these things."

"Please stop holding my wrist so tight." I tried to pull away gently. He gripped harder and twisted until my skin burned.

"None of that, now," he said. "You don't want the Grunster to notice you, do you?"

"Who?"

"The Grunster. Bernie the pervert."

"I really have to go to the ladies' room," I said, looking for a chance to get away.

"No, you don't."

"I really do."

"You want to see the movie or not?"

I tried to stand and pull away. He wouldn't let go, so I sat down again.

He leaned back in his seat. "Man. It's 12:20. I got to get back to work by one o'clock."

I wondered what kind of job he had. I pictured him in a sewer, shirtless and sweaty, his hair matted down, his skin angry red.

"Let's get on with it, Bernie!" someone yelled from the front right corner.

"Yeah!" shouted a shrill boy's voice from the left.

Another five minutes passed before the curtain jumped open and jerked across the screen with a screech like pants on coat hangers. Sound crackled out of the velvet drapes that lined the theater walls above us.

"Ladies and gentlemen," said a halting nasal voice over the sound system. It was Bernie, trying not to sound like Bernie. "Welcome to the Shining Valley Orbitron."

A hazy aerial photograph of a valley jiggled above us on the screen. A wiry hair danced from one curtain to the other.

"Enjoy your movie. And don't forget to say thanks to the employee of the month, Bernie Grunstra. And now . . . our feature presentation. In stereophonic sound!"

"Here we go," said Doug. He pressed my hand tight against his wide thigh. "Bet you ain't seen a dirty movie before."

"I shouldn't be here," I said, but I didn't close my eyes. I was still half thinking that I'd like to see a movie in French. I might broaden my horizons, like the elderly ladies who listened to foreign language records on the coconut-sized earphones at the library. Maybe someday I'd go to Paris and order chocolate mousse at a fancy restaurant.

It hardly mattered, though, what language the movie was in. Nor did it matter that the actors' voices burst from the speakers seconds after their mouths opened. I wondered if Shirley and Victoria had ever seen anything like this. I wondered if Uncle Jim knew that such things existed. Did Grandma know?

"Dear God," I prayed suddenly, moving my mouth silently like the shadowy faces on the screen. "Dear God, I shouldn't be here." Doug had slipped his arm around me. He began to pull me to him.

Just then there was a loud "Bvwippp!" Doug stopped and turned back to the screen. "What's going on?" The theater had gone dark. Bernie's faint cry rose from the tiny windows at the rear, above the last row of seats:

"Please be patient and remain in your seats. The movie will start in five seconds."

Suddenly I felt my hand free in the air. Doug had twisted around to stare at the projection room. I jumped up. My seat thunked shut.

"Hey! Hey!" he whispered loudly, and grabbed me again. "Get back in your seat."

"In the name of Jesus," I said, "I command you to let me go!"

I ran as fast as I could away from him, across the row and down the side aisle. I was sure he had followed. I ducked into an empty row and scurried toward the center aisle, heading for the side door across another row of seats. But it was dark. As I crossed the center aisle I didn't see a man making his way from the back with a box of popcorn. I flew into him. He spun off his feet and fell into a row of empty seats.

"What do you think you're doing?!" he shouted.

"I'm sorry," I said, and covered my face as the emergency lights blinked on. "A man back there is trying to grab me or something." I turned and pointed behind me up the aisle, but Doug had vanished.

"Carla?" said a voice nearby. A woman with thick glasses stood in the half dark, holding a large drink in each hand and a cigarette between her teeth. The cigarette bobbed up and down when she talked.

I moved toward her slowly. "Mrs. Jordan? Is that you?"

"Carla, is that you?"

I burst into tears. "I'm so glad to see you here!"

"What are you doing here? This isn't a movie for you."

"I know," I sobbed. "A man made me come in here. He wouldn't let go of me."

"Calm down, kiddo. Calm down."

"Ginger," said the man I'd knocked down, and as he stepped closer I noticed his long shorts and leather sandals. He looked like a camp counselor. Then I realized that it was Mr. Ferring, the church pianist. He wouldn't meet my eyes. "Are you coming or not, Ginger?"

"You go on, Bob," she said. "Here's your Coke. I'll make sure Carla's O.K."

"I wanted to see a movie," I said weakly, wiping my tears on the shoulder of my shirt. "If I could just sit with you, maybe we wouldn't have to leave right away."

"No way! I'm taking you right home, you little devil. Let's go."

Outside, Mrs. Jordan took off her glasses. She dropped her cigarette in her drink and tossed the full cup into a trash can. We walked around the building twice looking for Doug, but the street was empty. She went to the ticket window alone and shouted for Bernie. When he finally came out, they had words there. I saw him rub his wart and twist his big head apologetically. She walked briskly back to me; his eyes followed her.

"Now," she said to me in a motherly tone at the edge of the sidewalk, facing a traffic light, "Bernie tells me you snuck in there without his permission."

"Yes," I said.

"What did you think you were doing in a movie like that—and with a weird guy like that? He could be one of those psychos—didn't you ever see *Psycho*?"

I looked down, embarrassed, at the bright pavement. "No," I said.

"Why did you go in with him?"

"I thought maybe I could witness to him," I said meekly.

"What?"

"I thought I could witness to him. I thought I could share the gospel with him."

She turned up her nose. "You thought you could witness to him? Oh, right, and I'm Mrs. Billy Graham."

"I *did*."

"Don't lie to me, kiddo, because I'm not stupid."

"But I really did witness to him," I said. "He let me go because I said I was a Christian. It was like a miracle."

"Do you always go to dirty movies to witness to people?"

I shrugged my shoulders. "I just went because I wanted to hear people speak French. If it was a dirty movie, why were you there?"

She scowled. "None of your business."

"Oh."

We looked at each other and she burst into laughter. "Come on now and I'll walk you home. Bobby will understand. I'm always doing this to him."

We crossed the street and kept along the sidewalk together. Her high heels clipped against the cracks. I wondered if Doug was still around, watching us from some dark doorway.

"Look at your wrist," said Ginger. "It's all red. How are you going to explain that?"

"I don't know."

"Does it hurt?"

"Not really."

We kept walking and I pointed to my house as we passed it. "That's where I live," I said. "I don't really feel like going home yet."

Ginger was looking the other way at the public library, staring at it, not blinking. A wisp of dark hair fell out of the french braid under her hat and she let it fly in the breeze against her cheek. "I don't blame you," she said. We kept walking past my house, past the Chinese restaurant, past Kingsma's Laundry.

"Mrs. Jordan," I said, "are you very good friends with Mr. Ferring?"

"Well, Bob is just sort of—just sort of my baby. He needs me. He's a real artist. Really, you should hear his music. I'll have him play you the song he wrote for me. It even made Frank cry."

"Frank doesn't mind if you go to movies with Bob?"

"With Bob? Oh, no, no. Bob's only interested in art. That's why he dragged me to this movie, for the cinematography or something. Besides, Frank won't let me have a dog so I have to have Bobby."

"Oh. Who baby-sat for you? Did you talk Frank into it?"

"Are you kidding? No, a friend. I asked a friend."

"Oh," I said, disappointed that she hadn't thought to ask me again.

"How about you?" she said. "Do you have any pets, kiddo?"

"No."

"Too bad. I'm trying to ease Bob into the theater. I've got him in a show in Richmond. I think I can get him started on something really good. I mean who's to say how far he can go with his talent? Today he's conducting a small orchestra, tomorrow he's Leonard Bernstein. It's exciting; don't you think so?"

"Yes, it's very exciting."

"Do you want a hamburger? We can talk more about you and your choice of movies."

I let her take me to the Rainbow Diner, three buildings down from the hardware store. She bought me a cheeseburger and chocolate sundae, which I ate as slowly as I could, hoping to make the afternoon last. But the clock above the chrome barstools at the back was already chiming two. She said she needed to get home to her children.

"Remember," she said, "the next time you sneak in a dirty movie, you should go with a girlfriend. Don't go in alone. There's too many perverts out there."

"Like Bernie Grunstra?"

"Absolutely. Stay away from Bernie Grunstra."

"I'm not allowed to go to the movies at all," I said. "If my Grandma finds out, she'll kill me."

"Who's going to tell her they saw you there? That'd be like telling her they saw you with your eyes open during a prayer. If they saw you there, that means they were probably there, too."

I sat forward on my seat. "Can I ask you something before we go? Were you really on Broadway?"

"Hah. How did you know about that?"

I didn't want to say I'd been reading her scrapbooks. "Um, I think Mr. Hagedoorn told me. He knew about it, I think."

"Oh, he did, did he? Hmmm. Interesting. Tell me what you know about that guy," she said. "That Arnie—what's his name—Hagedoorn. I can't get my tongue around these Dutch names."

"His wife just had a baby."

"Is she cute?"

"It's a boy," I said.

"No, I mean the wife."

"Oh, Mrs. Hagedoorn. She's pretty nice. I had her for Sunday school twice. My father said it would take a real prayer warrior to hook Mr. Hagedoorn."

"Is your father a good friend of his?"

"They were best friends in high school."

"Isn't that interesting. Lucky you."

I went on to tell her about Mr. Hagedoorn's history, his suicide attempt, his health problems. She shook her head and clucked her tongue. She pushed back the stray hair.

"Poor baby," she said. "You don't know what it does to me to hear these things. I'm looking for a new friend. Maybe I'll make friends with Arnie."

"So were you an actress, Mrs. Jordan?" I asked. "Were you famous?"

"I had my big break. But . . . it just didn't work out." She fumbled in her purse. "Where are my cig—? Have you got a cigarette? No, of course you don't. You're a good girl."

"Wow," I said, "so you're a real actress."

"Oh, yes. It's in my bones. Problem is my husband hates it. Tell you a secret, though. I'm about to get back into it." She smiled, found her cigarettes, and lit up.

"You're going back to the theater?"

"Yes, kiddo, I am, but you're sworn to secrecy about this. You're my confidante. You know that little theater opportunity I've got Bob into in Richmond? Well, I think I'm in it, too. It's a musical comedy thing. There's a lot of money behind it. Dick Danson, this poultry millionaire over in Roanoke, is trying to help out his son-in-law, who

79

wants to bring back old-fashioned musical comedies. Dick is just a doll. And Al Palia is coming out of retirement to direct."

"Who's Al Palia?"

"An old guy who was on Broadway I think before they invented electricity or something. He must be about a hundred years old by now. The thing is, Carla, old men love me. I have a rapport with old men. I don't know why. But that's how I got the part."

"What's the musical about?" I asked, kicking my legs under the table like a younger child.

She rolled her eyes. "Do you really want to know?"

"Yes, ma'am."

"Don't 'ma'am' me. Let's see. It's called *Lady Don't Laugh.* I'm the lady, so it's about me. And it's about Henry Harrison, who's the biggest name in the show. You've probably never heard of him; he was famous for about twenty seconds once on Broadway. I never even saw him in anything. And there's an actress named Mary Burrows, who wants the girl lead. But Henry can't stand the thought of doing love scenes with her, so he wants me for the lead instead." She rubbed her lips with the tip of her fingers and smiled at me.

"But what's the plot?" I asked.

She looked uncertain. "The plots of these things don't matter, kiddo. It's the songs that count. Why don't you come watch rehearsal sometime and find out?"

"What? Really?"

"There's a real cute kid in it. Walter something. I should introduce you to this kid, Carla. He can sing and dance like a little star."

"I'd really love to come," I said. "Can I really come?"

"Absolutely. We'll have to arrange it. And I want you to meet Walter."

"I just love acting. I'd really like to be an actress when I grow up. Just like you."

"Aw," she said, "isn't that sweet. Hey, Donny! Could you bring the check?"

A pimply boy with a dishcloth skipped over to us and I drifted into thought. Recently my grandmother had suggested that I might grow up to become a librarian. Mrs. Ernst in circulation had even hinted that maybe one day I should have her job, as I seemed to know so much more about it than she did. But now I saw myself, a tall, dark woman with an armful of roses, taking bows to brilliant applause. Could that really be me, ten or twenty years from now? Was that my grandma cheering in the audience, and my father? Did I see my cousins, green with envy, and the library staff, including Mr. Hagedoorn, shaking their heads regretfully at the one that got away? Was that Mrs. Jordan in the wings, weeping tears of joy and pride over me?

"One thing I do need desperately is a baby-sitter," Ginger sighed, as Donny whisked away our plates.

"A baby-sitter?" I asked.

"Well, it's not the normal baby-sitting routine. I need someone who can come with me to Richmond on Wednesday nights from seven to ten and watch the baby. Which is incredible, Carla. They wanted me to commit three nights a week to this thing, so I told them about my little problem with Frank and it was like a miracle. Mr. Danson said he really liked me, said he'd let me off for the other two nights if I promised to pick up the choreography on the side. And Wednesday is just perfect, because Frank and the boys are at—of course—prayer meeting. Frank will think I'm at my sister's. I'll tell him she's pregnant again."

"I could do it," I said. "I'd go to rehearsal with you and watch the baby. I'd do it for free."

"I don't know, kiddo. It's—no, it's too much trouble for you."

"No, it's not."

"You don't want to do this. You're just feeling sorry for me."

"I want to do it," I said. "I really want to."

"You'd have to keep it a secret. What would you tell your mother?"

"Oh, my mother's dead," I said. "I just live with my grandma." I watched her face carefully. Her smiled dropped away momentarily.

"Well, what would you tell your grandma?"

"I'll think of something."

"Yeah," she smiled again. "I bet you will. All right. I feel kind of guilty, but who knows, maybe it'll be your ticket to stardom. And it's only for a few weeks. I'll give you a call when I know how things are going to pan out."

"O.K.," I said. We had finished eating and the tip had been calculated. The glorious lunch was over, and as we walked back to my house I was bursting to tell someone all about it. But of course I couldn't. I waved good-bye. "Bye, Mrs. Jordan."

"You can call me Ginger from now on, Carla."

"In that case you can call me Carrie—" It was too late. Ginger had turned and crossed the street quickly, barely avoiding a Thunderbird. The driver shook his fist out of the window but took a second look at her and whistled. Ginger was gone, across the street toward the library.

I went inside. The front door slammed behind me. "Grandma!" I shouted, ready to offer to do anything she wanted me to—cook dinner, clean the bathroom, wash the windows, whatever. I sailed through the living room, full of hope. For a little while I had forgotten the troubles earlier, the argument with my father, the unpleasantness in the back of the Valley Orbitron.

"Grandma? Oma, where are you?" I went into the family room. It was empty. I checked the basement stairs; they were dark. Finally I went to my grandmother's bedroom and knocked on the door.

"Come in," she said.

"Grandma?" I opened the door.

"Hello there, darling." She sat in the dark on the edge of her bed, her face in her hands, her shoulders shaking.

"What's wrong?" I asked. "What happened?"

She dabbed at her eyes with the corner of her sleeve. "Carolyn," she said, "we've got a lot to talk about. Sit down beside me here."

I sat down next to her on the soft mattress and she put her arm around me, hugging me close. "Your father," she began, "has just told me something which has, frankly, shocked me to pieces." She picked up a clean sock from the top of the laundry basket next to her and wiped her nose on it. She must have thought it was a handkerchief.

"What do you have to tell me?" My heart was still racing with good news, but her tone was ominous.

"I don't even know how to tell you." She paused for a long time and then heaved a sigh and dropped her shoulders. "But I have to tell you. He hasn't given me any time." She paused again and took a breath. "Oh, my sweet Carolyn, I've thought for a long time that I'll be get-

82

ting too old to take care of you soon. You'll be in high school before we know it, and you'll need someone to watch over you closely. You'll need good advice from someone closer to your own—your own era. You see, what I'm trying to say is that I've hoped that when your father came home from overseas. . . . Well, I've hoped that he would marry again. He's still young. Plenty of dear Dutch girls would have been interested. You and I are so close, Carolyn, but I wouldn't have let my jealousy get in the way of your best interests. Not even if you had to go away."

I thought of all the women at the homecoming party. "Who will he marry?"

"It's not a question of *who* anymore. I'm afraid to tell you. The fact is, Carolyn, your father has informed me this afternoon that he already has married."

"Oh."

"Carrie, I'm very upset at this, nearly at the end of my tether. You see, your father hasn't married a Dutch girl, or even an American. I'm so sorry," she said, dragging out the words in a sorrowful moan. "This must be a shock for you, at your age. Your father has married a Vietnamese." She sobbed and quivered on the last word.

I waited a long time for her to collect herself. "I don't really understand," I said. "You don't like her because she's Vietnamese?" It was Grandma who always pointed at the pictures of the dark people on the refrigerator and spoke of how much they had suffered. It was Grandma who proudly said that my father must be a great comfort to them.

Grandma put her head in her hands and pressed her eyes with her fingers. "I don't have anything against those people," she said. "The Lord said to show hospitality to the stranger in your land. I've even considered taking in a refugee. But I do feel . . . I do feel that your father has betrayed me. He has lied to me, not telling me this before. How could he lie to me like that? Why would he do it when we've always been so close? And I don't know anything about this woman. I don't know the first thing about her. We must be so different. We have to be."

I thought of the refugee children who were bussed to our Vacation

Bible School each year—three skinny Vietnamese boys who played kickball. I had seen their craft projects on the table at parents' night. Their macaroni maps of the Holy Land were neater than mine, without thin ribbons of Elmer's glue showing at the edges or clumps of blue felt clinging to the salty strip of Dead Sea.

"I refuse to live with her," Grandma said. "I just refuse."

I had never heard Grandma speak this harshly before. She had always cautioned me against talking badly about people. She had never complained about relatives, even Aunt Betsy with her health food and leather sandals.

"Will I have to live here if you leave?" I asked.

"Oh, of course not. I'm just talking." She hopped up from her bed and wiped her eyes in the mirror. "I just don't know if I can live with this, Carolyn. I'm getting too old."

"It'll be all right," I said. "I'll help you."

"I just don't know. I'm demoralized, to be honest. The world's going to pieces. This family's coming apart at the seams. What's it all going to come to? I just feel so betrayed."

I had no answer. It was strange to think of having a mother again, any mother, but I would think about all that later. I gave her a pat on the shoulder, and then I went quietly out of the room and closed the door. She was still standing in front of the mirror when I left.

The three of us sat moody and silent at dinner that night, breathing salty steam from grilled hamburgers. While a radio drama from Grand Rapids spattered tremulous organ music over the kitchen, Father got up to fetch himself milk, ketchup, relish, and sliced cheese singles from the refrigerator. And Grandma allowed this. She stared into her plate, just stirring the gravy on her mashed potatoes, and allowed her son to fetch his own food. I had never seen such a thing.

"Grandma," I said, "why is it wrong to go to the movies or to the theater when it's O.K. to watch T.V. and listen to the radio?"

"Because people don't see you watching T.V.," she said, without lifting her eyes from the gravy. "You can't cause a brother to stumble when you're watching in your own home."

"What if you hired actors and singers and dancers to come and entertain you in your own home? Would that be O.K.?"

She winced. "No."

"But you wouldn't be causing a brother to stumble. No one would know about it."

She winced again. "You wouldn't want that sort of people in your house, Carolyn. Remember that the Lord is the unseen guest at every meal. Would you want to invite the Lord to the cinema? No, and you wouldn't want to invite the cinema to the Lord's table."

"But you could invite them to church, couldn't you? That's the Lord's house."

"You could invite them, but they probably wouldn't come. People like that don't feel comfortable in a holy place."

My father looked up and smiled but said nothing.

"Isn't that right, David?" she said, suddenly fixing her eyes on him.

"Whatever you say, Mama."

"No, it's whatever you say," she said sharply. "Carolyn's got to hear your opinion, not mine only."

"My opinion," he said, "is that you're probably right, as usual."

"Then tell me why you were smiling."

"I was trying to picture us hiring singers and dancers to come and entertain us in our own home."

"I don't see that it's funny," said Grandma. "It would be a terrible testimony." After saying so, she was silent again. When dinner was finished, Father announced that he would wash the dishes. Grandma thanked him coolly and spent the rest of the evening in her room. I heard her sewing machine rumble loudly. It made diagonal lines on the television.

The next morning, Father came to wake me. I lay curled up in a wad of sheets, half dreaming, with my back to the door. I heard him whisper, "Carolyn?"

"Carolyn?" he said more loudly. "Carolyn?"

I turned over and met his eyes. He smiled, slipped into the room soundlessly, and closed the door behind him. Not once in his first few days home had he visited me here. He took a moment to look around at the portrait of my mother, a snapshot of Grandma, my school medals, and my rock collection. He stared at my bookshelf and cleared his throat.

"Carolyn," he said, coming over to the bed. "Did you ever hear the one about the little boy who went to the eye doctor with his mom and his older brother?"

"No."

"This boy cried and kicked his feet, and it was all the doctor and the mother could do to keep him quiet while the older boy got his glasses. Finally, the doctor cut two holes in a paper bag and plopped it on the little boy's head. And for a few seconds, he was quiet as a mouse, just looking out and blinking and all. Then he started to howl like nothing you've ever heard. 'What in the world is the matter?' his mother said. The boy looked up at her and howled, 'I wanted wire rims like my brother!'"

"Oh," I said as he laughed. I assumed there was a hidden message in the joke, but I couldn't see it.

Father shrugged his shoulders. "Figured you heard that already. Hey, how come you don't have any pictures of me in here?"

"There's pictures of you all over the house."

"I'll have to give you one. I've got some snapshots from Hawaii."

"You were in Hawaii?" I asked.

"Yep," he said.

"Did you surf?"

"Nope, but I ate raw octopus."

"What time is it?"

"Time you should be getting out of bed." He swept around in a circle looking for a place to sit and finally sank down on my bed. The mattress tilted and I put my hand out to keep myself from rolling. My fingers touched his. We both drew away. "I wanted to talk to you a minute," he said, "while Grandma's out at the grocery."

"O.K."

"Has your grandma talked to you?" he asked.

"Yes."

"About me?"

"Yes, and she's pretty upset at you."

"What did she tell you?"

"That you're married."

He nodded. "Did she say anything else?"

"She said you're married to a Vietnamese lady."

He nodded again and scratched his moustache and the rough hair on his unshaven cheeks. It was hard to think of anything then but my mother's portrait above us. She stared down at us, her tinted eyes blazing on the back of his neck. He scratched around his ears, as if he felt something, too. "What do you think about that?" he asked.

"I don't know."

"Have you ever met any Vietnamese people?"

"Yes." I told him about the boys from church, how neat and smart they were and how good they were at sports. I described their pictures of the Holy Land and their missionary key chains with Art and Gayle Steketee's pictures fitted so neatly into the tiny metal frames. He clapped his hands together.

"That's good," he said. "That's real good. It's good to start out with a positive view of people. It's going to be a little awkward around here for a while. The main thing I want to do is fight the negative. We're going to keep smiling, no matter what. We're going to be kind to each other, no matter what."

"Is she supposed to act like my mother now?"

"Who, Phuong?"

This was the first time I had heard her name, but I wasn't surprised by it. All Vietnamese names sounded strange at first—Lum, Trong, Nguyen, Tam, Son. There was a family at the Presbyterian church by the name of "No" who didn't speak English well. Sometimes when they voted on matters of politics or practice in their congregational meetings, the ballots would come back saying unanimously "Yes," except for two ballots saying "No," written in tiny handwriting, and always in the same red marker. So the minister would tell people privately that the No family had misunderstood the question. Their name was a long-standing joke now, though their children spoke English better than most in town.

My father cleared his throat, a gesture of clearing away the question. "Do you know my main concern, Carolyn? My main concern is to make sure your grandma is happy, whatever it takes. Never in my whole life have I disappointed her, and I don't want to start now. So let's all be on our best behavior. Like I said, let's fight the negative. Keep smiling." He smiled as he stood up and wiped his hands on his pants, looking down like he expected me to dismiss him from the bedroom.

Grandma was home now and calling me from the hall. "Carolyn, you lift yourself out of that bed. Annajane's at the door. She's been up an hour if she's been up a minute and there you are still sleeping."

"Coming!" I shouted.

"I'll give her something to eat and tell her to wait for you."

"Just keep all this in mind, Carolyn," said Father. "Remember, what are we going to do?"

"Fight the negative," I replied.

"Amen."

"O.K., I'll remember. Is that all?"

"Yep. See you at lunch. I'll be out all morning."

I got up and dressed quickly, worried that Annajane would leave before I got downstairs. She rarely visited me at home. I had spent more nights at the Ten Kates' than I could count. They lived in a rickety wooden house built in 1800 out of shipyard scrap hauled over from the James River on bumpety wagons. The house didn't have a street entrance. It sat behind the bakery, its two teardrop towers hanging over the bakery dumpsters. In the parlor on the second floor was a picture of an ugly great-aunt whom everybody called "Old Golie." According to legend, she had died in the cellar a hundred years ago, locked up there for a month by accident while the rest of her family vacationed in Baltimore. Annajane said that her spirit haunted the bakery at night and gnawed on the day-old donuts. Mrs. Ten Kate had once seen six apple tarts dance by themselves in the display window. The story had made it into the Dutch Falls *Trumpet,* with a picture of Sadie Ten Kate standing beside the deep-fry vat.

"I don't know what you saw," Mr. Ten Kate would often say, "but it wasn't tarts dancing by themselves." He was a gentle man, a tease, an elder for life at the church. He had lost his legs to diabetes and had to be trundled around in a wheelchair with a blanket in his lap.

I dressed and went into the kitchen. There was bacon on the stove. Grandma and Annajane were drinking coffee together.

"You must grind this at home," Annajane was saying. "Do you buy the beans from Mommy?" She habitually called her mother "Mommy," which seemed odd, since it was always her mother who made childish mistakes at the bakery and Annajane who did most of the scolding and comforting.

"I buy it fresh ground at the A&P," Grandma said appreciatively. They looked up at me as I came in, and raised their cups to their mouths. I didn't bother to ask for one. "I'm loathe to see you start on a bad habit," Grandma would say. "Remember, Carolyn, that your body is the temple of the Holy Spirit."

"Good morning," I said.

"Good morning," answered Grandma. "Listen to Anna's news."

"Mommy's got a job for us," Annajane said. "She wants us to do some advertising. And she's going to pay us."

"When? Today?"

"Right away. You can have breakfast at my house. Mommy made plum fritters."

"Doesn't that sound plum delicious?" said Grandma, who was bad at jokes. Of course Annajane laughed. They raised their cups like old friends. I waited for them to finish and then Anna and I walked across the street together, through the long tree shadows. It was only eight o'clock and cool for a July morning. The library windows remained dark. Bamboo blinds blocked the glass door of the Chinese restaurant. Around the bakery, sugar maples glowed emerald-green in the early sun.

"Come in! Come in!" Mrs. Ten Kate waited for us with fresh pastry. She placed it in our hands in napkins and the steam seeped through and burned my skin. "So, Carolyn, how have you been? I haven't seen you in almost two weeks."

"I've been busy. We had relatives in town."

"That's right! For the big homecoming! I just had such a lovely time there. Too bad your Aunt Josephine couldn't come. She used to visit me when she was a girl, you know, a high school girl, and I was a new wife. I would read the Bible and pray with her. Yes, I remember Josephine, always chasing those boys, chasing that Arnie Hagedoorn all over this world and the next. I hoped to disciple her, and often I regretted, well . . . But thank your grandma for me, won't you? And your father. We all have such admiration for him. Doyle can't stop saying what a great fellow he is. How do you like your fritter? Tasty?"

"Tastes fine," I said. "But what's wrong with it? Why are you giving it away?"

"Nothing's wrong with it. What do you mean why do I give it away? I give it away because I love you so. I've made it fresh this morning. Now, Carolyn, about my little proposition."

Mrs. Ten Kate sat down at a little desk behind the main counter,

90

winking at me. She was a stocky woman with large wrists and short fingers. Her hair was always teased and polished. It had the luster and shape of a golden bullet, with two coils springing down from it on each side of her flat face, bouncing in front of her ears like Slinkies. If she had been a pie in the bakery window, she would have been stiff, sweet lemon meringue.

"My dear, I want you and Annajane to do a little advertising for me," she said, "and I'm going to pay you for it. Does that sound fine?"

"Yes, ma'am."

"Well, dear, this is a job right up your alley, so to speak. I want you to take this box of chalk—" She handed me a big green box that rattled in her nervous fingers. "—Take it out to the sidewalk and write 'Ten Kate Pastry Pies and Sandwiches' as many times as you can until you run out of chalk. Go down to Church Street and over by the pharmacy on DeGroot. You can get yourself a soda; I'll give Annajane a dollar. Just stay away from that movie theater, you know, that Orbitron. There's a bad crowd down there, and I don't want you mixed up with them. The church will be calling us to picket that place soon, unless the dominie wants to spare his brother. Shame, shame on our heads for allowing the world to have its foothold here. Christians will rue the day when they didn't stand up to call their own country to repentance!" She twirled her big pinky in the air.

Annajane went to the back of the store and returned with a Bible under her arm. She collected her box of chalk and we went outside.

"Come back before lunch," Mrs. Ten Kate called after us. "Annajane has to practice her piano."

"Let's start by the library," Annajane said. "I'm keeping an eye on someone."

"Who?" I asked. "What do you mean?"

"I can't discuss it."

We walked to the library and began scrawling our advertisements about twenty feet apart on squares of sidewalk. When I had finished writing exactly what Mrs. Ten Kate had dictated to me, I stopped and looked over Annajane's shoulder.

"Annajane Ten Kate's Homestyle Pastry And Pies," it read. "Drop in on Your Lunch Hour. A Thief Shall Not Enter Heaven."

"Are we supposed to write Bible verses?" I asked.

"I like to tailor my message to the audience," she said. "There's been some theft here recently."

"What kind of theft?"

"All kinds. For instance, my souvenir two-dollar bill. I got it for a bicentennial present from Papa. Somebody stole it yesterday."

"Oh," I said cautiously, "where did you lose it?"

"Somewhere over there, by the flagpole. It must have slipped out of my pocket."

I thought of the two-dollar bill on my dresser at home. I hoped Annajane hadn't marked it.

"Let's go down to the Orbitron," she said. "We can write a warning on Mr. Grunstra's Impala."

"Your mama said not to go there."

"Now you can't save sinners by following the letter of the law, Carolyn Grietkirk. It's grace that I listen to, not law."

"But isn't it a sin to disobey your mama?"

"Remember what Jesus said to his parents when they went looking for him at the temple—'Did you not know that I must be about my father's business?'"

We reached the Orbitron and stood next to a dull gold Impala, which Annajane said belonged to Bernie Grunstra.

"Where is he now?" I asked. I looked up and down the empty sidewalk.

"I don't know," she said in a dry tone, "probably up to no good. How much do you know about this man, Carolyn?"

"Not very much. He's the dominie's brother."

"Did you know that he was once a *voorlezer* at the church?" *Voorlezers* were one step above deacons at the F.R.C. of V. They could preach on occasion, if the dominie was ill or called out of town. I could not imagine Bernie Grunstra in the pulpit, scratching his wart and looking up at the chandeliers, sighing.

"What happened to him?" I asked.

"He fell under church discipline."

"Oh, really? What for?"

"Immorality."

"What kind of immorality?" I asked.

"I don't know," said Annajane. "All I know is they took his Sunday school bell away and denied him the communion cup until he showed repentance, but he never showed it. So they deleted him from the church roll."

"Oh," I said, looking at the clothes and junk piled in the back of Bernie's rusty Impala. Doug had called him a pervert, and even Ginger had said to stay away from him. But I didn't tell Annajane any of this. "So what are you going to write on his car?" I asked.

Annajane raised her chalk and poised it above the front hood. She tossed out her hand and wrote, dramatically but neatly: "Flee Youthful Lust."

We stared at it together, cocking our heads to the side like birds.

"Aren't you going to mention the bakery at all?" I asked.

"This message is more important, Carolyn. A man's soul is at stake."

"But how old is Bernie Grunstra? He doesn't seem very youthful to me."

"I don't know," she said. "What does his age matter? It's the age of the heart that's important. Now don't go telling anyone about this. Remember what Jesus said: 'Go thy way and tell no one what has happened to you.'"

I shrugged my shoulders, then went down the street and wrote "Come Fill Your Tummy, Our Crullers Are Yummy" in front of the post office. I could be creative, too. I made my way down the street, scrawling something on every fifth square of sidewalk. Meanwhile, traffic had picked up and Annajane had disappeared. I caught up with her on DeGroot at Brinkerhoff's Pharmacy. It was a small, wood-paneled store that smelled like sour damp carpet. Over the door stood a five-foot tall, red neon hot dog with a top hat and tap shoes, leaning on a mortar and pestle. The door jangled shut behind us as we went inside. A young clerk looked up.

"Two chocolate sodas, please," Annajane said.

"Fountain's closed," he said.

She stared at him coldly. "How about a couple of cones?"

"It's too early for ice cream," he said.

"Now, no sir, it isn't," she said firmly. "I'll have strawberry cheese-cake in a cone. And my friend will have chocolate mint."

The young man sighed and hunkered down to the freezer under the restaurant counter, where he pulled out two big brown tubs. I agreed with him that it was too early for ice cream. Why did people give in to Annajane this way? We sat on barstools and twirled around. Her skinny neck was as straight as a broom handle under her blond ponytail.

"Do you miss school?" she said.

"No," I said. "I hate school."

"Why?"

"I don't know." It was because I didn't like the other children at Falls Christian Elementary. Why that was so, I didn't really know. For the most part, they were average Dutch children, smart and cheerful like Annajane.

"Maybe if we could be in the same class," she said, "you'd like it better." Annajane was about to start at Falls Christian High School, about a mile away from the church, on property once owned by the Hagedoorns. The elementary school met in the church building. My seventh-grade classroom looked out on the playground.

I let some time pass and then I said, "Do you want to hear something?"

"What?"

"My father got married again."

Annajane's mouth dropped. "Are you kidding? To who?"

"I don't know her yet. She's from overseas."

"From Holland?"

I shook my head. "No. She's a Vietnamese." I was proud to see that I'd surprised Annajane. She swung her body around and gave me her entire attention.

"You mean a missionary to Vietnam, don't you?"

"No, she's a real Vietnamese. Her name is Phuong."

"Phuong? Is she saved?"

"I told you, I haven't met her yet and I don't know anything. I just know that my grandmother doesn't like it, but my father's bringing her anyway."

Annajane turned slowly back to the counter and frowned. "Mommy had a good plan for your father," she said. "She was going to marry him to my cousin Roberta Jay. Then you and I could have been cousins."

"Oh, that's too bad," I said honestly. I would like to have been related to the Ten Kates.

"It's not an easy job taking in a Vietnamese. When my aunt was a sponsor for some Vietnamese, she had to take a sample of their stools to the doctor. They weren't even grateful."

"That's disgusting," I said. "Don't tell me about it. I'll never do that."

"You'd never make it on the mission field then."

"Who said I wanted to be on the mission field?"

"What if God calls you? You might have to eat grubs, or pull tapeworms out of people."

"Annajane, you're making me sick and I'm trying to eat."

"I'm surprised at you. What if God calls you?"

At that moment the door jangled again and into the drugstore walked Bernie Grunstra, with Arnie Hagedoorn just behind him. Annajane grabbed my arm.

"There he is," she whispered, her neck rigid and her face as pink and pointed as a new pencil eraser. She watched the two of them sharply as they moved through the aisles of the store. Bernie Grunstra picked up a magazine and paid for it at the counter. Arnie Hagedoorn looked around and ambled slowly out again, whistling, without buying anything.

"Let's follow him!" Annajane said.

"Follow Mr. Grunstra? Back to the Orbitron?"

"I don't mean Bernie Grunstra. I mean Mr. Hagedoorn. You go follow him and report back to me at the bakery. I'll pay the bill."

"But why? Where am I following him?"

"I don't know where. Just go on." She pushed me off my stool and into the aisle. I hurried out the door, where I nearly collided with Mr. Hagedoorn, standing dead still on the sidewalk, staring at Bernie Grunstra's car. The car squatted in front of the pharmacy now. Annajane's message was still there in chalk: "Flee Youthful Lust."

"I can't believe this," said Mr. Hagedoorn to me, or at least to the person he thought I was. I stood quietly in back of him. "It just burns me up. Now is that fair? Hasn't it been long enough? You know what

95

I'd like to say to the self-righteous guy who wrote this? I'd like to say, 'Physician, heal thyself, mister.'"

I shrank back, under the green awning and the five-foot hot dog. Arnie Hagedoorn turned and blushed deeply when he saw me. "Oh, excuse me. I thought you were Bernie."

I shook my head. I was not Bernie Grunstra.

"Well, my mistake," he said, still blushing. "See you later."

I started walking just after him, so he stopped a few yards down the street and turned. "Going to the library, Miss Grietkirk?"

"Yes, sir," I said. "That's where I'm going."

"I hope you're not going over there just to stare out that window all morning."

"Oh, no sir, I'm going to look at books on Vietnam."

"Why don't you just walk alongside me, as long as we're going the same way, huh? I feel like I'm being followed."

"O.K." Was there a better way of following him than this? Should I have given him a lead and then dashed from building to building, out of sight, weaving a serpentine path to the library?

We walked slowly. He breathed hard and went from warm red to hot crimson but never sweated a drop. "It's some kind of hot already," he sighed. "I shouldn't be out in this heat for more than ten minutes, but my car broke down. Had to walk this morning." He turned onto Church Street and bought a newspaper, which he lifted over his head as we walked. While he held his arms in the air I studied his big hands, his freckles, the orange hair on his wrists that curled and crinkled under his watchband. I studied his nose from the profile, bony and large. The skin over it was milky pink.

"Do you know Ginger Jordan?" I asked.

"Who? Doesn't sound familiar at all."

"The lady who sang at Bible school—the real pretty lady."

"Oh, yeah, O.K. The day after Arnie Jr. was born. I was practically in a coma that day; I hardly remember. What about her?"

"Nothing. I just wondered if you knew her."

"I've seen her a few times around town," he said coolly, no interest in his voice. "She's a fine person. The dominie says she and her husband have a fantastic testimony, but I don't know her well enough to ask about that."

"You should talk to her," I said. "She told me that she'd like to get to know you better."

"What?" He sniffed. "How did that come up?"

"She asked me about you. I guess she likes you."

He shook his head at me. "I don't need a social coordinator. Don't go around talking to people about other people—that's gossip."

We turned the corner onto Beatenbough and reached the library door together. He pulled it open and stood out of the way, but I stepped back.

"Good-bye," I said. "See you at church."

"Aren't you coming in? It's blazing hot out here, Miss Grietkirk."

"No sir, not today. Maybe tomorrow." I was going to the bakery, to meet Annajane and to be paid.

"Tomorrow's the Lord's Day," he said. "See you at church. And don't think you can just run in here any time to use the women's bathroom. What it is about you young ladies, I don't understand." He went inside grumbling to himself.

When I reached the bakery, Mrs. Ten Kate was not to be seen. The big brass door stood open and a breeze drifted over the threshold, as if she had torn out of the shop in such a hurry as to stir the wind. I went around back and called up at the windows of the house, "Hello? Hello? Anyone there?"

"*Dag*, Annajane—over here!" Mr. Ten Kate appeared in one of the first-story windows. He didn't see well at a distance. "Come here, Annajane."

"It's Carrie Grietkirk," I called. "I'm looking for your wife!"

"Oh, *dag*, Carrie. *Dag*. Forgive me, but Sadie is hysterical. Why don't you come in and see if you can talk to her. Tell Annajane to hurry."

"She's not with me. I just came for my money."

"Sadie's upstairs. She's got her purse up there. She'll see to you."

I went in and climbed up to a tiny octagonal room that teetered high above the largest dumpster in the parking lot. Mrs. Ten Kate was having her *kopje koffie* over the sweet, sulphuric smell of moldy dough and rotten eggs.

"Hello," I said.

"You came to be paid, didn't you?" She pulled three quarters out of her change purse on the tea cart nearby. Her hands shook as she handed them to me. She was perspiring enough for herself and Mr. Hagedoorn both. "Don't go back in that store, dear. Not until Doyle has ordered her out. He's the only one she ever listens to."

"Who?"

"You know," she said. "The O.G. I dropped a sack of flour this morning, Carolyn, and when I turned around to get a cloth—" She leaned in the direction of the door to shout down the stairs. "YES, DOYLE, WHEN I TURNED MY BACK FOR JUST ONE SECOND AND NOT FOR FIVE MINUTES, what was I to see when I turned around again, but two black handprints, big as life, on the counter!"

"The Old Golie?" I asked. "You're sure you didn't accidentally put your hands in the flour?"

"Of course, I didn't. Doyle asked me the same thing; now don't ask me again. I know what I saw."

"And there was no one else in the store?"

"No, no, no, and no! There was no one else. Do I have to swear it in blood, dear?"

"No, ma'am."

"If you don't believe me, go on down and see for yourself. Just be careful. And tell Annajane she'll have to clean up that mess for me. I can't do a thing, I'm so nervous. I can't clean a thing."

I wound my way down their steep staircase, waved to Mr. Ten Kate in his wheelchair, and returned to the street. Annajane was already waiting for me outside the bakery. She skipped around clutching her sides, about to break open with laughter. The skirt of her denim jumper was white. She clapped her hands together and flour mushroomed up in a cloud around her eyes.

"I followed him," I said over her laughter. "I followed Mr. Hagedoorn. Why did you tell me to follow him like that? He wasn't going anywhere but the library."

She laughed harder. "Don't you want to hear my joke? I did something *so* funny! Now, don't you want to hear it?"

"I'm tired of jokes," I said impatiently. "I can tell what you've been doing; you've been scaring your mother half to death." I sounded the way my grandmother had sounded the night before, irritable and humorless. Annajane didn't stop laughing, and so I turned and walked back across the street toward home. Why did everyone listen to Annajane? I knew better.

"Come back!" she shouted. "What's wrong with you, Carrie? Don't you have any sense of humor?"

"Nothing's wrong! See you later!" I shouted.

"Will you sit with me at church on Sunday?"

"O.K. Good-bye."

When I arrived at home, my grandmother put a grilled cheese sandwich in front of me and said that Aunt Jo had called. "She'll be coming to town around the beginning of the month, Carolyn, so let's just pray that we'll all say and do the right things. Let's pray that your father's 'plans' won't cause any problems."

I knew that she was talking about the marriage. Before we ate, we bowed our heads together and Grandma asked forgiveness for our sins, along with knowledge of how to do better. She had a hot garlic and onion sandwich with pickles on the side. The steam from it made my nose run, and so I had to lift my head and sniff loudly while she was still praying that we would have a blessed time of fellowship with Aunt Jo.

oday is the day," Grandma said one morning a week and a half later, over grapefruit and coffee. Her voice sounded neither sour nor bitter. Father had already left for Richmond to meet a nine o'clock coach from New York City. The bus would be late, of course, because buses were always late. But it would arrive today, and it would bring my stepmother. She would be staring out of a dusty green Trailways window as my father watched anxiously from the station door, breakfast smells leaking from the dilapidated diner next door, truck brakes hissing on the street. Father had gone for her in Grandma's Dart. Before he left, Grandma prayed that the car would hold together at least for the trip home from the city. She acted cheerful enough until he was gone and then went to her room for a short time and came back with her eyes brilliant blue and rimmed pink, like the sky opening up again after a quick shower.

For our small welcome party, Grandma had decided that I should make one neat welcome sign on white posterboard. She had bought the markers herself. All by herself, she had scanned the *Saturday Evening Post* and *Reader's Digest* for pictures of hot dogs, American flags, and apple pie. But I was to put the thing together and come up with a message.

"What should I write?" I had asked her.

"Write something like, 'Welcome to America,'" she had said. "That's all you need to put. Something short. Because there's no reason why we have to make a big to-do about this. She can't expect much on

100

such short notice." As if Phuong might expect us to paint the house for her.

But I had asked for help on Sunday from Lum Ha, a quiet Vietnamese boy with cool black eyes and smooth hair that gleamed blue in the sun. He didn't know much English yet, so I tried to explain that I wanted to say something like, "Welcome to your new family." He nodded and scrawled something on the back of a Bible crossword. Now I copied it onto my poster with a blue magic marker, leaving room for the hot dogs and flags and wedges of pie, all cut out of the magazines at sharp scissor angles.

"Phone for you," Grandma called from the kitchen. As I started toward her, she whispered loudly, "It's a lady, someone who doesn't pronounce your name right." Grandma had dressed to the hilt, her red blouse bolted tight at the neck with a white pin and a blue scarf folded into the collar. "I wouldn't be surprised," she said, "if it's somebody from the MTC asking about that camping trip." MTC stood for "More Than Conquerors." It was the Dutch Falls version of the Girl Scouts. Instead of cookies, we sold placemats decorated with scenes of the Holy Land.

"Don't tell them no this time, Carrie," whispered Grandma. "I couldn't face Mrs. Ronald Steen asking questions."

"Hello?" I said dully into the receiver.

"Carla?" said a low female voice.

"Hi, Mrs. Jordan," I said quietly, hoping Grandma hadn't heard.

She groaned. The receiver rattled in my hand. "Mrs. Jordan my a—, well, my avalanche! You make me feel sixty years old. It's Ginger, kiddo, please. Listen, day after tomorrow is my big Wednesday, in case you forgot. I'm counting on you for baby-sitting. You won't let me down?"

"Day after tomorrow? I didn't know you would need me so soon."

"Come on now, kiddo, I'm counting on you."

"Well, I can come, I guess."

At the sink, Grandma nodded and smiled. She thought I was agreeing to a wholesome camping trip on some sunny North Carolina mountain, eating melted Hershey bars and marshmallows between graham crackers.

101

"You sound strange, kiddo," Ginger said. "Is it fine or isn't it?"

"Oh, it's just fine. Yes, um, let me switch phones." I put my hand over the receiver and turned to Grandma. "We have a bad connection. Could you hang up for me when I get in the bedroom? I'll only be a minute."

"Take your time, dear. Tell them you have your own sleeping bag."

I slipped away and picked up the phone on Grandma's nightstand. "I'm back," I said.

"Well, kiddo," Ginger said, "can you come or can't you?"

"I think I can, but Wednesday is prayer meeting night. Grandma will get mad about that."

"Tell your grandmother you're coming to our church."

"She wouldn't understand that."

"Tell her Frank is going to pay you to keep the nursery. I'll pay you a dollar a week."

"She wouldn't want me to make money during prayer meeting."

"Oh, brother, and they say money makes the world go round. Tell her it's your ministry. That'll do it. You're committed now, kiddo. I'm counting on you."

"O.K., I'll do it. I'll do it. Ginger—"

"Huh? What? Speak up."

"Today is the day," I said.

"What? Today is what day?"

"Today is the day that my father goes to the bus station."

"Yes? And?" She held the phone away from her mouth. "Peter, now! Now! Pick it up!"

"He's going to the bus station to pick up his new wife."

"His new wife?"

"Yeah. He got married again. And my grandmother is pretty upset."

"Oh, really."

"Yes. I haven't met her yet or anything. Today is the first time." I waited for her to say something. While I waited, I wrote my name nervously on the writing pad beside the phone: Carrie, Carla, Carolyn, Carrie, Carla, Carla. I twirled the hem of Grandma's dust ruffle in my fingers.

Ginger held the phone away again and shouted, "Peter and Paul, I have told you to leave your brother alone! If you cannot keep your hands away from him, I will wrap all three of you together with duct tape. Listen, kiddo," said Ginger to me, "what you need is a little more faith. Things will work out."

"They will?"

"I just know they will. They always do."

"O.K.," I said, "if you say so. I'll try to trust."

"Why don't you just call me up when you feel bad and we'll talk through it together? That's what most people need, I've found, just a shoulder to cry on. And I'm real good at that. My shoulder's always soaked from little lost sheep crying on it day and night."

"I can call you anytime?" I asked. "You won't mind?"

"Well, anytime after ten in the morning. I don't get up early for anybody. And I'll see you tomorrow night at six thirty. We can talk more then."

"Um, Ginger—"

"Peter! You take that screwdriver out of his ear right now or I'll—" There was a click and then a lonely buzz. In another part of the house, somewhere upstairs, the vacuum cleaner droned and clattered on a wood floor. Grandma was cleaning again.

I went up to her, following the cord of the vacuum from the hall outlet into my father's room. She was feminizing there after spending the previous weeks masculinizing. She had replaced the African violets on the window sill with mums and snapdragons. She had hung Victoriana on the walls—milky-skinned girls climbing naked out of bathtubs, running through fields of lavender in bloomers and hoop skirts, buying fruit at the market from kindly vendors. A rose-patterned comforter and dust ruffle had replaced the old blue spread.

"What is it, Carrie?" Grandma yelled over the vacuum cleaner.

"Somebody from another church wants me to keep their nursery on Wednesday night."

"What? Another church nursery? When you should be at your own prayer meeting?"

"Yes, ma'am."

"Don't they have their own nursery workers?" Grandma said, still shouting. "Why do they need to steal our people?"

103

"It's a very small church. They need help. They're struggling. It would be a ministry."

She punched the vacuum cleaner with her foot and the motor moaned and whirled off like a spurned lover plunging over a cliff. "Who are these people? They're not Dutch. How do you know them?"

"Oh, they're just nice Christian people," I said.

"And what are they called?"

"Mr. and Mrs. Frank Jordan. I met her at the library and she told me that their church needs a baby-sitter every Wednesday night." I hoped Grandma wouldn't remember Ginger's name. I hoped she had forgotten about Bible school.

"Every Wednesday night? What church do they attend?"

"I don't know. I can ask."

"Well . . ." She frowned and fluffed a cushion against her knee. Dust motes floated in the glassy light of the window. "They're not Jehovah's Witnesses, are they?"

"No, ma'am, I don't think so."

"I'll have to speak to your father about it. He's the man of the house now, after all. I don't know why you even think I have anything to say about it."

"Will you ask him as soon as he comes home? I already told them yes."

"Now you know better than to do that without permission. What got into you, Carolyn, making someone a promise before you'd asked me?"

"I don't know."

"As if I didn't have enough to worry about. This whole thing is wearing me out. Do I have to be responsible for everyone around here?"

"No, Grandma."

"Go on and make us both some lunch. I don't want anything but a slice of bread with a little mayonnaise and pickle relish."

"Yes, ma'am."

"Because I already feel as though I ate a handful of hot peppers."

"Yes, ma'am."

After lunch I hung my sign over the knocker on the front door so

104

that Grandma could wince at it for a long time in the full sun. Bits of glue and glitter sparkled at the edges—my usual carelessness.

"Looks just fine to me," she said, "but how can anybody read that stuff?"

"Maybe Vietnamese people think English looks hard to read, too," I said.

"Well, your father says she's smart. She'd have to be to read that. I just hope the neighbors don't think we've gone out of our senses."

She and I sat down on the porch and waited. We watched the cars pass for ten or fifteen minutes, and we talked about where they might be going. I decided that some of them were on their way to New York or Philadelphia, but Grandma pointed out that none of the license plates said anything but Virginia, so most likely they were just headed back to work after lunch. The traffic thinned out gradually as the lunch hour ended. I was about to get up and fetch a book from upstairs when at last Grandma said, "Here he is! I hear him!" and the old Dart rumbled up the street. It swerved into our driveway and glided to a stop with a bleat and a thunk. Father jumped out.

"Hello!" he called happily. He ran around to unstrap luggage from the top, beckoning to us to come over. "Mama, Carolyn, you come on now!"

We looked at each other and stayed seated. Grandma tucked her hair into her bun and pulled at her scarf. I squinted to see the dark head in the car.

"Come on!" Father called to us in a happy voice. "Look alive! Come on!" We smiled and waved but hung back until he had tossed down all of the luggage, setting it aside under an apple tree.

"Well," said Grandma, "I guess we can't wait forever. Carolyn, you go ahead."

"Me?"

She put her hand on my shoulder and guided me in front of her like a walking stick, down the steps onto the grass. Father opened the passenger door. Out of the car came a small woman, unfolding slowly like an umbrella, leaning on his arm. She was black-haired like the Vietnamese boys from church but darker skinned. She had a figure like a child's but a face older than my father's. She stood no taller than me, and perhaps she was shorter. Her pink polyester pantsuit looked like it had been bought at a *Lawrence Welk Show* auction. It had stiff orange ruffles around the neck, fringe on the sleeves, and bell-bottom pant legs. The pockets glittered with rhinestones.

"I wonder if that's some kind of national costume," whispered Grandma.

Father spoke softly to his wife and led her toward us. We all walked together, converging at Grandma's rose bushes under the front bay window.

"Phuong," said my father to her gently, "this is my mother, Dorothea Grietkirk." He gestured from one to the other, and Grandma stepped forward first, towering over the Vietnamese woman.

"Welcome to your new home." Grandma wrapped her large pale hand around the small dark one. I remembered how often Grandma had bragged about her reach on the piano. Her hand stretched ten white keys easily, plus two black ones if she tried hard.

"I am Nguyen Ngoc Phuong," replied the woman, with only a hint of an accent. She smiled, squinting and showing her teeth, which looked brittle, yellow. Her smile was more like a grimace. I wondered if my grandmother had crushed her hand or pinched her fingers, maybe on purpose. I didn't think so. The woman's shallow black eyes darted back and forth over the landscape, among the houses, green lawns, shops, and cars.

"Win Goc Phong," Grandma said. "Did I say it right?" It was a good try. She was trying.

"Phuong," said Father.

"Phew-ong," said Grandma.

Phuong bowed her head, not meeting my grandmother's eyes at all. "Yes, Mrs. Grietkirk. It is a great honor to meet you." She bowed her head toward my father, also, and I noticed a shining white line that curved up from her lip to her ear like a spaghetti noodle. It was a scar, or maybe a birth defect.

"Phuong, this is my daughter, Carolyn," said Father.

"Yes, she look just like pictures," Phuong said. Her eyes flitted up, met mine, and dropped again. We all stood there then, in silence.

"Oh, dear, it's hot out here," said Grandma. "Shall we go inside?"

106

"Yes, ma'am," said Father. "Phuong could probably use a drink. We've been broiling in that car for an hour. I'll get the suitcases; you all go on in."

Grandma led us into the house and I came in last, scrutinizing this woman from behind. She passed through the front door, right beside my welcome sign, without turning her head half an inch to notice it. However, once inside the living room she began looking around again, glancing quickly up and down from this corner to that corner, from the chairs to the bookshelf to the piano. Her eyes settled on a painting over the sofa, a churning ocean scene. I had always been proud of its big gold frame and scaly brush strokes. She stared at it and then looked away without saying a word. Grandma gestured that we ought to sit down. She offered Phuong the couch. I slumped on the piano bench, my hands under my bare legs.

"Did you see Carolyn's sign that she made just for you?" said Grandma to Phuong. "It says 'Welcome to America.' She spent most of the morning working on that, didn't you, Carrie?"

I rubbed my nose. "Oh, Grandma."

Phuong nodded, staring down at her hands. "Thank you. Thank you. Very nice."

"Thanks," I said, and shrugged my shoulders.

"You must be very tired after all that driving," Grandma said to Phuong.

"She is," said my father, coming in the door. "Carolyn, why don't you get her some lemonade?"

Phuong's eyes darted back in his direction. Maybe she didn't like lemonade.

"Do you want something else?" I asked. "There's Coke, orange juice . . ."

She shook her head rapidly. "Oh, no, nothing. Nothing."

"No drink at all?"

"Oh, no. No."

"Carolyn, get her some lemonade," said Grandma. "She's got to be dry as a bone after that hot drive."

"But if she doesn't want anything . . ."

"Get us all something."

Father had seated himself on the sofa three feet from his wife. Grandma's eyes rested on the space between them. Meanwhile, I went into the kitchen and took out four tall glasses, listening to their conversation on the other side of the swinging door.

"Are you comfortable there, Phew-ong?" asked Grandma.

"Yes."

"That was Davey's father's favorite sofa. He was called home eight years ago."

"Oh, yes."

"Are your parents—do they live in Vietnam?"

"I think so, yes. I have not see them in very long time." She spoke slowly, taking some trouble over the words.

"Oh, my, that's a shame."

"Yes."

"That's a very interesting outfit you have on there. Did you make that yourself?"

"My good friend has give me in Guam."

"A friend? How very nice. Is she some kind of performer?"

"She is Presbyterian missionary lady."

"Oh, a missionary! How nice."

"Yes."

There was a long pause. "Well," said Grandma, "why don't you tell us a little bit about yourself, Phew-ong. Davey has told us so little. You met at one of those camps, I understand?"

"Oh, more or less," said Father. "She was in Guam for a year. I spent a few months there."

"Oh, really? Is that where she learned English?"

"No, she went to an English school as a girl; isn't that right, Phuong?" The sofa creaked. "Excuse me, a French school."

Father cleared his throat and called to me. "Is that lemonade ready, Carolyn?"

I brought it in on a silver tray, a family heirloom. I offered Phuong her glass first. She took it, saying "Thank you" again and again, but she only sipped it before she set it beside her on a wooden end table. Grandma scooped up the glass and threw a *Reader's Digest* underneath it to catch the condensation. Father and I gulped at our lemonade.

108

After a minute, Grandma rose up in her chair and, like Phuong, set her glass aside having only sipped it. She licked her lips, drummed her fingers on her knee, fluttered her eyelashes. I knew this behavior. She was straining for words. She was debating with herself. There was something she had to say.

"Were you going to say something, Mama?" asked Father.

"Oh, yes," said Grandma. "What I—I wanted to invite you to our church this Sunday, Phew-ong. Are you—do you have a house of worship in your country? Of course, we don't expect that you're all Reformed over there."

"Thank you," Phuong said, nodding at my father with that look of panic again.

"Did you think I was going to forget to ask her to church, Mama?" asked Father, winking at Grandma.

"Where has she been attending in Vietnam?" Grandma asked Father.

"In Guam she was sort of Pentecostal."

"Pentecostal?" Grandma asked uncertainly. "You mean like those preachers on television?"

Father shifted in his seat. Phuong looked confused. "I believe in the Jesus Christ," she said, "and I believe in the Holy Ghost. I pray every day and read my Bible. I am trying to live the holy life."

"Aren't we all," said Grandma.

Father shifted in his chair. "You see, Mama, over in the camp where she got saved it's just not the way it is here. Since there's usually just one minister for everybody, everybody worships together—Baptists, Presbyterians, Catholics, and Pentecostals. Everybody. Unless you're Buddhist, you go to the same church as everybody else. So it doesn't matter what you are. Too bad we can't be the same here, huh?"

"Well, that sounds a little idealistic to me," said Grandma. "But you know I'm all for unity. I'm not like some of these Dutch who think the F.R.C. of V. is God's only church. I've always said that the main thing is evangelism. That's why I've always been so interested in missions. Phew-ong, I thought about going overseas myself as a young girl, before I married. That's very unusual for us Dutch here in Virginia. Most keep to themselves."

"I've told Phuong that my mother is the most godly woman I know," said Father.

"I just want her to feel welcome here," said Grandma. "I guess this is where the Lord wants her to be since he brought her here."

"Amen to that."

"And, Davey, I want you to realize that this is your home now, and you shouldn't worry about what I think about anything. You just go about your business. From now on, don't give me a second thought." Grandma leaned over and began rearranging knickknacks on the coffee table.

"Come again?" said my father. "What do you mean by that?"

"I said it very clearly. This is your home now, David, and I won't get in the way. In fact, I think I should start making plans to find my own place somewhere."

"And where do you plan on staying?"

"I could stay with your brother for a little while."

"You couldn't stand living with Jim's family for a half an hour. What's this about, anyway? You know you don't want to live anywhere else."

"I want you to feel that you're the master here."

"No. No more of this, now. I don't want to hear another word about your leaving."

"Davey." Grandma's voice was plaintive.

"No. Not another word; do you hear me?"

"Well, all right."

Phuong slept through dinner that night. It was jet lag, Father said. He told us he had ordered her to stay in bed against her protests. While we ate, I brought up the subject of baby-sitting for the Jordans again. I explained what nice Christian people they were and what a ministry it would be to them, especially to Mr. Jordan as a seminarian, if I became their regular Wednesday night nursery keeper for their church. No one would want their babies to fall into the hands of a non-Christian.

"I told Carolyn I didn't like her missing prayer meeting," said Grandma.

"I don't recall you ever forcing Josephine or me to go to prayer meeting," said Father. "At least not at Carolyn's age."

"That's because you always went on your own."

"Not Josephine, that's for sure."

"Yes, well see how your sister turned out," Grandma said. Father laughed. "Joking aside," Grandma said impatiently, "are you going to allow your daughter to skip our prayer meeting or aren't you?"

"Oh, I expect I'll allow it," said Father. "But I'd like to meet the Jordans sometime. Carolyn, did you say that Mr. Jordan is a vet? Maybe we could have them over to dinner one night."

"Oh, me!" said Grandma. "Just let me get over one thing before I have to think about another!"

$\mathcal{I}$ was allowed to go with Ginger, but still there were miles of ordinary life to get through before Wednesday evening. I spent most of Tuesday at my library window, looking out at the rain. I looked down at my house and saw a light in my father's window that remained there all day. It must be Nguyen Ngoc Phuong at that window, I thought, sitting under the lamp at the reading table, looking out as I did now on the rain. I wondered whether Vietnam was a rainy country and whether she was thinking about her home. That was as far as my wondering took me. I didn't ask myself what had happened to her family, why she had left her country, or why my father had decided to marry her. I didn't wonder at the strangeness of her sleeping with him in the bedroom next to mine, though she was as small and frail as a starved child, as weary-eyed as an old woman. Grandma and I had hardly spoken to her, and she had hardly spoken to us. She padded around the house like a frightened animal. Because she was so silent and bashful, I assumed that we would never get to know her. I thought maybe even my father knew her no better than we did, but that out of some kindness he would keep her forever in our house, a mournful and distant old creature, staring out a window.

I counted the hours until I would see Ginger again, and when Wednesday night arrived and it was six thirty at last, I pushed open the screen door to the porch and stepped outside, breathing in the summer air. It was a dry, breezeless evening, only mildly hot after an afternoon shower, with a purple sky. I sat on the swing with my purse in my lap. There was a dull roar of air conditioners from all directions and a faint hum of insects from the tall grass in the yard next door. A hanging geranium dripped water on my head.

"Wasn't your Mrs. Jordan supposed to be here a while ago?" said Grandma as she headed off to prayer meeting with her purse over her arm and a flower pinned to her dress.

"It doesn't matter," I said. "I'm not in a hurry." Grandma walked like a woman rowing a boat. She threw out her purse and hauled it back with each step. I watched her go and scooted across the swing to get out of the path of the dripping plant.

"You ask those folks about their church," she called back. "Why don't they have people to watch their own children at that church?"

"Yes, ma'am."

Father appeared a few seconds later and dragged a bicycle out from under the porch with a rusty shriek. "Good-bye, Miss Carolyn. Enjoy yourself. We'll miss you at prayer meeting."

"Good-bye," I said.

"So long." He hopped on his bike and rode off in Grandma's direction. I checked my watch. Someone in the neighborhood was grilling steaks. Another neighbor washed his car, twirling a garden hose in the air in time to a song on a tiny transistor radio.

Down the street, Annajane left the bakery with her mother and father and got into their old blue Nova. Annajane waved as they drove away, no doubt wondering why I wasn't on my way to church. For a little while I enjoyed the fact that people might wonder about me. But soon it was seven thirty. I could only imagine that something terrible had happened or else that Ginger had forgotten me. I imagined my grandmother coming home from prayer meeting, Annajane driving back by with her head out the window, staring, and I would still be sitting here, waiting.

At last I saw the yellow station wagon. I jumped up and the swing swung off balance. I bounded down the porch steps.

"Hiya, kiddo!" Ginger called as she stopped along the street. She opened the car door, dropped something on the ground, and kicked it away into the bushes. I ran across the lawn to the car.

"Hey," she said, "who's that up there?"

I looked straight up behind me and saw Phuong watching us from

113

her open window, her head pressed against the screen. "That's her," I said in a low voice.

"Who?"

"That's Phuong. Remember, I told you?" I climbed in and slammed the door shut again. The car smelled like cigarettes. Little Floyd was fast asleep in the back.

"Is she Chinese or something?" said Ginger, squinting up. "I need my glasses."

"Vietnamese."

Ginger leaned over me and unrolled my window. "Welcome to America!" she shouted. "Hope to see more of you soon. Drop over anytime!" Ginger sighed as we pulled away. "Phuong? Her name is Phuong? I'll tell you one thing. She has gorgeous eyes. I'd kill for eyes like that."

"You already have beautiful eyes," I said.

"No, my eyes are boring. There's no mystery to me. What you see is what you get."

"I think you're mysterious."

"Thank you, kiddo. It's nice to know that someone thinks so."

"I'm kind of mysterious, too," I said. "Grandma thinks I'm going to a prayer meeting at your church tonight. If she found out the truth, she'd probably die."

"Is she in generally good health?"

"I think so."

"Then don't worry about it." Ginger laughed. "Hey, it's like I tell Frank. I can't spend my whole life with my eyes closed."

I laughed, too, though I felt guilty when I thought of Grandma. I told Ginger that I understood exactly what she meant. What I didn't tell her was that I would rather spend my life just this way, with her, roaring down empty highways in a rickety station wagon, through hills and woods, over the Powhatan Bridge, to the outskirts of Richmond. The drive took us thirty minutes, and as we rode along, we talked about our favorite movies. Ginger liked musicals—*Carousel*, *Music Man*, *Camelot*. She also liked anything romantic. She had seen *Gone with the Wind* twenty-five times.

114

"I like anything with Julie Andrews in it," I said. "I wish I could sing like her."

"Oh, she's the greatest," said Ginger. "I met her once in New York, at a birthday party for Rex Harrison. She autographed my cigarette."

"Do you still have that cigarette?" I asked.

She wasn't listening. Her face shone as we pulled into the parking lot of the Dela Fox Biddle Memorial Theater. We climbed out of the car and she put on her glasses to look over the building.

"This is where I'm going to jump-start my life. The year I left show business, that was the same year they built this place."

"Maybe it's been waiting for you all this time," I said.

"I think it has. It's more than coincidence. God wants me here."

I rested Floyd on my shoulder and the three of us made our way along a concrete sidewalk past a sculpture that looked like a half-eaten apple fritter on a plate. We walked past a fountain, a flag, a row of eucalyptus trees. Ginger gestured at a pair of glass doors under an awning as large as a tent.

"Tell people you're my daughter," she said quickly as she rushed in ahead of me. "And don't get in a car with anyone without asking me first."

She didn't have time to continue. Voices exploded near us. "Ginger, baby. It's been too long!"

"She looks like a million, doesn't she?"

"I'm not a million, Myra, I'm only half a million. Hah!"

I blinked in the light. We stood in a large lobby, a lemon-yellow room with a staircase at either side. Dancers in black leotards lounged on bright furniture against the walls, stretching their legs. The women wore their hair slick against their skulls, yanked back in buns or nets.

"Look at that gorgeous child!" A handsome man came toward me with his lips pursed. I stepped back, afraid, but he leaned over me and gave a wet kiss to Floyd.

"Henry Harrison!" Ginger cried. "I've been just dying to talk to you. I'm Ginger Jordan."

"I know," he said, turning from me to put his arm around her. "I was here yesterday for line rehearsal and I say, 'Al, where is my costar?'

115

and Al says, 'Henry, this gal can only make it one night a week, but brother is she worth it.'"

"Oh, my," Ginger said with a huge laugh, "I hope he's right. I've been looking forward to this so much. I'm so thrilled to be working with you." She took his arm and stepped away from me. "Here, Carla, hold the baby for a second."

I was already holding the baby. They talked in low voices and then Ginger burst out laughing again. I went to an older woman standing nearby in a long skirt, the one Ginger had called Myra. "Excuse me," I said, "can you show me where the restroom is?"

"What?" she said in a shocked voice. "Who are you? Are you supposed to be here with that child?"

"I'm her daughter," I said and pointed to Ginger.

"Oh, how sweet," she said, showing her sharp teeth. "I didn't know Ms. Jordan was bringing her family." She gestured to a side hall with a sharp yellow fingernail. I went down the hall quickly and entered the small restroom, juggling the baby from arm to arm while I washed my face and combed my hair. I looked terrible, nothing like a daughter of Ginger's. When I came out again, I saw a pair of white wooden doors open between the great staircases. They looked just like sanctuary doors, but instead of a deacon, a handsome young man without a shirt put his head out and shouted, "Last call for Ginger Jordan, Henry Harrison, Tommy Depew, Mary Burrows—Al's looking for y'all everywhere; better get down to the green room."

"Oh, Bill, leave us alone," said Henry Harrison. "Leave us alone; we're coming. Can't you see I'm talking to a beautiful woman? Ginger, it's tremendous to be working with you. I've heard—no, I remember—great things. I saw you twice off Broadway. And of course I remember Frank, before the accident. You know what I mean."

"Before he became a preacher," said Ginger.

"That's the word." Henry Harrison smiled and winked. "You were both sensational. I said to Al tonight, 'Brother, you couldn't have done better. This girl is terrific.'"

Still holding Floyd, I followed Ginger and Henry Harrison and a handful of other people through the doors into a wide, dim auditorium. We marched below the balcony, down a central sloping aisle under bulky chandeliers, toward the rectangle of light at the front of the theater. A big frizzy-haired woman in jeans stood alone there on stage with a yardstick. She squinted up at us, turned on her heels, and went quickly into the wings, calling in a deep voice, "Hey, Al!"

We kept going through a door at the side of the stage into a long hallway and down the hall to a long, bright room like a fellowship hall—except that instead of tile it had dense green carpet that held footprints like moss. You could have planted a rock garden in this carpet, the kind of garden Grandma always dreamed of, with a tiny blue stream winding and cutting among green ferns. The rivulet would have stretched from the small platform, where a director's chair sat empty, to the other end of the room. A fuzzy-haired, heavy-faced man greeted us at the door.

"Mr. Palia! Oh, Mr. Palia," said Ginger. She threw out her arms and pressed her cheek to his. Loose flesh bulged from the other side of his face.

"It's just so great to be here," she cried. "I was so nervous at my audition that I didn't have a chance to tell you how thrilled I am to work under you."

He shrugged off the compliment. "Heard a lot of good things about you, Ginger. Audition was great. Danson loved you, couldn't stop talking about you."

"You're kidding. I was terrible."

"No way. I was there."

"But I felt—you can't imagine. I went home crying. I couldn't believe they liked me. I mean, you really liked me."

"Just get yourself to rehearsal on time next week, honey, and you'll do fine."

"Oh, yes, sir!"

"I'm killing myself to schedule you late on Wednesdays. Making all these poor girls in the chorus line skip dinner to be here at six. These are working girls. That ain't nothing for them."

"Oh, no, sir. My heart goes out to them. It means a lot to me, it really does." Ginger was still smiling, but she dropped her arms from his neck.

Henry Harrison walked in the door. He had been held up by someone in the hall and looked out of sorts.

"Problem, Henry?" asked Mr. Palia.

"No problem."

"Listen, pal, how do you put up with what you have to put up with?"

"What are you talking about?"

"You know what I'm talking about. It gets worse every year."

"Oh, that," said Henry, with a glance at Ginger. "Let's keep it to ourselves, O.K., Al?"

"Fine," said Mr. Palia. "But it could be a challenge this time. I mean you're not on your own here."

"Yeah, don't worry, Al. It won't be a problem; you have my guarantee."

"I hope not, because, uh, you know how it is."

"Believe me, Al, I know. I know how it is."

I didn't understand a word of this. Mr. Palia winked a heavy gray eyelid at Henry, with a nod to Ginger. "Myra's going to work on the choreography with Ginger after rehearsal. You two get together and go over the rumba alone sometime, huh?"

"I'll be more than happy," said Henry, looking at Ginger. "I'm a good teacher, and the rumba's not hard. Do you know how to rumba, Ginger?"

"There's nothing to it," said Ginger. "I look beautiful while you do all the work. Is that right?"

Henry smiled and tossed his hair back. "Yes, something like that."

"Uh, excuse me, Mr. Palia," said Ginger. "I think this is a good time for me to introduce you to some little people. This is my son, Floyd—" She pointed at the limp child on my shoulder. "—and my daughter, Carla, who'll be taking care of him."

Mr. Palia turned to us and suddenly looked as though he wanted to spit. "What?" he said. "These belong to you?"

"Yes, sir. And they'll be no trouble. I guarantee it."

"They already are trouble. I don't want them here."

"Is it a problem?" asked Ginger. "Listen, Mr. Palia, if they are any problem, any problem at all—"

"I don't want them here."

"But I swear they won't be a problem," she said. "If they're any problem—"

"I don't want them here."

"Really, Mr. Palia, if you're that concerned, I can send them over to

McDonald's or something. But it is getting dark, and Carla doesn't drive yet. I suppose she could try. Or maybe I could give them cab fare or something. You tell me what you want. Anything."

He stamped his foot where he stood, scratched his chin, and said, "If they're any problem at all, you're out of my show."

"They won't be a problem," said Ginger. "Listen everyone. Hey!" She called out loudly to the ten or eleven people still at the back of the room. They looked up with blank eyes and she pointed to Floyd and me. "If my children get in your way or in anyone's way, you have my permission to get them out of your way. All right?" She turned sharply and looked me in the eye. "Do you hear that, Carla? Do you understand that? You are not to get in anyone's way. Do you understand that? Otherwise your father's going to hear about it."

I nodded. I had faith in Ginger. I trusted her. I would have driven her car to McDonald's and waited with Floyd if she had asked me to.

"Time is money!" shouted the frizzy-haired woman who had seen us from the stage. "Time is money! Let's get on with it! Act 1, scene 2!"

I sat on the floor, far at the other end of the long room, with Floyd on my lap.

"All right, you heard the boss," said Mr. Palia. "Let's block this thing." There were a few moments of script flipping and then Ginger stepped up to the platform with an elderly woman, a woman of my grandmother's age or even older, with a short haircut and large, frightened eyes. Mr. Palia sighed and closed his mouth. His lips stuck out like rolled-up cold cuts. "Dianne?" he said to the frizzy-haired woman. "What do you think? Any comments?"

Dianne frowned. "The young one has big teeth. Keep her upstage, away from Grandma. People might think she's dangerous."

"Who has big teeth?" he asked. "Ginger? Big teeth? I like her teeth."

"They're like tusks."

"The things women see that I don't see. All right, Ginger, honey, keep your mouth shut as much as possible and stay away from Grandma."

"Excuse me, Al," said Ginger, with a sharp eye on Dianne. "I don't believe that I have been introduced to your lovely assistant."

119

"Oh, excuse me," said Mr. Palia. "Ginger Jordan, meet Dianne Bane, my stage manager. Dianne, meet Ginger."

Dianne gave Ginger a fierce look, but Ginger said in a thick, sweet voice, "It's lovely to meet you, Dianne. I appreciate any advice you can give me." And Ginger moved back as Mr. Palia had suggested.

"That's good," he said. "Stay there. Center stage, face the door—that's the red line. Now, Mr. Ferring, put us in the mood for this. Give us something light on the piano."

At the edge of the small stage, the piano broke into a melody. I looked that way to see Bob Ferring, our church pianist and now the musical director of *Lady Don't Laugh,* hunched over the piano bench. His drowsy eyes darted back and forth across the score.

"No, Mr. Ferring," said Mr. Palia. "I need it light, not woebegone. That's better. Ginger, honey, Mrs. Blaha, honey, let's talk. You'll find I like to talk about these things. I like to delve into the philosophy of acting. Call me an artist." He bowed to the elderly woman. "By the way, you look lovely tonight, Mrs. Blaha; you look lovely tonight. I adore the haircut. Takes ten years off."

"Oh, thank you, Mr. Palia." Mrs. Blaha returned the bow.

I put my cheek against Floyd's hot forehead and closed my eyes while the blocking moved along in fits and starts. It was the songs I couldn't wait to hear, because no one could sing like Ginger. But Mr. Palia had said that doing songs in a blocking rehearsal was not the way he did things, and so tonight there was only his mumbling and shuffling through the score.

After a while, I opened my eyes and looked around at the others who were not onstage. Most of the young dancers had cleared away. Only a few remained at the back of the room. At the front, near the platform, sat a young blond man with broad shoulders like a swimmer. Near him stood a short woman with a big straight nose and thick pink lips. Bob Ferring had nodded off at the piano. His long nose hovered near C-sharp. In a corner, Dianne stood against the wall, blowing big, flesh-pink bubbles with her gum.

"O.K., let's go," said Mr. Palia. "Henry's in the wings. Chorus line runs offstage. Chorus line, where are you? O.K., so you're already offstage. Places everybody. Ginger, throw us that line again."

"Speak of the devil," said Ginger. "There's Bill coming up the driveway."

"I thought you said he was bankrupt," said Mrs. Blaha. "Why is he still driving that fancy car?"

"You know Bill. It'd be easier for a camel to get through the eye of a needle than for Bill to get through the door of a Ford. Remember, don't say a word to him."

"O.K., Henry," said Mr. Palia. "You can ring that doorbell."

There was a pause.

"O.K., Henry," said Mr. Palia, "we're ready."

Nothing happened.

"Henry!" shouted Dianne Bane angrily behind me. "Henry! Where on earth is he?"

"Right here!" called Henry, appearing from the hall door, pushing back his hair. It flopped into his eyes again.

"You're supposed to be in the wings," Dianne growled.

"Oh, calm down. Someone asked me directions backstage and I had to be polite."

"You liar," said Dianne. "I told you twice that Al wanted you onstage."

"Yeah, well you're not Al, are you?"

"Henry," said Al. "Henry, get control of yourself. Ginger, honey, throw Henry the cue please."

"And this time tie a stick of dynamite to it," said Dianne.

Henry started to say something but stopped with a look from Mr. Palia.

"Time for a break," said Mr. Palia. "I'm starting to perspire."

"Oh, me too," said Mrs. Blaha. "I want a soda pop."

During the break I saw a door open at the back of the room, where it was now dark. A man appeared in the doorway, silhouetted in the lights so that I couldn't see his face. He looked around, smoothed back his hair, and slipped out again. While the others went for drinks, Ginger climbed down from the stage and disappeared through the same door. Five minutes later, she was back again from the hallway with a ginger ale in her hand. She winked at me.

"Who was that?" I asked, standing up and shifting Floyd to my shoulder.

"Who was who?"

"Who was that in the doorway?"

"Nobody, I just went out for air."

She must not have seen him. She smiled and winked again. "Kiddo, you think this is what you want to do when you grow up?"

"Sure!" I said, because I imagined myself onstage with her. She would throw me my cue, praise me for saying my lines so well, and laugh lightly when I had them wrong. She would introduce me to the audience for a bow and an armful of roses.

"I wish he'd let me sing tonight," Ginger whispered so that Mr. Palia wouldn't hear her. "I'm going to ask him again." She walked back to the platform at the front of the room, leaving bruises in the mossy carpet. I sat back down with Floyd.

"Oh, Mr. Palia," Ginger said, lifting her dark eyes up to him pathetically. "Can't we just have one song? I'm afraid I'll lose the spirit."

"Well, which one do you want to do?" asked Mr. Palia. "Maybe I'll let you do something from another act."

"Let's do the title song. Before everybody comes back. Bob and I have been practicing all week. I can't get it out of my head." She hummed a little bit of it and swayed her hips. Mr. Palia smiled at her with his curled up lips.

"That's the attitude I like," he said. "Did I ever tell you you remind me of a niece of mine? Well, she was actually a third cousin, so I guess it was all right. O.K., go ahead and sing it for me."

So Ginger sang.

> Lady don't laugh
> And lady don't sing,
> Just cut open your heart
> And show them everything—
> The diamonds inside,
> And the arrows too.
> Did he really think nothing
> Could hurt you?
> Lady don't laugh,

You'll forget your pain,
And forgetting it
Will just bring it back again.
You'll go back to that man
For another try,
Back to the lover
Who said good-bye.

Mr. Palia clapped wildly at the end. "That was wonderful, Ginger, darling. Absolutely beautiful. I think she gets a round of applause. Don't you?" He swung around to Dianne and the others. "Wasn't that gorgeous?"

Most everyone clapped. Even those who had been there long before us and looked like they could eat Ginger alive for taking up extra time clapped in a bored way. Only Dianne stood to the side not clapping. Henry Harrison clapped harder and louder than anyone. Ginger's eyes were shining.

When that scene and two others were finished, Mr. Palia said that he would send Ginger home for the evening.

"You worked hard tonight," he said. "Go home."

"But I thought you wanted me to rehearse choreography with Myra," said Ginger almost pouting, though it was already ten thirty. "Did I do something wrong?"

"You kidding? I just don't want you getting tired out. You be here half an hour early next week. You're making old Al a very happy director."

She bounced up and kissed him on the cheek. They talked for a moment in low voices.

"Wait for me in the lobby," said Ginger to me. "I'll be right there."

In the big, brassy, yellow lobby, Floyd and I waited for a long time. Floyd was awake now and cranky, ready to toddle off barefoot on the tile in every direction. It was thirty minutes before Ginger came bursting through the doors, laughing with Henry Harrison.

"Oh, hiya, kiddo." She almost seemed surprised to see me. "I need to get you home to bed, don't I?"

"What time is it?" I asked, worried about my grandmother.

"Nearly eleven."

"Oh, no."

123

"Let's go. Bye-bye, Bill! Hah hah!"

"Bye!" Henry Harrison called and left by another door, still in his leotard, with a leather bag over his arm. As Ginger and I left, Bob Ferring came running through the lobby after us. His heavy sandals flapped softly on the carpet. "Ginger," he said, "I have to talk to you right now. Can I meet you somewhere for coffee?"

He had a tortured look on his face. I didn't worry about Bob Ferring mentioning any of this to my grandmother. He always turned and ran at the sight of her.

"Not a good time, Bobby, not at all," said Ginger. "But I'll call you tomorrow. You were just fabulous tonight." She kissed his cheek and he sulked away. We went quickly to the car. The air was thick and cool, stinking with loamy mud and mushrooms. Ginger rolled down her window as we started home. Floyd sat in his car seat peacefully. He winced up at the streetlights flickering by.

"My poor, pitiful little baby," Ginger said, glancing back at him. "He's got a hard life, dragged here and there."

"He slept for a long time tonight," I said.

"Praise the Lord. So tell me about the rehearsal. What'd you think of it?"

"It wasn't like I expected."

She laughed. "You mean you hated it."

"Oh, no," I said. "But I didn't know the theater was so much work."

"Frank used to say it was like getting ready to fight a war."

"I just love listening to you sing," I said. "I wish—I wish I could grow up and learn to sing just like you." What a joke to think that I could ever sing like Ginger, who could heft her voice like a church organ or glide weightlessly on air. She threw her cigarette from the window and pulled out the lighter by the radio to light another one. Its red coil was the only bright thing in the car.

"I like you, Carla," she said. "You make me wish I had a daughter. From now on I've decided that you're my confidante. Who else have I got to talk to, anyway? For some reason women my age don't really like me that much."

"You're kidding," I said. "Who doesn't like you?"

"Oh, just women. Women such as that stage manager, Dianne Bane.

124

I know she'll make trouble. And what's her problem, anyway? Most women worry about me stealing their husbands." Ginger laughed and winked. "What's she got for me to steal? Anyway, is it a sin to be attractive to men? Most gals think they shouldn't have to do anything. They think their husbands should love them for themselves."

I stared at her. "Shouldn't they?"

She frowned. "How old did you say you are, kiddo?"

"Twelve," I said.

"Well, just remember one thing. When you grow up and get married, don't do what I did."

"What?"

"Don't marry a guy you love. It's too much trouble. Marry a guy who loves you, who worships you, Carla. Make sure he can give you everything you want before you even think about walking down an aisle."

"But what if I want to love him?"

"Too much trouble." She shook her head. "I married for love and look where I am today. I'm a sweet Christian doormat. 'Oh, yes, my lord and master, I've done your laundry, I've washed your dishes, I've made your dinner. Just please, please love me. That's all I ask. A little crumb from the table for the dogs, please.' Now isn't that biblical? I tell you what, I know my Bible."

I was laughing.

"Hah," she said, "just spend ten long minutes with Frank sometime. He thinks breathing is sinful. He didn't used to be that way. Not in the old days." She rolled her eyes. "Before he was—saved."

"You married him before he was saved?" In my family we didn't yoke up with unbelievers. Except for Aunt Jo. Maybe.

Ginger's face softened. "He was a really great guy once. Oh, he was the best. Those big, brown eyes, those shoulders—like a swimmer. All the girls were crazy about him. I saw him for the first time on Broadway, and, kiddo, I thought he was a god. The first time I saw him in a show I fell in love." She sighed. "Sometimes a girl knows. You feel it's right before you even talk to the guy. I went up to him backstage and I said, 'We're getting married.'"

"You asked him to marry you? You didn't even know him and you asked him that?"

125

"I knew what I wanted. I thought I did. I was working off Broadway, traveling, trying to get into a big show. I thought I was going to be a star. So did I have time to wait? To play the lady? No. Here was this guy that I wanted and I knew I wanted him and I knew it was right. So."

"You didn't play the lady," I said.

"No. I played the star. I had confidence in myself, and I went for what I wanted, and that's important. I mean it was smart business, too. Bill had already made it, and he knew people. Right away Bill pulled strings to get me into *The King and I*. Not a big part, but wow, kiddo, Broadway. And then—well, that's the great tragedy of my life. I only did a year before I had to leave it, anyway."

"What happened?"

"Oh, what happened. What happened. Well, we'd been married a few months and I got pregnant. But that wasn't so bad. Then by some chance one day Frank ran into a guy on the street with a Bible and within two hours he had prayed the sinner's prayer. We're talking about a big sinner here, my Frank. I wouldn't have thought Billy Graham himself could do the job in two hours. So Frank decided we both had to get out of New York. I could have divorced him or something, I guess. But there I was pregnant. And I was in love with Frank, like I said. You don't just give up like that. So I stuck with him. Little did I know." She shook her head.

I just looked at her, with my hands on my lap, waiting for more of this. But we drove back across the Powhatan Bridge, with the moon shining on the sinewy river underneath us. And soon we were on my side of Dutch Falls, and before long we were in my driveway. I opened the car door. I hurried to climb out. I didn't want Ginger to meet my grandmother, not yet.

"Bye," I said in a rush. "See you next week!"

"Enjoyed it, kiddo," she said. She opened her door, tossed her cigarette out on the ground, and stamped it. She gave me one last smile and said, "Sweet dreams. See you next week."

No one had waited up for me. I slipped upstairs without reproach, though it was half past eleven. Grandma must have gone to bed too early to notice. It seemed like a miracle.

*O*n Sunday morning before church, Grandma brought out a high-necked, navy blue satin suit with a Tallheimer's tag in the back. She stood in wait around a corner for several minutes before Phuong slipped from her bedroom door and padded across the smooth planks of the hall floor in bare feet, leaving small moisture prints behind her. Phuong was on her way to the bathroom. She wore a white sundress that was old and transparent. It had no sequins or fringe. She accepted the suit with thanks when my grandmother offered it, hardly lifting her eyes to look at it, and changed in the bathroom.

"I picked it out at a yard sale years ago," Grandma said to me. She waited again. "How does it fit?" she called through the door. Phuong didn't answer, but at last she came out in the suit. "There!" Grandma said. The coat was fine, but the skirt hung low.

"It long," said Phuong softly.

"It looks just fine," Grandma said. "I can take up the hem later. But it'll do for today."

My father met us at the kitchen door and looked at Phuong's clothes in shock. "I think she'll be hot in that," he said. "You know how the sanctuary heats up, Mama."

"We have air now, Davey," said Grandma.

"Well, still."

Phuong looked frightened. Grandma said, "If she gets hot, she can remove the coat."

"I don't want her fainting in church," he said. "Her health isn't good. If you could see what she's been through."

"No, O.K.," said Phuong, nodding. She turned to Grandma. "O.K. Thank you, I can wear this lovely clothes." She sat in the living room in her bare feet until it was nearly time to go and then put on a pair of flip-flops with large plastic sunflowers curling over the straps. And in that outfit, she made her first appearance at the First Reformed Church of Virginia. We sat together in our family pew, the fifth pew on the left. Grandma sat nearest to the aisle and beside her, Father, and beside him, Phuong, and beside Phuong, me. While the other ladies fanned themselves in light flower print dresses, Phuong sat stiff and erect with her hands folded on her knees, holding down the stiff fanned pleats of the skirt. After the service there were hundreds of old friends for Father to greet and hug. Phuong disappeared and we could not find her again until it was time to leave. Out in the parking lot a few loyal friends of Grandma's introduced themselves to her through the windows of our car. Mrs. Ronald Steen told her in a loud voice that she could and should help herself to anything she liked in the missionary clothes closet. Louise offered to take her to get a perm.

"What a lovely suit," Mrs. Grunstra said. "So lovely."

"Thank you," Phuong said quietly.

And that was Sunday, the most important day of any week.

On Wednesday, the second most important day, Grandma arose early from the breakfast table and began bleaching counters. I complained of the smell. Father looked up pleadingly from his eggs and sniffed, but she was not moved.

"My ladies are coming for Circle at eleven," she said. "I apologize for the smell, but this has got to be done."

In three hours our living room would be full of elderly church women balancing coffee cups on their Bibles and snacking on *gehakt-ballen*. Grandma would listen hard to overhear them whisper, "Those counters—did you see how white those counters are? What does she use, a special family recipe?"

Phuong sat across from me at the breakfast table, quietly chewing. After a few minutes she pushed her plate away and set her silverware on it gently, without making a sound. A piece of toast lay untouched next to a wedge of orange. Grandma looked over.

"Well," she said, "I guess this will have to wait, since you folks have such delicate noses. I don't see why a little Clorox should stop anyone from enjoying a good breakfast." She put down her bucket of bleach water, turned, and disappeared through the swinging door to the dining room. As she left she said to Phuong almost under her breath, "By the way, you're welcome to join in on our Circle meeting." A few minutes later I heard the vacuum cleaner in the back of the house. A small pile of dirty dishes sat soaking in the sink. My father and I looked at them and back at each other. Usually Grandma had washed them by now. Usually she had finished the dishes before anyone else had finished breakfast.

"Carolyn," said my father, enjoying his food again, "I think Grandma must be expecting you to do the dishes."

"I don't think so," I said. "I don't have to do them because of my eczema."

"Eczema?"

"I get a rash on my hands," I said. It had happened once a long time ago.

"Maybe she expects me to do them." He looked dismal.

"Grandma likes glasses first, then silverware, bowls, plates, and pots," I said.

He finished his breakfast quickly and started to roll up his sleeves, but Phuong stood up ahead of him and went to the sink. She rolled her yellow blouse sleeves up to her elbows and thrust her hands down in the water. She stood still for a moment, looking down, and then she began washing. She washed the glasses first, as Grandma required, with a bottle brush. She scrubbed vigorously, vibrating from shoulders to hips. With a final grunt she gave each glass a hard, squeaking shine on her pink cotton skirt. Then she moved on to the silverware. Painstakingly, she scrubbed each prong of each fork. Soap suds ran freely off her elbows while she examined the spoons in the sunlight. Meanwhile, Father and I had seconds on breakfast. Finally, he slurped his coffee down and jumped up from his chair. He leaned against the sink and smiled at Phuong.

"You like to do that?" he said quietly, close to her. "Wash dishes?"

"Yes," she said.

129

"I have to tell you that hard work is the way to my mother's heart. At this rate, you'll be good friends by the time I get home tonight."

She stopped for a moment. "Where you are going today?"

"I've got an interview at a church over in Chester. Why don't you do what Mama said and jump in on her Circle meeting?"

"I don't know," Phuong said.

"Go on, she invited you."

"I don't know what is Circle."

He looked to me for help. "Carrie, what do the ladies do at those meetings?"

"They sew quilts," I said.

"There you go," he said to Phuong. "You know how to sew. Why don't you jump in. You'll make some friends that way."

Father had his suit jacket on now and was walking out the door. "Carolyn," he said, "you talk her into it." He left the kitchen and Phuong mumbled to herself in Vietnamese. She picked up the dish drainer and moved it to the other side of the sink. Then her hands flew faster on the soapy water, silhouetted in the brilliant sink window. It was like watching a swimmer from the bottom of a pool, a rippling shadow against the glassy sun. She was picking up speed, nearing the end of the dishes. She washed the plastic orange juice pitcher, a stoneware plate, a frying pan. She dried them, put them away, and picked up a large serving plate. It was just a plate, not a valuable dish or an heirloom, just an old blue ceramic plate decorated with windmills and Dutch girls in winged caps. Still, Phuong sighed and stopped, staring at it. Her wrists hovered in the air. Her mouth formed a word. And then, she cried out. The dish slipped from her fingers and cracked loudly on the hard tile floor. The jagged pieces twirled apart and drummed the tiles in circles until they slowed and lay still. Phuong gasped and pressed her hands to her ears.

The vacuum cleaner whirred off, a few rooms away. "Carolyn?" shouted Grandma. "What has happened?"

"Nothing, Oma," I called.

Grandma appeared in the kitchen doorway with the vacuum trailing after her like a small pig. She looked at me, then at Phuong, then down at the floor, where wet fragments sparkled in the shadows.

130

"I very sorry!" cried Phuong, who had been standing rock still with her hands up to her face. She dropped to her knees and cringed with her arms crossed against her chest.

Grandma looked down in disbelief. "What in the world are you doing? Get up, dear. This is America; we don't do that in America."

Phuong stayed on her knees. "I so sorry. I break this plate. You lovely plate."

"I couldn't care two cents about that plate," said Grandma, "but may I ask why you felt that you needed to move my dish drainer to the left side of the sink?"

"I left-hand," Phuong said.

"Then why don't you just leave the dishes to me from now on."

Phuong began to cry.

"Now, don't cry," said Grandma. "I told you, it doesn't matter two cents about the dish."

Phuong sobbed and shook. She put her face in her hands.

"Oh, my goodness." Grandma's face went crimson. "It was just an ugly old dish I bought at a clearance sale." She said it sharply. Her nose was pointed like a spear. "Please do not apologize to me anymore. Get up. Have a glass of lemonade. You can bleach my counters if you want something to do."

Phuong nodded and stood up with her head still in her hands. Grandma left in a hurry. I thought then that I might say something comforting, something diplomatic to smooth things over or make Grandma seem less frightening. I could say to Phuong, "My grandmother is really nice when you get to know her," or "Don't worry, she likes you; I can always tell," or "Dutch women are short-tempered but long-suffering." But Phuong stood with her back to me. Her shoulders heaved up and down. She didn't make a sound. She heaved the bleach water up on the counter and moved the dish drainer back to the right. When she had finished her work she hurried away to the stairs.

Later that morning I sat in the kitchen again, waiting for Annajane. I heard the ladies talking in the living room, Mrs. Grunstra's voice rising above the others as she tried to impart the Bible lesson. Annajane would probably come in by the front door so that she could stand in

131

the middle of the living room and be admired by them all, like Jesus in the temple with the elders. I got up from my chair, intending to disappoint her by meeting her on the street, when suddenly the kitchen door opened and Phuong came in with a package under her arm. She unwrapped the brown paper and held out a crystal plate far lovelier than the one she had broken. It was oval in shape, long and nearly as thin as paper, gilt on the edge and bordered all the way around with tiny green and white ginkgo leaves.

"It's beautiful," I said. "Where did you get it?"

She frowned. "Don't breaking it. Put it away."

"All right." I climbed onto a stepladder and put the plate deep in a cupboard, where it would be safe until I had an occasion to explain it to Grandma. "Don't be afraid of my grandmother," I said while I was facing the other way. "My grandma likes people who stand up to her sometimes. It's people who give in too quick that she can't abide. She likes to argue a little. She says it's her Dutch blood."

When I turned back around, Phuong was staring angrily at me.

"What did I say?" I asked.

She left the house again, without answering. I climbed down from the stepladder and watched her through the pane of the kitchen door.

A minute later I saw Annajane crossing the street. She had a new haircut. It was a Dorothy Hamill, heavy and straight around the bangs, feathered on the sides, tapered down the back of her neck. Though she waved happily, my spirits sank low. She was not beautiful anymore. I imagined her long, shining hair clumped in sweet piles on a dirty floor somewhere. Her neck looked so skinny now, swaying alone under that large head. What would I say? I worried that I would be blunt like Grandma and tell her how ugly I thought it was. I wouldn't be able to help myself. I would burst with the news—"It looks terrible."

"Well," she said as she approached, "aren't you going to invite me in and introduce me to her?"

"Introduce you to who?"

"You know. I saw her at church. She was wearing your grandmother's old suit."

"She just left. I'm surprised you didn't see her. Why are you so late?"

"I just got back from Richmond. I went to get my hair cut."

132

"All the way to Richmond for a haircut?"

"It was an early birthday present. Mommy thinks I need a more womanly look."

"And did you just throw it away, all that hair?"

"Of course not. We put it in a jar. Mommy says she'll have it woven into a tiara for my bridal veil. We'll lock it in my hope chest."

"Oh," I said.

"Do you like my haircut? It's for high school. Don't you think I look older this way?"

"Maybe," I said. Her head was like a melon now. She looked deformed. I couldn't keep my eyes on her.

"I can tell you don't like it," she said sadly.

"I'll get used to it," I said.

"Well," she said a little sadly, "let's go to the library. I just want to read today."

We walked over to the library and went inside—around the corner past the circulation desk, past the reference section, past Mr. Hagedoorn's large office next to the stairwell. He sat at his desk, shuffling through catalog cards. He looked up as we went by and smiled at us.

"Good afternoon, Miss Grietkirk," he said to me. "Staying cool, I hope. How's your daddy?"

"Fine," I said.

He winked. Annajane pushed me forward, out of the doorway.

"You shouldn't talk to him," she whispered.

"Why not?"

"Everyone knows about him."

We entered the stairwell and let the big door boom shut behind us as we walked upstairs, slapping the steps in our sandals.

"What are you saying?" I asked softly.

"Everyone knows about Mr. Hagedoorn."

"Who's everyone? What do you know?"

Annajane wouldn't say anything else until we reached the second floor. We sat down on some orange lounge furniture out of the view of any windows.

"He's immoral," she said, crossing her legs. "He drinks and dances.

He's always chasing women. He had an affair once and everyone knew about it."

"When?"

"A long time ago. Everyone knows about it."

"He's not like that now," I said. "His wife just had a baby."

Annajane flipped her short hair and ran her fingers through it. "Mommy says Mrs. Hagedoorn is desperate to hang on to him. She's trying every way she knows."

"How come I never heard about any of this?" I said. "How come no one ever told me?"

"Because there's no one to explain the facts of life to you."

"There's my grandmother."

"She may not remember very well, Carolyn."

The buzz of the fluorescent lights was loud above us. I looked down at my knees pinned together childishly on the edge of the orange couch, my heels splayed out, my toes turned in. The white lights made my dark skin sallow.

"Come here, Carolyn," Annajane said. She drew me up by the hand and led me to my window, the one where I so often sat looking out over town. It wasn't the people or the shops she wanted to show me, but the steeple of the F.R.C. of V., shrouded in gray humidity. "I climb up to the bell chamber of the church sometimes," she whispered. "The dominie lets me. I can see everything up there. I've seen Mr. Hagedoorn meet a woman and get in her car." She was still whispering. "Doesn't that tell you something?"

"Who was the woman?" I asked.

"I didn't recognize her. But it wasn't his wife."

"I don't believe you," I said. "If everybody knows about this, why does the dominie let Mr. Hagedoorn be head deacon? They should exercise church discipline on him."

"They can't do it," Annajane said, "because his mother is still alive. You know what a saint she is, and she claims he's an ancestor of the founder. They're waiting until she dies to discipline him."

"My grandmother would have told me about him." I shook my head. "I still think it's just a story."

134

"I'm sure your grandmother's planning to tell you when you get a little older."

After this mild argument, Annajane settled down in front of the window with a teenage Christian thriller, *Tanya Tate and the Mystery of the Terrible Twins*. I wanted to read, too, but I couldn't stop thinking about Mr. Hagedoorn. Could it be true, what Annajane said? He was good-looking, and Ginger, who knew so much about people, liked him. I opened my eyes wide, stared into my book, and imagined him in dark upper corners of the library late at night, drinking wine from a bottle and dancing with strange women in his arms.

"What book are you reading?" Annajane looked up.

"Huh?" I hadn't been reading at all. But I sat up in my chair and let her see the title of the book in my hands—*Stage, Screen, and Tube: the Actor's Milieux*.

She glanced at it absentmindedly and then looked me straight in the eye. "I'm sorry," she said. "I'm sorry if I upset you, talking that way about Mr. Hagedoorn. I know he's your daddy's friend."

I shrugged my shoulders and nodded. "That's O.K., Annajane."

That night when Ginger came to get me for rehearsal, Frank and the boys were in the car. Frank sat beside Ginger, pressing his hands to the dashboard. I hadn't seen him since that first afternoon of babysitting. I had forgotten how handsome he was, so much handsomer than Mr. Hagedoorn, or even my father. His blond hair shone in tangles around his forehead. His cheeks were dark red, ruddy like David's on the day Samuel chose him from among his brothers.

"Hi, kiddo," said Ginger. "Have a seat up front here with Frank."

"I don't mind the back," I said.

"The boys stink," she said. "They've been at soccer practice."

"We do not stink!" yelled Peter from the back. He was shirtless, as usual. His ribs glistened. Frank slid over and I climbed in beside him.

"Hello, Carla," he said.

"Hi, Mr. Jordan."

As we drove, Ginger's eyes darted from the rearview mirror to me. "I just love playing taxi," she said. "I should charge a fare, Frank's Toyota is broken down so often. And here I am late as it is."

"Why don't you just come to prayer meeting?" Frank asked her. "You'd be early."

"Well, I couldn't do that to Carla, could I? She really looks forward to playing with Patty's kids."

"She likes playing with your sister's kids? Well then she deserves whatever she gets."

I considered this. Playing with her sister's kids? I supposed that Ginger needed an excuse for taking me with her to Richmond.

"By all means, hurry," said Frank. "I wouldn't want to keep Carla and my nieces apart one second longer than necessary."

"Ouch," said Ginger. "You know how to hurt me, don't you?"

"I'm not trying to," he said.

"I hate prayer meeting," shouted Peter. "I want to go to Aunt Patty's."

"I do, too," said one of the twins. "I want to go to Aunt Patty's. How come you don't take us?"

"This is your fault, Frank," said Ginger. "You explain it. And if George and Mandi aren't at prayer meeting, will you call and tell them eight on Friday night? Frank? That is if you're still willing to go."

He was silent for a moment. "You know they won't be at prayer meeting. You call them. They're your friends."

"No," she said, "it's your job to arrange things." She looked at me. "How about you, Carla? Could you baby-sit on Friday?"

"I think so," I said. "I'll have to ask my grandma."

"Frank and I are going dancing. Can you believe that? Me and Frank? I don't think Frank can remember how to dance. So I'm asking George along."

"Oh, you're funny, Ginger," Frank said.

After that, neither of them spoke. The boys made a lot of noise, but I didn't listen. The older you got the easier it was to think of younger children as a backdrop, a painted scene behind the drama of adult lives. We drove down a pitted country road and Ginger swung the station wagon hard right into the Food Angel grocery store parking lot. A hand-painted sign drooped to the side of the corrugated metal building, posted on a tree: *Templ of the Dov, Frnk Jrdan, Pstr. Come joi us fr pryr mting this Wedny.*

I stepped out of the car and climbed back once Frank had gotten out. "I'll see you later," he said to Ginger.

"Bye," she said. She kissed the boys, one at a time at the window, all but Floyd. He stayed with us.

"Don't stay away too long tonight," Frank said to Ginger. "I'll get bored alone."

"My heart goes out to you."

He shut the door and waved good-bye to us. Ginger waved. She shook her head as we left him shrinking in the distance.

"Is Frank a real dominie?" I asked. "He's the dominie of that church? I thought he was just studying to be one."

"He's the real thing."

"And your boys are allowed to go to prayer meeting without shirts?"

She ignored the question. "Poor Frank," she said, and laughed. But her face turned serious. "Wow, look at the time. Al will be furious—"

We put on speed. When we arrived at the theater, the parking lot was still full of cars from the line rehearsal. Ginger explained to me that line dancers were usually young and poor. The girls would give up and get married and pregnant, she said, before they ever made it anywhere. The guy dancers would find good jobs, the way men always could. She said it bitterly. "Men have what they want." We took a side door in and walked softly down a short hallway, around a corner into a longer crescent-shaped hallway lined with African art, then around another corner to the green room. The line rehearsal was just finishing. At the piano, Mr. Ferring tonked out the tune for the last verse steps of Henry's love song to Ginger.

> Give the man in the moon a ring,
> Tell him to bring
> A bottle of bubbly
> For our little fling.
> Tell the sky it's black tie,
> Tell the stars our affair will
> Call for formal apparel.
> Yes, this party is private
> So make sure you arrive at
> The stroke of eight.

Darling, don't be late,
'Cause the moon and the sky
And the stars and I
Wait for you.

The dancers finished and spread out slowly while Mr. Palia sat in his dingy director's chair watching. A pair of wiry men in suits stood in back of him, the younger of whom had bushy blond hair and a pencil behind his ear. Down on the floor, Thelma Blaha rehearsed a difficult dance step with Myra Woods, the sharp-toothed woman I'd met at the first rehearsal. Myra was the choreographer. She wore a flowing pink skirt that looked like window sheers, and underneath it, navy blue tights and running shoes. I sat down in my usual spot with the baby. I was near a pole, out of the way of the dancers. I could hear the two men in suits talking.

"I want to know what you're seeing in it, Dick," said the man with the blond hair to the other man. "Do you see the energy in it? Does it give you a kick?"

"Yes it does, Saul."

"What does it remind you of? Doesn't Henry Harrison make you think of anyone?"

"Joel Grey?"

"Exactly. That's why I wanted him."

"You're the genius, Saul. I thought you just wanted him because he has a name."

"Not that much of a name. He doesn't have that much of a name."

Myra Woods snapped her fingers. "One, two, three, Thelma. Four, five, six, Thelma. Bend your legs, Thelma. You look like you're dying, Thelma."

Suddenly Dianne Bane shouted from the door, "Listen up, listen up, everybody. Shut up. Cut the piano, Mr. Ferring. It's seven thirty, you dimwits. We're a half hour behind schedule. Again." She cast an eye at Ginger, who stood on the platform stage now, talking to Henry. "Is everybody paying attention? Mrs. Jordan, are you paying attention?"

"What is it you'd like to say, Dianne?" asked Ginger sweetly.

138

"I'd like to say get offstage. You and Henry both. You're not in this scene."

"What scene is that, Dianne?" asked Henry in a dry voice.

"Act 2, scene 1. I want Tommy and Mary. Tommy and Mary!" she called. "Where are Tommy and Mary?"

I noticed then that Dianne was wearing a wedding ring, just a plain band. Ginger had said she wasn't the marrying kind. I wondered who in the world would marry her.

Tommy and Mary took their places onstage. I looked them over carefully. Tommy was the blond man I had noticed at the last rehearsal, the one with broad shoulders and pale skin. He looked friendly. Mary Burrows was the woman with the big nose and thick lips. She looked less friendly, and she said nothing to Ginger as they passed on the short flight of steps. At the top of the steps she giggled quietly at something Tommy whispered to her, so that Dianne shouted, "Attention! We're working on a time deficit. Attention!"

"All right," said Mr. Palia. "Let's take it from Tommy's line to Mary about the snow-capped mountains; that's on page 28 of your script."

"Excuse me," said Mary Burrows with her big eyes wide open, "what page is that in the script?"

"Page 28!" shouted Dianne.

"That's right," said Mr. Palia. "Page 28, Mary. By the way, I'd like to introduce all of you to our writer, Mr. Saul Anderson, and our producer, Mr. Dick Danson." He pointed out the two men in suits, who nodded and smiled to everyone. Saul Anderson was the one with the bushy hair. He was the genius. Mr. Danson looked like a rich man, with big teeth and slicked-down sandy hair.

"Shouldn't Tommy and I be at center stage?" said Mary again in a breathy voice.

"Mary," said Mr. Palia, "the diamond stands in the middle of the ring. And you, darling, are just a zircon in this show. Stand back by that garbage can, slightly to stage left. Let's groove. Mr. Ferring, give me a spooky intro, some ghost music. 'Night on Bald Mountain' kind of a thing."

By now I knew the basic plot of the musical. Ginger played Shelley Douglas, a popular comedienne estranged from her playboy husband, Bill (Henry Harrison). Bill had squandered his fortune, and so he made a deal with Shelley. If she faked her own death, he would give her half the life insurance money plus complete custody of their son, Little Billy (Walter Pinkney), under an assumed name. They arranged for her to drown on the night of their fifteenth wedding anniversary, during a Hawaiian cruise. But Shelley got the night wrong and went overboard when there was no lifeboat waiting to take her to shore. She climbed back on the ship, convinced that Bill had actually tried to kill her. The rest of the show was about Shelley pretending to be a ghost in order to get even with Bill—poisoning his vodka, leaving razor blades in his fruit, driving his fiancée (Mary Burrows) into the arms of another man (Tommy Depew). In the end, of course, Bill and Shelley realized that they actually loved each other, not to mention Little Billy, and they got back together.

I watched now as Mary Burrows worked on her romantic scene with Tommy Depew, just after Ginger's fake drowning. When Tommy finally leaned over to kiss her, I stared with hawk eyes.

"Enough!" said Mr. Palia. "No mush tonight. I'm already nauseous."

Tommy smiled and kissed Mary anyway, and then we went to another scene, a scene that called for Little Billy. I hadn't seen Walter Pinkney yet, the boy Ginger hoped that I would like. Dianne began to call for him in the hall.

"You find him, Dianne?" called Mr. Palia. "Where is the kid?"

"I know I haven't seen him tonight," said Myra Woods. "And I keep a lookout for stray children." She eyed me from the hall, then came back into the green room.

"He ain't around," said Dianne. "Walter Pinkney ain't been around tonight at all."

"Oh, no!" shouted Henry Harrison, with his hands on his face. He stepped up to the stage platform holding his script between his thumb and forefinger like a dirty diaper. "Child actors! This always happens with child actors. There ought to be a law!"

"Well, let's block the scene without him," said Mr. Palia. "We'll have to pretend the kid's here."

"Do the father speech with no son?" Henry asked frowning.

"That's what I said."

"And I just talk to nobody? Nobody?"

"You can say it to me," said Dianne. "Stop whining or we'll have to call your mama to come fetch you."

At that very moment, as if on cue, a woman came in the door and walked right up to Mr. Palia, swishing in a black slit skirt. Her right knee peeked in and out of the slit like a winking eye. Her white polyester blouse glittered with red satin hearts on the chest pockets.

"Well, Mrs. Pinkney," said Al Palia. "How good to see you again. Where's your boy Walter? We were just talking about him."

"Walter's a little bit sick," she said. "Won't be able to make it. Not this week or the next."

"Not next week either?!" asked Henry. "Where does that leave me, Al?"

"How sick is he?" Al asked Mrs. Pinkney.

"He's in intensive care over to the hospital."

"Oh," said Mr. Palia. "Real sick."

"Got hepatitis from dirty lake water."

"No! No!" wailed Henry. He threw down his script. "This is too much!"

Mr. Palia drew up to his full height. "I'm sorry, Mrs. Pinkney, but I'll have to drop Walter from the play. Hope he gets better soon, I really do. Give him my best."

"Well, I've come to collect on his pay."

"What?"

"We was told he'd get twenty-five dollars."

"Uh, no. Not if he doesn't work."

"You said he'd be rewarded." Mrs. Pinkney folded her arms.

"Well, experience is its own reward, isn't it, Mrs. Pinkney?"

"He ain't had no experience. I got to have the money. Where's the money?"

"There won't be any money," said Mr. Palia firmly. "Not if he doesn't act."

"Listen here, Walter's daddy is out in the parking lot right now waiting for me. Do you want me to get him?"

"Ma'am, are you going to force me to throw you out?"

"Are you going to force me to call Walter's daddy?"

"Now listen!" Mr. Palia screamed frantically. He threw down his script and stomped both feet. "I don't have the funds to pay another child actor. Your kid only made it to one rehearsal. I'll pay him four dollars from my own pocket, if that'll make you happy—that's almost a sixth of it. Here, take it. That's all you're getting."

"That ain't enough. I got two babies besides Walter."

"Hey, I've got an idea!" I shouted up at them from my small place with Floyd. The shrillness of my voice must have surprised them. Mr. Palia squinted and bent forward. "What? Who said that?"

I walked forward quickly. "Mr. Palia, I'll play the part. I can do it. And Walter Pinkney can have all the money. I don't care about that. I want to be an actress, I really do. And I can play the part."

"And who are you again?"

"I'm Ginger's little girl."

"Oh, Ginger's kid. Forget it." Mr. Palia sneered. But then he brightened up. "Ginger's kid. What a great idea. Can she do it?" He looked me over.

"I can't work with her," said Henry Harrison, turning up his nose at me. "No offense, Ginger. She's too plump and squeaky."

"Ginger," said Mr. Palia, "can this kid do Little Billy?"

Ginger laughed and put her hand to her mouth. "Carla is very talented, Al. But I need her to watch the baby. I need her to watch little Floyd. That's why she's here."

I thought Al Palia would bite his lower lip in half. "Your baby-sitting needs are secondary to my needs. I need Little Billy. Can she do Little Billy? Walter Pinkney could sing and dance circles around Henry. I want another kid at least that good. I figure if she's your kid—"

"Of course she's that good," said Ginger. "Al, it's just that I wanted to keep Carla off the stage until she was ready, you know. But oh, well, let her try if you want. Whatever you want."

I would show them that I belonged on the stage. I let a dancer take Floyd for a moment and I took a script from Dianne, whose hands, when they touched mine, were ice cold.

Mr. Palia coughed. "Henry and the kid. This is a big moment in the show. You're standing on this baseball diamond in the park, you've just done a big dance number in the last scene, and now you're fac-

142

ing each other alone for the first time. Center stage, Henry, Little Billy at his left elbow. No, that's the other elbow! Henry, take it from 'I've always done my best to be a good father to you.'"

Henry adjusted the waist of his lemon-lime leotard, took a deep breath, and gripped me around the shoulders.

"Bill Jr., I've always done my best to be a good father to you. I know I haven't been perfect, but I've tried. I see a lot of myself in you. You're getting older now, son. Pretty soon you'll be a man. And I want you to know that, no matter what happens, you're my boy. Nothing can change that."

"Where's the rest of my money?" shouted Mrs. Pinkney.

"Quiet!" said Dianne.

"Son," said Henry, "I want to tell you something about your mother. It's not an easy thing for me to say."

I read from my script. "She's dead, isn't she?"

"Louder!" shouted Mr. Palia.

"She's dead, isn't she?" I shouted.

"Yes. I'm sorry."

"I don't want her to be dead."

"I know. I don't either. I'd give anything to bring her back." He put his arm around me.

"You're lying. She told me you didn't love each other anymore."

"Louder, Billy!" said Mr. Palia. "Make your nose vibrate!"

Henry dropped to one knee and put his face close to mine. His breath smelled like paint. "Grown-ups are like children on a playground," he said, "fighting in the sandbox, calling names, running away in tears. After a while we forget why we're fighting but we're so angry and hurt that we can't make up and be friends again. That's how it is for your mother and me, Billy. For years I've wanted her back, but she didn't know it, and I could never tell her because I was too proud."

"You're not proud anymore?" I tried to make my nose vibrate.

"No, not anymore. I just wish I could tell her. I wish I could tell her how I loved her. If I had it all to do over again, I'd never let her go. Never. I know what it is to love, now. If I only had another chance."

"Oh, Bill," said Ginger, who had been hidden behind us. "That's

143

the corniest speech I've heard in my life. Is that really how you feel?" She walked slowly into the spotlight but hung back.

"You're shocked, Henry," said Mr. Palia. "Remember, you think she's a ghost. Jump back and grab Billy."

"Bill, it's me," said Ginger. "I'm alive."

"No, it can't be you. I'm hallucinating."

"No, you're not. I'm alive, Bill. Touch me."

"You start to touch her," said Mr. Palia to Henry, "and then you pull your hand back. Then Ginger, reach out that beautiful hand of yours and put it on Henry's shoulder. That's it, doll. Terrific moment. I can feel the heat all the way down here."

They looked into each other's eyes. Ginger took her hand away from Henry's shoulder and held it trembling against her lips. Then she fell against him, with both arms around him. They stepped away from me and held each other kissing.

"Shelley, I've been a fool," Henry said. "But I'll make it up to you, I swear I will. I'll never hurt you again. I'll remember my mistakes forever, and I'll never let them happen again. I swear it. I swear it."

They kept kissing and Al Palia called, "Enough! Sickening! Little Billy, I do like the horror in your eyes. Remember how you did that."

"Do I get the part?" I said to Ginger after a moment, when Henry had turned away.

"Does Carla get the part, Al?" said Ginger.

Mr. Palia turned to Mr. Danson. "What do you think, Dick?"

Mr. Danson said, "I wasn't really watching the little girl; what did you think, Saul?"

"I think Henry's right," said Saul Anderson. "She's a little squeaky."

"But she is Ginger's little girl," said Mr. Danson. "That counts for a lot."

"Can she sing?" asked Saul Anderson. "Can she sing my lyrics?"

"Of course she can, she's Ginger's girl," said Mr. Danson, and he smiled and winked at Ginger. "I think we can let the little girl in until further notice. Right, Al? Right, Ginger?"

"Until further notice," said Mr. Palia to me, "you are Little Billy. But I want you to work with Myra. Do you know who Myra is?" Myra waved at me. "Myra will work with you on choreography and vocals," he said. "Don't give her trouble."

"O.K.," I said. I was ecstatic; I was jubilant. But it was time to move on to Henry's song. Dianne showed me how to walk gracefully backwards out of the spotlight, lifting my toes last from the floor as if I were magically held there.

When Henry had finished his song, Mr. Palia waved us away and I went back to where the dancer was holding Floyd. I flipped through the script, looking for my lines. Where were they all? I flipped to the beginning and caught an "L.B." a few times in the first act and two or three times in the third. That was it.

"My money!" shouted Mrs. Pinkney, still breathing down on Bob Ferring at the piano.

"Here," said Dianne, throwing her a dollar bill. "Go buy yourself something nice." Mrs. Pinkney took it and swished out of the room and down the hall, marking her exit with a crash of the lobby door.

I looked back at my script again, despairingly, and noticed a single phrase at the end of the third act—duet: Bill/Billy.

*T*he next morning I asked Grandma about spending Friday night at Ginger's. She raised one eyebrow and sniffed. "What will these people be doing that keeps them up so late at night?"

"I'm not sure exactly."

"Something decent, I should hope."

"He's a minister, Oma."

"Are they Baptists? Could they be attending the evangelistic meeting over in Chesterfield?"

"Maybe, Oma."

By Friday morning Grandma had declared it a disgrace that the F.R.C. of V. never conducted revivals, especially now that there were so many people in Dutch Falls who needed reviving.

"I worry like a Baptist about the unsaved," she said to my father. "Jim wouldn't like that, but you just can't teach an old dog new tricks."

"Mama, you just keep worrying," Father said. "I'm all for it."

Specifically, she worried about the young English moving into our subdivisions, the Richmond commuters. They would all die in darkness, she thought, if the church didn't stop singing "Immortal Invisible" and lure them in with popular choruses like "Kumbaya" and "Pass It On." We saw these young people mowing their lawns on Sundays as we drove with Louise to Springeldam's Cafeteria by the river— Louise would shake her big dark wig and transparent pink hat and say, "Not when I was a girl, Dora, not when I was a girl. People honored the Sabbath then." And Grandma would say, "When we were girls, Louise, we would not have been allowed to visit an eating establishment on the Sabbath." It worried Grandma to eat at a good cafeteria right after church. She kept her Bible in the center of her tray and crowded her salad, meat loaf, and chocolate cake around it. It worried her to think of all those lost souls by the river. She always left a tract in the bathroom at Trudy Zeger's salon, where she had her hair permed. The tract was called "What If He Came Today?" It was about Jesus coming back and finding that Americans had abandoned the faith of their fathers for worldly diversions such as going to the cinema and mowing grass on the Lord's Day.

Ginger was supposed to pick me up at seven o'clock that night, but it was Frank who came at seven forty-five and then made me wait in his old car for a half an hour outside the Food Angel grocery store/Temple of the Dove while he supposedly got a few things together. He came out with an armful of books and a black suit, both of which he tossed carelessly in the back of the car. We said not a word to each other during the trip, from the time he picked me up until we arrived at his house. Walking up the front porch steps with his suit over his shoulder, he clenched his jaw. Ginger clomped into the foyer to meet us in thick heels and a green pantsuit.

"Hiya, kiddo," she said to me, and then turned to Frank. "You're late. You have a lot of nerve, Frank. How do you expect me to watch four kids, make dinner, and put on makeup at the same time? My face looks like modern art."

"Sorry, Ginger."

"I'm in a bad mood. I've got a splitting headache. Now I have to give these dratted fish sticks to these dratted kids. Peter, Paul, John!" she yelled. "Dinner!"

I followed her into the kitchen hesitantly, and as soon as Frank was out of sight, she became pleasant. "How do I look?" she asked. "Stunning?" She twirled around. Green was her color.

"You look beautiful," I said.

"I guess you noticed that Frank is in the worst mood. I don't know what's wrong with him and I don't care." She opened the oven door and tossed in two trays of paste-colored fish sticks.

"Where's Floyd?" I asked. It always seemed possible to me that Floyd

147

was dead, lying in an empty room somewhere with a wet finger in a light socket, sparks shooting out.

"Floyd is in bed. Now listen, kiddo, the older boys are out playing. They can eat dinner whenever they get back and they can stay up as long as they want. Just have them watch television. And don't let them outside after dark." She hurried past me, sighing. "I have to put on more eye shadow. Will you call me when George and Mandi come?"

"Sure," I answered. I went down to the family room and sat at the piano, playing hymns from a book I found in the bench. The hymnal was dog-eared. On the inside front cover it was stamped, "Ex Libris Frank Jordan." I didn't know what "Ex Libris" meant. I thought it had something to do with the zodiac.

"Hello?" called an unfamiliar voice. "Hello? Anybody home?"

I started up the steps. A middle-aged woman appeared at the top, smiling. "Hi there," she said. "No one answered the door so I let myself in. I'm Mandi. And what is your name?"

"Carrie," I said. "I'm the baby-sitter."

"Well, it's nice to meet you, Carrie," she said in a sweet, sing-song voice. "Frank and Gin around?"

"Upstairs," I said.

"Oh, upstairs." She lingered on the steps for a second, smiling at me, and then turned and said to someone out of sight, "They're still changing. Come on in."

I climbed up the steps to the kitchen as her companion came into the house. He was a tall, curly-haired man with a long nose. He jingled the change in his pockets.

"This is Carrie," said Mandi. "Carrie, this is Mr. Manning. Well, I guess we'll let you call him George."

"Hello, Carrie," said George. "And how old are you?"

"I'm twelve," I said.

"You look just like your mommy."

Mandi squeezed his hand. "George, she's the baby-sitter. You know Frank and Ginger have four boys."

"Oh, I see."

The front door opened again behind George and in walked, of all people, the Hagedoorns. Though I knew them well, I didn't recog-

148

nize them at first. It was like walking down a street and bumping into someone who was supposed to be dead. They didn't belong here. They weren't even dressed like themselves. Nancy Hagedoorn wore dangling silver balls on her ears and a glittering, green sequined dress that stood straight out from her thin body like a half-raised umbrella. She looked like a Christmas tree. Arnie Hagedoorn wore a yellow and black plaid suit with a bow tie. They didn't see me first. They went straight to the Mannings and introduced themselves, shaking hands and complimenting clothes. Nancy Hagedoorn giggled with Mandi about being so dressed up.

"I almost never go out like this—" she said, "so fancy. I'm home with the baby every day. Half the time I can't even get a shower."

"This is little Carrie, the baby-sitter," said Mandi, finally, pointing at me. "George thought she belonged to Ginger."

Mandi laughed in a way that hurt my feelings and Mrs. Hagedoorn looked down at me, smiling expectantly, and suddenly her lips caught against her teeth. Mr. Hagedoorn looked, too, and his face went red before he turned away quickly to say something to George.

"Hello, Carrie," said Mrs. Hagedoorn gently, as she put her chilly arm around me. "We already know each other very well, don't we? I've known Carrie since she was just a little thing in diapers."

"We go to the same church," I said. Mrs. Hagedoorn gave me a long look and I knew what she was thinking—"Please don't tell anyone at church about this."

"Church. Isn't that wonderful," said Mandi. "I used to go to church—back when I was a good little girl." She laughed again. "That's how I met Frank and Ginger. Frank is our minister. Can you believe that? We're going dancing with our minister."

"Frank will surprise us all," said George. "I heard this guy can really cut the rug."

"I know Ginger's a terrific dancer," said Mandi. "Watch if every man there doesn't have his eye on her."

"The Jordans sound like marvelous people," said Mrs. Hagedoorn. She had licked her teeth and was smiling again. "I haven't even met Frank or Ginger yet. I've just heard about them from Arnie. They sound so youthful and fun. How is your father, Carrie?" she said to

149

me. "I'm so glad we have him back at home now. The Lord brought him home safe, just like he promised."

"My father is fine," I said.

Frank came down the steps in ordinary clothes and Ginger followed after him.

"Hi, hon," Ginger said to Mandi. "You look terrific. George, it's good to see you. And Arnie, this must be Nancy."

"Yes, this is Nancy," said Arnie, and Mrs. Hagedoorn took Ginger's hand. Ginger looked at it, probably wondering at the temperature.

"I've heard a lot of wonderful things about you, Ginger," Nancy Hagedoorn said.

"What a beautiful woman, Arnie," said Ginger. "I can't believe this beautiful woman has a brand-new baby at home. She doesn't have bags under her eyes or anything. It's not fair. What's your secret, Nancy?"

"I'm just so grateful to get out of the house," said Mrs. Hagedoorn. "Arnie was so sweet; he talked his mother into watching the baby and so I said, 'O.K., Arnie, I guess I'm out of excuses.' And he said, 'That's right, Nancy, you're just going to have to force yourself to have a wonderful time for a change.' So that's what I'm going to do."

The whole group moved for the door. Mr. Hagedoorn didn't look at me at all. He put his hand around his wife's arm and pulled her away quickly. I watched them all go. Their long skirts and wide pants sailed behind them down the porch steps and disappeared, tucked into car doors. I watched a final moment as they pulled away in the Hagedoorns' white Oldsmobile. How cool it must have been inside that air-conditioned car, cool enough to accommodate Mr. Hagedoorn's defective sweat glands on a hot night like this. I remembered what Annajane had said about him.

I went back to my hymnbook and hardly noticed that it was growing dark outside as I played and sang:

> Jerusalem, in sorrows dressed,
> How oft I longed to shield thee.
> With tender wings of righteousness
> I could have succoured, healed thee.
> Though thou unwilling, thou unyielding

150

Never should receive me,
'Tis still my plea—Oh come to me,
That I may yet relieve thee.

The shadows had grown long on the patio when I looked up. A few lightning bugs throbbed yellow on the weedy, tall grass. I went outside and called loudly for the boys as Ginger had. I called again and again, but only when I was ready to give up and go looking for them did three short figures appear out of the swampy woods behind the house.

"Oh, it's you," said Peter. "Where did my father go?"

"Dancing," I said, because I didn't think it was a secret from the children. "Are you ready for fish sticks?"

"You eat them," he said. "We're not hungry."

The twins didn't contradict him. All three boys came in and sat on the family room couch side by side with their legs crossed at the ankles. Peter turned on the television and sank back into the arm of the couch with his eyes closed.

"You don't like fish sticks?" I asked.

"No," said Peter.

"Then why don't we order a pizza?" I had said it on impulse, because I wanted the children to like me. The twins looked up. Even Peter looked up.

"You got money?" said Peter.

"No," I said sadly. "I guess it was a bad idea."

"I know where we can get some money," said John.

"Where?" I asked.

He led me upstairs to show me. In the back of his father's top dresser drawer was a knotted-up sock with a small hole in the toe.

"This is where Daddy keeps money from Mama so she won't spend it," he said. He pried a bill out of the toe of the sock, rolled up as thin as a matchstick.

"Well, this is a twenty-dollar bill," I said in wonder. "And there's more in there—gosh, a lot of money. How'd you find out about it?"

John shrugged. "My daddy showed me."

"You mean he told you about this money on purpose? But he didn't tell your mama?"

"Naw."

"Why not? Doesn't he trust her?"

John shrugged his shoulders again. "I don't know if he trusts her or don't trust her. She knows all about his money, anyway, so it don't matter. She's always ordering out."

While we waited for the pizza to come, I sat in the living room shuffling through Ginger's photos and scrapbooks again. I came across a stack of yearbooks from the late fifties and located both Ginger and Frank in their senior classes. Ginger had a girl's face, round and eager. Frank's class voted him most likely to marry a rich old woman. As I opened another yearbook, a newspaper scrap fell into my lap. Written on the top was: The Ciletauna *Guardian*, Church Chatter, June 28, 1972.

When You Have the Lord, That's All You Need

by Cheryl Beth Cudney, Religion Desk

Ginger Jordan had it all. She had a burgeoning Broadway career, a handsome husband, and an expensive apartment in Manhattan. But her life, she reports, was empty. "I was like a desert inside," she explains. "Everything I had ever done was for selfish reasons and I didn't even know what it was like to feel love. I had Frank, but I didn't know how to love him. And he didn't know how to love me. We were man and wife, but we had no love."

Today, with a twinkle in her eye, the lovely brown-eyed mother of three gives God the glory for grabbing her out of the success race and refocusing her on the road of real happiness. While she was starring in *The King and I* and her husband, Frank, was scaling to the pinnacle of the acting profession with a lead in the Broadway musical *Eenie Meenie,* Mrs. Jordan was picking up her Bible at home and reading the words of Jesus.

One night on the way home from Broadway, Ginger Jordan stopped her taxi on a rainy street and started walking. Miraculously, she met a minister from a local church. He invited her to a revival, and there she accepted Jesus Christ as her personal Savior.

That night she told Frank what had transpired. "He just dropped to his knees right there and started weeping," she acknowledges with a zest-filled laugh. "It was just a tremendous testimony to the Lord's transforming power. He wanted to commit his life to Christ right on the spot."

Today, Ginger Jordan lives for others and not herself. The choir director at Church of the Apostles Assembly on Main, she also supports her husband in his full-time lay preaching ministry. She also takes care of her three small boys, including mischievous twins, and teaches youth Sunday school.

This month, her church has chosen to honor her as a "Proverbs 31 woman," as a faithful partner of a husband being faithful to God.

"I've never been happier and I just praise the Lord for leading me out of the desert," she reports. "I just thank the Holy Ghost for showing me how to truly love Frank and love my children. And I just thank all the Spirit-filled Christians who have given so generously out of their own pockets so that Frank could keep healing people. It's like a miracle, how when you think you don't have the money, it just keeps rolling in."

Ginger Jordan says that she would never trade her little yellow house on Brownkennel for an expensive apartment, or her life with her three children for the biggest Broadway show in the world. Smiling her wide, bright smile she claims, "God is the only one who can get you out of the desert and out of the rat race. Lean on him, and you'll make your life a real success."

So Ginger had led Frank to the Lord? But she had told me so clearly that Frank gave his life to the Lord first. Maybe it didn't matter how it happened, as long as they were both saved now. The doorbell rang. A delivery truck sat in the driveway. I put the scrapbooks away and went to answer the door.

After I had checked Floyd, we ate the pizza in the family room, with the television turned up high. I looked at the faces of the three boys and tried to imagine them much younger, in a place called Ciletauna.

"Stop looking at me," Peter said with his fierce face that was so like Ginger's. "I said stop it! Why do you keep doing that?"

"I'm sorry," I said. "You just look so much like your mother."

"Of course I do. I look exactly like her. Everybody knows that."

153

"You're lucky. People will always like you for your looks."

"Who cares? Just stop looking at me."

I stayed awake for a while after they went to bed at midnight. The night air was sticky and cool, drifting in through the screen door of the patio. I had forgotten to ask where I was supposed to sleep. I curled up on the couch and turned off the lights, letting the T.V. flicker on in the darkness. There was an old movie starting, something about a World War II soldier meeting a beautiful woman in Italy and longing for her later when he was back in New York with his wife and children. He had just returned to Palermo when I drifted off.

A car engine woke me, deep in the night. I sat up and opened my eyes, expecting to see shadows of venetian blinds and maple leaves stretching back and forth in car lights across my own bedroom walls. But this room was wide and dark, and the bullfrogs were loud outside. I couldn't remember where I was until the front door slammed and Ginger and Frank walked into the kitchen upstairs, arguing.

"I never called you that," Frank said. He was at the top of the short steps behind me, in the dark. "That's your word. All I said is you cheapen yourself, talking to a man that way with his wife sitting in the same room."

"Cheapen myself?" Ginger was loud. "I'm just trying to enjoy myself for five minutes. I guess I'm just not as holy as you are, Frank, because I like to have a good time now and then."

"You had a good time. I felt like a fool. How do you think it makes me feel, watching you come on to men like that? And I'm just sitting there smiling like an idiot."

"So now I come on to 'men'? More than one? Do you think I come on to all men? What is it you want out of me, Frank?" Her voice moved back and there were clattering sounds in the sink, silverware being thrown and shifted. "You want me to (crash) play the little minister's wife all the time, go to prayer meeting and do crosspoint—"

"Needlepoint."

"—and make friends with all the (crash) good girls and never speak to another man? That's not me, Frank. So stop preaching to me."

"If anybody's preaching to you, it's your own conscience."

"Who needs a conscience when you're around? You've never let me think for myself."

"I'm not trying to think for you," Frank said. "It's just that whatever's going wrong between us is ruining my ministry, Ginger. Doesn't our church mean anything to you?"

"Don't blame me for your problems!" she shouted. "That church is just a bunch of mental cases anyway, Frank! You attract those people. But I'm sick of losers. I'm sick of needy people. I need, I need."

"Ginger, you're drunk. It doesn't even bother me anymore, it's so crazy."

"You're the one who's crazy. You're a loser! You're not even man enough to make a real living. I wish you were dead."

"Don't ever say that again."

"Or else what? Will you hit me? That's some way for a minister to talk."

"I didn't say that."

"Go ahead." They were both quiet for a long time and then Frank's muffled cry floated downstairs. A second later, the front door slammed.

I couldn't sleep after that, but I didn't dare make any noise. For a long time I lay shivering, until there were footsteps in the kitchen again, then on the short steps behind me.

"Ginger?" I said quietly, hoping it was her and not Frank..

"What? Who is that?" Ginger's voice was slow and morose. She was smoking a cigarette.

"It's Carla."

The T.V. was still going. She kneeled close to it and the pale outline of her face flickered and danced on the darkness. "They playing that one again?" she said, looking at the screen. "Oh, yeah, this is the one. Always makes me cry. Every time." She sniffed loudly and stood up. "You want a drink? How about a glass of sherry?" She was offering me the cup of sin.

"I don't know," I said. "I've never had it before."

"Well I need one, so you might as well have one, too."

"Do you think I'm old enough?"

"If you're old enough to hang around with me, you're old enough to drink." She switched on a light and poured golden sherry into a pair of jelly jar glasses, which she steadied on top of the television.

155

She put a glass in my hand and I took a sip. I shivered and then felt warm.

"My grandma would kill me for this," I said.

"Frank would kill me for this, but then I'd like to kill him right now. I'd like to scratch his eyes out. But, Frankenstein's body is after all the temple of God, as he reminded me several times tonight. One does not scratch out the eyes of the temple of God." She lit a match near her face and it flamed bright for a few seconds, then with a wave of her hand the match went out and she set her cigarette in an ashtray next to her elbow. It burned slowly without touching her mouth.

"Can I have one?" I said.

"What?" She stared at me. "A cigarette? Absolutely not. You're only thirteen. I have my limits."

I had lost track, myself, of how old I really was. We sat looking at the old movie that still chirped softly in the corner. The soldier lay on his deathbed now. His Italian lover, white-haired, rocked him in her arms.

"Ginger," I said slowly, "did he hit you?"

"Who?"

"Frank. I thought I heard him hit you."

"Oh, I'd like to see him try."

"But he was so mad at you."

"Frank enjoys this. He's outside waiting for me to ask forgiveness so he can forgive me."

"Are you going to?"

"No, I'm going to bed. I don't enjoy this anymore. It's old."

I wanted to say something that would cheer her up. "Ginger," I said, "I've decided that you're my best friend."

"Well," she said after a long pause, "I'll tell you something, kiddo. I need a best friend, so it might as well be you." She didn't sound enthusiastic. But I was getting sleepy so I pushed it out of my mind. I rested my head on the pillow and fell into a dream.

When I got up the next morning, everyone was asleep but Frank. He sat in the kitchen, reading from a gigantic book. He drove me home again without saying a word. At least he remembered to pay me.

At home I found Phuong doing dishes again, this time from left to right as Grandma did. She wore her pale orange sundress. This dress she always wore backwards, so that the flesh-colored bust darts in the back looked like the stumps of amputated limbs. Why she had such poor clothes I couldn't imagine. I had seen other Vietnamese women, some of them much older than her, dressed in simple American clothes and wearing them correctly. An old woman who worked at the supermarket wore a clean white blouse and neatly pressed black pants every day. It was like a uniform. It looked good on her.

I walked softly behind Phuong. I would go straight to my bedroom.

"Your grandmother pick beans in the garden," she said loudly. "She wanting you to help it." Through the kitchen window I saw Grandma's broad-brimmed hat casting a shadow over the garden soil, her flowered gloves tearing through tangled green vines.

"Well, I have to take a shower," I said.

"You don't have to take it now," said Phuong, staring out the window. "You can working in the garden first."

"I do need a shower," I said."

"You going out to your grandmother."

"I can't right now," I said forcefully. "I just got home."

Phuong kept her back to me. Her shoulders looked pinched. She said nothing. After a moment I remembered what my father had said, that I should treat his new wife well and make things easy on Grandma. I should fight the negative.

"I'll go out there," I said. "But first I need a cup of coffee. Would you like a cup of instant?"

"Yes."

I put the water on to boil and sat down, with my overnight case beside me on the floor. I felt old enough for coffee today. I was like that American soldier in the movie, coming back to New York from Palermo, lighting a cigarette for the first time in his mother's kitchen.

"Why don't you teach me some Vietnamese?" I said to Phuong.

"Excuse me?"

"You could teach me some Vietnamese. I like languages. I want to learn French. And I know how to say some things in Dutch." I said several words to her quickly, hoping that my bad pronunciation wouldn't show. Only my grandfather had spoken Dutch with any skill.

"What are you saying?" asked Phuong.

I translated. "Don't tell the neighbor how fat are the pheasants on your own acre."

She lifted her head into the sunlight and said, in a sing-song voice, "Một, hai, ba, bôn, năm, sáu, bay, tám, chín, mười—."

I tried to repeat but couldn't follow. "What does it mean?"

She held up her fingers. "One, two, three, four, five, six, seven, eight, nine, ten."

"Say it in Vietnamese again and I'll try."

"Một, hai, ba, bôn—"

"Mop, hi, ba, bum."

"Một."

"Mope."

"No, một." She made a face like a fish. I was going to try again but my father walked suddenly in from the carport, singing.

"Good morning," he said. "Where's Grandma? Working herself to death outside? Guess what. I've got good job prospects, very good prospects. And I'm happy, and it's Saturday. So I had a wonderful thought—how about we all drive to the beach?"

"I don't have clothes," said Phuong.

"A bathing suit? We'll find you something."

She shook her head. "I can stay home and read my Bible. I supposed to read it today."

He smiled. "You can bring your Bible with you. Read at the beach."

She sighed and didn't argue. Father sent me outside to find Grandma. She had already walked up the back porch steps, her garden shoes caked with brown mud.

"We're going to the beach," I said.

Grandma stopped beside me. "Why do you smell like cigarettes?"

I looked her straight in the eye. "Mr. Jordan picked up a hitchhiker on the way home and he was smoking like a chimney."

Grandma's jaw dropped. "A hitchhiker! These days? That's just not safe, anymore. I want you to tell him that I forbid him to pick up hitchhikers when you're in the car with him."

"Yes, ma'am," I said.

158

"So dangerous. The beach, did you say? Well, all right then. If your father wants to." She hugged her tools and went inside.

Grandma picked out an old blue bathing suit for Phuong, with a high-necked collar and three layers of black ruffle around the waist. It had been sitting in a cedar chest for at least thirty years, probably since the last time Grandma had entered a body of water bigger than her bathtub. Phuong kept pulling nervously at the ruffles, so that from a distance on the lake she looked like a big woman trying to wedge an inner tube over her bottom. She sat right down in the sand with a Bible on her knees. Father stretched out on a purple towel a good distance from her and went to sleep, turning from brown to deep brown while he lay there with his arms over his head. It was an hour after lunch and the beach was dense with bodies. Most people lay on blankets—skinny boys looking around for girls and girls in bikinis waiting for boys.

"I brought something along to read," said Grandma. She reached down into her bag, over the arm of the chair she had brought from home. Grandma always wore long red culottes to the beach with a white blouse and a red cameo pin. Her white beach hat swept out in a ten-inch brim. "It's a prayer letter from the Zinkits, David. Do you remember them? Dolores was my best friend when we were just school girls. She and Del are ministering in France."

Father let out a snore. "I was going to take another nap, Mama."

"Well, I'll read it to myself and you all can just listen if you like or sleep if you like," said Grandma. She began slowly:

Del and Dolores Zinkit
Claire, France

Dear Colaborers in Christ's Harvest,

In our Lord's parable of the sower, some of the seed falls on dry ground where it cannot be nourished. How accurately that describes the situation here in the modest-sized village of Claire, France. Some villagers endeavor to justify themselves before God by their own works—confessing their sins to human mediators and subscribing to every jot and tittle of the law of the RoMAN Church. Paradoxically,

159

others apostatize, abandoning themselves to hedonism and despair. When Dolores and I attempt to educate them to a saving knowledge of God's free offer of justification, they harden their hearts and stop their ears (Romans 8). At times we wonder: Does God really have his "elect of every nation"—will he call his people from France, or is it time to shake the dust from our feet and go where people hunger for the gospel?

Grandma paused and took a sip of lemonade from our cooler.

These are the thoughts that burden our souls. How difficult it is for us to trust God. But then, in our human weakness, his sovereignty is suddenly made manifest. Yes, God has his remnant. Brethren, we exhort you to beseech God on behalf of the nation of France, and for Dolores and myself as we struggle with the ubiquitous xenophobia which hinders our ministry.

"Excuse me," I interrupted. "What's 'xenophobia'?"
"I don't know," said Grandma. "I need a thesaurus to read these letters. I don't understand half."
"It means fear of foreigners," said Father out of his sleep. "Xenophobia is the fear of strangers or foreigners."
"Dolores always makes it sound like Del writes these letters," said Grandma, "but I can tell her writing by the vocabulary. Now where was I—"

Pray especially for DOLORES—

"See," said Grandma, "she mentions herself first, so you can tell it's Dolores writing."

—who is endeavoring to reach out to the village women with an American cooking class and Bible study; in the first session, five of our neighbors (including one man, who misunderstood our sign!) came with their children to learn how to make Cincinnati chili and Boston creme pie. Fortunately no one realized the truth—that Dolores had never made either recipe before and that furthermore they were witnessing

160

her first attempts at cooking with the metric system. But grace abounds. All turned out well.

On a more serious note, Del, who continues to suffer from allergic rhinitis, finds it difficult to preach outdoors without sneezing continuously. His nasal passages are quite inflamed. Pray that he will learn to cope with this thorn in his flesh, if God should not heal it.

Most of all, covenant with us brethren to support our little church here which endeavors to proclaim to the world the whole counsel of God and the fullness of Reformed doctrine in the midst of so much spiritual darkness. Through your prayers and gifts, the Word goes out. How often we think of you all, and rejoice in the inheritance of salvation which is ours through the matchless generosity of our Savior and Master, Jesus Christ, who gave himself up as a sacrifice of atonement, a lamb without blemish, to pay the penalty for our transgressions against the law of God.

Yours in the Name of the Author and Finisher of our Faith,

Del and Dolores Zinkit
Missionaries of the First Reformed Church of Virginia
in Claire, France

Grandma folded the letter and put it in her bag. "Dolores has always had an outstanding vocabulary. You can't deny that. She's been doing 'Word Power' in the *Reader's Digest* ever since I can remember and she rarely gets one wrong. And she really believes in the power of the mind. She used to tell me that she could make a cold go away by concentrating."

Father made a noise, something like, "Mmmmmmm."

Phuong looked up from her Bible, squinting. "I believe in the Holy Ghost," she burst out. "I am trying to live of the holy life of faith and love." She put her hand over her eyes like a visor and looked back and forth between Grandma and me. I didn't know what she meant or what she was against, though she seemed to be against something. Grandma gazed down from her chair and slowly tilted her hat back.

"Holy life?" said Grandma. "Would you like to tell me what you mean?"

"Oh, Mama," said Father quickly. "Let's not get into a theological discussion on a day like this. Look at that gorgeous sky. Clear as a bell. Just enjoy it."

"I'm very interested in what my daughter-in-law has to say, David Grietkirk. I don't often get to talk about important spiritual things, and I'm sick to death of small talk. Aren't you, Phuong? Tell me exactly what you mean."

Phuong bowed her head. She looked ashamed. "I mean—"

"Do you think we are not filled with the Holy Spirit and you are?"

She shook her head. "I just wanting to live of the holy life."

"We all want to live a holy life," said Grandma. "You're no different from anyone here."

"It don't seem same," said Phuong. "You have never talk about Holy Ghost."

"It's a little different here," said Father to her softly. "It's not like the refugee camps, where people were coming to God left and right. You have to understand that this is a different kind of place. Not better or worse, just different."

"Why?" said Phuong.

"Because the people here have always believed in God. The Spirit's always been here. We don't talk about it all the time because we're so used to it."

"It's fine what happens over in the Far East," said Grandma. "But this is the United States of America." She pursed her lips.

I was hot, and the water looked murky-cold. I wanted to go in. Father stood up and pulled Phuong by the wrist toward the water, smiling. "Come on, you. Lighten up. Let's go swimming." I decided to wait for them to come back and then go in myself. I lay down on my towel, reached over and picked up Phuong's King James Bible. It was full of neon pink pen marks and handwritten notes—in Vietnamese, of course. I looked up John 3:16: "For God so loved the world, that he gave his only begotten Son, that whosoever believeth in him . . ." She had drawn a circle around "the world" in bright red, and added five exclamation points after "should not perish, but have everlasting life." Out in the water, she and my father paddled over to a diving pier. They hoisted themselves up and sat for a long time, dripping in the sun, talking. Phuong waved her arms wildly, explaining something to him. I wondered if other people on the beach were staring at the two of them as I was.

"Carrie," Grandma said, "I hope you won't pick up any strange ideas."

"What do you mean?"

"That's all I'm saying. I don't want you to pick up strange ideas."

"You don't like her, do you?"

"I have absolutely nothing against her. And I'm not raising you to be a gossip, and I'm not raising me to be one, either. So here's a quarter for an ice cream sandwich. And a quarter for me, too. Why don't you run up to the snack shop."

"Aren't you going to tell me what you were about to say?"

"I said here's two quarters for ice cream sandwiches. Why don't you run up to the snack shop."

I plowed through the hot sand, wishing I knew what was on her mind.

"Hey, look who it is!" said a voice right in front of me. The couple on the blanket near us had turned their heads and I saw that the tall man was Henry Harrison, the star from Ginger's play. The woman with him I didn't recognize immediately. Her hair was pulled up under a black hat. She wore red sunglasses that rested on a white blob in the middle of her face.

"Well, it if isn't Ginger's darling child," said Henry, sitting up and throwing out his arms in a theatrical way. "Come to Papa," he laughed. The woman slapped his knee and snarled. "Don't tease children."

I stopped in shock. It was Dianne Bane under the hat.

"What are you staring at?" she asked.

"I'm kind of surprised to see you two together," I said.

"Why?"

I couldn't think of a polite answer.

"Well, put your eyes back in your head," she said.

Henry laughed. "Don't listen to Dianne. She's got her hair pulled too tight under that hat. So little Miss . . . I forget your name—"

"My name's Carrie."

"I thought it was Carla," said Dianne.

163

"Well, where's your mother, anyway?" asked Henry, looking around anxiously. "Where's Ginger?"

"She's not here," I said. "I came with some family friends." I pointed in the direction of Grandma.

"Oh." He looked around and located my grandmother. "That woman over there, she's a friend of Ginger's? Any friend of Ginger's is a friend of mine. Why don't you introduce us?"

"I can't introduce you to that lady," I said quickly.

"Why not?"

"Because she doesn't speak English."

"What does she speak?"

"Only Dutch. She's Dutch."

"Oh, I see." Henry laughed. "Little Carrie," he said, "let me give you some advice about the theater, long as we're here."

"Oh, spare the kid," Dianne said.

"She needs to hear this," he said. "You see," he said, "the business of the theater is make-believe, real make-believe. That's how you make the madness work. Just say to yourself at the beginning of each rehearsal, 'I believe in the magic, I believe in the mystery, and I believe in me.' Because that's what it's all about, Carrie. Fooling yourself. Accepting the miraculous lie."

"Listen to the king of showbiz," said Dianne.

"Shut up," he said.

"O.K., Mr. Harrison, I'll remember," I said, anxious to get away before Grandma saw me.

"Just don't get egotistical," Dianne said to me. "I hate stage brats."

"Hey," said Henry to me, "want to swim out to the dock with me? Look at those kids on the slide. Let's go out there."

"I don't know how to swim very well," I said. "I was going to get a Coke."

"I'll buy you a Coke later. Let's swim out, if your friends don't mind."

Grandma's nose got that sharp look as we passed her, but I made the O.K. sign and she said nothing to us. Henry and I walked out in the water until it was shoulder-deep on me. Then we backstroked toward the slide. The water lapped in and out of my ears, breaking Henry's chatter into nonsense over the shouts of the children—"a

164

friend of Ginger's—know her better—possibly the three of us—get into character, you know?"

When we reached the slide, I climbed up and he waited at the bottom. He tried to catch me when I came down, but grabbed too hard and pinched my arms. I had bruised his head with my bony heel, he said. The slide wasn't that much fun, anyway. Dianne thumbed her nose at us in the distance. It was an odd sight, Grandma waving and Dianne behind her waving a beer can and thumbing her nose. I could see Father and Phuong off to my left, still talking on the platform.

"Are you married to Dianne?" I asked.

He frowned. "Yes. I hate to say so. There's nothing much romantic between Dianne and me."

"I didn't know you were married. I didn't think you even liked each other."

"We can't stand each other. Don't ask me how it happened. Can you see a guy like me ending up with a woman like that? I guess even a kid knows it's all wrong. But it's kind of a stage secret. So keep your mouth shut about it. Anyway, it won't last much longer."

"You're getting a divorce?"

He squinted over at the beach. "She drinks too much. I can't take care of her anymore. I always think kids are wiser than grown-ups about love. What do you think I should do?"

"I think you fight with each other too much," I said. "I'm getting sunburned out here. I'm going to go put on a T-shirt."

"Good idea," Henry said. "Let's go back. This water is putrid."

When we returned to Henry's blanket, Dianne was asleep under a copy of *Lady Detective True Confessions*. I said good-bye and hurried back to my grandmother to explain that Henry and Dianne were just a nice couple who attended the Jordans' church.

"Still," she said anxiously, "you're almost a young lady now, Carolyn. Before you go running here and there with grown men you and I need to have a talk. If your father hadn't been out in the water, I would never have allowed it."

We didn't say much to each other on the way back home in Grandma's old Dart. Father drove, and as we flew along it was difficult to talk over the wind and the roar of the wheels. Then it began

165

to rain, so we rolled up the windows and simmered silently for a long time on the hot vinyl seats. Grandma watched the road carefully and gave Father driving tips. Phuong was next to me in the back, her hands folded around her knees, her eyes off somewhere.

"Sure wish this car had air conditioning," said Father finally, only a few miles from home. "Think I'll look into getting it."

"I get chilled easily," said Grandma. "I don't want cold air blowing on me."

"You could always wear a sweater, Mama."

"You not hot in Guam," said Phuong to my father.

"My David has always been very sensitive to temperatures," said Grandma defensively, turning around. "If he wants air conditioning, I'll just have to make do. After all, it's his home now. Not mine."

"But this is your car," I said.

"Well, not for long. The day is coming when I won't be able to drive myself anymore, and if this car is still running, this car will be his."

Everyone had to be silent again after that. And then Grandma changed the subject and said, "Why don't we have those Jordan friends of Carrie's over soon? If she's going to be spending so much time with them, I think I'd like to know them a little better. Davey, remember that Mr. Jordan is a minister and a former soldier. You said something about wanting to meet him. Maybe he could be a new friend for you."

"Why don't I just invite him over to spend the night, Mama? We can play cowboys and Indians in the backyard."

She ignored his joke. "I'll call them when we get home. It will have to be this week because Josephine promises me she's coming sometime before her birthday. Of course, we wonder whether that will really happen, but just in case, we should plan accordingly."

At home, she told me to call Ginger and invite the Jordans for Wednesday night, before prayer meeting. I had a fierce desire to see them in my house, the Jordans whom I loved, especially Ginger. But I worried what might come to light about our Wednesday night activities. I went to bed after the phone call that night and could hardly sleep on account of everything that had happened, everything that was going to happen. Before I fell asleep, I heard Father and Phuong talking faintly in the next room. Every so often there were gentle sobs.

10

The next day at church I watched the Hagedoorns closely during a sermon on the temptations of the flesh. Dominie Grunstra had several occasions to lean over and say, "I think you know to what I refer," but I never did know to what he referred. The Hagedoorns listened for the whole thirty minutes without moving so much as an inch. They sat five pews in front of Father and Phuong and me, Arnie Hagedoorn with his arm loosely around Nancy's shoulder on the walnut pew. I gazed at his thick fingers, his hairy red wrist, his rough, freckled neck and thick sideburns. During Bob Ferring's post-communion interlude, Mr. Hagedoorn coughed and yanked at his nose. Nancy Hagedoorn put her long bony arm up and pushed a cough drop into his mouth with her thin fingers. They exchanged a silent glance. They shared a hymnbook as we sang, "A Pure Vessel Is Thy Church." The service had finished. Grandma motioned to me from the choir loft to see her immediately. I cut through the organ room in the corner of the sanctuary to get to her and passed Bob Ferring on the way.

"It pays to have friends at the top," he said airily.

"What?"

He closed his eyes and lifted his eyebrows, stretching his eyelids tight like sheets on a pair of twin beds. "You're the new protégée. Is Ginger teaching you everything she knows?"

"What do you mean?"

He smiled. "If you knew Ginger like I know Ginger, you'd know what I mean."

167

"I think I know her as well as you do," I said.

"Oh, just wait. There's more to her than anybody knows."

"I know almost everything about her," I said. "I'm her best friend."

Bob's smile straightened. "You and a lot of other people. That's a woman for you."

"What's 'a woman for you'?" demanded Mrs. Vander Weert, our organist, a few feet away. She was a short woman with tiny feet. When she played her instrument, she sat on the edge of the bench and rocked back and forth to reach the pedals. Right now she had pulled a choir robe over her head and only her legs showed, like two plump radishes under a big green leaf.

"I don't mean anything, Karen," he said.

"Yes, you do."

"Oh, no, I don't."

"I know you like the back of my hand, Robert. What's a 'woman' for you?"

"Well, some women are like cats," he said. "They have no sense of loyalty. They'll jump into anyone's lap to get their head scratched."

"I've been jumping for years and I can't get my head scratched," said Miss Vogel.

I left Mr. Ferring snickering wildly. I hurried to the choir room, where a crowd of men and women were climbing out of green robes and gold satin collars. I made my way to where my grandmother was whispering to Louise.

"Oh, Carrie, there you are," she said. "Your father and I have to meet with the dominie right after Sunday school. I want you to go home with Annajane and wait at her house until we get there."

"Can't I go with you?"

"No, dear. You run along to Sunday school now and be a good girl. Tuck your blouse in and pull your socks up. Remember who you are."

The meeting lasted longer than a half hour. I ate dinner with the Ten Kates in their dusty-ceilinged dining room, surrounded by portraits of dead relatives. The air was full of furniture polish and fibers wafting off old newspapers under the buffet. I sat in a tall-backed chair on the right of Mr. Ten Kate, who sat in his wheelchair, resting one hand on the hub of a wheel while he ate with the other.

168

"Glad you could join us, Carolyn," he said. "Tell your father I want to take him fishing one of these days and have a long talk. I have a great respect for your father, a great admiration for him. We all do, you know. He's a real spiritual giant."

"Thank you, sir."

"By the way," said Mrs. Ten Kate, "speaking of spirits, we never did see the Old Golie again after that day you were here. I went back to the store and that counter was spotless, clean as a whistle—no flour, no handprints. She must have cleaned up after herself."

"Yes, ma'am," said Annajane with a small smile, "she must have."

Mr. Ten Kate's eye flitted over to his wife. "Is that what you think, Sadie? That she cleaned up after herself?"

"Don't vex me, Doyle," said Mrs. Ten Kate.

"It's amazing what happens when the imagination gets working."

She set down her fork. "Why are you such a skeptic? You ate those fritters that danced by themselves in the deep-fry vat, didn't you? You ate them yourself. Did they taste like imagination to you?"

"They tasted just like my old mother's fritters. Maybe my mother is haunting us, Sadie. You used to complain that she could never keep her nose out of your kitchen."

"Doyle!" She turned away from him and addressed me, sweetly. "Carolyn, dear, wouldn't you like some pear sauce?"

"No, thank you," I said.

"Are you sure? It's just scrumptious."

"No, thank you. I better save room for whatever Grandma makes."

"You're going to have two lunches? Don't I wish Annajane would think that way. Then she wouldn't be so skinny and we wouldn't worry so. What will your grandma make, Carrie?"

"I don't know," I said. "Maybe pot roast."

"Isn't that wonderful—pot roast! So English. Imagine."

"Mommy always cooks Dutch," said Annajane. "Nobody cooks Dutch like Mommy."

Mrs. Ten Kate chuckled into her napkin. "Why thank you, Anna dear. A compliment from Annajane always means so much, she eats so little. By the way, Carolyn, dear, how are you and your new stepmother getting along? Are you getting just perfectly acquainted?" She smiled and the coils of her hair bounced around her ears.

"Yes, ma'am," I said. "We get along fine."

"Well, isn't that wonderful. I'll have to speak to her one of these days. Does she speak English? I'm curious, Carolyn. Where did your father meet your stepmother? Do you happen to know?"

"I'm not sure," I said.

"Maybe they became friends in the war," suggested Mr. Ten Kate.

"Oh, I think friendship is so important in a marriage," said Mrs. Ten Kate. "Most of the time romance doesn't last. It's the friendship that lasts. Isn't it, Doyle?"

"You're saying I'm not romantic?"

"Did I say that? All I said is that it's the friendship that means the most. You remember this, girls, when you choose a husband. Choose a man who will be your friend. Romance fades, but friendship lasts."

"Yes, ma'am," replied Annajane. "We'll remember."

"I remember your mother very well, Carrie," said Mrs. Ten Kate. "She was a pretty girl, like you. I know your father loved her very much. He could have gone with so many girls, but he chose her."

"Oh," I said, and I wanted her to say more. But I didn't know how to ask.

After dinner, Annajane and I went to her bedroom on the backside of the attic. We sat in the open windows in our Sunday dresses, stretching our bare legs over the roof slanting below. The tiles were warm but not hot. The sun made our skin dry as it tanned our legs slowly. From these heights we saw black rooftops and empty parking lots, early-blooming crepe myrtle soaking up color from cracks in the sidewalk, and bermuda grass withering spiky brown in yards like the shells of ocean creatures. Just over our bare feet and beyond three rows of rooftops and trees were the homes of some of our Black neighbors. Though the dominie preached against prejudice, we rarely visited their streets. Their houses were shabbier than ours. A few Black children bussed to our Christian school with the Vietnamese refugees, but we didn't know them well. I wondered what their houses looked like inside.

"Carrie," said Annajane, "I don't think I'm going to get married."

"Why not?" I was surprised.

"I think I'm going to the mission field."

"Oh. That's a good thing to do." I saw her there, across the sea, in some shaggy meadow with thick yellow trees in the sunlight. Skinny foreign children ran out to meet her in the glade.

"I know it's a good thing to do," she said. "That's why I'm going to do it."

"Have you told your parents?"

"No, because they might try to talk me out of it. I want to learn a foreign language first. Then I'll tell them."

"Are you going to take Spanish?" I asked.

"No, I don't want to go to South America. I had a call at the missions conference last spring. The dominie was talking and all of a sudden I felt God calling me."

"Where to?"

She turned to me and squinted against the hazy sunlight. "China."

"You want to go to China?"

She nodded. "Someday maybe. I know it's crazy, with all the Communism over there and everything. But I feel God calling me, like a voice talking right in my ear, saying, 'Go to China.' I just know that's what I should do."

"China," I said slowly, knowing nothing about it. "That sounds like a good place." The Sunday afternoon air was still. I wondered if we would separate someday and then meet again much later, as old women. I pictured her with black hair and dark skin.

"What are you thinking?" she asked.

"Right now," I said, "I'm wondering who I'm going to marry and what I'm going to do."

"Oh, you're going to be a dominie's wife," she said, "and you'll have ten children. You're predestined to have ten children."

"I don't want to be a dominie's wife," I said. "I want to be an actress. I want to be on Broadway someday."

Annajane frowned. "An actress?"

"I've been praying about it," I said. "I think there are a lot of people in the theater who need the gospel. I could witness to them."

"Well," she said thoughtfully, "that's true. That sure is true. I'll pray

171

for you, Carolyn. If God is calling you to be an actress, you're going to get there, all right. But you'll face a lot of temptation. Mommy says that Hollywood is like a modern-day Babylon."

"I already have faced temptation." I was thinking of the liquor I had tasted at Ginger's.

Annajane stared at me. She opened her lips with a question and hesitated because we heard her mother step out on the back porch and call, "Girls? Come downstairs. The dominie is here!"

"Let's talk about this later," she said.

We went downstairs quickly to see what Dominie Grunstra was doing at Annajane's house, but it was my father waiting in the living room. I had never heard him called a dominie before. I had never even thought of him as a dominie. He saluted me and shook Anna's hand.

"What a beautiful young lady you have here," he said to her parents. The Ten Kates had already pushed a big bag of day-old jelly donuts into his hands. Mr. Ten Kate was showing him a polished rifle from a rack on the wall.

"She is a beautiful lady," said Mr. Ten Kate. "Oh, I guess you're talking about my daughter and not my gun."

"Doyle, don't tease," said Mrs. Ten Kate. "You be careful. Annajane is our pride and joy. And Carolyn is just a dear. She's like a second daughter to us. We want her to feel welcome here anytime. I hope you're going to tell me you're in town for good, Davey. You wouldn't move away and leave your mama by herself, would you?"

"Not if I can help it," said Father.

"Good! I know you must have super job prospects."

He smiled. "I have a few possibilities. I'm trusting the Lord on that."

"It's the only thing to do," she said, her hair coils bouncing again. "Absolutely the only thing to do. Can't you stay and have a cup of coffee?"

"Got to get home," he said. "Got to get home or else my mama will tan my hide. Sadie, Doyle, Annajane—see you at the service tonight."

We walked outside together. Mrs. Ten Kate waved until we reached the end of the driveway. My father's smile dropped as she closed the door. He looked up and down the street, frowning, and steered me across.

"I don't feel so good," he said. "Maybe lunch will do the trick. Wonder what your grandma's got cooking." He undid his tie, pulled it off, and shoved it in his pocket.

"How did you meet my mother?" I asked him suddenly.

"What? Your mother? Well, I can't really remember, Carolyn. That was a long time ago. We were children."

"You don't remember how you met your own wife?"

"I wish I could. I don't remember. We knew each other most of our lives."

"Well, how did you meet Phuong?"

"Now, that I do remember. I already told you, didn't I? At a refugee camp in Guam. That was one of the many places I visited. We got well acquainted there."

"Did you date her there? Was it romantic?"

He laughed and shook his head. "In wartime, anybody who doesn't try to kill you is practically your best friend. You have to be careful all the time, and sometimes you end up making the best friends of your life just because you're trying to stay alive together. And it's not much different in those refugee camps, either—at least the worst of them. It sure would be nice if every place in the world were just like Dutch Falls, wouldn't it?"

As we walked the last few yards to the house, he relaxed. He was turning red like Arnie Hagedoorn. "You know what I'm remembering," he said, starting to laugh. "I'm remembering my sister Jo, this one time when we were kids. She was a little older than you are now. She got it in her head that she wanted to be a ballerina. Your grandpa and grandma couldn't stand the thought of women and men dancing together in tights, but they let her take lessons as long as I went along. I had to dance around with her in my gym shorts. I never realized how fat my sister was until I had to run across this great big room with her sitting on my shoulders."

"Am I like her?" I said, wondering again if he thought I was fat. "Do I remind you of her?"

He looked at me and laughed again as we stopped in front of our house. "Not a bit," he said. "You look like your mother, and praise the Lord for it. Grandma couldn't stand two of Josephine."

"I don't even remember what she looks like. I just know her from that picture on the wall." I was talking about my mother, but he thought I meant Aunt Jo again.

"She was always changing her hair color. She wanted to be a movie star. And do you know, Carolyn, that's the ugliest picture anybody ever took of Jo. Why do you think Grandma put it on the wall?"

I didn't try to answer. I thought about telling him that I was going to be in a play, a real musical at the Dela Fox Biddle Memorial Theater in Richmond. But I didn't tell him. I would bring him there somehow, and he would find out that night, when Ginger and I stood onstage, shining in the spotlights.

As we went into the kitchen together, Grandma said, "Wash your hands, dinner's almost ready." We sat down to pork chops and creamed carrots with bread. Most of Grandma's Dutch cooking was out of a book from the library, but it was as good as Mrs. Ten Kate's. Phuong joined us for the prayer and then returned to the kitchen quickly afterward to wash the pans. She wore her flesh-colored dress with the bust darts in front, where they belonged. Grandma must have said something. Perhaps it had been Grandma who had fixed her hair, too, sweeping it back in a ponytail with a leather brooch and wooden pin. The ponytail stretched the skin around Phuong's eyes and gave her face a younger look. Her scar glowed white against her dark skin, but her cheeks were full and healthy. Her body, too, looked younger—her arms were thick and her chest had filled out. She returned from the kitchen and sat down next to me, eating quietly while Father and Grandma talked about the sermon. It was an excellent message, they agreed. I couldn't remember any of it.

"Oh, I forgot to put the butter on the table," said Grandma suddenly.

Phuong stood up and sprang away through the swinging door into the kitchen. "She never stops moving," said Father. "Just like you, Mama."

"She only does as much as she wants," said Grandma. "I've told her many times that she's one of the family. She doesn't have to wait on us hand and foot." The door bumped open on its hinges and Phuong returned with the butter.

"Thank you," said Grandma. She looked at Father. They were both quiet then. I hoped they might discuss aloud the meeting after church, whether it had to do with some sin in the congregation, and whether the sinners might be Mr. and Mrs. Hagedoorn, who had lately taken to dancing in nightclubs. Sometimes we shared news during Sunday dinner, asking forgiveness later at devotions if our news had crossed the boundary into gossip. But no one mentioned the meeting. We finished our meal with very little conversation. Phuong took the plates, but Grandma stood up and insisted on washing them. Father went away for a nap. I lay down with a book on the couch.

I spent most of the afternoon reading, and then it was time for Sunday night church. We walked there together, with our Bibles under our arms. Few people attended the service. The Hagedoorns were absent. I sat with Annajane, watching her take careful notes on the sermon in the margins of her Bible. When the service had finished we went into the courtyard, where two pear trees grew. The sun was as red as teacher's ink on the horizon. Finger-shaped clouds drifted through it, smearing color over the flat, white sky.

Annajane looked straight into my eyes. "I've been thinking about what you said this afternoon about facing temptation."

"Yeah?"

"I'm a little worried about you, Carrie. If you're really facing temptation, I think you need someone to be accountable to. Accountability means—"

"I know what it means," I said indignantly.

"Then you know that when you fall into temptation, you should always tell another Christian right away so you can pray about it together."

"Who am I supposed to tell?"

"You can tell me," she said. "We shouldn't have any secrets."

"And are you going to tell me if you fall into temptation, too?"

"Yes," she said firmly. "I've prayed about it and I think it's the right thing to do."

"O.K.," I said. She turned away, looking satisfied. I had let her talk me into something again. I wondered where it would lead, whether I would ever really confess anything to her and whether I might one day learn something shocking about her. I didn't think so. A few yards away, the last adults had drained from the sanctuary onto the east steps. Grandma was among them, with Father at her side and Phuong following closely, her head bowed.

"I'm going to go say 'hi' to your stepmother," said Annajane. "Someone should be friendly to her."

"Be my guest," I said, and I watched her run down the sidewalk and part the crowd to greet my grandmother and talk to my stepmother. Grandma patted her on the head. Phuong nodded to her hesitantly, but smiled and walked down the steps with her, talking.

At home, as it became dark, we had a small supper—a few leftovers from dinner that had been stored in tiny white margarine containers with masking tape labels. When we had finished, Grandma took out the family Bible and gave the first call for devotions. My father made a quick trip to the bathroom.

"He's always done that," Grandma whispered loudly, "ever since he was a little boy."

He heard her as he came back into the room. "It's because you always pray too long, Mama," he said. "I could never wait."

Then Grandma closed her eyes and said that we would pray. After Father prayed, she let a long silence pass. Then she addressed God in a slow, soft voice that she did not use for anyone else, asking prayer first for Aunt Jo and Nathan as they traveled to see us, if they actually did come. She asked prayer for the unsaved, prayer for the young people who didn't go to prayer meeting, and prayer for the Zinkits in France. She finished by saying, "Teach us, Lord, if there's anything we need to be doing that we're not doing. And help us to listen for your leading. In Jesus' name." She didn't say, "Amen" because it was now my father's turn.

He took up the prayer like a baton in a relay. His voice grew quicker and louder. He mentioned that his job prospects were still not good. "It's your will that I want to do, Lord," he said, "so just bring me a position that will serve you, wherever you want to send me." He prayed for the men still in Vietnamese dungeons and for the Vietnamese people laboring under Communist oppression. He finished and Grandma took up the baton again.

"Oh, dear Lord," she said, "I ask you to bring our brother to repentance."

Who was she talking about?

"Yes, Lord," echoed Father, "I agree with that prayer. Please bring our brother to repentance."

"For I am persuaded," she said, "that neither death, nor life, nor angels, nor principalities, nor powers, nor things present, nor things to come, nor height, nor depth, nor anything else in all creation will be able to separate us from the love of God which is in Christ Jesus our Lord. You're going to bring him back to you, Lord. I know that you are. In Jesus' name."

A long silence elapsed. Someone was being urged to take the last lap. Our chairs squeaked against the linoleum as we shifted on our haunches. Grandma elbowed me, but I shook my head. Phuong sat stiffly beside me. I could almost feel her stiffness, her hard edges.

"Dear Lord," said Grandma at last, "I pray that you will forgive our hard hearts and pride. Forgive us if we don't want to come to you in prayer like we should, with humility. In Jesus' name, amen."

We lifted our heads and opened our eyes. Phuong picked up the plates and went quickly to the kitchen. Grandma wiped her eyes. Had she been crying?

"Who's the brother you were talking about?" I asked her.

"What?"

"Who's the brother who needs to repent? Is that why you had a meeting this afternoon? Is someone going to be disciplined?"

Grandma looked at Father. "Davey, help me here."

"Carrie," he said, "why did the elephant paint his toenails different colors?"

"So he could hide in a bubblegum machine. I already know that one."

"You're too smart for your own good," he said. And then no one would say anything else.

*O*n Wednesday afternoon, the day the Jordans were to come for dinner, Grandma sat on the porch with Louise shelling peas until a rain shower drove them inside. Then they sat in the dark kitchen whispering into their stainless steel bowls. "So where is she now?" Louise whispered loudly over the rain. I could hear her all the way in the living room, where I sat embroidering "D.W.G." on my father's handkerchiefs.

"She's in her room, I expect," said Grandma. "That's where she stays most of the time. Davey says she studies her Bible."

"She should be out here helping you," said Louise.

"She does her part."

"Well, at least she doesn't argue with you like my son's wife. But what will happen when the children start to come? She'll have her own way of doing things and it's not like ours, I guarantee."

"Children?" said Grandma. "At her age? At least I don't have that to worry about."

"She doesn't look so old to me."

"She's old enough. She was married once before to a Vietnamese. Lost him in the war, Davey says. It's a pitiful thing."

"I'm sure it is," said Louise. "You're just a saint."

The storm fled away, the afternoon sky turned rosy and blue, and a breeze lifted the curtains over the kitchen sink. When Louise left, I helped Grandma prepare the *gehaktballen*. My hands smelled of pepper and nutmeg when we finished. I set the table then, but left her to chop the cabbage and make a hazelnut cake for dessert. I went to take

178

a long bath. Phuong knocked on the door and I called that I would be out soon, but I didn't hurry. I was thinking of what I would wear tonight. I would wear a red satin dress, and I would sweep half of my hair back in a black comb and tease the other half with hair spray. I would wear plum rouge, jet black mascara, and bite my lips until they were blood red.

"Hey, there!" my father called, banging on the door. "Your friends are here and other folks need to use the bathroom. Get out of that bathtub and help your grandma."

"But they can't be here already," I shouted.

"It's six o'clock. That's the time you told them."

"But they're always late."

"Get out of there before your skin rots off."

I pulled myself up from the bath and the bath came with me, parting in glittering v's like geese around my fingers. The water fell in sheets from my arms. My knees drew up in shriveled bumps. Where were my clothes? Had I thrown them down the laundry shoot? How foolish. I stepped out, dripping and shivering, and pulled a towel around me. My heart pounded. I wondered how the conversation would proceed in the living room without me to guide it. Grandma might say something like, "Would anyone care for something to drink before dinner?" Ginger would say, "Sure. I'll have a double," and laugh heartily. And then they would all sit down and Ginger would say to my father, "Has anyone ever told you that you look a lot like the young Gregory Peck?" And Frank would say, "All men look tall, dark, and handsome to Ginger." And Ginger would say, "All men except you, Frank."

To get to my bedroom I would have to walk into the foyer just off the living room and mount the stairs. Anyone standing near the foyer archway would see me walking by in my towel, so before I left the bathroom I should make sure the living room and foyer were empty. I waited, listening and gathering courage, and stepped out into the hallway. Already I heard Ginger's laughter.

I padded down the hall dripping and turned the corner silently into the empty foyer. The laughter and din of voices was on the other side of the house, in the kitchen. Quickly I started up the steps. There was a noise below me. I turned in surprise.

It was Frank, standing at the bottom of the steps.

"Excuse me!" I said, and stood still on the stairs when I should have kept going. I held the towel tightly around me. My bare white shoulders felt large and ridiculous, like wings that I had been hiding under my clothes.

"Excuse *me*," he said, with a handsome smile. "I was just looking for the bathroom."

"It's that way." I pointed.

"Thanks," he said.

Before he turned to leave, Phuong appeared at the top of the stairs above me. She opened her mouth in surprise. She looked at me and then at Frank.

I smiled with embarrassment. "I didn't mean for anyone to see me like this."

"You come," she said, running down and grabbing me around the shoulders. "Come."

"What are you doing?" I shouted. "Stop it." But she wouldn't let go. She yanked me up, digging her fingernails into my flushed skin. I struggled to hold my towel on. As we went around the corner on the landing, I looked back to be sure Frank was gone. The foyer was empty.

"You're hurting me," I said. "Why did you do that?"

"Go to the room," Phuong said furiously. "Put your clothes on."

"I didn't mean for anyone to see me. It was just an accident."

"Bad, bad!" she said. A strand of black hair floated down across her face. She swatted it away. She pushed me into my bedroom, stepped out, and slammed the door behind her. I listened to her hard footsteps receding. Through the air vents I could still hear Ginger's laughter.

How could this have happened? I sat on the edge of my bed, hugging my arms. If it had been Grandma who had seen me in the hall, she would be sitting on the other bed now explaining why the Lord counted on her to teach me better manners. But I was on my own, and trembling.

"I didn't do anything wrong," I said aloud. It was true that Dutch

Falls girls did not ordinarily let themselves be seen in scanty clothing—except on the beach or in beauty contests—but I was still a child and I had made a childish mistake. What to do now? I wouldn't be able to look Frank in the face again after such a scene. I crawled into the sheets of my bed and thought about staying there all night. Then the laughter began to draw me downstairs again. I dressed slowly in jeans and a T-shirt and went down with my hair still wet, my face pale. I looked for Phuong lurking around a corner. The stairs were empty.

"There you are, Carolyn," said my grandmother as I came into the kitchen. "You look pale. And why are you shaking like that? What's happened?"

"Nothing," I said. I wanted to tell her what had happened, but not now.

"Why are you shivering? Are you catching cold?"

"I'm fine."

"Then why don't you go into the living room and show the Jordans our things?"

She referred to our Dutch family heirlooms. It was her custom to take English guests around, pointing out everything in the house that made us different from them. As I went slowly through the swinging door, I met Frank coming the other way. He smiled before I had a chance to look away.

"Carolyn," said Grandma, "aren't you going to be polite and say 'hello' to Mr. Jordan?"

"Hello, Mr. Jordan," I said.

"Hello, Carolyn," he said, and the door swung shut between us. His easy way of saying my name made me like him all the more. Maybe he had seen other Dutch girls in towels. Maybe he sympathized with me against Phuong. Sometime I would talk to him about her, tell him how mean she had been.

In the living room I found Ginger talking alone with my father. The two of them stood next to the piano sipping tomato juice. "Carolyn," Ginger said as I came in. "Why didn't you tell me your real name?"

I shrugged.

"For weeks I've been calling this poor kid 'Carla'!" she said to my father, and exploded in laughter. "Now I hear that her name is Carolyn."

"Or Carrie," said my father. "She likes her nickname."

"Kiddo, you should be smarter than to hang around with me. I'm dense." Ginger winked and took a sip from her glass.

"I like 'Carla'," I said. "I think it sounds nice."

Father smiled. "Glad your mother can't hear you say that. She was the one who named you."

"Really, Mr. Grietkirk?" asked Ginger. "And what did you want to call Carla?"

"Donald."

She exploded again. "You wanted a boy, didn't you? Typical man."

Father nodded. "Where's Phuong?" he asked me. "Is she upstairs?"

"How should I know?" I said.

Father went to the foyer and called upstairs. "Phuong? Come down and meet the Jordans." We waited. When Phuong finally came it was with her eyes down and one hand brushing the wall beside the staircase, as if she would dive into a crack as soon as she found one. Father held his hand out. "Come here," he said. "Don't be shy." Phuong came over slowly and stood next to him, taking a step back from me. I took a step away from her.

"Mrs. Jordan," he said to Ginger, "this is Mrs. David Grietkirk. Mrs. Grietkirk, meet Mrs. Jordan."

"I'm please to meet you," said Phuong. She glanced up briefly and then down again. The tone of her voice was cool and flat. Her mouth was straight, unsmiling. I wished her away from there, I wished her a million miles from this house. But Ginger smiled at her warmly. When Ginger stepped between Father and me to shake Phuong's hand, she smelled dense and sweet, a mix of cigarettes and perfume.

"I waved to you one day from the car. Do you remember?" Ginger asked. Phuong nodded.

"In Vietnam," said Father, "a wave doesn't mean 'hello.' It means, 'Come here.'"

"Really?" Ginger seemed interested. "Well, I do want Phuong to come—I want her to come see me one day. Listen, I know what it's like to be in a new place. Come on over with Carrie sometime. Bring your handsome husband, too."

"Oh, goodness," said Father.

"Mr. Grietkirk, I want you to know that Carrie is like a daughter to me. No one could be more special to me. I feel like you all are already family."

"Mrs. Jordan," my father said, "I understand that you have four rambunctious boys of your own."

"Oh, yes," said Ginger. "I keep looking at all these cute little knick-knacks around here, thinking what damage my boys could do in this room in about five minutes."

Father laughed. "That's boys for you. Rambunctious boys."

"They're staying with my sister tonight," Ginger said. "Why don't you come over sometime and be a good influence on them? We haven't grilled out in just ages, have we, Frank. Frank?"

"What?" Frank yelled from the kitchen.

"We haven't grilled out in just ages."

"What about it?"

"Well, we better get on the ball, don't you think?"

He didn't answer.

"Oh, that's right," she said. "We had a big yard sale when we became Christians and sold the grill. Got rid of the Ouija board and most of Frank's magazine collection, too." She winked at my father.

Father coughed. "Listen, I think I'll find out what your husband is up to in the kitchen. You ladies can get a little more acquainted. Here, Carolyn, finish my tomato juice." He trotted out, leaving the three of us alone. We stood stiff and practically useless, like three corners of a pot-holder loom.

"Grandma wants me to show you around," I said to Ginger.

"Excuse me," said Phuong quietly. "I can help in the kitchen."

"Oh, no," said Ginger. "Let the men worry about that. This is ladies' night."

I took Ginger's hand and she took Phuong's. We wound our way through the house, stopping to look at windmills and wooden shoes, delft china, and my great-grandmother's chifforobe. Ginger snickered when I pointed out curtains with embroidered scenes of Dutch children skating on frozen dikes. "I tried to learn embroidery," she said, "but I've got ten thumbs. That's what my home ec teacher used to tell me. She'd say, 'Ginger, honey, you'll never catch a fella if you can't sew.'"

"But you're so pretty," I said.

She threw her arms around me there in the dining room and hugged me tight. "Oh, kiddo, you are the sweetest. Mrs. Grietkirk, I want you to know that this girl here is just the greatest thing in pigtails. Hope you don't mind me stealing her away now and then."

Phuong shook her head.

"What's the matter?" Ginger laughed. "Don't you want her?"

"Carrie!" called my grandmother. "Have you shown Mrs. Jordan the house?"

"Yes, Grandma."

Grandma breezed past us to the buffet with a bowl of rice in the crook of her right arm and the meatballs in her left. After her came Father and Frank with the boiled cabbage and bread. Phuong moved quickly to help them.

"Oh, let Frank do his part," said Ginger loudly. "Frank, don't let this woman rescue you."

"I can't help it," he said, as Phuong took away the cabbage and waved him to the living room.

"Carolyn," Grandma said, "have you washed for dinner? Has anyone shown our guests the washroom? All right then, come to the table, everyone; we're ready. It's not much, just a humble little supper—Dutch food, plain and simple. We're simple around here." She took her position at the end of the table nearest the kitchen and waited while everyone shuffled up to the table. Father stood at the end opposite from her, with Phuong on his right. Ginger and Frank stood at his left, and I squeezed in next to them.

"No, Carrie," said Grandma. "You're over here by Phuong. I don't want to hear a word of complaint. Mr. Jordan, will you kindly lead us in the Lord's Prayer?"

"Wouldn't that be your son's place, ma'am?" Frank asked.

"Go ahead," said Father cheerfully. "Guest preachers get the honor."

"O.K., then," said Frank, "let's bow our heads and pray together."

He sighed and waited until we were completely silent, when the only sound was the clock ticking in the living room.

"Oh, Holy Jesus," he prayed, holding up his arms, "You are so great, so mighty, so wonderful. We just praise you for this table, Holy Lord Jesus, spread with so many good things to eat. We just praise you for the hospitality of our hosts, Lord Jesus, for the lovely hands which have prepared this wonderful meal. We just ask you to bring light into the dark places and salvation to the lost. Jesus, seek out the lost and bring them back like sheep to your flock. Gather them up, Jesus. Forgive them, Jesus. Forgive us. We ask you all this in your holy and precious name. Amen."

We opened our eyes and sat down in rhythm, shuffling our feet as we drew up our chairs. Frank pulled out a chair for Ginger but she scooted it away from him toward my father. Father seated Phuong, and she sat with her hands folded on the table, looking down away from me. I held my right arm tightly against my side, lest our bare arms touch.

"Apparently Frank doesn't know the Lord's Prayer," Ginger said.

"What?" said Frank.

"See," said Ginger, "he doesn't know it. It's too short for him. He'd rather say a long one of his own."

"Mr. Jordan, I appreciated your prayer very much," said Grandma. "I appreciate the reference to 'the lost.' Are you by any chance a Baptist?"

"No, ma'am, I'm not."

"Well, like me, you have the soul of a Baptist."

"Maybe so, ma'am."

"That's good. My son tells me that in these refugee camps where he's been, the Christians all worship together. He thinks that's just great."

"I've never quite figured out where you preach, Frank," said my father. "Carrie's been there so many times, of course—she says your church meets in a grocery store."

"Yes, the Food Angel." He flashed me an odd look.

"And what kind of church is it?"

"The small kind," said Ginger.

185

"Yes, it's a small church," Frank said, pushing back his hair before he took a bite of food. "We have regular worship together. About fifty of us."

"Temple of the Dove?" asked Father.

"You've heard of it?"

"I think I've seen the sign. That's an interesting name."

"Some of the folks chose it before I came. I don't care for the word 'temple,' myself. It sounds kind of formal. We're very informal."

"I expect you are," said Grandma, "if you're meeting in a grocery."

"I'd like to change the name," said Frank. He hesitated, nodding and toying with his food. "I have some ideas, nothing just right yet."

"I suppose you're Pentecostal," said Father. "Is that right?"

"We're Spirit-filled," said Frank. "But we don't like labels. Or legalism. We're very free."

"Maybe I'll drop in sometime," said Father.

Frank smiled and stammered, "Well, you'd be welcome. But it's probably not what you're used to. I haven't been to your church, but I expect you all have a rather formal service there."

"Oh, yes," said Grandma, "we're just too formal, I'm always saying."

"Well, our service is *very* informal."

I looked at Grandma for a response, but she had her mind on the food. She pushed the *gehaktballen* to Frank. "Try these, Mr. Jordan. They're authentic Dutch fare."

"Oh, thank you, ma'am. Yes, very delicious."

"How is your church able to support you, Mr. Jordan?" Father asked.

Ginger snickered as he said soberly, "We operate on faith."

"And my mother's money," she mumbled.

Father stared at Frank over the table. "You were in Vietnam?"

Frank nodded. "I was there with the army for nine months in 1970. Got shot in the abdomen and they sent me home with one kidney. I was pretty lucky. Course, it's not so good to lose a kidney."

"There are worse things to lose!" said Ginger with a snort. She covered her mouth with a napkin. Frank frowned.

"I wouldn't call it luck that you got shot," said Father. "Where'd it happen, anyway?"

"I don't remember the name of the place."

"You think he'd remember where he got shot," said Ginger, rolling her eyes.

"I couldn't pronounce it if I remembered it," Frank said. "Just one of those little villages in the South. Everybody had died or left, anyway, so the name wasn't important. It was like a ghost town, all ruins."

"Somebody must have been there if you got shot, Frank," said Ginger.

"I never saw anybody. We set up camp there one afternoon because it was too hot to march. We saw some pigs running around wild, and a few of the farmer boys got this idea to butcher everything on four legs and have a decent supper for once. But I didn't know anything about butchering pigs, so I went to find a well, and I washed and then I sacked out under a tree. All of a sudden, I heard a shot and I felt this pain in my side—that was it. The next thing I knew I was back in the States with one kidney."

"The Lord spared your life that day," said Grandma.

"Yes, ma'am, he did at that. I was one of the lucky ones, getting out of there the easy way. It was the Vietnamese I felt sorry for, especially the old people. They couldn't leave. You could see it in their eyes—they were just waiting to die."

"Oh, enough war talk," said Ginger. "Unless we can have a story with a happy ending for once."

Phuong's fork shrieked on the china and dropped to the floor. She bent down to pick it up.

"Davey can tell a story with a happy ending," said Grandma proudly. "Tell them about all the people you saved, Davey."

"I don't think this is the best time, Mama."

"Sure it is. Davey's not one to brag."

"This isn't the best time. I wasn't a real soldier like Frank. I was just a preacher."

"Anybody who can get a bunch of wild young soldiers to church on Sunday morning is a hero in my book," said Frank.

"My mother likes to think that I stepped right into my daddy's shoes," said Father. "He was in France on D day."

"I remember the letter I got from your colonel, Davey," said Grandma. "He couldn't say enough praise for what you'd done—

snatching women and children from the jaws of death. That's how you got the Silver Star."

"I'd like to hear about it," Frank said.

"Please?" said Ginger, leaning across the table with her chin in her hand, smiling at Father.

"Maybe another time," Father said. "I don't like to tell war stories with ladies present."

"We understand," said Grandma. "But if you knew the pain women go through at childbirth, David, you wouldn't think us so delicate."

Father and I looked up and stared. While it was always acceptable to talk about disease or death, it was almost unthinkable to mention childbirth at the dinner table.

She recognized the error of her ways soon enough. "Excuse me," she said, and got up quickly from her seat and went back through the swinging door. I knew that she must be reviling herself in the kitchen. I sniffed the air for Clorox.

"She is exactly, exactly right," said Ginger, mainly addressing my father. "Childbirth is something men wouldn't endure for two minutes. My last labor and delivery was like a twenty-two-hour war. Frank says it's as bad as anything he ever went through in Vietnam. I was screaming in pain. And ever since, I can't walk without a slight limp. It's a good thing I'm not doing musicals anymore. I'd break my neck in a chorus line."

Father bent down almost to his plate. Frank pushed back his hair. Grandma came back just in time to hear Ginger mention being in shows.

"Do I understand correctly," Grandma said to Ginger, "that you were a theatrical person at one time?"

"That's how Frank and I met," said Ginger. "Frank feels real bad about it now."

"And tell me," said Grandma, "how did the Lord pull you out of the worldly life?"

"Tell her, dear," said Ginger.

"Well, ma'am," Frank said, "the theater is an empty life, and I was about the emptiest person there ever was. And then one day, Ginger heard the gospel. She brought the Good News home to me. I knew

188

from that first day that it was for me. It was Ginger that convinced me to quit the stage, too. I guess I loved it as much as I hated it; you know how that goes. But we went from New York to Alabama to preach, and then we moved here a few years back so I could attend seminary."

"Pay no attention to him," said Ginger, dropping her long eyelashes against her cheekbones and smiling. "Frank was the one who did the evangelizing. He told me the gospel first and I just accepted it like the submissive wife I was."

Frank sniffed.

"That's a wonderful testimony for you, Mrs. Jordan," said my grandmother. "So many young women today don't respect anything their husbands tell them."

"Pay no attention to Ginger," said Frank "She was the one who shared the gospel with me."

Ginger lifted her eyebrows. Frank frowned and sipped his coffee.

"Listening to you all is like watching *Truth or Consequences,*" said Father, with a laugh. "Did you ever hear the one about the wife who thought she could read her husband's mind? She thought she knew how to read his mind because she could always finish his sentences for him. If he said, 'I'm going to the—,' she would say, 'bank.' If he said, 'I just called the—,' she would say, 'plumber.' One day he tried to fool her. He made a fist and said, 'Honey, you tell me what I'm holding in my hand, right now, without any help, and I'll give you a hundred dollars. But if you can't guess what I have in my hand, then you get—,' and his wife said, 'nothing.'"

Frank and Ginger broke their stare and laughed. What the truth was, I couldn't tell from their faces. Maybe I would have a chance to ask Ginger later, on the way to rehearsal. Right now it was time for the *hazelnoottaart.* Grandma served it on a china cake plate, with baked pears to the side.

"Are you going to prayer meeting with the Jordans tonight?" Grandma asked me as Phuong cleared away our plates after the dessert was eaten. I looked at Ginger for help, but Frank answered.

"We're not having prayer meeting tonight," he said. "I do visitation in homes on the first Wednesday of each month."

"Well, then," said Grandma, with a slight frown. "Carolyn, you may attend our church tonight." I looked into her triumphant face, her blue eyes smug and her pink lips firmly together. I looked at Ginger and looked for an excuse to get away.

"As a matter of fact, I'm taking Carrie to Richmond with me," Ginger said. "The fact is, Mrs. Grietkirk, I'm trying to witness to my sister. Patty's not saved yet, but I'm working on her. And we certainly can't talk about God with those children of hers running around, those awful children, so I just have to have a baby-sitter. Carrie may not be attending prayer meeting, but she's doing the Lord's work."

My grandmother's eyebrows sank down over her nose like an overloaded clothesline. "Carolyn never mentioned to me that she would be going out of town sometimes, Mrs. Jordan."

"Oh, Mrs. Grietkirk, I'm really sorry. It was my intention to keep Carrie here in town, but then I just felt God calling me in a different direction."

"So you'll be taking Carrie to Richmond tonight?" asked Grandma.

"Yes, ma'am."

"And this has happened before?"

Ginger ignored the question. "Tonight I'll be taking Patty to a Christian concert. I really hope she'll find the Lord there."

"Who is giving the concert?" asked my father.

Ginger put her hand to her head. "Right when you said that I forgot the name of the performer. What is it, Carla? Do you remember?"

"The child's name is Carolyn," said Grandma.

"That's right—I'm just so terrible with names, like this concert. What is it?"

"I don't remember," I said.

"Well," said my grandmother, "I'm not happy about Carrie's dishonesty. But I guess I'll let her go, if it's for a Christian ministry."

"It's for the sake of a lost soul," said Ginger. And so ended the conversation.

After dessert, Father volunteered to drive Frank home so that Ginger and I could go straight to Richmond.

"I appreciate this so much!" Ginger said, standing with Father in the driveway. "I'd hate for my sister to miss any of the show; do you know what I mean?"

190

"No, we can't let that happen," agreed my father.

"What a wonderful time we had. We'll have to have you all over soon. We'll have to grill, right, Frank?"

Frank stood behind her. "Right," he said.

"And Phuong," said Ginger, "I do mean it. I want you to call me anytime you just need a friend!"

Phuong nodded from the porch. She seemed such a small person hovering behind, like an image in the wrong end of a telescope.

"And Mrs. Grietkirk," said Ginger, kissing my grandmother last of all, "I just want you to know again how much I appreciate Carolyn. She's a real credit to you."

"Well, that's fine then," said Grandma. She accepted the kiss awkwardly. "Drive carefully."

Ginger did not drive carefully. We were late again, and worried what Mr. Palia might say. "I'm not really worried," Ginger said, but she sped up and swung the car against the sides of the road like a log in a flume. She knew a country shortcut, past severed gas pumps and broken-down shacks, scrap metal yards and chunks of grassy rock leaning into the highway. Old men watched us with raised hats. I put on my seat belt.

"You never told me how handsome your father is," said Ginger, racing through a yellow light.

"Well, he's married now," I said.

"Yeah," she laughed. We were speeding over the Powhatan Bridge. The ruts in the road thumped under our wheels.

"I thought you liked her," I said.

"Who?"

"Phuong."

"Of course I like her. I'm just kidding about him, kiddo. You don't have to worry."

"I'm not worried. I don't like her. I wish you were my mother."

"I can tell. I can also tell when a man's not interested in other women. And he's not interested. Now your grandmother, she keeps her guard up but I could tell she liked me. She was a beauty once. That's where your father gets the good looks."

"You think everybody's good-looking," I said. "You even think Mr. Hagedoorn is handsome."

"Who?"

"Arnie Hagedoorn."

She smiled, surprised. "Arnie? Yes, he's very handsome. He's got something wild underneath. I get the feeling that he's always walking a line, just waiting to cross over. There's this quiet anger about him all the time. I can feel it."

"It's because of his sweat glands."

"I don't know, but Carla, the way he looks at me. He's looking for something. He's frustrated because he can't get it from church and he certainly can't get it from the library."

I imagined Mr. Hagedoorn in dark corners of the library late at night, angry and bitter, tearing books off shelves because he needed something neither God nor the library could give him. What the something was I didn't know for sure. "You could help him," I said. "He would fall in love with you in a second." What would Annajane say if she could hear me now?

"Hah! That wife holds his hand everywhere he goes."

"Are you in love with him?"

She shook her head vigorously. "No. I don't claim to be perfect, but I have my standards. He's married."

"Why don't you just have a fling with him?"

"What's the difference?"

I explained to her something I'd read or seen in a movie, that a fling is temporary and meaningless. You didn't have to love the man you had a fling with, you just had to have chemistry with him. I pictured Ginger and Arnie Hagedoorn together in the library, maybe in the remote ladies' room on the third floor that no one ever used. The light was always off there. The water took ten minutes to get hot. Forever the same rolls of toilet paper sat untouched in the same place.

"You're pretty worldly wise," Ginger said. "Are you sure your father is a chaplain?"

I wanted her to think of me this way. "Are you sure your husband is a preacher?" I said. And then I added, "I don't think Mr. Hagedoorn's all that great, anyway. Frank's handsomer than him."

She smirked. "Big deal."

"Don't you think he is?"

"Oh, sure. All those little girls at his little church think so. And Mandi thinks so. My friend Mandi. She comes over just to stare at Frank. It makes me sick. Nobody knows what I have to put up with. They think, how can she complain when she has this handsome husband? Ten years with Frank, that's how I can complain."

"Are you and Mandi close friends?"

"Oh, sure. She's my oldest girlfriend. You know, someone to hang around with when Frankenstein's driving me crazy. We smoke and chew and go out with boys who do. Hah!"

"You never smoke and chew with me," I said sadly.

She laughed. "Why don't you and I go out sometime soon, as a fun thing? Maybe we could have dinner next Wednesday before rehearsal, just the two of us. I'll make Frank take the baby. Would that be fun?"

"Yes!" I said.

"Let's do it. We'll plan on it."

When we got to the rehearsal room, Mr. Palia was in the middle of a fight with Dianne Bane. Dianne had threatened to kill Henry Harrison. Mr. Palia had pushed them apart, and she had pushed Mr. Palia into his chair. Actors and dancers stood around now, arm to arm, watching.

"Dianne, you've pushed me too far this time," Mr. Palia said, standing up again. "I'm going to give you the New Jersey handshake if you try me again." Whatever the New Jersey handshake was.

"Go ahead. I couldn't care less," she shouted. She jumped off the stage, tore a piece of sheet music from Bob Ferring's piano, and ripped it into pieces.

Bob looked at her woefully. "What did I do?" he moaned. "Mr. Palia, this woman is insane. Why do we have to put up with her?"

Dianne crumpled the music in her fist and threw it at the stage.

"Come back up here, Dianne," said Mr. Palia.

She beaded up her eyes. "Not until you tell Henry that I'm in charge. He can flirt on his own time."

"All right," said Mr. Palia. "Henry, keep your mind on the job."

"She's just jealous," said Henry from a doorway at the other end of

193

the room. He leaned in with his arms folded, his hands stretched across his thick biceps.

"Jealous of you? That's a joke," said Dianne, and Mary Burrows cackled out loud at the very idea of it.

"Henry," said Mr. Palia, "I'd like to get rid of you and Dianne both, but it's too late. What is it about you two that makes it so impossible for you to work together?" He looked around pleadingly at the rest of us. "What," he asked, "could be so hard about a man and a woman spending a few hours together every week, working on a simple, happy, family-oriented show like this one? How did I allow myself to bring both of you into this show?"

"It was Dianne," said Henry. "She talked you into it."

"Well I must have been out of my mind," said Mr. Palia. "She's like a crazy woman. I've never seen her this bad. Dianne, would you get hold of yourself?"

Dianne sat slumped over a metal folding chair at the foot of the stage, facing the corner, her arms hanging loose by her sides. She didn't move. Tommy Depew went down and put his arm around her.

"There, there," he said soothingly. He helped her up and led her away through an exit door into a side hallway. Before the door boomed shut behind them, her harsh sobs echoed back into the auditorium.

"Oh, for Pete's sake," said Mr. Palia in a tired voice, "makes you want to get a day job. Come on everybody, let's get the lead out. Henry, I want to talk to you. Stay out of other people's dressing rooms for a while, huh? Dianne says she caught you in somebody's dressing room."

"It's none of her business," said Henry, and he went away smiling. We got to work. Things were hopping tonight. The dancers had stayed to rehearse a couple of scenes with us. Now that the fight was over, they cleaved together in loud packs in the dark hallways, around the water fountains. From a big workroom across the hall came the sounds of saw blades, like runners wheezing toward a finish line. The hammers crashed so loudly sometimes that the actors had to pause in the middle of lines and wait for a few seconds of silence.

"Where's the prima donna?" shouted Dianne when one of Ginger's scenes was next on the board. Dianne had recovered from her outburst, but her eyes looked bruised. Her hair was still matted against her cheeks.

"Excuse me, Mr. Palia," I said. "I'll find Ginger." No one ever seemed to think it strange that I called my mother by her first name.

"You?" he asked uncertainly. "Well," he sighed, "O.K., kid, go find Mama."

I wandered back into the maze of corridors. The dancers were lined up against the walls, stretching and laughing. I picked my way through their outstretched legs. It was like walking over train tracks.

"Anybody seen Ginger?" I asked.

They laughed and didn't answer me. In the largest dressing room, Myra Woods flossed her teeth. Her gums throbbed from pink to red as she attacked each crevice. It looked hopeless. She must have been sixty, Myra Woods, but she wore her shoulder-length hair like a child's, pressed straight back in barrettes behind her ears.

"I'm looking for Ginger," I said.

"Not here," she said. "Try back in the stalls."

Ginger wasn't in the stalls. I ran out of the bathroom again and nearly tripped over Bob Ferring.

"Stop sneaking up on people," said Bob. "There's no privacy in this world."

I returned to Mr. Palia. "I couldn't find my mother," I said. "I don't know where she is."

"Oh, great. Just great," Mr. Palia said, and he put his hands high on his hips and kicked over his chair. His elbows stuck fiercely out of his olive-green rolled-up shirtsleeves. They were blunt and crusty. I looked at Henry Harrison, who had reappeared while I was gone.

"Henry," said Mr. Palia, "what do you people think this is, anyway? A pickup basketball game? We can't do the scene if we don't have the actors."

"So somebody missed a call," said Henry. "Calm down."

"Where's Ginger?"

"I haven't seen her. How would I know?"

"Never mind. Let's have Bob and the kid run through the 'No More Tears' song from the third scene in act 3. A cappella. I'll fry Ginger's bottom later."

I jumped to my feet and went to my mark. I had run through my songs with Bob and Ginger in a couple of short vocal workouts, so I sang just as they had taught me, with a voice as big as I could manage. I dug down in my diaphragm and yelled the high notes at the top of my lungs—just like the kids in "Bye Bye Birdie," Ginger had said, and she had laughed when we practiced, remembering some outdoor theater in Atlanta and an almost date with Xavier Cugat. Right now, I thought I sounded wonderful, and I grinned, but Al gnashed his teeth and pulled out his hair.

"Stop!" he shouted right in the middle. "Stop! Stop! I'm going to cut my throat. She couldn't carry a tune in a bucket. Why didn't somebody tell me this?"

Henry Harrison closed his eyes and looked away, with his tongue in his cheek. Bob Ferring smiled smugly. I had no friends here. These weren't church people, who were bound to come to your aid if someone spoke ill of you. In a worldly theater with a bunch of worldly dancers and actors, who gave a rip about a little Dutch girl, especially with Ginger out of the room?

Then Dianne said, "Aw, the kid sings O.K."

"She doesn't sing," said Mr. Palia. "She screams. You heard her."

"That's why Dianne can appreciate her," said Henry.

"You shut up!" said Dianne, and pointed a heavy finger at him.

"I want something extraordinary," said Al. "I don't want screaming; I want Judy Garland."

Dianne turned to Mr. Palia but kept glancing back at Henry, to see if he would pick up the gauntlet. "Most kids don't sing like Judy Garland," she said. "They sing like kids."

Mr. Palia sat down in his chair and jiggled his lips with his finger. He was thinking what to do about me. I was standing in front of him, my arms at my sides, trying to look endearing.

"If you don't sing better by next week, you're out of the show, kid," he said quietly.

"Oh, look," said Dianne suddenly. "Mama Bear's back."

Ginger came running into the green room. "Al!" she said, out of breath. "Al, honey, I'm sorry."

Mr. Palia didn't lift his head.

"I am so sorry, believe me." She stopped at the corner of the stage. "I can explain later. I know you've been waiting."

"Mrs. Jordan," he said, looking over at me, "how many children do you have?"

"This one plus two more at home," she said calmly.

"Next time you make me wait—I mean it!" His voice rose to a yell. "I will come and kill all of your children!"

Ginger stared at him. "For your information, I was out saving your car. It was about to be towed away because you're parked in a fire zone. I had to pay ten dollars out of my own pocket."

He stared back. "Did you really save my car?"

"Yes, I did. But I wouldn't do it again."

He stood quietly for a long time, and then he shoved his hands in his pockets. "I don't blame you. Here's ten bucks. Thanks a lot. Let's get going."

Ginger held her hand out to Henry Harrison, who hoisted her up. She smiled as her feet touched the stage. They went on with the rehearsal. It was a long one that night. I sat through the rest of it sadly, thinking that I would never learn to sing.

Later, while I was waiting for Ginger in the hall, Bob Ferring passed me and said, "Has she dumped you yet?"

"What?" I didn't know what he meant.

"Nothing." He shared a small laugh with himself and kept going.

The next morning, I spoke to Grandma about the Jordans.

"Carolyn," she said, "did Mrs. Jordan enjoy her concert last night?"

"Yes, ma'am, I think so."

"You know, I just don't like you coming home after eleven."

We were working on a flannelgraph lesson for poor children in Richmond. I drew the Bible characters in magic marker. She cut flannel to glue on their backs, so that they would stick easily to another piece of flannel draped over an easel. Each summer, she and Louise packed up their flannelgraphs and traveled to the Fan district in a van with ten or fifteen ladies from Dutch Falls churches. Harold McQuick was their leader, an elderly child evangelist who had sold half of those ladies hearing aids in his spare time. He organized five-day clubs on

197

inner-city street corners, including a free lunch made by the ladies. Louise feared for her life when she went downtown. She carried an atomizer in her purse filled with ammonia. Grandma only worried about David and Jonathan cartwheeling off the flannel in front of a mob of laughing children.

"Yes, ma'am," I said, "it was an interesting evening. Did you like Ginger?"

"I like Rev. Jordan very much. In spite of his hair. I can tell he's a godly man; he's got the air about him. She worries me a little."

"Why do you worry about Ginger?"

"See there, to think of her letting a young person refer to her as 'Ginger.' I don't think she ever got all the show person out of her."

"No, ma'am."

I held up my magic marker drawings of David and Saul. Saul was tall and handsome, with a proud straight nose and a black beard. He was the first king of Israel, the king who loved David like a son and later hated him because of his popularity with the people. His purple cloak gleamed white in the shallow places and dark in the folds. The drawing was supposed to have a 3-D effect. You should sense the contours of the robe, at least from a distance. Perhaps his neck was too thin. I would make him another neck and glue it on. David was short and thick-necked. God had loved him, in spite of his adultery and murder. Everyone who had ever read the Bible loved him.

"The Lord is nudging me," Grandma continued, "that I need to warn you, young lady, not to compromise your Christian principles by falling in with the wrong crowd. I'll just have to trust him to help you sort out the good from bad in the people you meet."

"Yes, ma'am."

"This Ginger Jordan reminds me too much of your Aunt Jo."

"Yes, ma'am."

"And that's a problem."

"Yes, ma'am."

"Carolyn." She draped a piece of blue felt over her fingers. On it she let fall five neat drops of glue. It would make the backing for my drawing of David running from the cave after he had cut a piece from

198

the cloak of Saul. What a wild and gentle man David was. I began to draw him looking out at Bathsheba in her bath.

Grandma shook her head—or was it a shudder? "Carolyn, I have something important to talk to you about today. Much more important than anything we've talked about in a long time."

"Yes, ma'am?"

She hesitated for a long time, fitting flannel against paper, then rubbing dried glue from her wrinkled hands. "This is even more important than those troubles you had at school last year with Mrs. Van Zandt. It's a little difficult though. It's embarrassing for me, as an old lady, to talk to you like this. But it looks as though the job is still up to me."

"What is it, Grandma?"

"Carolyn," she said in a very low voice. She scooted her chair close and leaned near me, but kept her eyes on the flannel and glue. "I'd like to know how much you understand about . . . sex."

"Sex? Oh, Grandma, I've known about that for a long time. There are a lot of books at the library."

"Well, praise the Lord. Tell me what you know."

I began to describe reproductive organs and she held up her right hand to stop me. Her fingers were still covered with glue, like peeling skin.

"Oh, dear," she said. "I'm not really talking about the nitty gritty, Carolyn, I'm interested in what you know about men. About men's urges."

"Well, is there something you think I should know, Grandma?"

She hesitated for a long time. "Phuong told me that you were walking around practically naked the other night."

"That's it!" I said furiously. "She told you about that. I hate her. I can't stand her."

Grandma put down her work and folded her hands on her lap. "Calm down."

I couldn't calm down. In a loud voice I explained what had happened. "It was Phuong's fault," I said. "I was only trying to get back to my room and she came yelling at me from upstairs. She dragged me up and my towel just about fell off. If I was walking around naked, it was her fault and not mine!"

"Carolyn," said Grandma, "it's very immodest to run around in scanty clothing in front of a grown man. We have to take care about our behavior in front of men, Carrie. They're—" (she whispered loudly again) "—more subject to temptation than we are."

"I didn't know he was there," I said. "I had to get back to my room."

"From now on I want you to be careful around the Jordans, especially at their home. Do you understand that men are easily tempted?"

"Yes, ma'am."

"So you do understand that." She sat back in her chair and rubbed her index finger against her chin. "Well, that's fine then."

"Grandma," I said, "why do people get married if they'd rather be with other people?"

"Oh, my. Who are you thinking of Carrie?"

"No one." I was thinking about Arnie Hagedoorn storming around the library late at night, furiously desiring what God wouldn't allow him.

"Well," she said, sticking straight pins between her lips as she prepared to sew flannel backing on a strip of sparkly nylon, "it's not that people shouldn't get married. It all has to do with women becoming too much like men. Working gals are just like hothouse flowers, soaking up all that attention from men with no wives around to compete. Women and men ought to keep apart, or there's trouble in store for everyone."

Now I pictured the women who worked with Mr. Hagedoorn in the library—Mrs. Ernst in circulation, with her skinny white arms; Miss Dolly at the lost and found desk, eighty years old; Mrs. Atchison, slightly green and always pregnant. "Is it true what they say about Mr. Hagedoorn?" I asked. "Has he fallen into sin? Is he the Christian brother you were praying for the other day?"

"What?" she looked at me sharply. "Don't go around listening to gossip. I'm not raising you to be a gossip."

"Yes, ma'am. Then what was that meeting about on Sunday and who were you praying about?"

She looked up. "Oh, that was nothing. It was about your stepmother. The dominie wanted to examine her for church membership, and he asked your father and me to come along. But the dominie doesn't think she's quite ready. Your father needs to work with her on some doctrinal matters. It's all that Holy Spirit business. She says she doesn't feel comfortable at our church. She wants to attend another one part-time."

I thought there must have been something else to it, but just then Phuong came in from outside with a stack of books. After passing through the room with a quiet bow, she returned empty-armed and began sweeping up threads and swatches of flannel that had fallen under the table. Grandma lifted her feet to make way for the broom.

"Did you find those books for me?" asked Grandma.

"Yes," Phuong said. She hummed softly as she swept in the corners and pulled down cobwebs from the high places. She swished dust from the blinds over the kitchen door. I continued drawing. I drew Bathsheba to look like Phuong, with a scar on her cheek like a thin noodle.

"Where are my books?" asked Grandma.

"In you room," said Phuong with a nod.

Grandma left the room and came back with three novels, which she set on the table. "These are for you," she said to Phuong. "They'll help you learn about American culture."

I looked at the titles: *Trouble in Triage, The Heart Is a Lonely Surgeon,* and *Love's Healing Glance.*

"Those are just nurse books," I said. "That's not how you learn about America."

"Lora Elegan Braun is my favorite author," said Grandma. "She speaks the language of the heart. Why don't you recommend something of your own, since you're our family librarian?"

I shook my head. I wasn't interested in doing anything for my father's wife. I went back to drawing David and Bathsheba.

*T*he world from my Sunday school window was motionless and bright, hanging under my teacher's voice like a pendant on a chain. She explained it to us from notes on an illustrated card, where it came from and where it was going, why we were there in that room on a Sunday morning and why we should plan to be there again next Sunday. I looked out into the still pear trees and believed that the world in the window was just like the one on the card. The deep green of the holly on the walkway was the green of the sea that Jesus once put to rest with a single word. The earth in the garden was deposited there by oceans slipping back into place after forty restless days and nights, and even now men of great scholarship were pillaging Mount Ararat for splinters of gopher wood. Meanwhile, the yellow buses lurched forward on the street, getting ready to carry the poor children home to their unchurched parents. I saw Arnie Hagedoorn walk out to the street and look around, alert to something. A car pulled up beside him. The bell rang.

Annajane saw him, too. She nodded to me as if to say, "Go and see for yourself," and so as the boys hurried out of the room in packs, I grabbed my papers from under my desk and ran between them across the hall and down the steps. I plunged roughly through a mass of adults in the coatroom. From there I went straight to the vestibule, through the big oak doors to the courtyard, down the fan of steps and around a corner to the street. At the sidewalk I stopped. Arnie Hagedoorn stood on the curb a few feet away, leaning into the window of a rumbling red Karmann Ghia, one knee bent leisurely against the door and the other thrown back. His pants were tight and shiny around his thighs—he always wore them that way, riding up over his knees and catching on his ankle-high dress boots. Late-arriving women flooded around the car and up the steps. Their shoes scraped the pavement like cow hooves. Their eyes slipped over to Mr. Hagedoorn and back again. I turned and looked for Annajane sneaking up behind me, but she didn't come.

The back windows of the car were dusty, but through the yellow film I saw a red dress on a hanger and peacock blue suitcases stacked with a cowboy hat thrown on top. Above us the electronic chimes rang eleven o'clock, the call to worship. An old man walked out of the church and across the street to smoke a quick, forbidden cigarette. A car swished by and let out five or six teenage girls in skirts and striped kneesocks. They ran up the steps, through the doors, and into the vestibule. Still Mr. Hagedoorn leaned into the Karmann Ghia, talking. He rocked on his feet, shifted knees, scratched the back of his left calf with the toe of his right boot.

"Arnie?" called a voice in back of us. "Arnie!"

Mr. Hagedoorn and I both turned, and there stood Nancy Hagedoorn on the steps of the church, Arnie Jr. in her arms.

"What you doing out here, honey?" she asked. "I've been looking for you all this time."

I looked back at him. He stood up and a small Bible popped out of his back pocket like a piece of toast. When he leaned over to get it, laughing, I looked into the car. A woman sat inside with a square face and floppy pigtails like the ears of a cartoon dog. Her sleeveless yellow blouse hung limp from her neck and armpits as if she'd been traveling in it for days. Someone else sat in the backseat. A big head moved forward into the light for a second and back into the shadows again.

"Nancy, do you know who this is out here?" Mr. Hagedoorn shouted across me, not seeing me. "This is old JoJo Grietkirk. Remember JoJo?"

I looked quickly back at the woman in the car. My aunt? My grandmother had already given up on her coming.

"Isn't that nice," said Nancy Hagedoorn, waving. "Arnie, I need you. Little Arnie is crying and I have to go to the bathroom."

"Aw, Nancy. All right. Well, good to see you, Jo. You know I hoped maybe I'd see you at the reunion a while back, but you didn't come."

"No, I couldn't come," shouted my Aunt Jo after him, because he was now moving quickly toward his wife. "I wanted to, but you know my mama. I just couldn't. Let's see more of each other, O.K., Arnie?" Her voice was thick and slow, the kind of Southern accent people only had on television. I thought it was odd since she'd been in New York City so long.

"Sure. Yes, I'm coming, Nancy. I'm coming."

He trotted up the steps. My aunt put her hand out to change gears and I hurried over to the car.

"Excuse me," I said. "Excuse me."

"What?" She turned her eyes on me. They were heavy, watery eyes. Could there really be a connection between this woman and me? Did the wings of Providence have a shuttle between us, a freight line from her chromosomes to mine? She looked like my family—like my father around the shoulders, and Uncle Jim around the eyes. She had my grandmother's voice, though deeper and slower. But there was something out of line in her. Providence had made a rift between her and us; she had drifted away from our family like a wayward continent.

The person in the back was a teenage boy, slumped against the suitcases reading a comic book. My cousin Nathan?

"I'm Carrie," I said to my aunt. "I'm your niece." I stood before her, my hands folded over my Bible, my white socks folded daintily over the straps of my sandals.

"My niece?" she said. "You mean—you mean you're my Davey's girl?"

"Yes," I said.

"Well!" She threw her naked elbows over the steering wheel and stared at me. "Well, I can see it! You are Davey's baby. I'd know you anywhere. You're the exact spitting image of my Davey."

"Nice to meet you," I said politely.

"Your daddy. Where's your daddy? Around here?"

"Inside," I said. "The service is about to start."

"Oh, honey, I haven't seen your daddy in ten years. I don't want to wait another minute. Would you go get him for me, Carrie? Would you do that one little thing for me?"

204

"Yes, ma'am."

"Oh, thank you, honey, thank you! And I can even tell you which pew he's sitting on. Twelfth from the back on the right side. Run get him; tell him old Jo's outside. I'll wait right here. You go get him. Run, now!"

I went back into the church, past the deacons at the door of the sanctuary and straight down the middle aisle to the twelfth pew from the back on the right side. There in the center sat my father with Phuong. I climbed over to them across five or six pairs of legs. My dress crackled on Mrs. Riebersma's panty hose.

"Aunt Jo's outside," I whispered to Father.

"What?" he asked.

I whispered more loudly. "Aunt Jo is outside!"

"She is?" said my father. "That's terrific!"

"She sure is. She wants you to come out there right now. Be quick; she said she's waiting."

"Come on and sit down, Carolyn. The service is about to start."

"But she wants to see you right now."

"She'll wait. Have a seat. Get your heart ready for worship."

I sat down. Why didn't he get up? My heart pounded. Beside me, Phuong sat with her eyes closed in prayer. Her face was cloudy and hard like cold clay. Her lips moved soundlessly. She rubbed her palms together.

"I think you better go out there," I whispered across her to my father.

"Carolyn, not now."

"But she'll get mad at me. I said I was coming to get you."

"She can wait a little while longer. Don't think about your aunt right now. Get your heart ready."

"She will blame me," I thought. "She will think I haven't told him." Up at the pulpit, the dominie cradled a stack of sermon notes as thick as a dictionary. He smiled over our heads. "Shall we prepare our hearts in prayer?" he asked, and began his prayer with, "Lord as we consider this morning how thy hand has guided us through the turmoil of so many centuries, we thank thee for preserving thy church and fortifying it here not only with stone and girders of steel, but also with prayer and obedience . . ."

I looked over at my father once again. In the middle of the dominie's prayer he opened his eyes and checked his watch but dropped his head again quickly. For the rest of the service—for the hymns and the sermon and the offertory—he sat as still as a statue.

When it was over at last, when the benediction had been said and the dominie had hurried down the middle aisle with his robes flapping, we headed outside together. Now Father made haste. He signaled to Grandma and she came after us, almost as quickly. "Oh, my goodness," she said, rushing through the vestibule. "You mean Jo is here? And I didn't even make up the beds. I didn't believe she would come. Oh, my goodness."

But when we stepped out of the church together, we found the curb empty. The sun was bright. Father put his hand over his eyes and looked up and down the street. He was tall enough to see much farther than we could. "Are you sure it was a little red car, Carolyn?"

"I'm sure," I said. "It was bright red."

"I don't see any car like that. I'll check the parking lots." He walked off full of purpose, pulling Phuong along by the hand. Grandma watched him go and shook her head.

"Did you ask your aunt to come into church?" she asked me.

"No, ma'am," I said. "I didn't think about it."

"Was your aunt dressed for church?"

"I guess so," I said. "She was wearing a skirt."

"Did she tell you why she wouldn't come and sit with us?"

"No."

"Well, what was she doing when you saw her?"

"Talking to Mr. Hagedoorn in her car."

Grandma's eyebrows arched. The corners of her mouth turned down. "What color is her hair this time?" she asked. "You best tell me so I won't be surprised."

"It's blondish brown," I said. "She was wearing pigtails."

"Pigtails? Well-a-dell-dell. She would never wear them when she was a child; now she's in her forties and she wears pigtails. Does she look happy? Was her face lined and wrinkled?"

"No, Grandma, her face wasn't wrinkled."

"She didn't look like a woman bent down?"

206

"No, Grandma. She looked happy. She talks very Southern."

"All those years with the Yankees and finally she learns to talk right."

"Yes, ma'am."

Silently we waited together on the curb until Father drove Grandma's car up. Phuong sat in the backseat.

"Couldn't find her," said my father. "But you know old Jo. She probably sneaked home and climbed through a window or something. Let's get on back home before she leaves again."

Grandma climbed into the front and slammed the door after her. I sat in the back, as far from Phuong as possible, hugging the door handle. As we left the parking lot, Annajane waved to us with her white Bible in the air. "Carrie!" she called. She wanted to ask me about Mr. Hagedoorn. I waved back. There was no time to call out to her from the car. We would talk later.

"Good-bye," Annajane shouted. "Good-bye, Mrs. Grietkirk."

Grandma waved and smiled, but a moment later, she was back on the subject of my aunt. "How was her weight, Carolyn? Was she too plump?"

"A little plump," I said.

"A little plump?" she asked. "What is that supposed to mean?"

"She's fatter than I am," I said, "but not as fat as Mrs. Van Zandt."

Our car was hot. It had been sitting for an hour in the sunny church parking lot and now the heat clung to our faces and made even Father squint irritably. "Let's not speculate about Jo," he said. "Let's start out on the right foot with her."

"I just don't see how you think she'll get in the house," Grandma said. "She hasn't lived there in ten years. She's probably been sweltering outside all this time with poor Nathan. They're probably half-dead."

"Please calm down, Mama. You're getting upset."

"Don't tell me to calm down, David. I'm not a child."

He sighed. "I'm sorry, Mama. You're right."

"Jo sets me on edge, Davey. I want everything to be perfect this time. For your sake."

"Don't worry about me, Mama. I just want you to be happy."

"Well, I just want *you* to be happy."

When we arrived at home, Grandma smiled and dropped her shoulders in relief. The red Karmann Ghia did indeed sit in the driveway waiting for us, perched at a slant on a slope of ground that drifted down into the neighbor's hedge.

"She's here!" said Grandma. "Look, Davey, she's here. And she must have gotten in somehow." Grandma jumped out of the car and urged us into the house. Phuong dutifully carried Grandma's purse and sweater for her, stepping quickly just behind her. Father and I came as fast as we could. The side door stood open. "Jo?" Grandma called when we found the kitchen empty. "Jo? We're home!"

No one answered. Father went into the living room with a broad smile but came back frowning and shrugged his shoulders. Grandma rushed through the family room, up the stairs.

"Jo?" I heard her calling upstairs, from one side of the house to another. "Hello there? Jo? Nathan? We're home!" She came back down the steps.

"She must have gone out for a little while," Father said. "She'll be back."

"If this isn't just like Jo," said Grandma, "I don't know what is. How does she expect me to know how many places to set at the table?" She slapped her purse onto the kitchen counter and went to the refrigerator. She swooped out a thawed chicken and swung it into the sink with a thunk. "Why are you peeling potatoes?" she asked Phuong. "Didn't I tell you I want to have rice today?"

"I think you say potato," said Phuong quietly.

"That certainly is not what I said, but if that's what you're making already it won't matter I guess, because it doesn't look as though we'll be having company."

"Yes."

"Now, Mama, don't get so disappointed and grumpy," said my father, who was still standing there, looking somewhat shocked. "She'll be back. Jo's going to come back; her car is parked in the driveway."

"I'm not disappointed," said Grandma. "You just go watch your football game, David. I have to make dinner."

"Mama, it isn't football season. Please try to pick up your spirits."

"No man need be in the kitchen at this time. Go on, go on, shoo! Carrie, you start a pot of rice."

Aunt Jo didn't appear again that day. Not that afternoon, that evening, or that night after dinner. We all went to bed before Grandma. She sat up in front of the television in her curlers and shiny blue robe and fifty-cent bedroom slippers, her mouth straight and her legs crossed. Phuong brought her a cup of warm milk before following my father to the stairs.

"Mama, you won't like that television program," said Father. "There's a lot of necking in it."

"Good night to all of you," Grandma said firmly.

Up in my room that night, I looked out the window at the empty Karmann Ghia reflecting moonlight like a red puddle on the grass.

In the morning I knew that she was there. Even before I saw her, I knew. I heard voices in the hall, my grandmother instructing, "Towels in the dresser, soap under the sink, breakfast in a half hour, if you're ready." I heard laughter, doors slamming. My father said, "I'll wake up the little one." He knocked at my door.

"Carolyn, get yourself out of that bed."

"But it's only seven."

"Wake up and greet the day."

When I went downstairs, I found my grandmother and Phuong in the kitchen making Belgian waffles. "Good morning, Sunshine," said Grandma in a happy voice.

"I thought Aunt Jo was here," I said, looking around.

"Praise the Lord, she is. She got in very late last night. She took Nathan on a bus to see Williamsburg and didn't get in till late. That's what they were doing all that time. Isn't that funny? And I was worried about I don't know what."

"Where is she?" I said. It seemed to me that my aunt could at least have left us a note before going to Williamsburg, just to spare Grandma some worry.

"She's on the porch with your father. Why don't you go and kiss her, make her feel welcome. Oh, I feel so cheerful this morning, Carolyn. I jumped right up and read my Bible before it was even light outside. God has blessed me with a good spirit."

"That's good," I said, but I didn't go onto the porch. I had no intention of kissing anyone.

"Will you set the table for me?" Grandma asked.

"I still have to take a shower, Grandma."

"All right, I'll do it myself. I'm in such a good mood." She picked up the plates and marched through the swinging doors singing.

Phuong turned around to face me from the sink. "Your grandmother have asking you to do the work," she said, "and I think you can do it."

"She didn't care," I said. "She didn't mind."

"I think you can always have respect."

Now that we were alone and there was time for us to speak, Phuong would not get the better of me. "Who made you the boss?" I said.

She put her lips together firmly and didn't answer.

"You are not my boss," I said. I stood exactly eye to eye with her.

She put her soapy hands on her hips. "You are a bad girl."

"No, I'm not."

"Yes, you are. My mother have spank a bad girl like you."

"Well, you're not my mother and you're not going to spank me. I'll tell my father if you try."

Her face tightened up. She was intent on something. "So you grow up bad, too, if nobody can teach you."

"Why are you so mean to me?" I whispered, and stamped my foot. My throat was hot. "I've never done anything to hurt you. I've tried to be nice to you since the day you came here. Why are you mean to me?"

"You need to teach you," she answered, and she turned back to the sink quickly, because my grandmother had just put her head through the door.

"Phuong?" Grandma said. "What are you doing? I need your help."

Phuong turned on her heels and followed Grandma out, with a bitter expression. I started to cry. I went into Grandma's bedroom and sobbed into my hands. Then the thought occurred to me that I could call Ginger. She would understand how I felt. I picked up the phone and let it ring ten, fifteen times before Frank answered sleepily, "Hello?"

"May I speak to Ginger?" I said.

"It's only seven thirty in the morning," he said. "Call back later."

"All right," I said. I hung up the phone and cried again. It was unfair, the way Phuong spoke to me. I didn't deserve it. Just then Grandma called us for breakfast. I wiped my face before I went to the dining room.

My aunt came to the table in dark glasses and a cotton blouse that sagged at the elbows. She sat down by me, and I got my first good look at her, my first smell of her. She smelled salty and soapy sweet, like soaking dishes. Her fingernails were long and glossy, red like the paint on her Karmann Ghia. She scratched the skin on her neck and it made a dry noise like insects in grass.

"I like the hair, JoJo," Father said. "I've never seen you as a blond."

"Things change, Davey," said my aunt. "Except old Mama's dishes. She's been using these same dishes for forty years."

"Fifty," said my father.

"Never mind the age of my dishes," said Grandma sharply.

"Well, Mama," said Aunt Jo, "I'm going to give you some new dishes for Christmas."

Grandma took a bite of her food and touched her napkin daintily to her mouth. "Does that mean you'll be here for Christmas, Josephine?"

Aunt Jo laughed. "Did you hear that, Davey? She's worried I'm going to move back home permanently."

"I am not," said Grandma. "I'm thrilled to have you and Nathan here."

"Well, JoJo," said Father, "are you or aren't you moving back?"

My aunt grinned and smacked her food with her mouth open. She looked over at my cousin Nathan, who was a shaggy-haired, hulking teenager, nothing like the small boy on the bad photograph I knew so well. Grandma had set him beside my father. Nathan was shaped like a butternut squash, big on the top and bigger on the bottom. His long legs hung pale and hairless and heavy from his shorts, like slabs of ham in a butcher's freezer. I liked to think that each one weighed fifty pounds, enough to crush your skull if they happened to fall out of a four-story window and land on your head.

"Nate," said my aunt, "you want to move in with Grandma?"

"I don't know," he said through his nose, like a Yankee. "I only been here one night."

211

"Listen, Nate," said my father, "I want you to get a good impression of us. Don't listen to anything your mother tells you; it's all prejudiced. Did she ever tell you about the time she painted the walls of her room with black and white stripes to look like a prison cell?"

"No," he said. "She did tell me that she used to lock herself in her room for days and you would slide food under the door."

"Oh, that's right," Father said with a laugh. "I tried locking myself in once, but I didn't care for the solitude. Jo liked being alone. Isn't that right, JoJo?"

"I just loved being away from Jim," said my aunt. "He made me miserable." She took off her sunglasses and wiped her watery eyes. Her skin was tan except for a pale yellow tint on the soft inner sides of her arms, like the yellow white centers of lemon snaps. I stared at her. She put her glasses on again and stared back at me.

"You must think I'm an ugly old witch or something," she said.

"No," I said.

"Carolyn," said Grandma, "how do you answer politely?"

"No, ma'am," I said.

"I sure haven't been called ma'am in a long time," said my aunt. "They don't say it in New York. It sounds good."

"Josephine," said Grandma, "tell us about your work. Is it something you can just leave if you choose to?"

"Well," said Aunt Jo, "there's not much to tell because I haven't been working in a long time."

"Then how do you manage to keep clothes on your back? On Nathan's back?" Grandma's voice rose to a squeak.

"Careful, Mama," warned Father.

"Ever heard of alimony?" smirked Aunt Jo. "And there's this and that. Old what's-his-name helps."

"That Roger fellow?" asked my father.

"Robert. Yes, he helps. Let's not get into that." Grandma and Father exchanged a look, but the subject passed away naturally. When we had finished eating, Phuong stood and cleared the table. Aunt Jo watched her quietly with a thin smile.

"All right," said Grandma. "I just don't know how to thank the Lord enough for what he has done for us today, bringing my children home safely. Shall we pray as a family since this is our first morning together?"

My aunt's smile faded. "Not this morning," she said. "I have to wash my hair. It looks like a rat's nest."

"There's always time to pray, isn't there?" asked Grandma.

"Not when your head's itching." Aunt Jo scratched her head.

"Just this one time. You just let us pray, Jo, and then we'll let you wash your hair."

"No, Mama, not today."

"Well, why not?"

"Because I don't want to. If you want to pray, go ahead. I want to bathe while the shower's free." Jo stood up, adjusted the wide mouth of her blouse, and left us. She had a firm, no-nonsense walk. The cut glass on the ledge of the bay window rattled as she passed. Grandma looked at Father and shook her head. He nodded.

I told Ginger about my aunt on Wednesday night at our dinner together. While I talked, she glanced around nervously. She examined her food and scraped ketchup off her sleeve cuff. She tapped her feet to the metallic music jangling over our heads.

"Ginger, I think you'd like her," I said, trying to get her attention.

"Just a second, I have to get another napkin," said Ginger. She came back and scratched her sleeve cuff with it furiously.

"You'll have to meet her sometime."

"I can't wait. Oh, this stupid ketchup! I look terrible tonight. Kiddo, I feel so ugly. This outfit doesn't work at all."

I looked at her in disbelief. She wore a purple lamé blouse with rhinestones, a purple velvet skirt, and black boots with little silver chains dangling around the heels. Her eye shadow sparkled—threads of silver and purple woven under a wavy outline of black pencil. Sitting with her in this yellow booth at McDonald's, I knew that all the men in the restaurant were watching us. I looked around to know for sure and I was right. A pair of soldiers, a man with a newspaper, an elderly gentleman sitting with his wife—they were all watching.

"But you look beautiful," I said to her. "Everybody thinks you're beautiful. I wish I was half as pretty as you."

213

"Oh, hush, kiddo." She snorted and blew her nose into a napkin. "You're just saying that. I'm just an old bimbo."

"I mean it. I wish I were half as pretty as you."

"Thanks. You know, Carla, all you really need is a makeover. I'll give you one as soon as you're old enough. Maybe on your birthday."

"I'll never be as pretty as you. I'm too fat."

"Oh, kid, you're not fat. You think men really go for those skinny chicks? Most men like substantive women."

"Well, then how come you're not fat, Ginger?"

"Because—" she said thoughtfully, "because I'm suffering all the time, kiddo. My broken heart keeps me skinny."

Suddenly I thought it would break my heart if it were true. I wanted to know why she suffered. I waited for her to tell me, while she slowly finished her french fries and slurped her Coke. She waved at the soldiers and giggled. A girl came by in a green knit uniform and mopped under our feet. I recognized her from football games at the high school. She had been a cheerleader once, with a big smile and an arched back, like a bow about to let go of an arrow. She was still pretty, but her smile was gone. Ginger winked at her.

"Ginger," I said when the girl was gone and the soldiers were pretending to look away, "are you really always sad?"

"Yes," she said, "I'm always kind of sad."

"Why?"

She put her finger in a pool of ketchup and smeared it over her lips and licked them. "Why not? What's there to be happy about?"

"You don't seem sad most of the time."

"I'm happy when I'm with you, kiddo. You lighten me up. And you see the best of me. I'm at my best on stage. I'm never at my best at home. At home I'm at my worst."

"Why?"

"I don't know. I guess it's Frank."

I sat up straight and looked her in the eye. "He's the one who makes you sad."

"Yeah, he's the one. You're so perceptive, you know that?" She reached into her purse for her cigarettes and lit one, smiling. "He just

214

doesn't love me, that's the real problem. I mean, what's so unlovable about me?"

"How can he not love you?" I said. "Everybody loves you."

She shook her head. Her eyelashes glistened black and wet and made a dark smudge as she wiped them. "That's not true," she said. "Oh, Carla, I wish it was, but it just isn't."

"Ginger," I said hesitantly, "did you ever—did you ever love anybody else?"

"What do you mean?"

"You know."

"You mean did I ever have an affair?"

I blushed. "No, that's not what I meant." It really wasn't.

"Yes, it was, and you know it. People always think I'm like that. I was never a good girl. I've always liked men. But that doesn't mean I don't have my standards. If a guy even asked me, I'd say, 'Sorry, pal, but I already have a lover. It's a soulmate I need.'"

"Frank should treat you better. I'll tell him. Do you want me to talk to him?"

She smiled at me and shook her head slowly. "Carla, you're crazy."

"What do you mean?"

She lit another cigarette. "Want one?"

"You're going to let me smoke tonight?"

"I feel indulgent. Maybe I'm getting too sentimental." She laughed while I tried to strike a match. My hands shook. I tried again, succeeded, and smoked. I liked it.

"It reminds me of softball," I said, trying to cheer her up. "This is just how the air tastes. At church basketball games the smokers have to stand outside because you're not allowed to smoke in church gyms. But at softball games it smells just like this."

"Don't get hooked. You'll grow up and get cancer and it'll be my fault. I couldn't stand the guilt."

"Maybe you'll have cancer by then, too."

"Hush. That's bad luck. Take that cigarette out of your mouth and finish your Coke. It's almost time to go."

Ginger put her arm around me as we stood. I held my cigarette down, just in case some acquaintance of my grandmother's was nearby, watching.

"You're wrong," I said as we got back into the car together, "when you say that I'll grow up and find out you're not so great. I'll always think you're great. You were almost a star, you were on Broadway. I saw the pictures in your scrapbooks."

"I'm afraid I'm going to disappoint you, Carla."

"You'll never disappoint me. There's nothing you could do to disappoint me."

"Maybe not. But I worry about it. Maybe you shouldn't hang around with me so much. I know your family—I don't want to ruin you."

"Sometimes," I said thoughtfully, "when I'm with you, when I'm in the theater, sometimes it's like I don't belong to my family anymore."

"That's what I'm afraid of."

"But it goes the other way, too. When I'm with them, it's like how could it be true? How could I be talking to you this way? It's like there are two me's now."

She shook her head. "You ought to stick with your family. They're O.K. Look at your grandmother, she's healthy and beautiful, and she must be a hundred years old. Righteous people live longer, Carla. Bad things don't happen to them."

"It's funny you say that," I said. "The dominie always says that if you're not being persecuted by the devil, then you're probably not walking with the Lord."

She smiled. "I guess I'm walking with the Lord, then. Because I'm persecuted all the time."

We smelled the sawdust already in the warm air of the theater parking lot. It was an important rehearsal tonight, our first on the main stage, under the lights. Two sturdy boys from the tech crew carried rough furniture and plywood back and forth, measuring from wall to wall and floor to ceiling before we began to rehearse. The floor boomed and popped under their hard boots. An older man with wiry arms like pipe cleaners held out paint swatches for Al to approve.

Backstage, Ginger and I were fitted for costumes with the other principals. I stood next to Mrs. Blaha in shorts and a T-shirt and bare feet, trying not to stare at the dimples and bruises on the backs of her

216

legs. Tommy and Henry were bare to the waist. Henry's chest hair looked dirty gray like a Brillo pad in the dim lights backstage, but Tommy was smooth and white. He lifted his arms for the costume designer and clasped his hands together over his head, flexing his biceps. Then Mary Burrows came over for her fitting. She pulled his right arm down and held it between her hands like a trophy, laughing and giggling at everything.

"You have lovely calves, Tommy," said the designer as she draped a tape measure around one of his legs. "I'm in awe of them."

"Thank you," said Tommy. "I'd give them to you, sweetheart, but you've got nice ones of your own."

Mary laughed hysterically. "Tom, you're such a flirt!"

"What about my calves?" asked Henry. "Aren't my calves just as nice?"

"Very, very nice," said the designer without looking. "Like two skinny drumsticks under your big ugly knees."

Now Ginger laughed. The designer left us all alone and Ginger held on to Henry's shoulder and bent over, laughing. Henry looked angry for a second, but then he threw his arm around Ginger's waist and twirled her against his chest. This I didn't like. She laughed harder and pushed him away. He held on.

"Henry, now stop it," she said, still sounding flirtatious.

"Keep laughing and I won't let you go," he said. "You have to stop laughing at me."

"Come on, you're embarrassing me."

"I don't care."

"I don't know what your problem is, Henry, but let me go right now."

"No, not till you stop laughing, you little flirt."

She struggled and screamed as he pinned her arms behind her back. I remembered the man who had held my wrist in the theater, and suddenly I hated Henry. "Please let her go," I said, in a voice too quiet to be heard. "Hey, please let her go."

"Come on, Henry," said Tommy, "that's enough. Let her go."

"Oh, lighten up," said Henry. Ginger was looking away now, pretending to ignore him, whistling some song.

"Stop ignoring me," said Henry. "Stop it. Kiss me and I'll let you go."

"Henry," said Ginger flatly. "Let me go right now or I'll kick you where it counts."

"Just try it." She did. He danced out of the way and dodged around, fending her off. His hair swung down over the bridge of his tall nose.

"Look what you've done!" he yelled. "You've messed up my hair!"

"I'm about to mess up something else. I'm serious, you jerk."

"Kiss me. That's all I'm asking."

"Hey, Henry," said Tommy, with a glance at me. "You're upsetting her little girl. Now cut it out."

Henry held on to Ginger's arm and swung around. He stepped right against Tommy, hairy chest to bare chest. "Gonna make me? Gonna? Huh? Come on, come on!"

"Sure," said Tommy. "I've got what it takes. Step up and fight."

"Henry!" said Ginger. "Let go of my arm, now! I'm yelling for Al."

"Go ahead."

But before she could, I grabbed one of Henry's big naked thighs, and bit hard. I held him long enough to gag on his rough hair, then I let go and jumped away. He looked down in horror. "Why you little—" I was smiling.

"It's O.K.," said Tommy, taking a stand between us. "You upset her; you had it coming."

"You did," I said. "Don't ever do that again."

Henry was licking his lips. I thought he might cry. Mary went to Tommy's side and held his hand.

I stood against the wall, out of their way. We were all quiet, even Ginger, who had a moment ago been laughing. Then Dianne Bane roared from the wings, "Two weeks till dress rehearsal! I'm not messing around tonight!"

"Who wants to mess around with her, anyway?" said Henry.

The silence broke. Ginger wheezed with laughter. Tommy slapped Henry on the back and kissed Mary square on the mouth. Henry kissed Ginger on the cheek. So was that it? Had it all been a joke? Was all forgiven? Maybe I had misunderstood—I had been the only angry one. There was a mystery about the theater people I had known so

218

far, the way they played at hating each other. I wondered how they knew who they really hated and who they really loved.

Just then Al came down the backstage steps, scratching his hair, which stood up in balls like the stuffing pulled out of a pillow. One of his sleeves was buttoned at the wrist and the other rolled up.

"What's so funny back here?" he asked.

"Private joke," said Tommy.

"In other words, you were laughing at me. Is that right?"

"No, Al, honey," said Ginger in a sweet voice, and swung her arm from Henry's shoulder to his. "We were laughing at Henry's calves. Look how tiny they are. Isn't that ridiculous?"

"Yeah, they are kind of tiny, aren't they?" Al laughed. Henry frowned down at his ankles. "That's enough," said Al, turning serious again. His eyelids looked like globs of stone. "I'm in a rotten mood tonight. I should be in a hospital, the way my back is killing me. Henry, I'm about ready to take the deep six. Can you believe Dick Danson is out there again tonight, him and that writer? And Dianne is acting like a crazy woman. I've got to do something about her, Henry. She's out of control this time. It's your fault."

"What do you mean?" asked Henry, smiling innocently. "What can I possibly do about her?"

"All I know is something has got her goat. The woman is foaming at the mouth, literally drooling. I'm going to try something new. O.K., listen up everybody. We're going to try something really different. Something really terrific, and I just know you're going to love it. Meet me in the green room in five minutes. All of you. You understand? Tech crew, too."

When we met, Al made us all sit in a ring. Actors, dancers, tech crew, props people, wardrobe department—we all sat in a large ring with our legs crossed yoga-style. "We're going to start out different tonight," he said. "We're going to start out on the right foot tonight."

"Looks to me like we're starting out on our butts," said Dianne.

"And I don't want to hear one word of complaint from you, Dianne. Do you understand? This is the newest thing; I read about it in a journal or somewhere, and it's called a vulnerability workshop. I should have done it weeks ago. It has to do with learning to be nice to each other for a change. We're going to hold hands, we're going to say nice things, and we're going to hug. Yes, hug. We're going to go around the circle and I want each of you to say something to the person on your right—something positive, something encouraging. Say 'I like the way you sing, Ginger,' or 'I like your legs, Tommy.' Anything at all."

Dianne sat between Tommy and Mary. "What is this, Al? Whose screwy idea is this? Did Henry put you up to this?"

"Dianne," he said, "just for that I want you to sit next to Henry."

"Have mercy!" said Henry.

"And I want you to hold her hand, Henry."

"She'll grind my fingers together. She'll make me cut myself with my own fingernails. She loves to do that."

"I'll make her go first. Dianne, sit down by Henry and tell him something nice."

"Sit down by Henry?" she grumbled. She sauntered around the circle and dropped her bottom on the stage floor between me and Henry. Henry shivered as she touched him. She drew back but he grabbed her fingers and held them.

"Dianne," said Al, "say something nice about Henry."

Dianne clenched her teeth. "Something nice? Well . . ." She shook her head and bit her lower lip. "It's too hard, Al. I can't do it."

"Sure you can, honey, just do it for me."

She tried again. "Well . . ."

"Well?" said Henry.

"I guess," said Dianne, "I guess I wouldn't run over him if he was lying dead in the road."

"Thank you very much, Dianne, for those touching words," said Al. "You think you're going to get out of this, Dianne? No way. Now try something a little less grotesque this time. It doesn't have to be original. How about, 'I will try to treat Henry more kindly from now on, Al.'"

Dianne's lips curled back. She sneered and said through her small teeth, "I will try to treat him more kindly."

"That's very nice," said Henry easily. "And as for me, well, I'll just keep praying every day that the doctors find a cure for her malignant personality."

220

Dianne's eyes flashed up to Al. "I did it! Make him do it."

Al wiped his face and nodded his head. "Henry, it's your turn now. Make peace; do it for me."

Henry tossed his head. He was wearing more clothes now, but he rubbed his chest hair through his shirt. "I will try to treat her more kindly," he said, sighing.

Al sighed too, a sigh of relief. "Anybody else want to go say something?" he said, already turning to the door. Obviously he didn't care too much about the rest of us, but it was only fair to ask. "Anybody have anything nice to say?"

"I do," said Mary. She squatted up on her haunches and steadied herself on Tommy's knee. "I think," she said, "that Tommy here is doing just an extra, extra, extraordinary job. I mean when I'm up there he's just so—you know—so warm and affirming. He looks over at me when he says the line and it's almost like his eyes are feeding me my line. He's that good. Some actors are so—into themselves, but with Tommy, it's so—different. It's like acting with your best friend. He's great!" Mary leaned over and gave Tommy a hug and a kiss on the neck.

"Now isn't that nice?" said Al, taking interest again. He began to clap. "Come on, everybody, clap for Tommy and Mary. Isn't that terrific? At least two people here know how to get along. Tommy and Mary, stand up and take a bow. I like to see young romance blossom. It adds to the show. Makes me feel like an old matchmaker. Anyone else? Anyone else have anything nice to say?"

"I think Ginger is just doing terrific, too," said Mrs. Blaha weakly.

"Thank you, darling," said Ginger, with a curtsy.

A blond beauty stretched out her hard, thin dancer's legs and rolled her ankles restlessly. Henry smiled at her from the left corner of his mouth, the corner Dianne couldn't see. A long silence followed. It was like the silence of prayer meeting, all of us waiting for the next nervous voice. But too many seconds had passed and now it was too late. No one would speak after all this time. I rubbed my eyes and prepared to lift my head again.

"O.K.," said Al. "If that's all, let's get to work. Tonight, let's just keep

221

on concentrating on the good things about each other, the nice things. O.K.? O.K.?"

"Wait!" said Ginger, looking up quickly. She had been twirling her finger in the dust on the floor. "I have something to say."

"Yes, honey?" Al asked.

She stood up, cocked one hip back, and smiled. "It's just, well, I think you're terrific, Al. And I want you to know that I think you're great. We all do. Don't we, guys? Isn't he great?" She clapped her hands.

"Hear, hear!" said Tommy, and we all clapped.

"And I'm going to do my best for you from now on," she said. "Because this is going to be an amazing show."

"Hear, hear!"

"So let's get our act together from now on and show Al and Mr. Danson and everybody else in this town what we can do. This is the best cast and the best show this theater has ever seen. Al said it. I believe it. Let's prove it!"

"Hear, hear!"

"Well, well," said Al, with an embarrassed grin, "my spirits are doing better. I guess I won't quit tonight. Let's get to work." We stood up. The dancers shook out their knees and rubbed their thighs. Henry put his arm around Ginger's shoulders and said something into her ear, laughing. Beside me, Dianne growled.

I wasn't called up for a long time, not even to stand mute on the stage, looking back and forth between Henry and Ginger as though they were batting a ball to each other. Eventually, Al sent the other actors home while Henry and Ginger rehearsed a few dance numbers with Bob on the piano, a few pieces of the orchestra down in the pit, and Myra Woods on the choreographer's stool at the side of the stage.

While Ginger and Henry danced, I sat in the hallway playing cards with a pair of dancers who were sisters.

"What's Ginger like at home?" they asked. "Is she always so bubbly? Does she always flirt like that? Is she real romantic with your dad?"

"She's just a normal mom," I said. "I don't know. I can't describe her very well because she's my mother."

"You're so different. You must be like your dad."

"Why? What's so different about us?"

"You're so quiet and serious. And you don't look anything like her."

"I've got her hands," I said. "See?" I held up my fingernails, which I had painted bright red the night before.

"Oh, yeah, maybe so."

Dianne called down to me from the wings. "Would Ginger Jordan Jr. get herself up here? Al wants to do the reprise now."

I climbed up on stage. Ginger and Henry stood over the orchestra pit breathing hard and streaked with sweat. They were laughing with Al and Bob over a dirty joke. Myra Woods sat on a stool in the corner looking over the tops of her glasses. She frowned at me and pushed her stringy hair behind her ears.

"O.K.," said Al in a weary voice. "One last time with the kid. Let's do it. And that's it for tonight."

I had no steps to learn, Myra Woods said. I should just run around on the stage with my arms out like an airplane, following Ginger and Henry.

We started into the song, skimming over the parts we didn't know well to the parts we could sing with great emotion. The orchestra made it easier. The music behind us was like the music I heard in my mind when I dreamed of doing great things. I sang heartily, riding the orchestra like a fast animal. I whooped out the song, I punched deep into the notes, I threw out my arms to send forth my words like doves, and I waited to hear them fly down again. When they came I thought they sounded fine, spinning splendidly off the high walls of the auditorium. I glanced out over Bob Ferring's hands and I closed my eyes and sang even more loudly. I was proud of myself. "Yes," I thought. "I can sing like a star. I can hitch this whole auditorium to my brilliance and carry it with me, moving faster than the world turns."

"Hold it, hold it!" yelled Al. I opened my eyes. The movement stopped. The orchestra galloped off without me, screeched, and clattered. "Hold it!" shouted Al to Bob Ferring. "Cut! Hold it! Now, what in the—what's going on up there, Henry? Why aren't you dancing? Why are you standing there like Mr. Potato Head?"

"This kid can't sing. You know that, Al. What's wrong with you?"

223

"The kid? Aw, grow up," said Dianne from the wings. "She's doing fine."

"Myra?" called Al. "I'm exhausted. My ears are numb from listening to Henry squawk. What do you think about the kid?"

"Well, she's doing her best," said Myra Woods. "What does Ginger think?"

Ginger didn't commit herself.

"I think I'm losing my mind," said Al. "I don't care anymore. If Myra has no problem—"

"No," interrupted a voice from the middle of the auditorium. It was Saul Anderson, the bushy blond writer. He stood up from his seat next to Dick Danson and ran his fingers nervously up the back of his neck. "Henry's right," he said. "This song is the epiphany of the entire show. The kid has to be great. This kid is whiny and stiff."

Whiny and stiff? But I was loud and free, like a songbird.

"I didn't think she was so bad," said Dick Danson.

"She was terrible," said Saul Anderson.

"This is Ginger's kid, right?" asked Dick Danson wearily. "Has Ginger tried working with her?"

"Uh," said Ginger, "well, we just haven't had a whole lot of time, Mr. Danson."

"Take her out," insisted Saul Anderson. "Take her out. It's the kind thing to do. Swift and merciful."

I shook my head desperately and looked at Ginger. "I can do it," I whispered. "Just teach me how, Ginger."

"Mr. Danson," she shouted back, "what if I give you my absolute and personal guarantee that Carla will learn this part? I absolutely promise you that I will without a doubt work with her on this. Is that enough?"

"Thank you," I whispered, "oh, thank you, Ginger."

Mr. Danson looked over at Saul Anderson. They whispered to each other. "We'll give the kid one more try," said Mr. Danson aloud, while Saul Anderson sighed and shook his head.

Al nodded at me. "All right, you. But I warned you before and I'm warning you again. This is your last chance. You better learn to sing between now and next week or I'm calling back that little Walter. That

224

kid was a genius. He knew the whole show and besides, I liked his mother. She had good taste in bowling shirts. Let's do it again. A one, a two—"

Bob Ferring mounted the piano again, charged up to the heights of the keyboard, and waited there for us. The three of us hurried back to the mark at stage left. On the beat we would hold hands and swing our arms down, touch the stage, and then leap and run apart.

"Come on now, kiddo," Ginger whispered, "I'm counting on you to be great."

"I'm trying my best," I said.

"Well, try harder. Don't squeak." The horns came in with the piano, the strings, and finally, the drums.

"On three," said Myra. "And a one, and a two, and a—there's your cue. Good. More attention, more attention, pick it up, pick it up."

We bent down and I looked into the gold and orange threads of the stage floor. I saw myself for a second, smiling worriedly, and then I was jerked up and to the left as Henry moved off with Ginger. The wings of the stage flashed across my vision, Dianne standing like a guard in the billowing folds of off-white curtain, Tommy and Mary waiting for their cues while Ginger sang:

> Hello, lover, it's been so long
> Since our hearts were singing
> The same glad song.
> I'm so tired of a cappella
> I've been longing for a fella,
> So join me now, sing it loud and strong.

And eventually we all came in:

> No more tears, no regrets,
> And no alimony checks,
> Cause he loves her and she loves him . . .

I would sing soon. Right now I was supposed to fall into Henry's arms and he would lift me up on his shoulder. Myra had shown me how. Ginger had said, "Oh, you lucky kiddo! I think he's cute." So here it came. I closed my eyes and let myself fall. The lights flew up above me—red, blue, yellow. Henry's face was over mine. He looked disgusted. He grabbed me around both wrists.

"What are you doing?" I said. "Why are you holding me so tight?"

"Pipe down," he said. "I've got you."

I tried to sing,

> No more tears, no regrets,
> And no alimony checks,
> Cause he loves her and she loves me
> And we're a model family . . .

Then it was Henry's turn. He went back to the chorus.

"Louder!" Al shouted. "You're dead up there! Find the beat! Try harder!"

"I'm going to fall!" I said quickly to Henry as he spun me in circles. My head flew out like a tether ball. "What are you doing? I'm going to fall. I have a cramp in my toe! You're going to drop me!"

"You're too fat!" he said, and then he started to sing.

"I'm going to fall!" I shouted.

Slam! The orchestra shot up above me and split in two jagged halves. There was a crack. I felt a hard, slick surface under my chin, a sharp pain in my shoulder. It was like turning circles in a swimming pool, doing somersaults, and then not being able to find the air again. I had struck my head against the concrete. My chest felt like a vacuum. I tasted something sweet.

"Somebody call a doctor!"

"My french horn! It's crumpled up like tin foil!"

"What happened?"

"She told you not to spin her around like that."

"Carla? Carla?"

A long time seemed to pass, with people talking all around me. I lifted my head, painfully, and felt someone gently press it down again. Al leaned over me, frowning. His breath smelled like an old hot dog. "Don't move your neck, kid. We're going to call a doctor to check you out."

"Did I fall?" I was still disoriented.

226

"You jackknifed into the orchestra pit. You're gonna be O.K., though, I promise."

"Where's Ginger?"

"There's no telling where she went. Don't try to talk. Mama's coming. You just rest for a minute. We want to make sure nothing's broken." He walked away mumbling something about a lawsuit.

"Are you hurt, child?" Myra Woods stared down at me from the stage. She looked like a frog, squatting with her knees up. All around me people moved, filing back and forth. I could see Bob Ferring in the corner of my eye, sitting at his piano bench.

"Where's Ginger?" I asked.

"I don't know," Bob said, with a flick of his hand. "She was onstage just a second ago."

"Can't you call her?"

"Oh, she's off somewhere. Don't try to talk."

"Well, where did she go?" I insisted. "Can't you find her? Go get her."

"I don't know where she is. Do what he said and don't try to move your head."

Al was talking furiously to Mr. Danson across the rows of theater seats. And so I just lay there alone, waiting for Ginger. And it was a long time before she came to me.

I would not be paralyzed, they said at the hospital. I would only have to wear a neck brace for a week. Ginger lied and said that she was my mother. The nurses watched her sign the permission forms and then wheeled me into an X-ray room. There, on the cold table, I drifted off in a half sleep and dreamed that I sat in a wheelchair on the stage of a Billy Graham crusade, singing.

> When I was sick and languishing,
> You just touched me.
> You just reached down and touched me.
> And just your wondrous touch
> Did wondrous much
> For my soul, yes, for my soul.

I left the hospital on my own two legs. My neck brace kept me from turning my head to look straight at Ginger as she drove. I wanted to ask her why she had disappeared when I fell, why she had left me in the hands of Bob Ferring, surely the world's least comforting person. But she was sweet and chatty, and I lost the will to accuse her of anything. "It's after one o'clock," I said. "My grandmother's probably worried. She's probably called your house by now and talked to Frank and they're both hysterical."

"Don't worry, kiddo," she said. "You've had a hard night and you need rest. I'll explain it all to your grandmother. Trust me."

"But how can I explain this neck brace? I can't lie about it."

"I'll take care of it. You don't worry."

"But it seems pretty hard to explain."

"Everything sounds harder when you're tired. What you need, sweetie pie, is a good night's sleep. I sure hope you're not in too much pain."

"No, I guess not," I said in a brave voice. My neck felt hot and pinched. "I think he dropped me on purpose, Ginger. He hates me."

"Well, I wouldn't be surprised if he did," Ginger said, shaking her head. "We were a little oversensitive tonight, weren't we?" I shrugged my shoulders and winced. Yes, maybe I was oversensitive, but only on her account. Didn't she see that?

We reached my house after one thirty. A light was on in the kitchen. I opened my door and paused as I got out, waiting for Ginger to turn off the ignition and come in with me.

"Bye now, kiddo," she said. "Take care."

"But Ginger, I thought you said you would explain."

"I'll give your grandma a ring in the morning. Don't worry about anything. Let me handle it. Love you."

I slammed the door as she pulled away from me. Her taillights flicked on and off and on again as she headed down the empty street, traveling in the opposite direction from her own house. Why that direction? Where was she going? The lights became tiny red points in the distance. I stood by the kitchen door, gathering my courage to go inside. The crickets chirped loudly in the hedges. That light, that light in the kitchen, who had turned it on? My grandmother or my father? My aunt? I thought it surely must be my grandmother. Maybe she waited there, tipped back in her chair in her bathrobe, sleeping until the turn of a key in a doorknob surprised her awake. I looked up and down the dark street before I dared enter. All these houses, these brick walls. If you pulled them down, you would find rows and rows of beds in perfect ranks like cribs in a nursery.

I opened the door and found Phuong at the table. As much as I disliked her, as angry as I had been recently, I felt glad to see her. I had feared seeing Grandma there, and had found only Phuong. She couldn't hurt me tonight, not the way Grandma could have hurt me, with just a look. Phuong's Bible lay open at her elbow. She was read-

229

ing intently. She looked up and gasped when she saw my face, my neck brace.

"Where's my grandmother?" I asked very quietly, because I stood only a few feet from Grandma's bedroom. I didn't want to wake her.

"You neck," Phuong gasped quietly. "And you eye." She stood up, and as she did, she lifted her hand to her cheek, to touch the scar there. I hadn't even noticed my black eye, but when I touched it, I saw stars.

"It hurts," I said. "But it's O.K."

Her hands shook. She came over to me and examined my face gently with cold fingers. "It hurt?"

"I told you it did," I said. "It's just a bruise. But where's my grandmother?"

"She go to bed. Don't wake her up. No, you go upstairs."

"But she'll see me tomorrow anyway."

"I think you can use some makeup. Make the face better."

"That won't fool Grandma," I said.

"How you—?" She pointed curiously at her own eye. She wanted the story.

"I just fell down," I said. "I'm tired. Good night."

"Somebody has hurt you?"

"No," I said. "I just fell down."

She stepped back and seemed to give in. "Good night, Carolyn. I hope you can sleep well."

"Thank you."

I slept poorly. The next morning I went to the bathroom for some aspirin and saw myself in the mirror. My eye was a black stain on my sallow face. My lower lip had swollen up, pink and tender like a plum. What would Grandma say? Of course she would be angry, but would she be sympathetic, too? Would she worry over me, would her pity soften her anger? I imagined her touching my temple the way Phuong had touched it, looking at me in tenderness and distress. The thought of it gave me hope. So, having taken my aspirin I went down to the kitchen. I found my grandmother talking with my aunt over coffee. Grandma looked up at me sadly, but unsurprised. Maybe Phuong had told her.

230

"I'm sorry, Oma," I said. " I'm really sorry."

"So you've been getting into trouble," she said, and she turned to my aunt and threw up her hands. "Coming in late, doing who knows what. I don't even want to know how it happened. It's Davey's house; he'll have to take care of this himself." And she stood up and went out of the kitchen.

I had never seen Grandma carry on like this before, pretending to give up on me. Only a week ago, hadn't she lectured me on the dangers of immorality? Hadn't she warned me about spending time with Ginger?

My aunt regarded me for a long time while I poured myself coffee and cereal. She sighed and gave a hard laugh. "Your grandma is pretty steamed at you, girl."

"I didn't do anything wrong," I said. "I just fell down."

She tossed her hair out of her eyes. "Now what on earth was Davey's little girl doing out so late?"

"I wasn't doing anything," I said. "I don't want to talk about it."

"Come on, honey, I won't tell on you."

"Well, I don't want to talk about it," I said.

Phuong had been doing something at the refrigerator. Now she came over and pressed an ice bag against my face. "Please, Carolyn," she said to me, "where is your neck?"

"My neck? You mean that brace for my neck?" She nodded. "It's upstairs. I don't need it."

She shook her head disapprovingly. I took a seat across from my aunt. Phuong filled a hot water bottle and laid it across the back of my neck. She pushed my head down on the table, so that my cheek rested on the brittle ice. A moment later my grandmother marched back into the kitchen, holding an open phone book. "Carolyn," she said in a remote voice, looking away from me, "I cannot find the Jordans' telephone number."

"Why are you calling them?" Suddenly I was frightened again. "They won't be awake yet."

"Just give me the number, please."

I did. Grandma sat at the telephone in the kitchen and dialed slowly. After each dial came a long whirr and then a deliberate pause. "Hello?"

231

she said at last. "Mr. Jordan? Good morning, this is Dorothea Griet-kirk, Carolyn's grandmother. I apologize for dialing you so early—oh, yes, you certainly may. I didn't realize I was interrupting your bath. Hello, again? That's right, it's Mrs. Grietkirk. Is your wife there, Mr. Jordan? Thank you. Hello, Mrs. Jordan? How are you this morning? I'm fine, too, thank you. I get up very early every morning. That's part of getting old, I guess. Oh, yes, I am. You know it when it happens to you; nobody has to tell you. Well, thank you. That's a generous thing to say. Listen, Mrs. Jordan . . . all right, Ginger. I'm very unhappy about last night. I'm talking about Carolyn's injuries. Yes, that's what she said. Well, I'm also talking about the fact that she was home so late. Are you going to tell me that she was baby-sitting for your sister again, for another of those hard rock concerts? Oh, you did, did you? I consider it irresponsible of you to take Carolyn without my permission. Immature, I should say. Apology accepted, but she won't be allowed to baby-sit for you anymore on Wednesday nights. I'm sorry. No, I won't reconsider. I'm sorry."

I knocked the hot water bottle and the ice away and looked up. "No," I whispered. "No, Grandma. Please let me go with Ginger. Don't make me stop. I'll never come home late again." I got out of my chair and bent down beside her. "Please, Oma? Please?"

Grandma was still talking to Ginger. "Do you hear that?" she said. "Can you hear this child? Do you see the problems you've caused me? I wish you could see her face this morning."

I wanted to interrupt her and say something to Ginger. I tugged at the receiver, but Grandma hung on hard. "Stop it," she mouthed. "Carrie, stop it." Finally she put a hand against my chest and held me at arm's length, like a boxer. I wrestled my way back, crying. Phuong came and held me away.

"Get away from me," I said, while my aunt mumbled something behind us.

"Mrs. Jordan," Grandma said over my protests, "I'm sorry but I'm having trouble hearing you."

Just then my father came downstairs in his bathrobe. He had slept late. His uncombed hair curled up over his ears.

232

"Help me," I begged him. "Don't let Grandma tell Ginger I can't come anymore. Please."

"What's all this about?" he asked. "And what happened to you, Carolyn?"

Grandma gave him a biting, blue-eyed stare like a cold wind and pressed the phone against her thigh. I heard Ginger's deep voice croaking away in the folds of her dress. "The Jordans have taken Carolyn to a rock and roll concert," Grandma whispered, "and she has been injured there. If you want her to continue seeing them, that's up to you, but in my judgment, she should spend Wednesday nights at her own church from now on, where she won't be in danger."

He rubbed his nose with the back of his hand and blinked. "Oh, boy. Well, it's up to you, Mama. You use your judgment."

"This is your house," she said. "I think you have the final say."

"No, Mama, it's up to you. What makes you happy is most important."

"What makes you happy, David, is what makes me happy."

"Well, it's up to you, Mama; I'm too sleepy to come to any decisions."

"I don't think she should go over there anymore."

"I trust your judgment, then."

"Thank you."

"I hate both of you!" I yelled. Grandma looked up at me, shocked, and I shouted it a second time. "I hate both of you!"

"Carolyn," said my father with sudden harshness. "Get yourself upstairs and stay there. You won't speak to your grandmother that way."

His face was stern. I could have run out the front door, across the street, into the library. I could have curled up on a couch in the remote bathroom of the third floor, where Arnie Hagedoorn took his lovers, or so I thought, and where the toilet paper rolls sat untouched, and the paper towel dispenser was never refilled, and the sinks were spotless, and the stucco ceiling looked like the surface of the moon. I could have sat there looking down on my house. But I obeyed my father and went upstairs without breakfast.

A while later he came to me. I had been thinking that I was a failure for obeying him. I wondered how Grandma had finished the call with Ginger. Wasn't I the impetuous girl who led a lonely double life as a true-hearted Dutch girl and a wild-hearted daughter of a stormy singer? Wasn't I the girl who had lied to nearly everyone? Was I, in the end, only another obedient Dutch girl, plain and simple, doing as I was told, not provoking my father? Even the lies I had told were all to protect my grandmother. I was no kin to Ginger, not even at heart.

"You've been very disrespectful to your grandmother," Father said as he came into my room. He sounded angry. "How do you account for that?"

"I didn't mean to hurt her feelings," I said quietly.

"How do you account for it, then?"

"I just wish things were different."

He hesitated for a moment, pushing his hair down behind his ears. It was wet from the shower now. Something about the motion of his hands, the way his own hair disobeyed him, told me how uneasy he was. He didn't want to be hard on anyone, but Grandma wanted it to be his house. "What do you mean, you want things to be different?" he asked.

Of course I meant that I wished I could pack up my things that afternoon and go to live with the Jordans. "I don't know. I know I wasn't a very good person this morning."

"Well, Carolyn, you sure didn't do what Jesus would have done, did you?"

"No, but I don't want Grandma to stop me from hanging around with Ginger. I would die if she did that. I would just die."

He sighed and folded his arms, leaning against my bookshelf. "Do you feel that Mrs. Jordan is a good influence on you, Carolyn?"

"Sure," I said.

"Let me rephrase the question. She's a nice lady, a very attractive lady, but do you think that she's a spiritually mature lady? Remember that the Lord tells us not to associate with people who might drag us down spiritually."

"She talks about God all the time," I said indignantly. "She tells me that I have to have faith, that God works things out. And she is a preacher's wife, isn't she?"

He frowned and shook his head. "I guess I'll talk to Grandma about

234

it. But Carolyn, try not to get your grandma riled, O.K.? With Jo here she's got all kinds of things on her mind. And Jim and Betsy are coming to town next week with the kids. She'll have enough on her hands without worrying about your problems, too."

"Yes, sir."

"Your grandma needs help and support, not a contentious spirit."

"Yes, sir."

He came over to my bed, bent down slowly, and kissed my bruised eye. My father never smelled of aftershave, cigarettes, or chewing gum. He had his own pleasant smell. "You apologize to your grandmother for what you said," he whispered. "You hear?"

"Yes, sir. I will."

When I went downstairs, I heard my grandmother and aunt talking to someone on the porch. This surprised me, since the porch was not my grandmother's territory at all. Unless there was a deck chair to be mended or flower boxes to be watered, Grandma spent her days in the kitchen and family room. I went slowly toward the porch. My aunt lazed on the swing, half asleep, with one leg stretched out over the length of it. And across from her, to my surprise, was Ginger, sitting next to my grandmother on an oak bench. I paused just inside the door of the living room and sat down silently on the sofa.

Ginger wore a denim jumper that splashed down almost to the toes of her flat-heeled leather boots. Underneath the jumper her voluminous pink blouse sprouted tiny hand-embroidered green flowers around the lace of its high collar. Her hair was brushed back in a shiny dark bun, with a barrette perched at the top. She looked like a dominie's wife.

"Mrs. Grietkirk," Ginger was saying, "I really believe that the Lord has led Carolyn into my life. I would feel so ashamed if something I had done wrong—if something I had, humanly speaking, done wrong—should spoil the Lord's work."

"I, too, trust that God is working here," said Grandma, "and yet, Mrs. Jordan, I've had reason to call your judgment into question."

"Life hasn't been easy on me, Mrs. Grietkirk. I haven't had the church background, the spiritual guidance that you folks have had. My mother and father were good people, but they weren't spiritual people. So it's hard for me to have judgment. I know I need insight. The Lord is showing me that just left and right. Well, I guess what I'm trying to say is that I want to learn from you, Mrs. Grietkirk, I truly do. I believe that the older women should teach the younger. Doesn't the Bible say that?"

"Yes, the Bible does indicate this, Mrs. Jordan. I have to say I think it's wonderful that you know you need help, that you're coming to me like this." Grandma's voice was softer.

"I have a special love for your granddaughter," said Ginger. "I wouldn't want any harm to come to her because of me. I'd sooner have a millstone hung around my neck than harm a little one like that."

Grandma nodded. Scriptural allusions always pleased her. "I think, Mrs. Jordan, that it's wonderful how you have taken such an interest in Carrie, because she does certainly need a motherly influence in her life."

"That's what I've felt. But I'm young and I don't always make the best decisions. If you could guide me," Ginger said, her eyes down.

"Well, I'd like that, Mrs. Jordan. I'm so glad you have the humility to come to me like this. That's important in a young woman. If we could pray together once a week, and have the *kopje koffie*—coffee, that is—maybe that would help."

"I'm sure it would. I'm just sure. Will you allow Carolyn to visit me, then? Will you allow her to accompany me to Richmond?"

"Yes," said Grandma. "If you come see me once a week, for prayer."

"Oh, yes, yes. But I want to be honest with you. Soon, beginning next week, I'll be needing Carolyn more than ever. Perhaps as often as three nights a week, Tuesdays, Wednesdays, and Thursdays. It won't last forever, just until Patty has her baby—"

"Your sister is expecting?" said Grandma.

"Oh, yes," said Ginger. "That's why I believe it's so important that she make a decision for Christ now, before she's busy with another little one."

Grandma paused. "I agree with your reasoning, Mrs. Jordan. But Carolyn will have homework soon."

"I can promise you that after school starts I'll only need Carolyn on weekends." Of course she would. The show opened just as school began. After that there would only be weekend performances.

"Well, dear," said my grandmother to Ginger, "I feel torn in two directions. But for now, I want to honor your good faith in coming to me this way. I firmly believe that the best way out of every problem is the direct approach."

"I do too, ma'am," said Ginger.

"So I'll give my temporary approval to this arrangement and hope that all goes well from here on out."

"Oh, thank you, ma'am."

"I shall call Carolyn then." She called loudly, "Carolyn?"

"Yes?" I called from the window.

"Oh! Why didn't you say something, Carolyn? Here we were rattling on—Jo, you saw Carolyn there; why didn't you tell me?"

"You're wrong, Mama, I didn't see her," Jo said.

"Well, you're staring right at her."

My aunt sighed and stretched. "I guess I'm just lost in daydreams."

"Carolyn, come out here," said Grandma. I stepped out onto the porch. "I've decided to let you visit Mrs. Jordan on occasion. I don't think I was wrong to stop you before, just looking at your face. Oh, my! But Mrs. Jordan has convinced me that it was an accident and that she'll be using better judgment from now on. And no rock concerts, right, Mrs. Jordan?"

"Absolutely not," said Ginger soberly. "Never again. Never again. I told Frank just this morning, I said 'never again,' and that's what I'm telling you. I would still like her to come to Richmond with me, Mrs. Grietkirk, if that's all right with you. But no concerts."

"From now on, Carrie will not be taken away from your sister's house without my permission?"

"I swear it," said Ginger easily, smiling. In her dark eyes shone the blue of the cut-glass slippers on the bay window.

"I don't ask you to swear," said Grandma, for whom swearing outright was as bad as drinking or visiting the cinema. "I'll let your 'yea' be your 'yea.' That's all I'm asking. Let's pray together now. That puts me in a better mind about things, if you don't object."

We all bowed our heads. Ginger put her hands together.

"Lord," said Grandma, "help me to put aside the hostilities I've felt. I pray that my little Carolyn will heal up fine. Help me to trust you for the things that I cannot control. I pray your blessings and your wisdom for Mrs.—for my friend Ginger here. Show her how to continually seek your paths. Lead her only in the true and right way. Have mercy, Lord, but let your justice be done, let the sin in our lives, seen or unseen, be rooted out. Let the weed of bitterness be torn from Dutch Falls and flung onto the fire. Start with me, Lord. And I especially pray, Lord, for this dear sister of Ginger's, Patty, this dear soul who has yet to see your hand in her life. Open her eyes, Lord. Move her by your Spirit to take hold of the promises you offer in your Word. In the precious name of Jesus, Amen."

"That was a dangerous prayer, Mama," said Aunt Jo lazily when we lifted our heads. "Makes me scared to stay in Dutch Falls, thinking what might happen to me. I don't want to be flung in the fire."

Ginger smiled warmly. "But it was a good prayer, Mrs. Grietkirk, very touching. Thank you for remembering Patty."

"I want to go get you something," said Grandma, now squeezing Ginger's hand in hers. "Do you have a minute? I want to show you something. And mercy me, I haven't even offered you the *kopje koffie*. What kind of person am I? Care for coffee? A pastry?"

"I'm dieting," said Ginger. "And I don't drink coffee. It's too strong for me. But thank you so much anyway."

When Grandma had left the porch, Ginger sighed and sat back on the bench. My aunt was still with us, and so we looked at each other but said nothing. Grandma returned shortly with a picture of my mother. It was a snapshot of her as a teenager squinting into the sun beside a black automobile. I had seen it many times.

"I want you to think of this lady when you're with Carolyn," said Grandma. "This is Carrie's dear mother. She would have taken wonderful care of her daughter if she had lived. I guess I feel a special trust, having to watch over my granddaughter practically all alone this way. Carrie is very special to me and I don't easily let go of her. We've been very close. You can understand, Mrs. Jordan, why I am so concerned about her."

238

"Absolutely," said Ginger. "Goodness, what a gorgeous woman her mother was."

"She was very beautiful," said Grandma. "Inside and out."

Ginger laid her hand on my grandmother's knee. "Thank you. Thank you for showing me."

"Yes. Well." Grandma sighed, looking at the picture again.

"And now I have something to ask you, Mrs. Grietkirk," said Ginger. She fondled the lace neck of her blouse and pulled a string of pearls from the top of her jumper. She rolled them in her fingers. "Would it be all right for Carrie to baby-sit for me this Saturday? Frank has to preach out of town and I have a ladies retreat. It would be a special ministry to us if Carrie could watch the children."

"A ladies retreat? A church function. Certainly," agreed Grandma.

"Oh, terrif." Ginger cocked her head stiffly toward my aunt, as though she were looking around the corner of a nun's habit. "Are you doing anything Saturday night? Would you like to come along on our retreat? It's just a bunch of sweet gals from our church."

"I don't know," said my aunt sleepily. She ran her fingers through her hair and put her feet down on the porch floor. "I'll have to consult my calendar."

"Well, you're as welcome as anything," said Ginger. She stood up, smoothed out the folds of her big jumper, and picked up her purse. "That's all settled. Mrs. Grietkirk, it has been lovely seeing you again."

"You too," said Grandma. "I have to admit, my impression of you is much changed."

"Thanks. I'll be going now. I want you to tell that little daughter-in-law of yours to come see me soon."

"You mean Phuong?" asked Grandma. "Oh, yes, I'll tell her."

"And tell her to bring her husband. Frank and I would just love to see them again."

"I'll tell them," said Grandma.

Ginger winked at me and walked off toward her car. Her hips swayed even under all that cloth. Or maybe it was just the movement of the trees around her. Grandma waved as the car pulled away. Aunt Jo smiled. The day had been pieced back together and there was some joy in all our hearts. When Father and Nathan came in from playing tennis later, they found the three of us still on the porch, talking pleasantly.

Later that evening, my aunt entered a dreary and somber state of mind, hardly talking to anyone. She offered no explanation for it. She was as quiet as Phuong across the table, in spite of my father's jokes, and went to the porch before the rest of us had finished dinner.

"What's wrong with Jo?" Father asked Grandma in the family room, when Nathan had left for a moment and I pretended to be distracted.

Grandma turned in her chair and whispered loudly, "She's just as stubborn as she ever was."

"What is she stubborn about?"

"She's stubborn about everything."

"But what in particular?"

"I've told her that she can't invite that man down here. I think he's an addiction, just like those cigarettes."

"What's so terrible about him?" asked my father, "besides the fact that he's a non-believer?"

Grandma whispered, "They've been living together. He led her astray."

"Well, she didn't have far to go," said Father.

"Anyway, I won't invite sin into my house. When she marries him, God forbid, he stays in this house. But not until that time."

The next afternoon I happened to hear my aunt talking with Phuong. Phuong had been an ethereal presence since my aunt's arrival, haunting the stretch of hallway between her bedroom and the bath, making silent visitations at mealtimes to cook or clean. She was sometimes seen or felt breezing through the back door, off on one of her solitary walks. But we hardly spoke to her, and she didn't speak to us. She seemed to me like an electric fan on the lowest setting, spinning gently but not enough to matter to anyone, never winding down to a complete rest.

I sat down with Phuong and Aunt Jo on the porch. "I was just telling your stepmother," said my aunt, "what a good man she got. Not many

240

are lucky enough to find somebody like your daddy." Phuong smiled slightly and stared into her lap.

"Are you going to get married again?" I said bravely to my aunt, thinking of my grandmother's ultimatum. Her eyes darted up to mine.

"I sincerely doubt it," she said. "I need another husband like I need a hole in the head."

Phuong's voice was meek. "I think God have made the woman to need the man," she said. "Some, the nun, can live alone. But most has to marry."

"Honey," said my aunt, "I'll tell you. I've been married twice. It was awful both times."

"I think you have the bad husband."

"Maybe so."

"You try good husband this time," said Phuong.

"I've got a pretty good old guy back in New York, but I've seen good guys turn into jerks."

"The Christian is never jerk."

"I don't know any Christians," said my aunt. "Arnie Hagedoorn got married. He's the only nice Christian boy I ever dated." She laughed.

"Would you marry if you found somebody like my father?" I asked.

My aunt perked up. "Not much chance of that. Not too many guys like that who'd marry little me. Maybe I'll just move in with you and your daddy. I might absorb some of that aura around here, some of that holiness. Then I can go on the mission field and meet one of those single Bible translators, the ones on motorcycles down in Ecuador, the ones who marry nurses." She continued to laugh and then we were all silent for a few moments.

"Well," I said. "I'm just going to the library. You want me to take your nurse books back, Phuong?"

"Yes, thank you." Phuong excused herself and went into the house to retrieve the novels. Aunt Jo and I looked at each other.

"Spend a lot of time at the library, don't you, honey?" she asked.

"Yes."

"Going to be a bookworm like your daddy?"

"No." I wasn't sure what she meant. I had never seen my father read-

241

ing books, only the newspaper. Also, I didn't read that much anymore. I usually stared out the window of the library, watching people.

"What kind of books do you like to read?" she asked. "Romance?"

"I want to be an actress," I said, out of nowhere.

She laughed and looked straight at me, then away again. "Yeah, you and every other girl your age. I used to pray and tell God I'd witness to Doris Day if he'd just let me get to Hollywood."

"But I'm really going to do it."

"Well, I guess it's good to have a goal." She beckoned me closer and I sat down on the porch swing next to her. It was late afternoon, near our usual suppertime, and Grandma was still at the A&P. The sun stood at my aunt's back. It lit up her blond hair like a candle flame around her ash-brown roots. A few yards away the afternoon traffic was light but constant. My aunt waved at a truck that beeped going by. "You're a good girl," she said. "That Ginger Jordan is a fine lady for you to hang around with."

"I'm not what people think," I said. "I know a lot about life. I know a lot of actors. I even smoke sometimes."

My aunt's face didn't change. "Oh," she said, "then I guess you're not a good girl."

"Ginger lets me," I said. "You'd like her. She's really a lot of fun."

"Well, honey, she sounds fun."

The door squeaked open and Phuong came with the library books. "I have finish," she said. She handed me the five or six dusty, yellow novels with pictures of blue-eyed, sharp-chinned nurses and big-boned doctors on the covers. I took them onto my lap, but I didn't want to move off the swing. I really wanted to say other things to my aunt. I wanted to tell her about the show and all about Ginger, who was going to teach me to be a star. But Phuong was there, sticking out dark and stiff between us like a poorly grafted branch.

A little while later, while Grandma cooked supper, Father returned from his interview and joined us all on the porch. He sat down in a rocking chair and kicked his shoes off. He looked depressed.

"Bad news on the job front?" asked Aunt Jo.

"My hopes are dashed," he said. "Got to start all over again."

"Something will turn up, Davey," she said. She and I were still on the swing, and Phuong sat on a deck chair. Phuong looked anxious to be in the kitchen, but Grandma wouldn't allow it. She insisted that she was nervous this afternoon. She had to be left alone.

"You want a Pepsi Cola?" Aunt Jo offered a can to my father. "Mine's still cold. I can't drink it all."

"No, thanks," he said. "You know, that's quite an accent you've developed up there in New York City, Jo. I don't remember you ever talking so southern when you lived down here in the South."

"I have to keep in touch with my roots. You don't like the way I talk, Davey?"

"I do like it, JoJo. I like it. You should have heard this English teacher in a camp over in the Philippines. Came from Macon, Georgia. 'Y'all gots to learn this grammar! Y'all gots to learn this grammar if you wants to talk English real good!'"

Aunt Jo smiled at him. She tapped her feet to the beat of a song coming from a radio in a passing car.

"I was surprised you didn't stick around at church the other day," Father said to her.

"Huh? When?"

"Sunday when you showed up. You didn't stick around to see any of your old boyfriends."

"That's high school stuff," she said. "I didn't want to see anybody. You know, I saw old Arnie Hagedoorn, that wolf in sheep's clothing. That was bad enough."

Father looked uncomfortable. "How about this Roger fellow?" he said.

"Robert. How about him?" she asked.

"Have you set the big date yet?"

"For Pete's sake, Davey, did Mama tell all of you to interrogate me or what? I had to sit here and listen to your wife an hour ago, telling me not to be unequally yoked. And now you."

"Oh, Jo," Father said.

"Just tell Mama to stay out of my business."

"Aw, come on, Jo."

"You too, David. Don't come along asking me questions she could ask me herself. You want to know the truth? It's over with Robert. I

243

thought I might invite him down here, try to get him into my life again, but he wouldn't have come anyway. So no more questions. That's all over."

I wanted to crawl away into the kitchen with Grandma. But we all continued there on the porch together, in crusty silence, until dinnertime.

On Saturday night, Aunt Jo announced that she would go on Ginger's ladies retreat after all. We waited an hour past the arranged time, until at last Ginger pulled into our driveway and honked her horn with gusto.

"You said she's fun, right?" asked my aunt.

"She's the funnest person I ever met," I said.

We hurried together from the front door to the car with nearly matching steps, lighting our hands on the heavy door handles at the same time, mine on the back handle, hers on the front. I normally sat in the front, but she was an adult. Grandma had taught me always to surrender the front seat to adults.

"Hey, y'all!" Ginger leaned out the window, flailing her arms at us like a wild schoolgirl. She wasn't wearing a high-necked blouse now. Not hardly. She had on a shiny yellow halter top, a black skirt, and those high-heeled purple boots. "Come on," she said. "Let's go. We're late and I'm ready to party."

"Yes, ma'am!" said my aunt. We both looked back at the house to see if Grandma was in sight. She didn't appreciate theatrics in the driveway. Ginger honked the horn. My father looked out the kitchen door and waved.

"That brother of yours sure is a cutie," Ginger sighed as Aunt Jo got in. "Wish I'd met him about fifteen years ago."

"Dream on, baby," said Aunt Jo in her lazy voice.

"I keep telling you all to send him over," said Ginger. "But he never comes."

"My brother doesn't get out much. Except to church, of course."

"Well, in that case," said Ginger, "I'm sure he's a stumbling block to many a fine Dutch woman around here."

My aunt laughed. After a moment she said, "So where is this retreat? What kind of people go to this thing? People from your church?"

244

"Oh, it's nothing like that," said Ginger. "Frank's out of town and I'm busting loose."

My aunt smiled widely. From the side I could see three brownish molars in the back of her mouth. "You have good taste in friends," she said in my direction. But that was the only thing either of them said to me. They talked steadily. I was quiet in the backseat.

"Here we go," said Ginger, rolling up into her driveway. "Not much, but it's home. There's my sister Patty. She's always early."

A tall redhead came out of Ginger's house to meet us, with a smooth and perfect face, like painted wax. She made her way down the driveway carefully in heels like chopsticks, taking tiny steps. Peter and Paul walked in front of her and John carried Floyd behind. Their faces fell when they saw me looking at them through the window.

"My boys have got a thing for Patty," whispered Ginger to my aunt. "They adore her. Personally I can't stand her. She reminds me of our mother—such a goody-goody."

My aunt cackled and introduced herself through the window. I got out and tried to trade places with Patty, leading the boys up the driveway as she climbed into the car, but the boys didn't want to hold my hands. The older ones ran off down the street with soccer balls. Floyd toddled into the weedy overgrown grass of the front yard and started to scream. I picked him up and brushed him off. I tried to hear what Ginger was calling to me. "Don't know when we'll be back," she said. "Don't wait up. And don't touch the wine. Frank's got the bottles marked. Hah hah!" The other two bent over laughing.

"Have a good time," I said. The car pulled away. I could still hear them laughing down the road. I held Floyd tightly, as tightly as I could. He flailed and screamed, and I pressed him even more tightly against my neck.

"You know how I feel," I said. "You know exactly how it is, don't you?"

I didn't hear Ginger come home that night. I slept on the couch downstairs and woke with strong morning sun beating down on my back. It was Sunday. Ginger had agreed that she would take me to church, so I expected to hear her footsteps soon on the stairs. I took a shower, dressed, and went up to the kitchen. It was nine o'clock already, but the house was perfectly quiet. I went downstairs again and sat at the piano bench. I pressed a few keys softly, thinking Ginger might hear and wake up. But she didn't. So I banged loudly on the keys, but Ginger still didn't come. Finally, I called home and talked to my father. "The whole family is sick with the flu," I said, "so you'll have to pick me up." At ten o'clock I heard the Dart rumbling steadily in the driveway. I gathered my clothes and went out to meet him. We drove to church together.

The dominie preached on the story of Ananias and Sapphira that morning. He said that God struck them down, man and wife, because there are few things more destructive than a lie. When Ananias laid his money at the feet of the apostle Peter and said that it was everything he had made on the sale of his property, he was holding back the truth not just from Peter, but from God. Lying to God is sinful, the dominie said, and besides being sinful it's just plain stupid, since God always knows what you're thinking before you even think it. The dominie explained that it's yourself you hurt when you lie, even if you get away with it. He said you become a child of the Father of Lies, who is Satan.

While the dominie said all this, I looked over the congregation and thought of myself, Mr. Hagedoorn, Mr. Ferring, and who knew how many others? We didn't fit in here, I thought. We lived with one foot in another world. Why, we had told so many lies to God and man that it was hard to figure out why we hadn't been struck down, all of us, a hundred times already! If there had ever been a group of people so worthy of judgment, it was us. We should either leave the church or repent, now, instead of sitting here like hypocrites week after week knowing what sinners we were and hiding it on account of our shame and guilt.

I held my Bible tight between my knees and told God that, after Friday, I would not lie again. In the name of Jesus Christ, Amen. What a serious thing that was, to use the name of Christ. I took a small pencil out of the roll book on the pew in front of me and wrote in the back of my Bible: "I will read my Bible and have my devotions every day. I will not sin anymore." I thought I would tell Annajane about this, too. I would confess it to her. That will keep me from lying again. I would do it that night, when I went to her house after the Sunday night service.

We had a miserable, stormy Sunday afternoon and evening. I told my grandmother that I would be going to church that night with the Ten Kates, but when I got to Annajane's house, I found out that she had been excused from the evening service on account of it being such a rainy night and her catching cold easily. "You girls stay home and watch television," said Mrs. Ten Kate in a jolly way to please Annajane. "*Wonderful World of Disney* is on. I made popcorn—have all you want. Why not grab a sandwich, too? Anna needs more flesh on her neck. Her head looks too heavy for her. And Carolyn, you put that neck brace back on. Your grandma is quite concerned about you."

The Ten Kates went out rattling umbrellas and whizzing up raincoat zippers. It was still raining heavily outside. The rain came down like a jungle rain, pummeling the big hydrangea bushes on the back patio. We sat quietly for a while, reading magazines. Then suddenly Annajane pitched up from her chair and went to the hall closet without saying a word. She took out two black raincoats and two black umbrellas. She threw me a set. "We're going out in that rain?" I asked. "I'll ruin my shoes."

"I have something to show you," she said. "You'll thank me later, believe me."

We walked out into the downpour, staying as far apart as the pavement allowed. Her face was expressionless. She walked stiffly, kicking up the rain behind her, with her neck straight and her nostrils flared like an animal on some scent. We wound our way through old neighborhoods. I didn't know them well because they verged on what Grandma called "colored town," which was a place we only viewed from a car window or a rooftop. We passed a Black church that was just ringing its bells. We passed the Health Department, a Safeway, the public kindergarten.

"We're heading for the river," I said nervously. "I'm not supposed to walk through this side of town by myself. Where are we going?"

"You'll see."

The rain slowed to an inky drizzle. We passed rows of small white

247

houses with yards full of junk—rusty clothesline poles thrusting up from waist-high weeds, swingsets dangling empty chains, bald tires, shutters torn from their hinges, ragged rusty truck beds. The people who lived here were poor Dutch. Their children went to public school, so I didn't know any of them well.

We walked what seemed like miles, until we had left the poor side of town behind us and reached the woods that ran along the river. We had been walking over an hour. I wondered when her parents would get home and what they would think about us taking off by ourselves. Here we were in the new subdivisions, where the forest had been shorn away and the hills leveled to make way for young families. Here the unchurched English waited like fruit to be plucked off the vine by anybody with an evangelistic spirit—which Grandma said we didn't have enough of at the F.R.C. of V. These were the people Grandma wanted to see at First Reformed, the unprayer-meetinged working men and women living by the side of the old river, not far from the Powhatan Bridge where my mother had been killed. Annajane led me down a rough, gray sidewalk, past newly seeded dirt lawns that were being washed away in the rain. The air smelled like paint and ply-wood.

"O.K.," I said. "It's getting dark. You better show me whatever it is or I'm turning right around and walking straight home without you."

"Now, Carrie, trust me. We have to keep our cover. Hold your umbrella down close to your face. And pull your raincoat around your cheeks, like this."

"That looks stupid."

"All right," she said, pointing, "just look up there."

In front of us was an unfinished house. The houses to either side of it were nothing but roofless cages, but this house lacked only siding and shutters. I stared at it as Annajane asked me to, and then I turned to her and waited for an explanation.

"My Uncle John was over here yesterday," she said, "inspecting for the fire department in some of the new houses. And while he was here, he happened to see something. I'm not sure I should tell you, Carrie." A taxi came by just then. It flew past the house, churning up the loose gravel. Its lights blinked on as it passed us.

"So what did he see?" I asked impatiently. It was getting dark. I didn't want to walk home in the dark.

"He saw a woman come out of this house. She was wearing a long raincoat and a plastic scarf and sunglasses, so he couldn't see her face. But she came out and got in her car and left. And then he noticed someone else's car parked right over there, in front of that Portajohn. See it? Want to know whose car it was? It was Mr. Hagedoorn's."

"So? That doesn't mean anything."

"My uncle waited for Mr. Hagedoorn to leave, and then he went in and looked around. Do you know what he found?"

"No."

"A woman's slip."

"Oh." I imagined it, Annajane's uncle picking up a woman's slip— a couple of yards of sheer, static-charged material—in one of his big, bony, dry fireman hands. But no, it was raining yesterday, and humid. There wouldn't have been static.

"I heard my uncle telling Papa that he must be a very desperate fellow, because the floorboards are full of splinters and tacks, and there's no furniture or anything. But Mommy said that they probably brought a blanket with them."

"Oh," I said. "And who do they say the woman is?"

"They don't know."

So, he really had done it. No longer would Mr. Hagedoorn walk among the shelves at night, weeping for what he couldn't have. But why would he meet a woman at this rough place, rather than take her to the upper ladies restroom of the library, where he could make love to her comfortably on an overstuffed couch?

It was completely dark before we'd gotten even halfway home. We walked shoulder to shoulder in the cool, rainy breeze, talking in low voices. Annajane said that she liked my stepmother, and I nodded. Annajane asked if there was anything we should talk about as each other's spiritual sisters and I shook my head and shrugged my shoulders. Annajane said she wasn't scared about walking in the dark through poor neighborhoods because she knew the Lord walked with us. I asked her if she thought that Mr. Hagedoorn's lover was as guilty as he was.

"She's not quite as guilty," she said.

"But she went right along with him, didn't she? It takes two." That's what Ginger would have said.

"Yes, but now you have to consider the emotional aspects," Annajane said, clenching her eyebrows together. "A man plays at love to find sex, but a woman plays at sex to find love." That was straight out of a tract called "Tuff Talk about Sex" on the vestibule book table at the F.R.C. of V. "The guilt is just the same," she said, "just like for Adam and Eve. But their punishments should be different because men and women are just, now, you know, different. God will probably punish the woman by stopping up her womb or putting a prideful nature in her children."

"Maybe she doesn't want any children," I said. "So she wouldn't care about her womb being stopped up."

"Every woman wants children deep inside," said Annajane.

As we walked back near the Black neighborhood, a voice called out to us from a porch. "What are you girls doing out in the dark there?" I turned and saw an old woman sitting behind us in the dim light of a porch lamp.

"We live over on Beatenbough," Annajane replied.

"What do you call yourself?" the woman asked.

"Carolyn Grietkirk and Annajane Ten Kate." Annajane answered for both of us.

The old woman waved us away. "Get on home," she said, "you got no business being out after dark. Get on home."

"The Lord is taking care of us," shouted Annajane.

The woman held up her hand and bowed her head.

When we reached Annajane's house, her mother bustled angrily out to the driveway. She had been opening and closing the front door for forty-five minutes now, she said, looking for us to come up the sidewalk.

"You worry too much, Mommy," said Annajane. "It's ridiculous."

Mrs. Ten Kate didn't answer this. She demanded that we come in and take off our wet clothes. We obeyed and said no more about our walk. But I was going to ask Ginger about it later.

Later that evening, I spoke to Phuong again. She was in the kitchen, washing up the last of the supper dishes. I talked to her while she sponged tiny droplets of water from the stainless steel sink knobs.

250

"How did you get your scar, anyway?" I asked. I had been curious about it.

She raised her eyebrows and kept her eyes on the work. "My scar?" she said in a sharp, high voice, the one she used more for me than anyone else. "A man giving it to me with the knife."

"Why?" I said. "How did it happen?"

"He has cut me."

"On purpose?"

"Yes."

"You mean he wanted to hurt you? Was he crazy or something?"

"Maybe."

"How did you get away from him?"

Her sponge flew furiously across the stainless steel. She grabbed a can of Comet and shook some out onto the counter. She attacked the formica.

"How did you get away?" I asked again.

"I have not get away."

"You mean—what do you mean?"

She pressed her lips tight together. The muscles in her chin dimpled up. I had seen it happen before, when she was working hard. Maybe that's all it was now, just a funny expression she made as she put more effort into the sink.

"O.K.," I said, "so don't tell me if you don't want to. But sometime you should tell me. I can understand anything." I turned and left the kitchen. For now I had no further thoughts on the subject.

eginning on Monday morning, I tried to live out my promise not to sin. I sat in the bath for a full two hours reading the Bible, until Grandma knocked on the door and called, "Carolyn Grietkirk? Are you alive in there? Have you drowned yourself?" I sat for just a second longer praying, "Lord, let me be conformed to the image of your son Jesus Christ." I got out and stood on the cherry red bath rug and examined my face in the mirror. Grandma gave a lot of credence to the way she saw herself in glass. My face this morning was a mystery. My eye was healing, slowly. It had turned from black to orange. But I looked uncertain. I stared at myself, wondering.

"Carolyn," called Grandma impatiently.

"Yes, ma'am, coming. Here I am." I opened the door, pulling a bathrobe around me.

"You must be a Baptist, Carolyn, the way you practice immersion. Now get your clothes on. This is my big cleaning day; I need all hands."

I put on overalls and sneakers and presented myself for service. There was no arguing. It was time to wash the walls, to polish the furniture, to beat out the rugs and brush-scrub them with ammonia water, then wax the planks underneath. Nothing would be overlooked, no strip of molding or window ledge. Grandma had sharp eyes.

"I need you, too, Jo," she said as my aunt moved slowly past us through the living room, fanning herself with a women's magazine. Aunt Jo had stayed in her room all of Sunday, claiming to have the stomach flu. This was my first sight of her since Saturday night, when I had waved good-bye to her and Ginger in Ginger's driveway.

"Mama, I'm hardly awake yet," she said. "You go on and have fun without me."

"Listen, you," said Grandma, and my aunt paused with her hand on the front door. "Your big brother is coming tomorrow. You know how fussy he is about everything."

"I'd forgotten."

"I'd like to have the house clean for Jim."

"I'd love to help but I'm still feeling poorly."

"Oh, you are, are you? Well, bless me; I'll have to let you off this time. But you tell me, before you disappear again, how was that ladies retreat with Mrs. Jordan? Did you have a good time?"

"I had a wonderful time, Mama," said Aunt Jo. She glanced at me as she pushed the door open. It clapped shut behind her.

Grandma sighed. "Let's just get to work then."

Together we hauled the big rugs out back, Grandma and Phuong and I. We slung them over the sturdiest clotheslines and whacked them hard with old brooms. I was the strongest of the three of us. My broom cracked loudly on the blue foyer rug with the verbina pattern. The noise rang on the Brinkerhoffs' tool shed. Father called out from the kitchen window, "Hit 'em again, ladies!"

And then it was back inside again, porting the rugs between us, one under each arm, until we had made three trips. Grandma handed a pail of ammonia water to Phuong. She gave me a pair of yellow gloves that came up above my elbows. They happened to be the only pair. Phuong wore a short dress and was prepared to work next to me on her bare hands and knees, which were already red and knobby from daily chores.

"Here," I said. "You take the gloves."

"No, no," she said, "you wear."

"But look at your hands. You'll rub them raw."

She shook her head and dipped her brush in the pail. Right away she got to work scrubbing the rug. Her arms were brown cords of muscle. No loose flesh jiggled under her elbows as she scrubbed, which is more than anyone could have said for me.

"Don't miss those spots in the corner, Carolyn," Grandma said. "You know the ones I mean. I want this house godly clean." Grandma's favorite Bible verse was Ephesians 5:27: "That he might present it to himself a glorious church, not having spot, or wrinkle, or any such thing; but . . . holy and without blemish."

Phuong abandoned herself to scrubbing. She grunted roughly at each jerk of her arm. Her whole body shook when she scrubbed at the gold stain in the corner of the carpet that had been there for years and years, probably put there by some long-dead pet. I scrubbed hard, too. I felt a sudden pain in my thumb and stopped to look at it. It was nothing but a little splinter under my fingernail, but I said "Ouch," and pushed it out easily, with a drop of blood.

"Well, now I see that you're overdoing it," said Grandma to me. She was dusting the top of the buffet, momentarily swooping up an African violet from a purple lace doily. "Jim's opinion of our house isn't so important that I want blood spilled for it. You know, I just realized that Phuong has never met Jim. You've not yet met my oldest boy, have you, Phuong? Well, you're in for an experience. Jim is something, isn't he, Carolyn?"

"Yes, ma'am," I said.

Grandma paused as we kept working. "I don't suppose I'll get to see my soap operas while Jim is here. You know how he feels about them."

"Why don't you watch them in your bedroom?" I said. "We won't tell."

Now Grandma smiled. She liked the picture of herself doing this, but of course she wouldn't do it. "I'd be just like Phuong here," she said. "I'd hide away in my bedroom all day and watch my stories." Phuong looked up, confused.

"Grandma's teasing you," I told her. "We all know you're in there studying your Bible." Phuong shrugged her shoulders and nodded, but her look said, "Am I shirking my duties somehow? Am I not washing enough carpets? Am I not sweeping, mopping, bleaching, mending, stripping, waxing, scalding, scouring, dusting, and buffing enough? Are you unhappy with me?"

"Oh, tell her it was a joke, Carrie," said Grandma. "She doesn't understand, then. That's how we are here. We like to joke about ourselves. We don't take ourselves so seriously that we can't laugh now and then."

"You work harder than anyone in this house," I said to Phuong.

The phone rang, and I went to it first. Nathan passed by me in his bathrobe, on the way to the television set with a bowl of Sugar Smacks. He had spent the last week watching a horror film festival. I felt glad to sit down alone in the kitchen, with the breeze from the window on the back of my neck. The sunlight fell full and sharp in the corners of the room. I saw more dust to be swept away, more gray grime to be bleached and eradicated.

"Hello?" I answered.

"Hey, kiddo." Ginger's voice was rough.

"Are you all right?" I asked.

"Listen, kiddo, I'm so sorry. I feel so bad about yesterday morning."

"That's all right."

"No, it's not. I told you I would get you to church and I didn't. I don't know what happened. I had an attack of selfishness. I just needed the sleep."

"That's all right."

"To be perfectly honest, I had the hangover of my entire life. It was like a truck ran right over my head."

I smiled, because I was her confidante again. "That's all right," I said. "I don't mind. Are you feeling better?"

"Well, I have to feel better now, because Frank's back. He doesn't have time for other people to feel bad. Did your aunt get home all right?"

"I guess so. She's here now."

Ginger laughed. "I like that old girl. I guess that's where you get your good nature, kiddo."

"From my aunt?" I asked.

"Don't you think so? She's a great girl. Like you."

"Maybe," I said hesitantly.

"Don't tell anyone about my hangover. I don't want Frank to know. Don't mention to Frank that I went out Saturday night."

"Of course not," I protested, "what do you think I do? Tell on my friends?"

"Well, Carla, I know you have a little crush on Frank."

"I do not." I was shocked at the suggestion. I did like Frank. He was handsome and kind. But he was Ginger's husband.

"Now, don't be embarrassed," she said. "A lot of women are attracted to Frank."

"I'm not embarrassed, Ginger, but I don't have any old crush on Frank. I couldn't care less about Frank."

"Come on, kiddo, you can tell me."

"There's nothing to tell."

"Yes, there is. Frank told me about the towel. Come on—"

"Shut up, Ginger, I don't have a crush on Frank." Had I really told Ginger to shut up? There was a pause.

"All right," she finally said, a little stiffly. "I'm sorry. Are you mad at me?"

"No," I said. "But I don't have a crush on Frank."

"O.K., you don't have a crush on Frank. Is that all you want me to say?"

"Well, I guess I'll see you on Wednesday night then," I said.

"No," she said, surprisingly. "On Wednesday I want you to go to prayer meeting like a good little girl. I'll see you Tuesday and Thursday."

"But what about Wednesday?"

"Al wants Henry and me for a private rehearsal that night." She giggled. "Sounds dangerous."

"Don't you need a baby-sitter on Wednesday?" I didn't want to leave her alone with Henry.

"No. It's just a little dance rehearsal. I'll make Al hold the baby. Won't that be just great?"

"Couldn't I come watch?"

"Got to run, kiddo. Remember, rehearsals on Tuesday and Thursday. Love ya."

"I love you, too, Ginger."

I hung up the phone and went back out to the living room, where Grandma had now removed the heavy drapes from an ancient and brittle set of curtain rings. It was a delicate job that she did only once a year. The rings would crack and come apart, and she would glue them together again with adhesive that was certainly more expensive than a new set of curtain rings. The warm air in the house was ripe with ammonia. This was the smell of relatives coming to visit, of the family being together after so many years. My eyes watered. I started to feel choked.

"Who was that on the telephone?" said Grandma.

"It was just Ginger," I said.

"What did Mrs. Jordan want? Did she want to speak to your aunt? Jo is on the porch."

"Ginger wants me to baby-sit tomorrow and Thursday instead of Wednesday."

"What? But your uncle is coming tomorrow."

"Remember, Grandma? Ginger told you she'd be needing me a lot this week. You said it was fine."

"No, it's not fine," Grandma said simply, and turned back to her work. "Your uncle is coming tomorrow and this time the answer is no." I began to argue. Grandma held up her long fingers. Meanwhile, Phuong worked away at a black rubber heel mark on some molding near the foyer archway.

"Oma, what if Father says it's O.K.?" I said. "Then would you change your mind?"

Grandma looked at me sternly. "Your cousins are coming, Carolyn. You can't run out at night with your uncle here. What will he think?"

"What does he care? He never talks to me."

"Of course he talks to you. He talks to everyone."

"No, not to me. He hates me."

"Ridiculous. He loves you. He's your uncle."

"He couldn't care less about me. Why do I have to stay here when he doesn't care one way or the other?"

Surely Grandma would have answered that it was plain good manners not to run out on your guests, that the Lord wanted us to show hospitality even to those who treated us badly. But something drew our attention away so that the conversation was forgotten. Suddenly Phuong reared up on her haunches and stared at me. For a moment I thought she was going to upbraid me again, in front of Grandma this time. But she only made a gurgling sound and flailed her hands against her sides like fins. Grandma turned. Phuong gave us a pleading look,

257

then slung her scrub brush sideways into the empty white wall by the piano and fell back on one shoulder. The brush clattered to the floor.

"Well, what in the world?" Grandma got up quickly. Phuong couldn't answer. She arched her back and snapped it down against the hard polished floor. She writhed and twitched, bicycling against the floor, leaving streaks on the wood with her neat black shoes, while on the wall three streams of dirty gray water arched out in random directions from a new crack in the plaster. Grandma would be mad about the crack, but that was nothing to think of now. She knelt down beside Phuong, trying to get a hold on her, studying her like an appliance that needed switching off. Phuong's thin body twirled around like a garden hose about to burst, a live wire. Her head thunked up and down.

"Settle yourself," Grandma said to her shakily. She sounded afraid. "Settle yourself. Carolyn, where's your father?"

"He went out somewhere," I said. I drew back nervously while Grandma stretched out her arms and took Phuong hard around the shoulders to stop her from pitching into a leg of the piano.

"Settle down," Grandma said. "You're just agitated. You're going to hurt yourself."

"Let's take her outside," I said. "She might need fresh air."

Grandma nodded. "Maybe you're right, Carrie."

We picked Phuong up under her armpits, still jerking helplessly, and dragged her out the front door onto the porch steps. There we laid her down and posted ourselves on each side of her. Aunt Jo came over to help. "Should I call a doctor?" she asked loudly. "Should I? What's the matter with her?"

"A little agitation," said Grandma. "She'll be herself in a minute." Grandma bent over Phuong again and held her. Aunt Jo and I stepped back and watched, shaking our heads.

"I bet it's a seizure," I said. "I saw a boy at school have one."

"If it is a seizure," said Grandma, "then there's absolutely nothing the doctor can do. He'll just charge your father thirty dollars to tell her to take it easy."

"Mama, that's crazy," said Aunt Jo. "That's just crazy. They have drugs these days."

258

"Call the doctor if you want," said Grandma. "It's up to you, but you'll have to explain it to Davey."

Aunt Jo grumbled. "Just because you haven't been to a doctor in twenty years, you think nobody else should go either." She went in the house.

Grandma frowned and blinked but didn't say anything. It wasn't long before Phuong seemed to recover. "Breathe, honey, breathe deep," Grandma said in a kindly way, patting her hand. "You'll feel all right in a minute. That's the way; just relax. You're among friends."

Phuong took deep breaths until her breathing slowed. Her eyes closed. Her mouth hung open. Her arms and legs were loose now and still, just twitching occasionally like the last kernels of popcorn snapping in a pot. She made a croaking noise and gasped for breath again.

"She looks pretty sick," I said. "We should make sure she's off her back in case she upchucks."

Grandma looked up at me and out at the cars going by. I knew she worried that Phuong might throw up right there on our front porch, right there in front of the whole world, right there beside our rose bushes. We started to lift Phuong to roll her over, but she opened her eyes and motioned to us that she was all right. She sat up slowly and breathed into her hands.

"Are you feeling better?" said Grandma loudly. "Phuong, are you feeling better?" Phuong nodded. "Why don't you get her walking?" said Grandma to me. "That'll free up her circulation."

"Oh, I don't think she's strong enough for a walk yet, Grandma," I said. "She needs to sit here and rest."

"I think she'll be O.K.," said Grandma. "Right now her blood's all dammed up. You need to get her circulation working." Phuong nodded weakly.

"She sure doesn't seem strong enough," I said.

"Don't take her very far. Just get her legs moving. Exercise is the best medicine for everything."

At first, Phuong could hardly stand. Together we hauled her to her feet and hung her arm over my right shoulder. She took a minute getting her breath; then we began to walk. Grandma nodded and waved to us as we went up the driveway. Phuong walked at a baby's pace, her knees slightly bent and the wide toes of her small feet pointed in. I kept my eye on her to avoid bumping heads as we walked close. She watched the ground, clenching her jaw shut. Slowly, the two of us walked down the path to the sidewalk, down the street a short ways, across the road at the pedestrian marks to a little dirt path that led back to the library green, where the librarians ate lunch in the summer. It wasn't far.

"Just a short walk!" Grandma shouted behind us.

"Can you make it?" I asked Phuong.

She nodded. I led her around the corner to a picnic table and she collapsed on her back on one of the benches. She squinted up into the sunshine, licking her lips in the breeze.

"Are you feeling better?" I asked, still worried. "My grandma really thinks that exercise helps everything. But I don't know." Phuong nodded. "Have you ever had a seizure like that before?"

"Yes," she said.

"How often does it happen?"

"Sometime."

I looked at the shadow of my own head and shoulders stretched across the red wood planks. Phuong closed her eyes as the wind lifted glazed threads of her pure black hair. She stretched her arms over her head as though she were sunbathing. What a strange picture we made. A few feet away was a high, smooth corner of the library, a fall line between red light and gray shadow. We sat in a silence that was so natural to her and to me, too, though at that moment I would have liked to hear my own voice or footsteps or cars or even an air conditioner buzzing away in a window. I could think of nothing else to say. It didn't seem polite to quiz her about the illness.

"If you're feeling better," I said to her after a while, "maybe we should go back."

She lifted her head a little. Her hair spilled over her neck. "I don't want to go," she said.

"Why not?"

"Your grandmother see me."

"That's nothing to worry about," I said. "What's the matter with that?" She groaned and started to cry. "Come on," I said. "It's no big deal."

"I'm ashame," she said.

"Well," I said, "at least your seizure didn't happen in church, or in the grocery store." She nodded. "Don't worry about my grandmother," I said. "You just rest, no matter what she says."

"I can wait here a little longer," she said. "That's better. You go."

"It doesn't make any difference," I said. "Whatever you want, I'll wait."

We did wait for a while, until we saw a pair of young boys staring at us from a second-story window. Then I helped her to her feet and we finished the circle around the library, crossed the street, and met my aunt coming after us.

"What kind of crazy idea was this?" she asked me. "What possessed you to take her off walking in her condition?"

"Grandma told me to," I said.

"Well, use your own good sense sometimes." Aunt Jo sounded disgusted. She took Phuong over her own shoulder and practically carried her back to the porch.

Grandma waited for us with her hands in her apron pockets. Her face was anxious. "How is she feeling?"

"She's better," I said.

"I told you so. I bet the blood was just dammed up, or she'd be worse by now."

"Is that how your medicine works, Mama?" said Aunt Jo. "Either the patient gets better or she falls down dead?"

"Well, you can take her over to see Dr. Wolcott this afternoon if you're so worried," said Grandma. "He'll have the right kind of medicine, I expect. I wish Davey was here."

"You go on to bed right now," said Aunt Jo to Phuong. "You need rest. I can help with the cleaning."

Phuong opened her mouth to say something, but she stopped short, glancing between my grandmother and my aunt. She nodded slowly and went upstairs. Later, she and Aunt Jo left for the doctor and stayed away most of the afternoon. Father came home before they did and listened to Grandma's version of the story in the kitchen.

"I wish you'd been here, Davey," I heard her say. "I wouldn't know what to do if this happened all the time."

"I'm sorry, Mama," he said. "One of these days we'll be off on our own and you won't have so much on your shoulders."

"Oh, Davey, don't even say such a thing. You're no burden. It's just that I don't know how to take care of these things by myself. I'm not trained."

"I think you handled it all just perfectly, Mama," said Father. "You're doing fine." And he kissed her on the cheek.

The next day Grandma boiled all the china on account of an article in the *Christian Woman's Almanac* listing twelve diseases that can breed in the pores of ceramic dishes. Aunt Jo slept late. Nathan woke up at noon and went back to the horror film festival.

My father was home and sat at the kitchen table writing letters on aerogrammes. I sat beside him and wondered what he was writing to his friends overseas, how he was describing all of us. Was he sending them jokes from the Dutch Falls *Trumpet*?

"What did you find out about Phuong?" Grandma asked. "What did Dr. Wolcott say?"

Father sighed again. "He wants her to take some medicine."

"For her blood?"

"I'm not sure just what it's for, Mama, but it's supposed to help."

"Well, that will be expensive, I imagine."

"No, because Phuong won't take it, anyway."

"And why not?"

"She believes in healing, Mama. She wants God to heal her."

"That's the most ridiculous thing I've ever heard."

"Then you need to go back and read your New Testament."

Grandma sighed. "If the doctor says she needs medicine, and we know what a good Christian man he is, then don't you suppose he knows what he's talking about?"

"You're preaching to the converted," he said. "I'm not against medicine. Phuong is."

"Oh, my. Foolishness, utter foolishness." Grandma shook her head.

At one o'clock the doorbell rang. No one doubted that it was my uncle at the door. Though he wasn't due to arrive until five, we knew to expect him early. We quickly prepared. We threw the last clean lunch dishes out of the drainer and into stacks on the cupboard shelves. We put away stray pens and pencils. We changed the calendar to August rather than July. This all took two minutes. Now who would go to open the door? Aunt Jo was presumably still in bed. Phuong was upstairs. So the rest of us went together. Father, Grandma, and I moved swiftly into the living room and opened the door to the porch, expecting to meet a row of glad faces. Instead we found Aunt Jo sitting on the porch swing in a dressing gown and curlers, staring quietly at Jim and Betsy, with Victoria, Shirley, and Zachary lined up sour-faced in front of her. After a quiet moment, the family shifted to face us at the door. They were all dressed up and tan from a weekend at Virginia Beach. Except for the sour faces they looked like a perfect picture in a church directory.

"Well, what are you all standing there for?" shouted Father. "Come in, come in. Jo, you're welcome to get up and act friendly."

My aunt stood up. "I am acting friendly," she said. "I just don't look friendly. I'm not feeling well."

"That the way they wear their hair in New York?" asked Uncle Jim, pointing to her curlers.

"That's the way *I* wear my hair in New York," she said.

"Welcome home, JoJo," said Aunt Betsy. She kissed Aunt Jo and made the girls kiss her. They gave her the small smiles they gave everyone else and turned away quickly. Then Jim came in and leaned down to kiss her, too, with a sniff. He looked like a dog sniffing a hand to make sure it was familiar. "Jo, you haven't changed a bit," he said.

"You've gotten kind of fat," Aunt Jo said.

"So have you." He ushered his family into the house. Victoria and Shirley started toward the T.V.

"Oh, no you don't," my uncle said. "No television until we've sat here as a family for at least—what do you think, Betsy—fifteen minutes?"

"Whatever you think, Jim," replied my aunt.

"I have to use the bathroom," said Shirley. "Daddy wouldn't stop at a gas station the whole way and I'm about to explode."

"Shirley," said Aunt Betsy, "that's not ladylike. Just run to the bathroom and come back quickly."

"No, she can wait a little longer," said Uncle Jim. "Shirley, you sit there by little Carolyn. Victoria, sit here by me. I'll hold onto Zach. Come here, buddy. Come here and sit with your old man."

Shirley sat down beside me with her legs crossed tightly and stared at the empty wall. Aunt Betsy came over and touched her thumb to my black eye.

"What in the world happened, Carolyn?"

"I had an accident," I said. "I fell down."

"I should say so! You're very blessed that it wasn't worse. Things are usually worse. Poor little precious." She patted me and went back to my uncle.

"Well, Josephine," said Uncle Jim, "it's been a long, long time." He hoisted his left ankle up to his right knee and slapped his shoe. "Yes, it has. How they treating you up North, Jo? Have they figured out yet that you're more trouble than you're worth?"

"Jim," said Grandma, "wait till you see Jo's boy, Nathan. He is so big and strong. But I'm a little worried about his asthma."

"Mama's worried about him breathing my cigarettes," said Aunt Jo with a smile, and Grandma sniffed and looked away.

"You still smoking those cancer sticks?" asked Jim.

"Why," she said, "you want one?"

"No, ma'am."

"Jo," said Grandma, "don't you want to ask Nathan to come and be social for a while?"

"If you want to try and drag him away from that tube. He's addicted to it, you know. He has seizures if you tear him away too quickly."

Grandma looked nervous, as if worrying that the mention of seizures would take the conversation in unpleasant directions. But she called out, "Nathan! Nathan, dear! Don't you want to turn that T.V. off and come meet your cousins? They're two very lovely girls."

"Nathan!" yelled my aunt, "get yourself in here!"

Nathan hunkered into the room and dropped his huge legs on the couch between Father and Grandma. Uncle Jim leaned over to shake his hand.

264

"Well, you're going to be a football player," said Jim. "You like football, Nate? Want to be a linebacker?" Nathan shrugged.

"He's too gentle-natured for sports," said Aunt Betsy. "He doesn't have the killer instinct like you, Jim."

"That's too bad," said Jim. "Nate, you come spend a summer with me. I'll teach you about killer instinct."

"Thanks," said Aunt Jo, "but I can teach him all he needs to know. He likes his comic books and he likes T.V. I guess those are his hobbies."

"Some hobbies," said Uncle Jim.

There was a pause. Zachary cried out.

"May I go to the bathroom?" asked Shirley.

"All right," said Uncle Jim. "But come right back. You hear?"

"Finally," said Shirley, and she bolted up from her chair. Victoria followed, giggling.

"What about Phuong?" I asked Grandma after they had been gone a minute. "We're all down here in the living room. Shouldn't she be here, too?"

"Oh, Phuong," Grandma said. "Well, I guess so. Did anyone call her? Davey? She's probably not well." My father shook his head silently.

"Remind me how you say that name," said Uncle Jim with a funny squint. "I've been practicing."

"Phew-ong," said Grandma, sticking out her lips to enunciate. He nodded. She started to get up, but Father said, "Carrie, why don't you run up and get her? Spare your grandmother a trip upstairs."

I obeyed gladly. The air in the living room was stuffy and pungent. It wasn't the smell of ammonia now. Maybe it was sweat, or garlic that somebody had eaten for lunch. I walked up the wooden steps in my bare feet to the second-story landing. The air was cleaner up here, but hotter and harder to hold in your lungs. I went to Phuong's door and knocked.

"Yes?" she said.

"It's Carrie. May I come in?"

"Yes."

Although my father's room was right next to mine, I had never been inside, at least not since Phoung came. I opened the door slowly and looked in.

"Come," said Phuong. She had been cloistered away most of yesterday and today, resting. Father had brought her her meals. Her color looked better now. She sat in a little chair at the desk near the window, watching the street. Here was her little lamp I had seen from the library window. It occurred to me that we must have often been looking out at the same time. If anyone had passed by below, they would have seen two faces, a woman's and a girl's, gazing at the world like strangers on a bus. A sewing machine sat on a little table in one corner. The double bed had been made neatly.

"Your room looks nice," I said. "I haven't been in here before."

"Thank you."

"Is this where you study the Bible all the time?" I pointed to her desk.

"Sometime."

"I used to play and read in this room when it was empty."

"You can sit down."

I sat on the side of the bed. I looked at the small photographs on the desk, next to a neat stack of books and a ticking clock. "Is that your father?" I pointed at a tiny, sepia-toned studio photograph of a sober, middle-aged Asian man, with a suit and a walking stick. She nodded, looking pleased that I had guessed.

"He's handsome," I said.

She nodded. "He was teacher, and businessman."

"Do you have any more pictures? I like looking at them. Grandma says I should be a photographer, the way I like pictures."

"I don't have more," she said. "I carry this a long way, sew it in my dress."

"Oh." We gave each other the vaguest smiles, and then I said, "I came to tell you that the family is all downstairs. My uncle is here. They want you to come down."

She looked fearfully at the clock. "I think he is coming at five o'clock."

"He's always early. Just like Grandma. I told them I'd go get you. You don't have to worry about anything. Aunt Betsy is nice; you'll like her."

266

She pushed in a drawer on her desk. Her face tightened. "Oh, I not coming, Carolyn. Because I feeling so sick. I feel so sick after yesterday."

"I told you not to worry about that," I said. "Nobody saw you except us. You shouldn't be embarrassed."

"Well—" She put her hands to her mouth. It seemed reasonable to me that a person wouldn't want to meet my relatives, especially Uncle Jim, who could be frightening. But there was a brooding sadness in her face. I tried to lighten the mood with a joke, the way my father always did.

"But what if you have a baby sometime and he looks like my Uncle Jim?" I said. "Don't you want to know what you're in for?"

She didn't laugh at this, so I said, "Excuse me, I have to go downstairs now." I left her room, and I realized on the stairs how sweet the air upstairs really was, how it only became bitter as I went downstairs again. I returned to the living room, where everyone sat perfectly still. A fan roared in the window. Nathan lay slumped down in the corner of the couch with his eyes rolled back in his head. Shirley and Victoria hadn't returned from the bathroom.

"Well?" asked Grandma. "Where is she? Is she coming?"

"Phuong can't come right now," I announced. "She's very tired."

Grandma looked relieved.

"Well, it is so hot today, I can't blame her," said Aunt Betsy. She sponged away sweat from her neck with the old pink pad of a compact. Uncle Jim grunted something about these old houses without air conditioning.

"Phuong hasn't quite recovered from jet lag," said my father. "She needs a lot of rest."

"She's been in poor health lately," said Grandma, shaking her head. "Just yesterday we had to take her to the doctor. I don't know what exactly he said, but I expect she'll need plenty of nursing from Davey and me. Davey is just a saint with her, bringing her meals. You know, she's been visiting another church on Wednesday nights. I don't know much about it. I don't say anything, either. I'm open-minded, or I try to be."

After a pause, my Aunt Jo snorted and laughed. "The doctor told me," she said with a sneer, "that Phuong's suffering from overexertion. In other words, she's been given the good old Dutch Falls welcome, which is basically a boot on the butt and an unspoken request to stay out of the way, please, until we need you to scrub a floor or wash dishes. And now she's laid up. What a surprise she doesn't want to attend church with us. It's a chore, isn't it Mama, keeping the servants in line?"

My grandmother's face suddenly went white, the way a blank screen pops up in the middle of a slide show. She fumbled for an answer.

"What in the world are you talking about, Jo?" said Aunt Betsy.

"Yes, explain that remark," said Uncle Jim, sticking out his lower lip like a bulldog.

"Record time, you all," my father said with a laugh. "Jim's in the door for ten minutes and already we're arguing."

"Oh, admit it, Mama," Jo said, turning to Grandma. "Phuong does five times as much work around here as anyone else and you know it."

Grandma stuck her own lower lip out and rose up in her seat. "She does as much as she wants and no more. If she's gone overboard, I'm sorry. I'm just stung by you, Jo. I never thought you held such a low opinion of me. The fact is that Davey has never said a critical word to me about anything."

"That's because Davey's your favorite," said Aunt Jo. "He would never say a harsh word to Mama."

My grandmother held up her hands. "That is not true. I do not have favorites. You must apologize, Josephine."

"Oh, come on now, you two," said my father, smiling nervously, "lighten up. Did you ever hear how many Yankee women it takes to screw in a lightbulb?"

"Who cares?" snapped Aunt Jo.

"Hey, that'd make a good punch line," said Father, and he laughed, but no one else did.

"I don't understand how Jo can say a thing like this," said Grandma in a trembly voice. "Right in front of my grandchildren. What has the devil put into her mind? What is she trying to do to me? Jim, you tell her that she's wrong about Phuong."

268

"You have a knack for rhyme, Mama," said Uncle Jim. "How do I know about the woman? I just got into town."

"I'm not trying to hurt your feelings, Mama," said Jo. "I'm just telling the truth as I see it."

"Oh, Lord," said Grandma. She looked up to heaven. "I've done all I could. I have tried to get along with Jo, but it will not happen." She stood up from the couch and went to her bedroom.

Uncle Jim looked at Aunt Jo. "Like I've always said, Jo, if you were mine I'd put you over my knee."

"Shut up, Jim," hissed Aunt Jo. "Stay out of this."

"Well, at least keep your big mouth shut from now on," he said, "so my kids don't pick up your rotten manners. Use a little prudence if you don't mind, in front of the children."

"I'll do as I please," she said. My father reached over and put his arm around her. Her face softened some, but her mind was not changed. She put her black sunglasses on, went out to her seat on the porch, and hardly spoke another word for the rest of the day.

Later that night, I decided that my only hope of going to rehearsal with Ginger was to tell another lie. So at the dinner table I told my grandmother that I had to spend the night with Annajane.

"Carolyn," said Grandma, "I told you you can't go out tonight."

"Well," I said, grinning nervously, "it's Annajane's birthday party, Grandma. It'd be rude not to go."

"Isn't anyone else going to her party?" asked Grandma.

"I doubt anyone else will come."

"But Annajane is such a pretty girl."

"She's a brat," mumbled Shirley near me.

I shrugged my shoulders.

"Isn't that just a shame?" said my father. "Nobody coming to that poor little girl's party. Let Carrie go, Mama."

"Please?" I said.

"Carolyn," said my father, "why don't you take Shirley and Victoria with you? Then Annajane would have three guests."

"Oh, well," said Grandma, "now there's a better idea."

"That's a beautiful idea," said Aunt Betsy. "The girls would love it."

"We would not," said Shirley. "I have to meet somebody tonight. I promised."

"Who?" boomed Uncle Jim. "I haven't heard about this."

"Billy De Ruiter."

"Who?"

"Jim," said Aunt Betsy, laying a plump pink hand on his large brown one, "you remember the De Ruiters. Phyllis used to work at the bank, years ago. Billy is her youngest."

Uncle Jim shook his head like a dog shaking off rain. "Phyllis De Ruiter from the bank?"

"Yes, Jim."

"Shirley," he said, "it's impossible for you to be seeing any De Ruiter boy."

"I agree," said Grandma.

"What's wrong with the De Ruiters?" asked Aunt Jo.

"It's that Phyllis De Ruiter," Grandma explained. "The gossip about her comes down just like rain around here."

"If you won't go to poor little Annajane Ten Kate's birthday party, Shirley," said Uncle Jim, "you won't go anywhere tonight. Victoria can go with Carolyn."

Shirley knocked over her chair and ran away in tears. My father turned to Uncle Jim and said, "Hey, Jimbo, little Shirley will be going back to Charlottesville in a week and what's to worry about?"

Uncle Jim looked at my father and shook his head firmly. "You don't know what it is to have girls this age, sneaking around with boys. I'll have a talk with her. She'll come around." He slowly placed his napkin on the table and went away with one large boiled potato uneaten on his plate. Leaving food was an offense in itself on most days. A silent conversation occurred among us now. Aunt Jo raised one eyebrow at my father as she drank a full glass of iced tea in large gulps. Grandma and Aunt Betsy locked eyes. Victoria sighed and chewed her food, glancing at me sharply. She certainly had no interest in Annajane's birthday party. I felt so sick over my ruinous lies that I could hardly eat.

*V*ictoria didn't complain aloud until we stepped outside together and I led her directly to Annajane's house. I had arranged for Ginger to meet us around the corner, out of sight. We walked quickly and crossed over a green yard and a row of bushes. We stepped into the back bakery parking lot. Victoria sighed and told me in her milky sweet voice that she would never forgive me for this.

"It won't be as bad as you think," I said.

"A whole night wasted," she said with a pathetic cry. "A whole night!"

I knew that she had been planning to wash her hair. It stood up hard in the air like a wire sculpture. Her face was stiff. I led us past the door of the house, into an alley, down a short dirt hill to a low wall built close beside the street that crossed ours.

"What are we doing now?" she asked. "Where are we going?"

"We're waiting for my best friend," I said, "and hoping we don't get caught."

"Who's your best friend? You mean Annajane?"

"No, I don't mean Annajane."

"We're not going to that dumb little party?"

"No."

"And your best friend has a car?"

"Yes. We're going to Richmond." This obviously encouraged her. She sat down and waited without further questions. While we kicked our feet over the wall and stared up and down the street at the passing traffic, someone walked up behind us. I turned cautiously, hop-

271

ing that it wasn't Annajane. It was Aunt Jo, picking her way carefully through the brambles on the hill, trying not to slide down into us. I made a place for her on the wall.

"I knew you weren't going to any party," she said. She sat down carefully. Her knees cracked and she groaned, "Carrie, you're in danger of hellfire for the way you lie to your grandma. Don't you know that?" She smiled. I was ashamed and so I didn't answer. I agreed that I was in danger of hellfire. I had asked Jesus into my heart three times before I realized I was only supposed to do it once. But maybe I wasn't a true Christian even yet—in 1 John it said, "Whoever abideth in him sinneth not. Whosoever sinneth hath not seen him, neither known him."

"Carolyn's turning out just like Shirley," said Victoria. "She'll be wild one day."

"Maybe so," said my aunt. "She's got good taste in friends, I'll say that. Ginger's the best." Just then Ginger's car scooted up. Aunt Jo threw open the front door and shouted too loudly, "Hey, Ginger! How's it going?"

"Hey, gal," said Ginger. "Climb in. Hey, kiddo. And who's this pretty girl?" She winked at Victoria.

"That's Vicky, my other niece," said my aunt. "She's a sweetheart."

"Good to meet you, Vicky," Ginger said with another wink. She pulled over a stack of Frank's books and a brush balled up with hair to make room for Aunt Jo in the front seat. Victoria and I settled on either side of Floyd.

"Is this cute little boy yours?" asked Victoria, smiling sweetly at Floyd.

"You mean Floyd?" asked Ginger. "Is he mine?"

"Yes, ma'am."

"He's mine all right, but I don't know if he's Frank's." She elbowed my aunt and they heehawed together.

"He's as cute as can be," said Victoria. "I have a little brother, just a teeny tiny bit older than him. I just adore babies." She smiled sweetly again.

"I bet they adore you, too," said Ginger. "Where did you get those looks? Is Grace Kelly by any chance a relative of yours?"

Victoria giggled. "I don't think so."

"Honey," said my aunt to Ginger, shaking back her straight blond hair and pushing it behind her large ears, "how'd you come up with a name like Floyd for that poor kid, anyway? I mean, you've got Peter, Paul, John, and Floyd. That's like wearing stripes with polka dots."

"I know," said Ginger. "It was cruel. I did it to irritate Frank."

"How so?"

"Frank said God had told him to call the baby Moses. So just for the heck of it I told him that I knew God wanted us to call the kid Floyd. I wouldn't back down, not for love or money."

"You mean you lied about God's will? You lied about it?"

"Yes, I did."

"And you led your poor husband astray?"

"It doesn't take much to lead Frank astray. Men are just children, really, aren't they?"

My aunt gave a rusty laugh. "Want a cigarette, Gin?"

"Not if they're those awful menthols of yours."

"You sound premenstrual tonight, Ginger."

"I sure am. I've got cramps. You know how it is."

"Honey, do I," said Aunt Jo.

They swapped stories about menstruation. During all of this, Victoria kept her face straight ahead, smiling and calm. I watched her from the corner of my eye, wondering what she thought about my best friend, about me.

"So how's Arnie?" said my aunt casually to Ginger. "Seen him?"

"Seen him?" sneered Ginger. "Not hardly. You know, I'm with kids all day. That's all I do. Why do you think I have time for librarians?"

"I thought about stopping over there—over to the library. It's just across the street."

"Why don't you?" said Ginger.

"Because I'm really not interested," said my aunt. "Like I told you the other night, I know he's just dying to talk to me. But I'm really not interested." She turned around and pointed her cigarette at me. "You don't listen to a word we're saying, Carolyn. Do you understand? Don't you ever tell a soul any of this or I will kill you."

273

"What about Vicky?" I said defensively. "Why don't you ask her not to tell?"

"Because she must know how to keep a secret. She lives with Shirley."

"So, tell me more," said Ginger to my aunt, with a slight smile at me in the rearview mirror. "Why do you think Arnie's so interested?"

"Oh," said Aunt Jo, "I know when a guy is interested. Thing is, Gin, I just don't want him. You know what I mean? I got a good guy back at home—or at least I had one—and I want him back. I don't need Arnie at this stage in my life, not when I'm down like this. He'd just wreck everything."

"No, of course not," said Ginger. She smiled at me again, quickly. I knew that she was playing a game with my aunt. "You wouldn't go out with Arnie if he asked you, Jo."

"No, honey, I wouldn't," said my aunt. "Not if you paid me. He's a loser. A loser librarian, that's what he is. I wish I'd known that years ago. I used to cry in my pillow over that loser. He's one reason why I left town."

"Oh, really?" said Ginger, clucking her tongue. "What a sad story. I'd like to hear it sometime over a beer. Beginning to end."

Neither of them said anything for a while. As we bumped along on an old road, I whispered some of my songs for the show. All week I had been practicing in secret for the difficult finale with Henry.

"Stop talking to yourself," said Victoria softly. "It's driving me crazy."

"I'm rehearsing," I said.

"Rehearsing for what?"

"You'll see. You'll see tonight. Ginger, is this right?" I said, and I started to sing, but Aunt Jo laughed so hard I had to stop.

"You better give up, Carrie. You're cursed from birth. There isn't a woman in our family can carry a tune in a bucket."

"I can," said Vicky. "I got my daddy's voice."

"Well, maybe you can be the next George Beverly Shea then," said Aunt Jo. "But Carrie here doesn't have a chance."

"Try singing a little lower," said Ginger to me, more gently than my aunt, but also smiling. I sang lower, but both Aunt Jo and Victoria still laughed heartily.

274

I mumbled, "If Ginger would teach me to sing like they told her to, maybe I'd get it right."

Ginger met my eyes in the rearview mirror. "I heard that. If it weren't for me, you wouldn't have the incredibly wonderful, incredibly unusual opportunity to be singing up there on a real live stage. How about a little gratitude?"

"I didn't mean anything," I said.

"The fact is I'm doing something very valuable for you."

"Yes, ma'am," I said.

Ginger shrugged and said to my aunt, "You know, I could refuse to drive this kid back and forth to Richmond, and then where would she be? What if I charged her for gas? Maybe I should. Maybe that would teach her how to be a little grateful."

I didn't have any answer. I leaned on my fist. My throat felt like a charcoal at the bottom of a grill, crushed and burning.

As we arrived at the Dela Fox, Ginger happily hummed the tune I had been trying to sing.

> See you in heaven if you ever drop by,
> We're building a mansion for three in the sky. . . .

She was still humming it later as Henry and I went over our dance steps with Myra. Al had called us up for a brief run-through of the finale while the rest of the cast took a break. There was no orchestra tonight, there were no dancers. Bob Ferring waited for us down at the piano, his eyes bulging up in his hollow cheeks so that he looked even more than usual like a martyr in the hands of musical infidels. I could see Mary Burrows and Tommy Depew gnawing on a chicken leg together back in a dark corner. Near them sat Dick Danson and Saul Anderson. Ginger and Al watched at the side of the stage, with Victoria and my aunt parked in the middle of the third row. I could see them across from us, just above the orchestra pit. They tapped their feet happily on the seats in front of them, gesturing at me and whispering into their palms. What were they saying? I looked to see if Victoria was awed by all of this, awed by me. I couldn't read her face. I almost never could. She looked calm and unsurprised, interested only in what my aunt was saying. I wanted her to be awed. I tried to look grand.

"Give us your attention, Carla!" said Myra Woods in her high, cackling stage voice. "Your mind is wandering!"

"I know, ma'am," I said. "I'm trying."

"Remember, you've got to make your leap on tempo, or you're going to throw Henry off. We don't want you down in the pit again."

"No, ma'am."

My aunt laughed out loud below me. I glanced down. Vicky looked dreamy and unamused. She yawned.

Henry seemed nervous. He tossed his head around, cracked his neck, pulled his knees up to stretch. Bob gave us an intro. Myra slapped out the beat on her wiry old dancer's thighs.

"O.K.," said Al.

"O.K.," said Myra. "And a one, and a two, and a one-two, up—"

I ran on tempo and vaulted into Henry's arms. Though his shoulders were slick with sweat, I got a firm hold in the spongy muscle around his neck. I wasn't going to fall. I threw my right leg over his back, pulled up, and wrapped my feet under his armpits, twisting them like keys in a lock. It was his turn to sing first.

> No more airplanes,
> No more ships,
> No more first class
> Business trips,
> I've deducted life away,
> Now I'm home
> And home to stay.

While Myra droned out the beat, Al called, "Don't slouch, Henry. Get those legs up."

Henry kicked higher and grunted with the effort. It was going well, I thought, but he cocked his head to the side and hissed at me through his teeth. "Stop digging your toes into my armpits."

"I can't help it," I said. "I don't want to fall again. Don't pinch my ankle like that."

"Get ready, Carla," said Myra. "Here you come, a three and—"

> No more nannies,
> No more rules,
> Good-bye expensive
> Boarding schools!
> So long to all of
> That forever,
> Cause Daddy's home and
> We're together—

Henry grunted like a pig.

"Come on, Henry," shouted Al, "you look like an old man up there. You look like a tired old man." He flopped around after us, clapping. "What's the matter, fatso? Pick it up."

"Choreography!" screeched Myra, "not boreography!"

"Forget it!" Henry cried suddenly, and stopped. He stamped his foot. "I won't! I just cannot do it!" He bent down and I slid off over the back of his neck, throwing my legs together before I hopped to the ground. It was like sliding off a horse.

"What's eating you now?" asked Al.

"I cannot do this scene with this kid. Either cut the scene or cut the kid."

"Come on, you're crazy. We open next week. I think she's improved a lot. Ginger's been putting her to the grindstone. Haven't you, Ginger, honey?"

Ginger wasn't there to answer.

"She doesn't jump on the beat," said Henry, "she doesn't come in on the beat, she can't sing, she strangles me with her feet. I'd rather have that Walter kid back, even if I have to pay him myself, even if I have to pay him a hundred dollars myself."

"Oh, I think you've got the performance jitters or something," said Myra Woods. "She's not so bad—Lord knows I've seen worse."

At the back of the auditorium, Saul Anderson piped up, "Once again, I cast my vote with Henry. Are there any other options?"

"Well, that's what I'm saying, Mr. Anderson," said Al. "There really are no options. It's just too late in the show to bring a new kid on."

"Let me be blunt, Al," said Henry, angrily now. "She's fat. There's no getting around that. She's fat. And I can't pick up some fat kid every show for three weeks. I'll throw my back out. I bet she weighs as much as Dianne. I want Walter."

"Why don't you just pick on somebody your own size for a change," said Dianne from the wings.

"The little girl's not that fat," said Al. "You're exaggerating. And it's too late to get Walter back."

"I just can't work with a fat kid," said Henry. "She's too fat." He put his head down and pouted. He turned his back to us and stood in a corner of the stage with his fists balled up against his thighs. It was a great dramatic moment, I thought. I wished I could have made a scene like that in front of all these people. The muscles on his back rippled under the lights. It was a beautiful thing. I stood there for a second too, but then I thought about my fat knees under my shorts. I went and stood beside Myra.

"You're not so bad," Myra said to me quietly. "You have no talent, but you're not so bad."

"I'm fat," I said morosely.

"You're plump," she said. "So what? Give Henry ten years. He'll be fat, too."

"Everybody out to the green room!" shouted Al. "Loosen up and wait for me. Five minutes, five minutes. Carla, you stay here. I want to talk to you." I shuddered at the thought of talking to Al alone.

"Oh, no," said Myra. "Not more of that vulnerability stuff. Good luck, little Carla." And she left me. The theater cleared. Dick Danson and Saul Anderson stepped out to the lobby, talking. Even my aunt left with Vicky. I watched to see the door close behind them.

When we were by ourselves, Al came and sat down next to me. This was the first time I had been alone with him. He was just the kind of man Grandma would have told me not to be alone with, big and perverse, with heavy lips and sinking eyes. But he only smiled weakly with his thick lips, like a man who didn't have much practice smiling at children. He caught hold of my collar and pulled me up against his side in a fatherly way, with his heavy arm on my shoulder.

278

"I hate to disappoint you, kid," he said. "You're not so bad. I can tell Ginger has been working on you real hard."

"I've been practicing all the time," I lied. "Even in my sleep."

"I'd give you another chance. In fact, you come around sometime and I might give you another chance. But not this time, honey. I feel like a big jerk."

I couldn't say anything. I stood there stiffly against him, looking at his oily leather boots, stretched ugly by his bunions.

"Who will you get to replace me?" I asked. "Walter Pinkney?"

"I have no idea. I don't have one single idea, but I'll have to find somebody."

"Oh," I said. That was the saddest thing I could have heard. I was worse than almost anyone.

"You can understudy," he said kindly, "if you want. I might get that desperate. I might need you."

"I don't want to be an understudy," I said, beginning to cry. "I want to act."

"Yeah, well. Why don't you come on in and do the workshop with us, anyway. You can say anything you want about Henry. Tell him what a jerk he is. It'll make you feel better." Al squeezed me twice, let me go, and I tried to smile at him. But I couldn't.

"I just want to go home," I said.

"I understand. I'd feel the same way. I'll tell you one more thing, in case it'll make you feel better. There's no way this show will last more than three weeks, not even with Danson's money, not even with Ginger."

"I think it can last," I said. "Ginger's the greatest. I bet it'll go all the way to Broadway."

He smirked and shook his head. "We got no nudity, we got no angst, no nothing. It used to be you could put a bunch of girls on stage in bathing suits and you had a hit. Nowadays you need girls in bathing suits talking about genocide or something. You need a neurosis. I ought to put Dianne on stage. She'd take me to Broadway."

I was surprised. "So why don't you quit?"

"Because it feels good to get back. Yeah, everybody needs a hobby. But three weeks; I give it three weeks."

"That's too bad," I said. "It was fun."

"Well, see you later, doll." A door opened somewhere in the hall and Al turned quickly on his heels. It was just Dick Danson in distress, looking everywhere for his precious Ginger. When anyone had shown faith in me, Al or Dick Danson or any of the others, it was because they believed that I was Ginger's daughter. Surely a daughter of Ginger's would sing and dance like an angel. But of course I wasn't Ginger's daughter, and there was no use pretending. I went into the enormous hallway behind stage and meandered for a while through the dark building. I saw a young male dancer holding Floyd, showing him the artwork on the wall. He described it in baby talk—"Pretty, pretty art deco, huh, baby? You like that, huh?" I passed them and went on. I went to the car and sat for an hour and a half alone.

Finally, Ginger came out with Victoria and my aunt. They came through the golden door laughing together. I wondered if my head looked pathetic in the car window, dangling sadly in the air like an old balloon. Maybe I looked like Phuong staring out at the world. They didn't seem to notice, though they became serious when they got close. Ginger carried Floyd and walked ahead of the others. She pulled the backseat door open with a loud creak and looked in at me.

"Pouting in here, huh?" she said. "Why'd you run out on us? I wanted to talk to you."

"I don't want to talk about it now," I said. "I couldn't find you."

"Al talked to me, kiddo. I'll call you tomorrow and we'll meet and discuss things."

I nodded. My aunt jumped into the front seat with a snort and adjusted her dress under her thighs. Victoria got inside and sat straight up on her seat, carefully guarding her hair. It was a long and quiet drive. When we reached my house, Ginger pulled quietly up to the curb, lights off. My aunt stayed in the car while we got out.

"Good night, Vicky," said Ginger. "Glad to meet you." She turned to me. "Night-night, kiddo, sleep tight. Don't worry about any little thing. I'll call you tomorrow. Love you." And she and my aunt drove away together, with no explanation as to where they were going.

Inside, Grandma sat in the kitchen alone. It was eleven o'clock, but she was drinking coffee. "Did you girls have a good party at Annajane's?" she said rather sharply. "I assumed you were going to spend the night." I thought that she must have called the Ten Kates and found out the truth.

"It was O.K.," we both said.

She nodded. Maybe she didn't know.

"Where is your Aunt Josephine?"

"We don't know," we said, and shrugged our shoulders. Did Grandma know that she had gone with us?

"That doesn't surprise me," Grandma said. "She just ran off tonight, without even a word to Nathan. I have no idea where she went. She has so little concern for her family's feelings. No better than when she was a child."

"Sorry, Grandma," I said, noticing that her lips trembled. I didn't want to see her cry again. I felt that it was my fault.

"I just want to know," she said, "do you think it's true, any of it, what she told me? Do you think I treat anybody disrespectfully?" She was speaking of what my aunt had said to her this afternoon about the way she treated Phuong.

"No, Oma," I said. "I don't think you treat Phuong badly."

"What do you think, Vicky?"

"I don't think you could ever treat anyone badly," said Victoria.

Grandma waved her hand. "I know I'm a sinner, but I do my best. I've opened my home."

"That's a lot," I said. "I think that's a whole lot."

Vicky and I kissed her and went upstairs without a word to each other as I turned off at the second floor and she kept to the stairs. That night I lay awake thinking about everything. When I drifted off to sleep, I was on someone's shoulders, singing to Grandma, to my father, to my aunt and uncle, and even to my cousins—"See you in heaven if you ever drop by, we're building a mansion for three in the sky . . ."

And then I was standing on a cliff. It jutted out from a mountain like a long finger or a hard fish stick. It plunged forward over clouds and flat, patchwork countryside thousands of feet below. A sign in the sky said, "On a Clear Day, See Seventy States." While I stood looking down, someone near me said, "Oh, look," and a girl rolled through my legs and over the end of the cliff quietly, without even a shout.

How strange. She dropped like a basketball, spinning gently in the air. A crowd behind me broke into applause. I took a bow and promptly woke up. But now I felt a weight on my chest, a choking warmth. Someone lay on me, stretched out flat and heavy like a dead or sleeping body. Someone! Had one of my cousins fallen through the ceiling? I opened my eyes and saw nothing. My hair stood on end. The air in my room was so dense that I thought I would die if I didn't get to a window. But I was pinned to the bed.

I closed my eyes again. "God," I said, "dear God. The Lord is my shepherd, I shall not want. He maketh me to lie down in green pastures; he leadeth me beside the still waters. He restoreth my soul. Yea, though I walk through the valley of the shadow of death, I will fear no evil; for thou art with me; thy rod and thy staff they comfort me."

I breathed again and my chest filled with air. I felt free now. I fell off my bed hands first, crawled to the window, and dragged it open with a shriek of the tight wood. Across the room lay my bed. I stared at it and then looked out the window, where the moon shone on our empty street. Over our lawn, over the library lawn, lay deep green quiet. But a panic came over me again. I ran out into the hall and down the stairs toward my grandmother's room. A light shone in the living room. Was Grandma still awake?

No, it was Phuong again. She sat on the couch, with her head against her hands. As I came in, she looked up at me. She seemed surprised, and almost smiled. "Oh," she said, "I am praying for you. God tell me. Will you come to church tomorrow?"

I didn't know what to say at first. I sat down.

"Will you come to prayer meeting tomorrow?" she repeated. "To my church?"

"Yes," I said. "O.K."

"Praise Jesus," Phuong said and held her hands up in a strange way, with her head tilted back as if the ceiling might drop down and kiss her on the mouth. I just watched, and pushed my hair down. Any company was welcome at a time like this.

16

*T*he next day, I could hardly eat. Ginger didn't call in the morning. I went to the library around lunchtime, expecting in a vague way to meet her there. But hadn't she told my aunt that she had no time to visit the library? When I came home, I asked Grandma if there were any phone messages.

"Well, no dear," she said. It wasn't her custom to take messages. She liked to say that she was no secretary. "What were you expecting?"

"I thought Ginger might call," I said casually.

"What about?"

"It doesn't matter."

"Why don't you call her?"

"Because she said she would call me." And it was true.

A short time later I mentioned that I would be going to prayer meeting with Phuong. Grandma looked perturbed, or maybe disappointed, and said, "I thought you were coming with us for a change."

"I'm sorry, Grandma," I said. "Phuong invited me. What could I say?"

"Carolyn. Why are you always going off to other churches? Is it because of me? Do I embarrass you?"

"No, Oma, of course you don't embarrass me." Why would she say such a thing? It annoyed me.

"You can go with other folks to those English churches if you want," she said. "If you want to go with your stepmother, goodness knows I wouldn't get in the way of that. It's out of my hands."

"I'm sorry, Grandma," I said. I walked out of the kitchen in mild

283

distress. For a while, I watched television with Nathan. Shirley giggled on the phone in the hall, probably to Billy De Ruiter. "What if Ginger were to call me right now?" I thought. "She couldn't get through." I went into the hall and tapped Shirley on the shoulder. She pushed me away. I tapped again and said, "I'm expecting a call." She rolled her eyes.

"I can tell on you," I said. "I know who you're talking to."

"Well, I can tell on you," she said. "I know all about what you did last night. I know all your secrets."

I left Shirley alone and went to see Annajane, but she was out of the bakery. I felt strangely abandoned. Mrs. Ten Kate sat alone, taking inventory. She was counting as I came in and held up her finger for me to wait. But after a minute of waiting, I got tired and went back home. I put on my modest bathing suit and sat and sunbathed in the backyard, near a patch of milkweed where a copper-colored butterfly skipped and hovered like a tiny kite. From this corner of the grass I would hear the phone ring, if it was going to ring.

Later that night after dinner, Phuong and I left the house and walked down Beatenbough. We kept going, past Bridge, past Church, past Deacon, toward the river. I assumed that we were taking a detour and that we would soon turn back to town. But we passed the convenience store and turned north. We kept going, toward the river.

"I've never seen any church down this way," I said.

"This is good church," Phuong said confidently.

"What church do you go to?"

"You can see," she said mysteriously. I thought she must be taking me to some church run by foreigners. She would translate the sermon for me under her breath and I would keep my eyes on my knees, embarrassed. We were heading north now by the same roads Annajane and I had taken just a few evenings before. We passed by the same dusty houses, the same junk piles and weedy carports that Annajane and I had passed by. We stopped short of the new neighborhoods, however, and turned onto a dirt road. A hundred yards down and over a mound of orange mud was the back of the Food Angel grocery store. Four giant truck shells snuggled up to its belly like nursing puppies. A big cooling unit roared and clucked at the side, throwing out meat smells. We passed around to the front and saw the sign thrusting up from the crumbly asphalt: *Templ of the Dov, Frnk Jrdan, Pstr. Come joi us fr pryr mting this Wedny.*

My soul rejoiced so that I felt gratitude even to Phuong. The idea of attending Frank and Ginger's church had never occurred to me, not in my wildest thoughts. It was a hopeful idea, now that I had spent a whole day wishing to talk to Ginger, unable to. Would she come to church tonight? Al had arranged for her to rehearse alone with Henry, but I felt that a miracle might happen. She might come. The parking lot sat empty. The windows of the grocery store were dark. Phuong led me up to the glass double doors of the store. We stood now on a little black welcome mat, the kind that led you to think the door would open automatically. When it didn't, I stepped forward and gave the door a push. The bolt thunked against the strike.

"How can the store be closed?" I asked. "It's not even dark yet."

Phuong shook her head. "The store is close early for church."

"Do you go here every Wednesday?" I asked her.

She nodded. "Two time."

"Is it really a good church?" I said incredulously. Because as far as I had seen, everything Frank put his hand to failed.

She nodded again. A van swung across the empty parking lot behind us. We both turned. The van stopped at the bottom of the parking lot, which was gently concave, like a shallow lake bed. Out of the trunk stepped a tall, skinny man. He sauntered toward us, his knees making sharp creases in his brittle jeans. He wore a plaid shirt unbuttoned to the chest and an oily braided leather strap around his neck. He was the sort of person I had met often at gas stations or at the softball field, but never at church. I had thought that such people didn't attend church.

"Y'all here for the meeting?" he called, coming up close.

We nodded.

"Praise Jesus," he said. "I been down at the river, for the baptism. Y'all going to see the rest of the folks coming any minute. It's just that I drive too fast for my own good. I always have to end up waiting for everybody else." He laughed and came over to stand with us. "Y'all been here before?" he said.

Phuong nodded. She held her Bible tight against her stomach.

"I go regular," he said. "My name's Oscar. My brother owns the grocery here, but he don't let me have a key. I don't remember you. What was your name?"

Phuong introduced herself quietly.

"And who's this little cutey?" he said to me. I didn't want to meet him. I stepped toward Phuong. When he put out his hand I smiled but bit my lips and looked away.

"We usually start by seven thirty," he said, "soon as they close the store down. But everybody's coming up from the river tonight." He looked carefully at Phuong. "You Korean?"

She shook her head again. "Vietnamese."

"Well I should of knowed that," he said. "But I was in Korea about twenty years ago and I can still speak a few words. I guess you don't know no Korean." He spoke a few sentences. Phuong shook her head. He leaned against the store wall with one hand above her head. She stared down and I turned away, pretending to watch the road.

Finally, a string of cars laced through the driveway like a funeral procession and circled the outer edge of the parking lot. Doors slammed. Men and women got out, hiked up their pants and yanked down their skirts, looked at each other in a familiar way, and walked over to us smiling. An elderly Black woman led the pack. Behind her came five or six White women with piled hair and long skirts, a young man with long blond hair and bare feet, a plump, pale girl with black hair reaching to her ankles, and a middle-aged Black man in a sports jacket and faded pink pants. Ten or twelve others straggled up gradually behind them. They looked at the orange-blue sky and murmured admiringly.

"You got here fast, Oscar," said the elderly woman to the man standing with us.

"Yes, ma'am," he said. "Where's Preacher?"

The man in pink pants came up quickly from the back of the crowd. "Preacher's bringing Mrs. Pritchett over himself," he said. "Worried about her driving alone." He turned to Phuong. "Ma'am, I've seen you here before but I haven't had the pleasure. I'm Dr. Peter Klingscales."

Phuong nodded and allowed him to shake her hand. I stood back.

"A blessing to meet you," said Dr. Klingscales. "You should have seen our baptism tonight." He turned to the others. "That was a beautiful baptism, wasn't it? Mrs. Pritchett was an inspiration."

"She's a sweet and savory offering to the Lord," said the elderly Black woman.

"Amen, Miriam," said Dr. Klingscales, and the woman bowed slightly. "Amen. Mrs. Pritchett is a savory offering, ninety-three blessed years of age."

"Ninety-four," said the plump White girl.

"Ninety-four and she got the Holy Ghost for the first time!" said Dr. Klingscales. "Praise the Lord. We praise you, Lord Jesus!"

There was something pastorly about Dr. Klingscales. Maybe he was Frank's assistant. I remembered that Dominie Grunstra had had an assistant one year, when Arnie Hagedoorn's cousin Fleming took a year off from his ministry at the Christian Reformed seamen's home in Norfolk. Fleming Hagedoorn always wore an oxford shirt and tie, even to Saturday ice cream socials in the summer. He always carried his Bible, even to church league basketball games, just in case he was called upon to teach someone something. Now Dr. Klingscales was looking up to heaven with raised hands. The rest of them, even Phuong, followed his lead. There was some throaty mumbling. "Praise you, Jesus; praise you, holy Lord Jesus." I stared at them, thinking that at the F.R.C. of V. the closest thing to mumbling was the doxology. Then Dr. Klingscales dropped his head and said, "Excuse me." He stepped forward, flattening his elbow to his chest to get around me. He stood up on the mat and tried the grocery store door. Did he think we hadn't tried it already? Did he think we'd been standing here outside for no reason? When the door wouldn't work, he looked up again and said, "That's O.K. Long as we're out here praising Jesus, that's what matters."

"Amen," they all said. "Amen."

He licked his lips. "Preacher's coming any minute now. He said he had the key; he told us we would just have to wait a little longer.

287

Reminds me of judgment day, people. Jesus is coming back, with the keys of the kingdom."

"Yes."

"Will you all be ready?"

"Yes."

"Will you all wait?"

"Yes. Praise Jesus."

I put my head down and stood against the wall. I wished now that I hadn't come. I had no faith that Ginger would appear among these people. Out on the street, a car pounded by, jangling loud music from its open windows. Preacher was a slow driver, someone in our little crowd said.

"Preacher drives godly," said Oscar, with a rattly laugh. "He sure does."

"That's why Mrs. Pritchett likes to ride with him," said Miriam. "She always wants to ride with Preacher. And she makes him go under fifty the whole way, even on the toll road."

While they laughed, the Jordans' station wagon came gently down the street. They waved to greet it. How many times had I ridden in that vehicle now? I knew it better than anyone here, I was willing to bet. Let them think it belonged to them. Let them think they owned the Jordans. I knew better.

"Is that the children with him?" asked Miriam, straining to see. She curled her fingers up like glasses and squinted through them.

"Yep," said the plump White girl. "He must have stopped at home to pick them up."

"How about Mrs. Preacher then? He fetch her too?"

"No, Mrs. Preacher ain't with him."

My heart fell. Of course Ginger wouldn't come.

"That's a shame then," said somebody.

The station wagon glided down in front of us. The passenger door opened in the front. An old woman climbed out carefully. Before she had both feet on the ground, three or four of the other women screeched and sucked her up in a long hug. Dr. Klingscales pumped her hand and kissed her right on the mouth. She wore a dry T-shirt, flip-flops, and culottes that showed thick crescents of blue calf under-

288

neath. Only her hair was wet. It was much shorter than the other women's. It lay straight down on her long forehead like a Roman senator's.

"Just as you were baptized with Christ in his death," declared Dr. Klingscales loudly, "so also live with him not after the flesh but after the Spirit!"

"Amen," said Miriam and the others. "Praise the Father. Praise Jesus. Oh, praise the Holy Ghost."

"Because I say unto you that the time is coming when they who worship him will worship in spirit and in truth."

"Amen."

Frank parked the car nearby and he and his boys got out of the car and ambled up to us. The boys were shirtless, as usual.

"Hallelujah," said Dr. Klingscales. "Preacher's here."

"Praise the Lord!" called Frank.

"Look at those fine boys," said Miriam.

"Yes, just look at them," said several other people, and they put out their hands and touched Peter, Paul, and John on their heads, saying, "Praise Jesus!" The boys followed close to Frank, holding onto each other.

"Preacher," said Miriam, "we're so sorry that Mrs. Preacher couldn't make it with you tonight."

"Well," announced Frank, "she sent you all her love." He walked behind Mrs. Pritchett and put his arm around her. How happy he looked in the middle of his friends. His hair was wet from the baptism, slicked back and reddish in the red twilight. "Sister," he said, "why don't you just do the preaching tonight?"

"Preacher," she said in a cracking voice, "I believe I could if you asked me to. I'm just so full of the joy and love of Jesus." She jumped and danced around in a feeble way and clapped her hands together.

"Amen," said Dr. Klingscales, and he clapped, too. His mouth twitched when he smiled.

"What a precious testimony," said Miriam.

"Bless you, sister," said Frank, and he kissed Mrs. Pritchett. Finally he took out his key and came toward the door. I tightened my smile, waiting to be seen. What difference did it make, anyway, if I was here?

Why should Frank care? He saw Phuong first and nodded. He kept coming then and not until he was exactly in front of us did he give me a blank look and stare for a second, in a kind of horror. After a pause, he smiled again, signaling that he was at ease again with everything. I held up my hand and waved, a modest gesture from someone who knew so much about him. I wondered if Ginger had told him that I had a crush on him. She would have announced it as a fact, not a suspicion.

"Well, hiya, Carla," he said. "This is a surprise. How you doing?"

"Fine," I said dully.

"Is she here to baby-sit?" asked Peter in a disgusted voice behind him.

"I don't think so, son," said Frank. "Carla, I'm glad you brought your stepmother back to us. She's really been a blessing to our fellowship."

Phuong smiled shyly and put her hand up to cover her mouth. Frank touched her shoulder. "Hope you'll share with us tonight, Mrs. Grietkirk," he said. "Tell these folks a little about yourself. They'd like nothing better than to get to know you." He fingered his keys.

Oscar said, "Nobody's shy when the Holy Ghost takes hold of them."

"I see you all met Oscar," Frank said. "He's a fine soul, aren't you, Oscar? You're looking fine. Where's your brother Orly tonight?"

"Orly sends his regards," said Oscar. "He had to run out for a truckload of frozen pizzas. Said he'd be with us in prayer."

"We're just waiting for the Lord to touch him," said Dr. Klingscales, his mouth twitching again. "The Lord told us a year ago that Oscar is going to be touched and his life will never be the same again. We're just waiting."

"That's what I'm waiting for," said Oscar. "I believe on it, if God said it."

"Said what?" said a woman standing off the curb, on the asphalt.

"Said he's going to be touched, said he's going to get the Holy Ghost," said another woman.

"But right now I'm just waiting for the meeting to start," said Oscar. "I'm willing to be touched or not touched, I don't ever say it'll be one way or the other."

290

I didn't know what Oscar was talking about, so I watched Peter, Paul, and John, who had gained confidence again and stepped away from their father. They shuffled around on the asphalt, kicking each other's feet. The younger two sighed and yawned. Everyone was looking at the lock on the door now and the shiny key in Frank's hand. But Frank stood there in a torpor, smiling.

"And, uh," he said to Phuong, "let me introduce you to a newcomer to our church, Todd Wilson."

"Hey," said the long-haired, bare-footed young man to Phuong. He shook my hand. His was warm and limp.

"Todd's my neighbor," said Frank. "This is his first time." Todd snorted. Frank cleared his throat again. "And Todd, let me introduce Rhonda—" The plump White girl waved coyly to Todd. "And this is Miriam," said Frank, to the woman I had been watching. "And this is—"

"Preacher," said Dr. Klingscales suddenly and rather loudly, "I'm not trying to trouble you, but Mrs. Pritchett might catch cold with her wet hair and all and if you'll just hand me that key, I'll be glad to let us all into the store."

"Now, Pete," said Frank with a slow smile, "you know I can't let that key fall into any hands but my own. Don't rush me folks. I'm coming." At last he put the key in the lock and opened the building himself. The smell of cold white bread rushed out. We quickly filed in.

It took a few long minutes for us to assemble in an open area just in front of the cash registers. Oscar and Dr. Klingscales and a large man, whom somebody called Irving, fetched chairs for everyone. The chairs crashed and screeched across the dingy tile floor. Peter, Paul, and John had disappeared. The only other children here were toddlers, the ones I would have cared for in the nursery, if there had been a nursery and if Ginger and I had told my grandmother a true story.

"Fetch me a *People* magazine off that rack, Miriam," said Rhonda in a husky voice.

"We're fixing to praise Jesus," said Miriam.

"I ain't going to read it now."

"You ain't going to take it home, neither, Rhonda. Not without paying."

"I done paid twice last week. You seen me leave a dollar bill on the register."

"Orly said don't do that no more."

"Aw, Miriam. They know I'm going to pay up."

"Hey, Rhonda and Miriam," called out Oscar, "attitude check!"

Rhonda's face cleared and she sighed and smiled. "Praise the Lord!" she said, lifting her hands.

"I taught that to them," Dr. Klingscales explained to Phuong and me. "That's what we used to do in my church back in Alabama. That was my own church there what I was pastoring in. It was a fairly large church—five hundred members. We had a number of problems getting along at the start. When a brother or a sister started to complain or get out of line, I'd just say to my congregation—'Attitude check! Hey, everybody, attitude check!' and they knew to let the garbage out and let the sweet air in. So all these folks knows to do it now, and y'all do, too."

"How come you're not a pastor anymore?" I asked.

"Oh," he said, bouncing his Bible and notes between his knees, "I lost my church when the Holy Ghost set me straight. They were lovely people, but their hearts were hard. I used to preach to them what to wear, what to say, what to do. Then the Holy Ghost set me straight— said, 'Don't make the law no god.' Those good people didn't want to hear it, so I came over here to make this man's life hard!" He pointed at Frank and slapped his leg, laughing. "This here hippy, here. Lot of folks wouldn't let Preacher walk in a church with long hair like that. But God has set us free."

"Amen," said Frank sincerely. "Thank you, Pete."

We were all seated in a circle now on cold metal chairs. Big lights hummed above our heads. The air conditioner chugged on and whirred off.

"Let's join hands and seek the Lord in prayer," said Frank. He leaned over in his chair, his legs pushing up on either side of his chest. He clenched his eyes shut and held hands with Todd on one side and a teenage girl on the other. I held hands with Phuong on one side and, on the other, Miriam, whose skin was rough like green beans.

"Holy Lord Jesus," Frank started out.

"Praise you, Lord," said Miriam. Her hand jumped in mine.

"Glory to Jesus," said someone else.

"Holy Lord," said Frank, "we come before you today like helpless babes in your arms, crying out for the pure milk of the Word. Send to us your comforter, Lord, your Holy Ghost to rest upon us and comfort and counsel us, that paraclete of your divine love, the Holy Spirit of God."

"Amen," they all said. The cry rippled out like a wave. "Praise to Jesus. Praise to the holy Lord Jesus."

Frank's voice rose in the air and trembled. "In the precious, precious, precious, holy, holy, holy name—"

"Precious Lord! Holy Lord!" The chairs creaked, the people swayed as Frank's own prayer drew to a close:

"—the name of Jesus—holy Lord Jesus. Amen."

When Frank said Amen, I realized that my hands were free again. Miriam had pulled hers slowly away, grazing mine with the jagged ridges of her fingertips. Phuong had dropped hers quickly. I opened my eyes for a second and shut them immediately, embarrassed, because without wanting to I had seen them all, the whole crowd of them, still worshiping, swaying, murmuring prayers of thanks and praise, with their arms in the air and their heads thrown back. This was not prayer meeting as I knew it, the decorous gathering of God's covenant people. Even Phuong was reaching up in the air for something, her eyes shut tight. The only exception was Frank. He sat bent over stiff and still, with his head resting on his knees.

"Oh, take it to the Lord, all of you," he said. "Take it to the Lord in prayer."

It was a long time in prayer meeting terms, maybe three or four minutes, before anyone prayed aloud again. There were quiet prayers around the circle. Then a short prayer burst out of a woman near me: "Heal my son, dear Jesus, heal him from this sickness that the devil has laid upon him. He's a burden to my heart. Won't you heal, won't you heal him?"

Another woman agreed with her. "This sister, Lord, cries out to you. Oh, holy Jesus, give the sister the desires of her heart."

A man prayed, "I got a secret sin, dear God, that I been hiding up

293

forever. I want to get it off my chest so I lay it down before you. I'm coming to your mercy seat."

"Yes, Jesus," they all echoed. "Yes, yes."

In my heart I prayed, "Lord, let me be in the musical again."

And then Dr. Klingscales prayed. "God!" he said, and I thought I could tell that he was standing up now instead of sitting down. "God," he said, "thou art so big, so mighty, so majestic, and we're just so puny and small. I want to thank thee for being so great, God."

"Amen!"

"There's no one like thee, God. Like I read in the Bible just this morning, there is no rock save thee; I know of none."

As he prayed, a woman began to sing a chorus softly, and the others joined in with the words:

> When my tears were not enough to wash away my sin
> The blood of Jesus made me clean within.
> And when I think of how he suffered on that tree,
> I wish my tears could heal his misery.

"Oh, Jesus, oh, Jesus," said Dr. Klingscales, "that's all I have to say right now. Just help me, Lord—" His full, thick voice swooped up in a falsetto and he began to sob. Sobs broke out around the circle. The song changed.

More people prayed and I had almost forgotten about Phuong when she put her hand on my arm and gripped it tight. "What are you doing?" I whispered.

"I want to pray," she answered.

"O.K., sure," I said, wondering why she needed my permission.

"Holy Lord Jesus," she began in a soft voice, "holy Jesus, hear me."

A woman across the room hadn't heard her. "Fill me!" she shouted. "Fill me up with all your loving, God!"

"Hear me prayer, Lord," Phuong continued bravely. "Hear me, Lord," she said, "because I calling on you. I have tried to be the good Christian. I asking you to hear me."

"Amen," said Dr. Klingscales. "Listen to this sister, Lord."

Phuong's voice sank down and rose up again. "Holy Jesus, help me, because I am so tire and empty. Holy Jesus, I need to be full."

"Give this woman the Spirit, Lord! Let her speak to us!"

I looked up quickly to get a glimpse of Phuong gripping her head, swaying with her hair in her hands. She got to her feet and began to whisper softly.

"Lord of God," prayed Phuong with anguish, "oh, Jesus Christ, oh, my Lord, my Lord, help me! I want the Holy Ghost!"

"Give her the Spirit," said Oscar again. "Just give her what she wants. Give it to me, too, Jesus."

"Amen," said several others. "Give her the Spirit, Lord. Give it to her, Jesus."

"Yes, Lord!" said Phuong. She smiled, and opened her eyes, and got to her feet, and then suddenly the familiar erupted into the unfamiliar. I was the only one watching. The rest of them bowed and mumbled with her in a strange tongue. She rocked and swayed on her feet, staring up at the ceiling with her arms out, her arms tense and rigid as twisted wire. The mumbling was like water. For all I knew she was speaking Vietnamese. Her face twisted up in a joyful agony. She grabbed at the air with her hands.

"Send her an interpreter, Lord!" called out Frank suddenly. He fell to his knees and stared up sorrowfully, with his hands clenched together. His knuckles were white. I had never seen him like this. He looked like a figure in stained glass. "We want to know what the sister's telling us, Lord. We can't understand it. Give understanding. Let me interpret. Give me back my gifts. Let me heal! Let me speak with the tongues of angels. Let me interpret—"

"You shall not interpret, Preacher!" shouted Miriam. "The word of the Lord is that you shall not interpret! God has taken away your gifts because of the sin in your heart."

"Oh, God!" he said mournfully. Everybody looked up at him, hanging his head, and at Miriam, whose chest heaved. She moaned, long and low.

Then Dr. Klingscales shouted, "I know what the sister's saying!" He came excitedly to Phuong's side. Her eyes rolled back, her mouth moved silently. It was another seizure, I thought, and suddenly I felt sick and afraid. I crouched in my chair. Dr. Klingscales put his hands on Phuong's shoulder.

"Give ear to the word of the Lord," said Dr. Klingscales, "for I tell you that this sister has a prophecy for us all." Phuong continued to mumble softly. "She tells us that the Lord says we are all sinners. Our hearts are stained with sin, and the day of cleansing has come. It has come for this woman. God has told her to confess her sin to us, because then her heart will be light and easy. Then she will suffer less."

"Confess it, sister!" someone said. "Get your heart washed clean! Get right! We don't want you to suffer." Everybody had their eyes open. Phuong was shaking with tears.

Dr. Klingscales helped her down into her chair. "Confess it," he said gently. "Get it out. I know just how it is. You need the Spirit." Frank sat quietly across the room. I saw his face so clear and unclouded. His features were not dull. They were sharp and full of torment.

"Confess," said Dr. Klingscales. "Confess it."

Phuong fell limp in her chair, her arms to her side. All of the wiry stiffness had left her. The others leaned toward her, waiting. Some still mumbled quietly. Some held hands, but I just clenched mine together in front of me.

"What is it?" said Oscar from across the room to Phuong. "What you've done can't be no worse than what I've done. I've killed ten innocent people in wartime. What you got to bear?"

"I'm afraid," she said.

"Fear is a bad sin," said Mrs. Pritchett. "It's a bad sin to fear, because then you don't trust God like you should."

"God will forgive the fear," said Frank, clearing his throat. "I know all about that. Fear comes because you're human and you can't help it. You need to tell us what you're afraid of, and why. That's the only way to find courage."

"That's right, Preacher," said Miriam, in a sad voice, full of kindness. She didn't chide him. Maybe she wasn't speaking for the Holy Spirit any longer.

"That's right," said Dr. Klingscales.

"I not want to tell," said Phuong. She sobbed so that she could hardly breathe. I had to look away. "I not."

"You have to tell," said Dr. Klingscales. "God commands it."

"She don't want the little girl to hear," said Oscar. "Isn't that right? You don't want the little girl to hear it."

Phuong glanced up at me, just for a second, and nodded. Why did she bring me here if she didn't want me? Still, I would have gone, gladly, but before I could move, Phuong stood up again from her chair in a solemn way, with her head bowed. She stood with her hands folded in front of her and her feet tightly together. Frank was still in his chair, looking up with his red cheeks shining. Again I wondered why she had brought me. I didn't belong here; I was Dutch. Phuong began to speak in a sad voice. While she spoke her eyes were always on the floor; her hands were clasped. She did not look at me or at anyone as she told her story. Standing while we sat, she was the tallest in the room. Everyone was quiet. There was no more mumbling.

"I want to tell my story," she said slowly.

"Yes," said Dr. Klingscales, "give us your testimony. Start from the beginning, child."

She thought for a moment. "I come from North Vietnam. When I was the child, my country poor colony of France, and my father a schoolteacher. It was revolution, a very bad time, but he want me to get school, and he go with France against the Vietnam revolution so I can go to the school. I go to an expensive school in the south of Vietnam. After the revolution, it has been discover that my father was go against the revolutionaries and he go to prison. Mother has hate me because he go to prison, so I leave home." Her face was steady. The others in the room nodded vigorously, encouraging her.

"I have been poor. Revolution over, but there is not much of food or job. I working as a tutor for high school student, and sometime I can only eating potatoes for a whole week. I living in Saigon alone, no parent, or the husband, or children. I have started to go downtown with the men, because they help me get food. So I was—I was prostituting." She glanced down at me and away, as one of the women moaned. "I have not know about Jesus Christ. Everybody so angry at the government. We can't get the job, but to bribe or prostitute. Then one time I meet a man who is coming from the North, coming near my village where I have grow up. He very educated and smart. He

297

telled me about Communism, about Russia, where the poor people can get land and food from the government. That man doctor and Communist. He told me all the time he can help the Vietnamese people recovering the proud and strength we have lose. And he giving me food and money, but he not have ask me for anything, not to prostitute.

"Then I have remember my father and the things he teach to me when I was a child. He say don't trust Communists. But that man say we can help every poor people. I was very poor. And I was seeing many people in my childhood who starves to death because the French people take their lands and don't let them grow crop. That man has convince to become a Communist." She took a deep breath. I studied her. She looked around at the eyes of the others, which were now blank, less sure. Somewhere at the back of the store, the boys were yelling and thunking around.

"Stop it, you idiot!"

"I didn't do anything!"

Phuong broke out in sobs again as she spoke. "I have marry this man and helping him because I have want to help the poor people. We live in the mountain, in the small village with ten of my husband friend, and telling people to believe in the Communism. First only teaching and talking and people don't listen. My husband want to be patient, but then one time my husband friends kill a man, a landlord who can cheat people. They say he can be an example. I have been so scare. They kill two men, and then three. The capitalist landlord afraid, who try to kill us, and my husband go with his friend to kill the whole capitalist families. They beat them to death or burning them houses. After that killing, there more killing. Sometime children and old people, and sometime not only capitalist. Poor peasant, too. My husband is been a bad, evil man. I was so afraid. One time his friends beat me and some soldiers when they are drunk have rape me. I want to die. Try not to think about it because I have my mother-in-law to take care of. My mother-in-law is sick and I taking care of her day and night. I know I have to take care of her, because she so old. But I hate my husband! This was my first thoughts about God. Have ask God, how can you let this man live? I want to know how God can kill the good people and let him live?" She stopped then. She clenched her fists together against her chest, shaking, looking out into the absolutely still faces of this small congregation.

"Come on, honey," said Dr. Klingscales. "You can finish the story. I know you can."

"Come on, sister," Miriam said. "In the name of Jesus. In the power of the Holy Ghost."

Phuong put her hands over her face. "One day the South Vietnamese soldiers have coming for the Communist. The Communists have run into the forest and they have set the houses and fields to fire. I think my husband is kill. I going to run away, but my mother-in-law old and sick, and she say she want to go with me. She say please don't leave her to kill by the soldiers. But I . . . decide to leave my mother-in-law." Phuong pressed her lips together, her eyes shut. She shook her head. "She old and sick, and cannot move herself out of bed. I have drag her into the forest and leave her there, like a dead body, for birds. I have not had Jesus in my heart. I have thought it don't matter because she was old anyway. I leave her there. She cry for me when I leave." Phuong choked and couldn't lift her hands away from her face. I looked around at the others.

"Oh, God," Phuong said, "God help me, I have kill her. I go to hell for this. I don't want to go to hell."

"The only salvation for you comes from above," said Miriam, jumping to her feet. "From God. Oh, praise to Jesus, praise to you, holy Lord, because I know now that you have saved me. He will save you, too, sister."

"Have you repented of your sins and been baptized in the name of Jesus, sister?" Dr. Klingscales asked Phuong in a loud voice.

"Yes," said Phuong. "I do it in Vietnam."

"Do you believe that he forgives you?"

"Yes."

"Then have peace in your heart," said Dr. Klingscales. "That's all you need. In the love of Jesus." He held his Bible over his head.

Phuong lifted her arms above her head. Out of her throat and up from her chest and from the depths of her body came a long, anguished groan. "No, I sinning! I want to be baptize again!" she cried. "I not really die to myself the first time. Now I am bury with him in death. I have die again and again. Now I want to raise with him in eternal life. I want to see my sins wash away again with water!"

"It only takes once," said Dr. Klingscales. Frank nodded. The others groaned and lifted their hands.

"But I have more sin."

"Just confess the sins," said Frank, in a softer voice than Dr. Klingscales. "He'll forgive all of it."

"It's Satan," said Miriam. "I can hear him telling her she's a sinner."

"Pray that devil away," said someone across the room. "Pray away that Father of Lies."

They all got up from their chairs, the whole circle of groaning, swaying worshipers, and started toward us. Dr. Klingscales hugged Phuong against his shoulder. His shirt was dark green with her tears. Frank came close and put his arms around the two of them, so that they stood in a huddle of three.

"Come close, honey," whispered Miriam to me. "She needs your prayers, too."

"I'm sorry," I said. "I can't. I don't know how."

"Oh, come on. The Holy Ghost intercedes for us with groans deeper than words."

"I'm not feeling good," I said. I slipped off the side of my chair and quietly ran outside to stand in the fresh, dark air. I didn't want to be in there anymore. I wanted to go home and sit with my grandmother and feel cleansed of it all. Did my father know any of this? Did my father know he had married a Communist? I thought of his constant prayer, "Lord, deliver those suffering in Communist dungeons in the Far East and in the Soviet Union." I wondered if the Communists would come for Phuong one day and find her here in Dutch Falls, at our house. What would happen then? I breathed in short gasps. A car passed and its lights flashed over me. My shadow raced across the front of the store. Another car came, and another. I felt like a guard on duty.

Then a little Toyota swished around the corner of the parking lot, sped toward the grocery store, and slowed when it came up near me. It was too dark to see the people inside until they rolled their windows down. It was Ginger, driving Frank's car, and there was my aunt in the passenger seat. In the back was my cousin Victoria, squeezed up against Floyd.

"Kiddo," said Ginger. "What are you doing here?" She sounded drunk. "I've been trying to get in touch with you. My rehearsal ended early and I wanted you to baby-sit."

I was unsteady on my feet. I felt the effects of all that praying, or maybe it was just that the air was lighter out here. "I can call home and ask," I said, trying to smile. I put my hands in my pockets and bent into the car. "I can probably still baby-sit."

"Well, we got Vicky now," said my aunt. "She can do the baby-sitting." Vicky looked straight ahead in the backseat, not even at me. She stared right into the back of Ginger's head.

"I could still do it," I said. "It's my job, isn't it? I'm the regular baby-sitter. Vicky doesn't need to do it."

"Vicky will do fine," Aunt Jo said. What else could I say? I frowned.

"So how have you been?" Ginger asked me casually. "I meant to call you today, kiddo. I'm sorry; you probably think I'm a rotten pal."

"I've just been around here," I said, pointing back at the grocery store.

"Why? What are you doing at Frank's church?"

"I came with Phuong," I said. "She goes here."

"Oh, really?" Ginger rolled her eyes. "I thought she had more taste. How's Frank tonight?"

"Fine."

"Fine, huh? Well he was supposed to be out thirty minutes ago. We're meeting George and Mandi and my sister. I wish I knew what was up with Frank these days. Hey, kiddo, you tell him Ginger couldn't wait all night, O.K.? I might just go on."

"I'll tell him," I said. "See you tomorrow night?"

"What?"

"I'll see you tomorrow. At rehearsal, remember? You said you wanted me there on Thursday night."

She smiled slightly. "Kiddo, I'll be in a big hurry tomorrow. In fact, I'll be leaving early. I won't have time to be a taxi service."

I looked down at my feet and back at her. So it was different now that I was out of the show. "Well," I said, "it's O.K. if I come to dress rehearsal next week, right? I'm still coming?"

"Do you really want to?" Ginger asked.

"Al said I could come."

"I'm just not sure it's a good idea. You're so sensitive. Somebody might hurt your feelings."

I was disheartened. "You might need me there to watch Floyd," I said. "You'll be busy that night."

"Oh, the dancers will play with him. They're used to it."

"I guess I won't see you anymore then," I said. I hung my head and struggled with tears.

"Oh, forget it," she said. "I can tell it's a big deal. If it's such a big deal, you be right out there waiting for me at six thirty Wednesday night or else I'll leave without you. Don't make me wait."

"Ginger, you're such a pain in the butt when you're drunk," said my aunt, laughing. "Lay off poor Carolyn. She'll be ready."

They waved and drove away. I looked behind me in the store window. The people inside were all on their knees around Phuong, all except the Jordan boys, who were kicking colored balls out of a big metal stand in a corner of the store. Even from outside I heard the metal yelp and the rubber springing on the tile.

17

Bible says a lot about a Dutch Falls girl—if she won it, for instance, in a school contest, being the first in her class to locate Hosea 2:9, or the first to realize that there's no such book as Hezekiah. Annajane Ten Kate's Bible was made from calfskin leather and had her name embossed in tiny gold letters on the front. Inside, glued over a map of the Holy Land, lay a slip of white paper like you'd find in a fortune cookie. It said, "Thy Word Have I Hid in My Heart, Dutch Falls Christian Elementary Sword Drill Champion 1975." Annajane could flip to any passage of Scripture within ten seconds. She could be on her feet shouting it out before the rest of the kids in chapel had decided whether it was in the Minor or Major Prophets, the Gospels, or the Epistles. My own Bible was a hardback, red King James Version that my grandmother had garnered from a barrel of used church stock for my tenth birthday. She had bragged about her economy as I unwrapped it. But later she told me that, when I was old enough, I would have her own black leather Bible with the silky paper and notes penned in at the sides from some of the greatest sermons ever preached on the radio. For now I could mark up my cheap hardback red Bible as much as I wanted. The morning after I went to Frank's church, I opened to the concordance at the back of my red Bible. I circled the verse I had looked up—1 Corinthians 14:5: "I would that ye all spake with tongues." I would ask my father what it meant.

It was still early, maybe seven or seven thirty. The backs of my legs felt sore where I had leaned over the edge of a metal folding chair at the Food Angel grocery store. I put my Bible aside and began a letter to Ginger. It was a letter that I had considered all night. Now that the morning had arrived, and before voices broke the peace of the house, I would try to put my thoughts into words.

Dear Ginger,

This is the hardest letter I have ever in my life had to write. You mean more to me than anyone in the world. I would never hurt you on purpose. You are truly my best friend in the whole world. I think I am your best friend, too, and I know that I understand you better than anyone else, because I know how good you are inside, even when you are hurting and lash out (which you don't do too often, mainly when you are with my aunt). You are my first and best friend. But I have a few things to say to you, and I can't hold it inside anymore.

Ginger, you say I'm like a daughter to you, but yet you turn your back on me again and again, it seems. You say we're best friends, but you never act like that anymore and when we're together you talk to my aunt or Victoria a lot more than to me. If you had helped me with my singing and dancing—I know I'm not naturally very good—maybe I would still be in the musical. I wanted it more than anything else. You probably might say, "What does this crazy kid want out of me any-way? Don't I give her a lot? Didn't I take her to rehearsals every week?" It really hurts not to be in the show anymore, but what really hurts is losing you. I feel like I'm alone, without your friendship anymore. We used to have great times together (you were my heroine). Last nite I realized that you've changed and I just wanted to die because I couldn't stop it. I know that probably everything is my fault, so I am sorry ahead of time for all the things you will say (if you don't write me back, I will understand). But I just love you anyway. I want to know that you love me, too.

Carrie

P.S. You don't have to write back. You can just think about what I said.

I folded the letter up and wandered into the hall to look around. I had an odd feeling, as though someone had been reading over my shoulder. But no one was up yet. I went back to my room to put on

304

shorts and a T-shirt. As I sat dressing, a voice suddenly called my name. I jumped and turned around. It came from the old intercom, an orange metal box that only worked half the time.

"Can you hear me, Carrie? I don't trust this thing—"

"Grandma? I can hear you. What?"

"I said don't punch that button until I'm finished talking." Her voice sounded harsh and shrill, like a blue jay squawking.

"Yes, ma'am."

"I'm trying to get breakfast on the table. Why don't you pick me some roses for the centerpiece?"

"Yes, ma'am." I went immediately down to the front yard and worked right under Phuong's window. The last words she'd said to me were in the backseat of Frank's car the night before, as I climbed out and left her sitting next to Todd, the neighbor.

"Don't tell them," she'd said.

"Are you coming?"

"I come up soon. Good night."

After a few minutes, my father tapped on the window and smiled down at me. I waved. My hands were dirty. He kept looking at me and finally pulled the window up and put his head through.

"Good morning, there," he said cheerfully.

"Hi."

"What do you call a lazy, one-legged woman?"

"I don't know."

"Eileen Dolittle."

He shut the window, tapped again, and went away. I was afraid Phuong might look out and try to catch my eye, so I finished quickly and took the roses in. Grandma put them in a china vase on the table. She laid out cloth napkins in silver rings beside each china plate. She poured the milk into a cold silver pitcher, which sweated on the beautifully embroidered lace tablecloth that Aunt Betsy had brought for us.

"Our prayer meeting was very sparsely attended last night," Grandma said to me sharply. "How about yours?"

"I'm sure there were more people at the F.R.C. of V., Grandma," I said.

"So tell me about this church that your stepmother prefers to her husband's."

"Well, it's kind of a Pentecostal church," I said.

"Oh, really?" She glanced at me. "I guess that's no surprise."

"No, ma'am."

"I've only seen the kind of Pentecostals they have on T.V. I imagine they're a lot different from the F.R.C. of V."

"Yes, ma'am."

"Are they anything like the Baptists?"

"I've never been to a Baptist church," I said.

"That's not true, Carolyn. You've been to a Baptist church once on vacation. I know you have. You went to a singing Christmas tree with Uncle Jim and Aunt Betsy."

"No, I never have," I said.

"I know you have."

"No," I said, almost angrily. "You've never let me go anywhere but Reformed and Presbyterian."

"But you've been to a Baptist prayer meeting."

"No, ma'am."

"Carolyn," she burst out, "you're stubborn!"

"Yes, ma'am."

"You know, a lot of people around here would take very ill to their daughters attending any church outside the F.R.C. of V. But I have a strongly open mind on that subject. Now go upstairs and get dressed for breakfast, Carolyn. I want us all to look nice. It'll put me in a better mood."

"Yes, ma'am." I did as she said, putting on a Sunday dress and white leather sandals with square heels. Since it was a humid day, my hair had already curled up tight. I pulled it back in combs.

"Don't you look nice," said Aunt Betsy, meeting me in front of the bathroom door upstairs. She stood in her worn leather sandals, smelling like alfalfa or some other herb.

"Thank you," I said. "Is Victoria in the bathroom?"

"No, Shirley's been in there washing her face again, drying her skin out like sandpaper. Oh, Shirley! Are you finished yet?"

"Where's Victoria? Is she awake?" I wanted to see her. I wanted to see if a night at the Jordans' house had changed her.

"I don't think she's even back yet," said Aunt Betsy. "She spent the night out, baby-sitting. Her father will be foaming at the mouth. Shirley! Excuse me, Carrie, honey, I've been waiting half an hour to use the bathroom. Could you run and see to Zachary? He ought to be awake by now." Shirley opened the door a crack and Aunt Betsy danced past me into the bathroom. "Excusez-moi!"

At the breakfast table, my grandmother tried to keep us on our best behavior. We were all there but Victoria and Phuong, who had begged a headache. Uncle Jim sat at the head of the table, in the only chair with arms. Father sat next to him, Aunt Betsy next to Father, and a weary-looking Aunt Jo still in her white gauze bed jacket sat next to Aunt Betsy. Aunt Jo probably had a hangover, I thought. Shirley, Nathan, and I squashed together on the other side, and Grandma sat opposite Uncle Jim. She fed Zachary on her lap.

"I'm hot," said Shirley. "Can't we turn on the air?"

"There is no air, dear," whispered Aunt Betsy across the table.

"How scrubbed and well dressed we all look," said Grandma. "Nathan, I declare you look so handsome this morning. Why don't you pray for us?"

Nathan had been coached on prayer by now and knew better than to refuse. He stood up at his chair with his hands in his pockets and sighed through his nose. "DearLordthankyouforthygraciousand-bountifulblessingsamen."

"Thank you, Nathan," said my grandmother, as he fell back down in his seat and tossed his hair out of his eyes.

"You ought to learn the Big Mac prayer, Nate," said my father. "Dear-Lordthankyouforthetwoallbeefpattiesspecialsaucelettucecheesepick-lesoniononasesameseedbun."

"My Nathan," said Aunt Jo hoarsely, "is getting downright spiritual. That ought to be a lesson to you, Jimbo. You should lay off your children and they'll turn out just fine on their own. I'd know how to handle them. They've got sensitive souls, underneath. Just like I do. You can't beat them down or someday they're going to get right back up and hit you in the face."

"You, Jo? A sensitive soul?" Uncle Jim smacked his lips on orange juice and clacked his spoon and knife against his bowl. "Hah!"

"Yes, I do have a sensitive soul. It took me years to realize it, years of not living with you."

"Aw, poor little Josephine; let's hear all about your poor pitiful childhood. I want to hear about every single precious thing that you were denied. Don't you, Davey? Aren't you just dying to hear all the terrible things we did to our sister?"

"I didn't say anything about Davey," said Aunt Jo. "I was talking about you and only you."

"Me and only me," said Uncle Jim. "O.K., go ahead and tell me everything I did to ruin your life."

"It would take all day," Aunt Jo said. "I don't have that kind of time, do you?"

"What a lovely table Mama has laid for us this morning," interrupted Father. "It's all so lovely, Mama, it looks good enough to eat. What's the occasion?"

"The occasion is," Grandma said, as my aunt and uncle eyed each other, "that I have my whole family home and I'm eager for us to put aside this bickering and learn to act like civilized people. Do you hear me, Jo? Do you hear me, Jim? More coffee, anyone? Anyone want eggs? I tell you Nathan here is outdoing all of you. Look at the way he puts away his oatmeal." Nathan grunted and nodded and shoveled more into his bowl, which had been full just a moment ago. Grandma smiled approvingly.

"If I had just eaten like that when I was his age," said my father, "I might have made quarterback."

"How much do you weigh now, Davey?" said my grandmother.

He patted his chest. "One hundred and fifty pounds of raw, hard muscle."

"You runt," laughed Uncle Jim. "How dare you be born into this family?"

"He takes after me," said Grandma. "It was your father who had the big people in his family. That's where you and Jo got your stoutness, from your father."

"Stoutness?" said Aunt Jo. "What a delicate way of putting it."

"Well, stout Jo," said Uncle Jim, grinning, "how much do you weigh now, anyway? Want me to guess?"

His eyes were smooth, unblinking, clear blue. Aunt Jo's were quick and gray. "I don't know and I don't care how much I weigh," she said. "And if you try to guess, I'll kick you under the table. You know I will."

"You must know your weight."

"I said I'd kick you. I'll hurt you."

"I'm trying to decide if it's worth it."

"Jim," said my father. "Don't."

"You can't tell me, Jo," said Uncle Jim, "that you don't know how much you weigh. All women know how much they weigh. Betsy can give you her weight by the ounce."

"Oh, yes," said Betsy. "I haven't been off a diet in ten years. But do you know, Jo, that this *Healthy Life, Holy Life* diet is the best thing that's happened to me? I've lost three pounds in four months. That's how you do it, just a little bit at a time. In five years, I will have lost forty-five pounds."

"See?" said Jim. "Betsy's obsessed with her weight."

"That's her problem," said Aunt Jo. "I told you I don't know how much I weigh and I don't care."

"Just a question," Uncle Jim said.

"It's never just a question with you."

"What do I care if you're old and fat? Look at me, I'm older and fatter. I weigh three times what I did in high school."

"You're a man. Who cares what you weigh?"

"Five dollars for your weight. Five dollars." He pulled out a bill and laid it on the table.

"Stop it," said my aunt.

"What difference does it make?"

"You know very well how you've been in the past, Jim!" Aunt Jo banged down her fist. Her plate spun like a quarter. "When we were in high school you never let me alone about being fat."

"Twenty years ago."

"Settle down, JoJo," said my father. "Don't let him get to you."

"Don't tell me to settle down. Tell Mama what he used to call me in high school."

"Josephine," said Grandma, "don't say a word. I want all of you to stop it."

Nathan looked at his mother. "What did he call you in high school?"

"Nathan, let's drop it," said Father.

"I'd like to know what he called my mother," Nathan insisted.

"Hamburger buns," said Aunt Jo. "He ruined my life calling me that. He made everybody call me that."

Nathan looked at Uncle Jim. "Did you really call her that?" There was a long pause.

"Oh, well *excuse* me," said Uncle Jim. "Excuse me. I'm to blame for everything that ever happened to you, Jo. Well, I want you to know that the tables are officially turned now and I welcome all of your insults. Go ahead, hurl them at me."

"All right," said Aunt Jo. "You've got three chins and a belly as big as a Volkswagen."

"Thank you," said Jim. "I accept that."

Aunt Betsy stood up and started to take Zachary from Grandma.

"That's enough," said Grandma. She held on to her grandchild. "You're talking like naughty children. Jo, I forbid you to hurl insults at my table." She shook her hands in the air. "Can you just imagine, can you, what your father would say if he were sitting at the head of this table? Can you imagine such a vain argument as this ever taking place within his earshot? I don't think he would have stood it for two seconds. He would have taken us straight to the Lord in prayer. We would have bowed the knee here and now. Why can't you—" She looked at my father and at Jim. "You boys both know the Lord. Doesn't either of you know how to lead a family?"

"Don't look at me," said my father, because everyone had turned to look at him. "I'm not at the head of the table."

"But you're the only dominie in the family," Grandma said.

"You can lead a horse to water," said Uncle Jim, "but you can't make him drink. Jo is just as wild and untamed as she was at the age of thirteen. You can't tell her to put reins on her tongue, like it says in the Book of James. You can't tell her to act like a lady. Not even our daddy could do that."

"And God knows he tried," said Aunt Jo.

"Please," said Grandma. "Have a little respect, everyone." She stared down at her food and began eating silently, with a grave face. Father looked ashamed.

"It's not that this family lacks a leader," said Uncle Jim. "What it lacks is followers."

"I'll never follow anyone," said Shirley, licking margarine off her fingers. "There's no one in the world worth following."

"Shirley," said Aunt Betsy. "You'll always follow Jesus."

"That's what you think."

There was a moment of horror at the table. Grandma and Aunt Betsy looked in shock at Shirley, waiting for her to say she was joking. Father shook his head. Uncle Jim growled, "Go to your room and wait for me there."

Shirley gave a funny grin. "You all think I'm the bad one," she said mysteriously, "but I'm not." With that she stomped away to the stairs. We heard her high heels knocking on the planks. I thought that we would discuss what she had said, sermonize about it, examine it, and pray about it. But Uncle Jim only looked and said, "Well!" He glanced from face to face. "Where's Victoria? Why isn't she down here? Is she in the bathroom again?"

"She probably is," said Aunt Betsy, which was as close to the truth as she could come.

"I told her about taking those long showers," he said. "She's been in the bathroom all morning, hasn't she?"

Aunt Betsy looked down guiltily at her food.

"Jim," said my father, "what do you call a lady who always stands up in a canoe?"

Uncle Jim stared. "What?"

"Felinda Waters."

Uncle Jim shook his head. "What my children need is a rod of correction. They need a hard hand on their bottoms. And I'm just the man to apply it."

Aunt Jo coughed.

"Don't be too hard on them," said Grandma. "Jim, don't be hard on my babies."

"Mother, your babies are vipers in diapers," he said.

311

"Oh, please, Jim."

"That's all I'm saying. Vipers in diapers. A brood of vipers."

Victoria came home soon after breakfast, while my uncle was in the upper regions of the house administering the rod of correction to Shirley. Grandma and Aunt Betsy lingered in the backyard, hanging up sheets and chatting. Aunt Jo had taken this opportunity to smoke on the front porch in full view of the Christian world, and Nathan sat with her. I was the only one who saw Vicky. I watched her face carefully as she rushed past me in the kitchen on her way to the bathroom. I saw nothing in her empty expression to tell me one thing or another about her night at the Jordans'. What had she done there? Had she found alcohol in the cupboard or read Ginger's old scrapbooks or smoked cigarette butts from the ashtray?

I followed her upstairs to the bathroom and waited in the hall. Finally I knocked on the door. "Vicky?" I said.

"Yes? Who is it?"

"Carrie. Can I come in?"

"Carla, give me a break. I'm in the bathroom."

"I just wanted to ask you about something."

"Ask me through the door."

"Well, did you have a good time at Ginger's?"

"Yes, I did."

"What did you do all night?"

"Nothing."

"Don't you think the kids are kind of bratty? I hate that Peter; he always drives me crazy."

She flushed the toilet and shouted over it. "I think he's cute for his age. He's just right for you, Carolyn."

"Oh, shut up; he is not."

She unlocked the door and looked down at me. "So," she said, "was that it? Was that all you wanted to ask me?"

"No," I said. I wanted to step into the bathroom with her and close the door, for privacy's sake. It was a very large bathroom, after all. You could have done calisthenics in that bathroom. There was space, but she didn't move to let me in.

312

"Your daddy doesn't know you spent the night over there," I said. "Your mama thinks he might be pretty mad if he found out."

"Oh." Her small mouth went round. Her eyebrows gathered over her perky nose. She seemed bothered and surprised. "Where is Daddy?"

"He's talking to Shirley upstairs. She's in trouble again."

"Because of Billy? Did she try to go out with him?"

"No, she blasphemed."

"Oh, that." Blasphemy didn't interest Victoria.

"Ginger's really great, isn't she?" I said after a second.

Victoria smiled and winked. "She's real special."

"Yes," I said, "she sure is special."

We stood there without anything else to say. Faintly, faintly we heard my uncle's heavy voice buzz in another corner above us. We heard a girl's angry shriek and a stomp. Victoria shuddered and started past me. "I'm getting out of the house while everybody cools off. Tell my mother I went to the library."

I nodded. "All right. So you really like Ginger a lot?"

She shook her head and started down the stairs. "You're a funny kid. Why do you ask these questions?"

"Because I think Ginger doesn't like me anymore."

"Oh, she likes you," Vicky called from the bottom of the steps. "Just don't be a brat and people will always like you."

"I'm not a brat," I called out. I thought about my letter to Ginger. I would give it to her in a week, and then I would know where we stood—if she did like me or didn't, if we were friends or if we weren't friends. Having thought about the letter, I had to look at it again. I went to my room and studied it. How I wanted to change it, to say everything more gracefully and easily. Or should I not send it at all? I put it in my desk and thought about it anxiously. I held it in my hand. Maybe I should mail it now. But then by the time I saw Ginger she would have read it, and I would know that she had read it, and every minute with her would be awkward. So I waited and thought about it, hour after hour.

For the rest of that week, Victoria and Shirley came and went according to their own plans and secret knowledge. I ignored them.

313

I went to the library in the mornings, visited Annajane in the afternoons, and watched television in the evenings with my father and grandmother and Nathan.

We lasted through a long Dutch Sunday and made it to Wednesday again. I had wanted Wednesday to come. But it passed slowly. In the afternoon, I sat with Grandma in the living room, for comfort or distraction. It was still early after lunch, and we were alone. She looked out past the curtains at Aunt Jo rocking on the porch swing. Grandma's mouth turned down naturally at the corners when she thought. She was pondering something now, probably a question of good and evil. She frightened some people who didn't know that her steeliness was the measure of her goodness. Today she was as distressed as I was, though about different things, and she seemed caught in a cloud. The afternoon light on the curtains made shadows across her neck, over the tender, wrinkled hollow of her throat.

"Carolyn," she said softly, with a smile, "there was actually a time when I thought we had conquered original sin in Dutch Falls."

"That's impossible," I said, knowing that she already thought so.

"It certainly is. We've got more sin here than I don't know what. I don't know what we could ever do about it either."

"I don't know either," I said.

"Well, we could pray and we could try to do better. That's what we've always done. But I've never seen so much sin in my entire life. If we were Baptists, we could have a revival. But we're too proud for that. Aren't we, Carrie?"

I had no answer for this. I felt like the worst of sinners, though she would never know the many things I had done wrong.

"People didn't sin in the old days like they do now," said Grandma.

"They sinned all right," shouted my aunt, who had heard us outside. "You're just not remembering."

"I didn't know you could hear me, Jo," called my grandmother. "Well, there is sinning and then there is sinning. Nobody caroused in the old days, drinking and dancing the way they do now. You would be shocked at the things I hear in choir practice."

"People always sinned," Aunt Jo called again. "You just didn't acknowledge it."

314

"Well, if they did then they paid for it. I'll tell you one thing, your daddy would turn purple if he came back from the grave and heard the way they carry on, without a word of discipline from anyone. He was as good as they come, a man in whom there was no guile."

"Oh, but Daddy was hard," said my aunt. "Too hard. He could always see sin where there wasn't any. Just folks enjoying themselves."

"Why are you arguing with me about this?" Grandma frowned at her folded hands.

"Because you're not telling the truth. It's not any worse now than it was twenty years ago. I remember how you complained about Bernie Grunstra."

"Yes, well," said Grandma, "let's not bring up that poor man. You of all people to bring him up." She sighed again and moved the sheers aside. Aunt Jo moved out of sight.

"Grandma," I said, "tonight is Wednesday."

"Yes, Carolyn. I suppose you want to go away somewhere with your friend Mrs. Jordan."

I nodded. "I want to go to Richmond. It's probably the last time."

"Oh, it's all right," Grandma said, and she stuck out her lower lip like a child. "I'm a tolerant old woman. You know, your Mrs. Jordan hasn't called me or tried to meet me once. She said we would study the Scriptures together. I suppose she's too busy with her children, isn't she? That's the excuse the young women give these days."

"That's right," yelled Aunt Jo, breaking in again, though we couldn't see her. "Her four children are just an excuse for getting out of studying the Bible."

"I didn't mean it that way," said Grandma. "I just think it's a shame, that's all. For her sake."

"Well, may I go with her?" I asked uncomfortably.

"Yes," Grandma said sadly, "you may go."

In the early evening, it became unbearably hot in the house. The sun blazed in our windows like a torch. The dust on our floors turned to salt. Our tempers were up. We ate dinner in front of the television, which was as rare a thing as Christmas in our house. Grandma brought out wooden tray tables and we straddled them over our cushioned

315

chairs. My uncle talked loudly through the evening news about the fact that God's old covenant with the Jews had been replaced by a new covenant with the spiritual children of Abraham, the church, and yet how the old and the new were mysteriously one and the same. He licked his fingers as he talked. The rest of us just ate.

Ginger picked me up exactly on time, at six thirty. Her car rumbled in the driveway just as Grandma set off for prayer meeting on foot with Father, Uncle Jim, and Aunt Betsy. They glanced sternly into the car, waved, and walked on by, still talking about the children of Abraham. I had been waiting for this moment all day, longing for it, and yet dreading it in a certain way.

"Hiya, kiddo," Ginger said cheerfully. She wore a red blouse that was velvety thick, like a choir robe. Really, the blouse didn't look so good on her. Her hair curved back in a bun, the way the dancers always wore it. It stretched her temples tight so that her eyes slanted up like apostrophes.

"Hi," I said at the car window. The letter lay in my front overall pocket. I put my hand against my chest to feel the stiff, dry envelope cloistered in blue cotton. When would I give this to her? How would she take it?

"Jump in," she said distractedly. "Just move all that junk aside on the seat there."

"Where's Floyd tonight?" I asked, noticing that the backseat was empty.

"Oh, I can't worry about Al and a baby too. I left him with Mandi."

I was confused. I hesitated before getting in the car. "Do you still want me to come then? If you don't need me to watch the baby—"

"Oh, get in, kiddo. You want to come, so come."

I felt something new in her mood. Maybe it had been there before, but I hadn't sensed it. We hadn't been alone in such a long time. As I sat down and buckled my seat belt, she grabbed a Richmond *Times Dispatch* from the back and tossed it in my lap.

"There's an article about the show in there," she said, "with a picture of me and everything. Frank read it. Yes, Frankenstein reads the paper one day out of the whole year and figures I'm back in show business. Great luck."

"Was he mad?" I asked.

She tossed her head. "Oh, it's not my problem if he is mad."

I opened the paper and saw Ginger immediately, without searching for her, though the photograph was small and tucked into an inner column on an inner page. It showed her dancing with Henry in skimpy shorts and a halter top, an outfit I'd never seen. The caption read, "Music and Romance at the Dela Fox."

"This is wonderful," I said in awe. I thought I would go home and cut it out of our paper before Grandma saw it. And I would save it forever.

"It's all right," she said. "Look at my teeth. I look like I'm about to eat Little Red Riding Hood."

"Frank should be proud," I said.

She snickered. "He's too busy acting hurt. That's the only role he's playing these days. Poor, hurt Frank."

I thought about Frank at prayer meeting, on his knees, begging God to let him understand Phuong. I thought about Dr. Klingscales and that woman Miriam. "Maybe he's upset about God," I said aloud, though I hardly knew how to explain.

"Why is that, kiddo?" asked Ginger. "Why is he upset about God?"

"I don't know," I said. "Maybe he's worried because he's not as close to God as he used to be."

"What gave you that impression?"

"A lady at your church told him that he had sin in his life."

"Sin in his life?" She nodded at herself in the rearview mirror. "He probably thinks he's married to it. It's like I told your aunt the other night—Frank's religion is just an excuse to hang a stone around my neck."

"Well, what about you? Aren't you a Christian anymore?" I asked.

She hesitated. "Of course I am, but I happen to have a brain, kid. I didn't check it at the door when I got religion. That's what I tell Frank. Everybody has their limit. I can't sit there and listen to that garbage anymore; I don't feel it. And I've faked it so long I'm going crazy." Her face went pink.

"So did you lead him to the Lord," I said, "or did he lead you?"

"What?"

"How did it happen? Who got saved first, you or Frank?"

"Why do you care? What's this all about?"

"No reason," I said, "but I never figured out who became a Christian first. One time you said one thing, one time you said another."

"And why is that important?"

"It's your testimony. That's important."

"Well, it ain't important to me. Let's drop it. I don't remember anyway."

"O.K.," I said. "I'm sorry, Ginger."

"All I remember is that Jesus was going to set us free. But look at Frank. He's God's policeman."

"I'm sorry, Ginger."

"He thinks I'm the one who talked him into going to seminary. I guess he thought he was Jesus or something. He says seminary makes him feel average."

"He kind of looks like Jesus," I said. "I mean his hair and everything."

"Well," she said, "I didn't talk him into anything. I just told him he might make something of himself. You can't preach to fifty people forever. Not if you want to eat." Her voice became softer. "Tell me how you're feeling. Are you disappointed about being out of the show?"

"Yes," I said quietly.

"You'll have another chance. This part wasn't right for you, anyway. You know, I doubt this show will last. I think I'm the only one around with the sense to see it. Well, Bob sees it. He hates it. But like I told him, we have to start somewhere. I'm hoping somebody will notice us."

"I like the show," I said.

"Just don't be too mad about it."

"O.K.," I said.

She looked at me and laughed a little. "You're very agreeable, aren't you? Everything's just O.K. with you."

"Yes," I said.

"I hope you're not going to mope around tonight. You know, kiddo, Al is going to find another kid. Don't be rude about it, all right?"

"I won't," I said. "I figure it's that Walter Pinkney. I hated dancing with Henry anyway."

She scratched at her mouth with a long fingernail and licked her

318

lips. "Oh, Henry's a baby sometimes—he'll drive you crazy—but he's a big sweety when you get to know him. I guarantee if he wanted to he could be best friends with you in a week. But you didn't handle him right; you go and bite him on the leg. No wonder he hates you."

"He was hurting you that night."

"No, he was not. Don't be so melodramatic. You need to learn to flatter a man, trust a man. Your problem is that you have no faith in people. Hey, don't tell anyone, kiddo, but I found out a big secret about Henry Harrison. He's married to Dianne Bane. Does that explain half his problems or doesn't it?"

"I knew about that," I said. "I just don't like him. He's always hanging on you."

"You have no sense of humor, kiddo."

"I do have a sense of humor," I said. I kept my hands together and looked out at the pastures zinging by, the forest, the river. Ginger turned on the radio. I would have said everything then, if I could have. Instead of handing over my letter or leaving it beside me on the seat as I climbed out later, I could just say what was on my mind—all of it—while we were alone with the soft thrum of the highway and the radio. I was just chicken.

In the parking lot of the theater Ginger pushed her purse into my hands and hurried us on. "Now we have to leave right after rehearsal," she said. "I have to be at a party somewhere, so I want you out there and waiting for me."

"O.K. By the car?"

"Yes."

I don't know why she gave me her purse, except that it was such a heavy thing, the size of a small briefcase. While she walked ahead I pulled out my letter and slipped it inside, into a soft inner pocket where she kept her cigarettes. I knew she would find it there.

As noisy as the theater had been in the past few weeks, it was quiet tonight. A morbid calm lay in the air. Ginger went straight back to the women's dressing rooms and I followed her. She opened the door from the darkness and quiet of the hall to the brilliant complaining of the chorus girls at porcelain sinks. Each girl rolled her hair into a perfect bun, pasted on false eyelashes, painted on rouge. The orchestra ladies stood around the corner in the laundry room, steaming out the crimps in their white blouses, pressing the hems of their black polyester slacks.

"How's it going, everybody?" Ginger shouted in a high, happy voice.

"Terrible," they all groaned. "Can you believe we open in two nights?"

"Well, we'll all be good and fresh this way," said Ginger. "I like to be fresh, don't you, girls?" She patted my cheek and swung out through the door. "See you later, kiddo. I have to find Al."

"Hey, Sophie," said one of the dancers to another, "are we doing workshop tonight?"

"Yeah," said Sophie. "I think so."

"Oh, brother," said a girl that I didn't know, who stared serenely at her reflection in the mirror with one black satin dancing shoe pointed out behind her. "And," she said, "you know he wants us to open up, open up, let it all hang out. But you won't hear who Henry's hanging out with."

"You mean there's anyone who doesn't know?" snickered someone else. Their laughter sprang off the mirror.

"Be quiet, Deborah," said Myra Woods, stepping out of a stall.

"Oh, Myra, you're a prude."

"Just keep your mouth shut. There's a child present."

The girls looked at me and at each other. I went out into the hall, curious and disturbed. Around a corner came Dianne with a clipboard hanging from her neck. She looked like a Saint Bernard. She punched the bathroom door open and shouted for everyone to get up to the stage. Al wanted to talk to them. I went into the theater and sat several rows back, out of the lights.

The actors were already in costume. They sat in a circle onstage, looking up at Al. Ginger happened to be the best-dressed of them, decked out in a crimson nightgown for the first scene. She sat next to Henry, who wore a black suit and wingtips. Their knees touched. Tommy Depew wore nice slacks, rough wool stretched taut over his muscular legs. His arm crossed behind Mary Burrows, his hand lying flat on the floor near her bottom. When the dancers came in and formed a second circle around the cast, I could only see a bunch of backs and arms, elbows inturned, fingers splayed out. Below them in

320

the pit, Bob Ferring wore a suit jacket and whispered sharp instructions to the orchestra. Dick Danson sat in the front row, mumbling fiercely to Saul Anderson. I wanted to be closer to all of it. I wanted to hear the murmuring and the jibes and gossip. I strained to hear, but could only hear Al.

"Well, you numchucks," he said, "tonight is dress rehearsal and I feel like we've got to dig our way out of about a thousand pounds of horse manure before we've got this thing up and running. You all dance like a bunch of potatoes rolling off a truck and you sing like a pack of dogs. We're going to stay here all night if we have to; we're going to work till we drop. But first, you have exactly five minutes to call me the worst pain in the neck you've ever run into in your life, tell me how miserable you are, whatever. Just get it all out, and then let's get on with it." He looked around, baggy-eyed, heavy-jowled, crusty-elbowed. The cast and chorus were quiet, no cracks tonight. "All right," he said. "let's put on the gas. Remember, our dear producer and writer are watching. Try not to trip over each other."

As they stood and dispersed, I saw something that took my breath. Among the crowd onstage was my cousin, Victoria. I opened my mouth and looked around for someone to cry to. I wanted to say to someone, "What? What's she doing here? How did she get here?" There was no one in the seats but Dick Danson and Saul Anderson. I rushed out of my dark row and went straight up to them. "Why is that girl up there?" I asked, pointing to Vicky, who smiled at Henry Harrison and said something I couldn't hear over Bob Ferring shouting to the violins.

Mr. Danson looked up at me with his teeth clenched. "Pardon?"

I repeated my question.

"Listen, you run along to Mama, O.K.? Mr. Anderson and I are discussing big people's stuff."

"She's a great-looking kid," mumbled Saul Anderson, and he turned away from me. By this time Vicky had disappeared into the wings with the others. I went backstage looking for Ginger and found her in a circle of people, talking to Al with her arm around Vicky's neck.

"She's got a lot of talent," said Ginger. "Reminds me of myself at her age."

Al chuckled. "You're a humble one, Ginger." He patted Vicky's cheek. Vicky giggled breathlessly.

"Places!" howled Dianne from the wings. "Places!"

"All right, you all heard Dianne," said Al. "Places. I want the curtain down and everybody ready to go in five minutes. Yes, Bob?" He climbed down in the pit to consult with Bob Ferring.

I started up the side aisle to the door of the lobby and saw Aunt Jo sitting in a back row. She was chewing gum and smoking at the same time. Of course she was here. She must have brought Vicky. I waited for a moment, then went up to her. I approached her slowly, letting her look at me and away and back to me for a long time before we stood a foot apart.

"What is it, Carolyn?" she asked. "What do you need?"

"I didn't know about Vicky," I said. "Nobody told me."

"I'm sorry nobody told you."

"I don't understand how Vicky can do the part. I thought it would be Walter Pinkney."

"Well, Ginger's been working her. Little Billy is Little Betty now. Vicky's a gorgeous little girl. You can't argue with looks, honey."

"I wish someone had told me."

Aunt Jo smiled a little. "I guess Ginger wanted to tell you. You'll have to forgive her, honey. She's a sweet, sweet woman but she's just a plain old prima donna when it comes down to it. She likes Vicky. Vicky makes her look good."

"I hate both of them," I said.

"I don't blame you. But that's life." My aunt shrugged and sat back. She patted the chair next to her, inviting me to sit down, but I kept walking, up to the lobby door. I waited for a few seconds with my fingers on the cool handle and it struck me for the first time that Ginger must be wrong about the age of the building. The Dela Fox couldn't possibly have been built in the early sixties. It smelled like vacuumed carpet, new paint. It smelled like a log of wood sliced open, wood so ripe that it still sprays out moist grain when you nick it, like an apple. Everything had that smell—the dressing rooms, clustered around the stage like cathedral chapels, the green room, the conference rooms, the classrooms that carved up the rest of the building. If you traversed the farthest halls in the muted light of this hour, you would notice the same new smell, like a hardware store.

Suddenly I wanted my grandmother. I pushed through the doors into the lobby and sat down on a vinyl couch under a huge square canvas streaked with paint. There were dancers in the design, bright and undefined like swirls of fish. In fact, dancers were like fish—you admired them but seldom learned to tell one from another. And they didn't bother to learn your name, either. Hardly anyone in the show had learned mine, not in five weeks of rehearsals. But certainly they would learn Vicky's name. They would all learn it. Wasn't that how God arranged things? Didn't Providence lift up the unworthy?

I got up and looked into the theater from a crack between the main doors. The curtain was down and everything was dark except the orchestra pit, where Bob Ferring stood flat-footed on a bright floor like a penguin in the snow. He looked pleased. He tapped out the beat of the overture with his right foot and both hands. The middle-aged orchestra watched him over their bifocals with trusting eyes. Maybe he would feel good about himself when this was all over—what if a great career came of it? If so, Ginger could feel that she had found a home for at least one of her little lost animals. To think that all this time, Bob had been feeling abandoned by her, when it was really all for his own good. Maybe even the pain was part of her plan to place him in the world, to push him out of his nest. And what if, right now, I was living the hardest part of her plan for me? I should grin and bear it. I should go back in the theater and watch Vicky, stupid Vicky, doing the first scene with Henry and Ginger.

I watched through the doors just long enough to hear Ginger's first song.

> Lady don't laugh,
> You'll forget your pain,
> And forgetting it
> Will just bring it back again.
> You'll go back to that man
> For another try,
> Back to the lover
> Who said good-bye.

The music was light and sad. Ginger's voice fell into it like a stone into a pool. When she had finished, the curtain went down and I made my way along an outer hall to the dressing rooms. What I would do once I saw Vicky I didn't know. Maybe I would smile and congratulate her like a good Dutch girl, always composed, always mindful of appearances. Maybe I would yell and cry and stamp my foot.

Before I reached the dressing room door, I heard Dianne calling "Places!" again in a miserable voice. A pair of dancers stood at a water fountain talking about the cast party that night at Al's place after the rehearsal.

"Are you coming?" one said.

"Drinks on Al?" asked the other.

"Drinks on Dick."

"Guess we ought to make hay while the sun shines."

A cast party? I wasn't in the cast and I wouldn't go, even if they asked me. I would go home with my aunt, unless even she had an invitation. Vicky could ride with Ginger. I returned to the auditorium and sat with Aunt Jo in the back. She wasn't going to the party, she said. She had an invitation but she also had a headache. So midway through the rehearsal we headed home together, without a word to the others.

18

These are our last hours with you," Uncle Jim said on Friday morning, the very day of the opening of *Lady Don't Laugh*. He pointed to his coffee cup, which Aunt Betsy quietly refilled.

"Oh, no, Jim," said Grandma sadly. "You didn't tell me you had to go so soon."

"Mama," he said, "I'd forgotten that I have a session meeting early tomorrow."

"Can't those Presbyterians do without you for one day?"

"Now, you'll be happier when we're gone," he said. "You'll have your privacy again."

Shirley moaned, no doubt thinking of Billy De Ruiter. The rest of us were thinking of him, too, thinking that her romance with him was half the reason for this quick departure. Yesterday, while Aunt Betsy and Grandma visited the Ten Kates for *kopje koffie,* Uncle Jim had caught Shirley hanging out Grandma's low back window in her bathing suit, flirting with Billy and an English boy from the public high school. I had only heard about the episode. I wished I could have seen it— Uncle Jim's neck popping out of his collar as he tripped across the backyard to find the gas can for the lawnmower and discovered two shaggy-haired males in patched jeans barking after his younger daughter.

This morning Shirley looked woeful and barely touched her food. Victoria, on the other hand, ate her breakfast in calm, though I knew that she had more to lose by leaving Dutch Falls than anyone. Tonight was her opening, her stage debut. How would she manage to stay near Richmond for the next three weeks of scheduled performances?

"Oh, can't you stay through Sunday, Jim?" asked Grandma. "You've only heard the dominie once this visit."

"We've outstayed our welcome already," said Uncle Jim, with a glance at Shirley. "Next time you all will have to come over to Charlottesville and let Betsy do the cooking. Jo will like the pool. I remember what a sun-worshiper you used to be, Jo."

"Women only get tan to suit men," said Aunt Jo. "I've turned over a new leaf—no more tans, no more men."

Uncle Jim snorted. "Speaking of tans," he said, "why don't we take the kids over to the beach today for a picnic? I'll man the barbecue. You all can just sleep in the sun."

Grandma put her hands together. She looked as excited as a child. "That's a lovely idea! Thank you, Jim! Thank you, thank you." She kissed the top of his head. "I've been wishing all week that one of you would come up with a good idea like that. I tell you, I am just out of good ideas."

"Jim is never out of good ideas," said Aunt Betsy. "He's just full of ideas." Aunt Jo rolled her eyes.

Later that morning, Uncle Jim went to the supermarket and bought a two-by-three robin's egg blue Styrofoam cooler, which he packed elbow deep with beef and pork. There was twice as much animal flesh inside the cooler as we could eat in a week and not room enough in Uncle Jim's station wagon for all of us plus the cooler too. We argued over the seating arrangements in the driveway—who would ride in the wagon and who would ride in the Dart. While we argued, we looked into the Dart at the black vinyl bubbling up on the backseat, the buckles glinting white hot on the seat belts. No one wanted to ride in the Dart.

"How about we let all the older children ride with Davey and Jo in the Dart?" suggested Uncle Jim. "Betsy, you and Zachary and Mama can go with me in the wagon."

Never mind that the station wagon seated eight comfortably, cooler or no cooler. It had air conditioning, a radio, and automatic windows.

326

Grandma said, "Well, all right, Jim; this is your day. We'll do it your way."

"I can't take so many in the Dart," Father said.

"Why not?" asked Grandma impatiently. "What's your objection to that, David?"

"Well, Phuong is going to come. She likes the beach. That'll be too many in the Dart."

"Where is she?" Grandma glanced up to Phuong's window.

"She's getting ready," Father said. "We'll be along a little later. Carrie and I will wait. You all go on in the wagon and get the grill going. By the time we get there, it'll be time to put the steaks on. You know how long it takes Jim to start a fire in a grill."

"I thought all he had to do was breathe on it," said Aunt Jo.

Victoria, Shirley, and Nathan climbed in the cool wagon. In spite of the heat, Aunt Jo wanted to wait with my father and me, but Grandma said, "Please Jo, ride with Jim, for the sake of family fellowship. It's our last occasion to be together." So Aunt Jo stormed over to the wagon and placed herself in the very back, staring through the window defiantly as they pulled away. Victoria and Shirley sat at her sides, like maids-in-waiting.

Father and I were left to wait alone. We went into the kitchen. After pouring us both lemonade, he began to read his paper. I sipped at my drink quietly. I ran my finger along the top of the kitchen table. Father sighed. Half an hour went by, an hour. What was Phuong doing? Washing her face? Praying? Speaking in tongues?

Finally, my father went upstairs. A short time later they came down together, she with her hair wrapped up under a short-brimmed, black-ribboned straw hat. She nodded to me with her eyes turned away. I nodded back politely, though she wasn't looking. We all proceeded to the car.

In all of these weeks, we had never been alone together—my father, my stepmother, and I. Without Grandma or Uncle Jim, there was a certain awkward peacefulness in the car. I felt it. My father may have felt it, too, because he shifted back and forth, lifted his knees under the wheel and put them down again, pulled one sandaled foot up tight between the door and the seat, and looked around, whistling. He pulled at his sunglasses and wiped the sweat out of the brown creases of his thin face. What was there to say? We drove along. Grandma's car felt wide and lonely with the windows rolled down. We didn't have to cross the Powhatan Bridge to get to the lake, but we saw it standing rigid in the distance, casting black shadows on the blue water. Father's eyes flicked up in the rearview mirror. He looked out over my head, and then forward again.

"I have to remember to have air conditioning put in this car," he said. "I just don't see how Mama can be comfortable in here. I remember when we used to go to the lake like this when we were kids, and we'd get so hot that we'd fight the whole way. My dad hated the heat." He looked over at Phuong, grinning, trying to get a smile from her. She held up her hand to keep her hat from being blown to the back of the car. Now that we were going sixty-five along a state highway, the air roared in our ears.

"You're quiet back there, Miss Carolyn," he shouted to me after a moment. He seemed determined to talk. "What are you brooding about?"

"Nothing," I shouted back. "It's just too loud in here for conversation."

"I've got one for you," he said, throwing the wheel back and forth as he tried to catch my eye in the rearview mirror. The car swerved like a bird over the country road. "Did you hear about the little boy who was told that Quakers were gentle, peaceful, softspoken people? He said, 'Well, my father must be a Quaker then, but I don't know what my mother is.'"

"That's funny," I said.

Phuong asked what a Quaker was, and after Father told her she covered her mouth and blew her nose into a small tissue from a plastic package in her pocket.

"Well, Carolyn," Father said, "how would you like to move to Pennsylvania?"

"Pennsylvania?" I shouted over the wind. "What?"

"Yep. We may have to become Presbyterians, Carrie. I know it's a fate that you wouldn't wish on your worst enemy, but we may just have to become Pennsylvania Orthodox Presbyterians."

I wished he wouldn't joke. I didn't know what was serious and what

328

wasn't, whether some terrible thing was about to happen or whether a punch line was forthcoming.

"I couldn't hear you," he said, rolling up his window. "What did you say?"

I put my hands over my ears, which were popping. "Nothing."

"Really," he said, "really and truly, how would you feel about moving to Pennsylvania?"

"Well, what about Grandma?" I asked. "Would she come?"

"No. I've already talked to her. She won't ever leave the Falls."

"But Phuong would come?"

"Oh, yes, of course."

What a ridiculous idea. Just the three of us. I looked over at Phuong, confused and silent on the seat, breathing into a tissue. I pictured us in Pennsylvania losing each other on an unfamiliar Yankee street corner. Father would go one way, Phuong would go another, and I would go still another. We would keep walking and never meet again. We would waste away and die in a place like Pennsylvania, where we didn't even know the streets, or the people they were named for.

"There's a nice little church that wants me," Father continued. "They have a Christian school. Probably a lot of Dutch folks around, not quite like us *real* Dutch, but similar. Hah hah."

"Well," I said.

"I would hate to take you away from all your friends and your school."

"I don't have any friends," I said honestly. "Just Annajane." And Ginger.

"Then you could make some friends. It's a good chance to start over."

"Can't you find a job around here?"

"No, Carolyn. I tried." He looked over the fields and water on either side of us. He nodded as if taking it all in, considering, and coming to his inevitable, logical conclusion again. "I had a few leads that didn't pan out. Of course, the dominie's getting on in years, and I'm sure my name will come up here when the pulpit is empty. But who knows? I can't count on that. God's called me to be a pastor, I guess. I can't wait here forever."

I remembered what Father had said to my uncle. He had doubted his call, or wondered about it. "Has God really called you?" I asked. "Do you really have a call?"

"I guess I do," he said.

"How can you tell?"

He laughed and shrugged his shoulders. "God gave me two left thumbs and a brain like a steel sieve. Can't do anything else. Guess I'm called to be a preacher."

I settled back against my seat. Father unrolled his window again. Phuong took hold of her hat and held it tight, with her brown elbow extended across the seat in front of me, so that I could hardly see.

When we got to the lake, Father said that he would rent three lawn chairs for us. He took off down the long grassy hill from the parking lot to the clubhouse, which sprawled along an overgrown section of the beach under scrawny pines. In his brown swimming trunks Father looked like a chip of sandstone, hurtling and bouncing down the hill. At the bottom, beside a rock wall, he took small steps to stop himself, and then disappeared into the trees. Phuong and I walked down slowly together, hardly saying a word. Because the beach was crowded and we had parked far away, it was a long walk to the picnic tables.

We reached my family's blanket on a shady hill just above the water slides. I waved to my grandmother and Aunt Betsy. Uncle Jim stood at a large brick grill, fanning away smoke with a spatula. As we approached, Phuong held her hat again. It flapped away from her forehead in the breeze, but she didn't take it off. She held it steady until we had reached the blanket. Then she sat gingerly on the ground with her sunglasses in her lap. Aunt Betsy stood up and offered her own chair, but Phuong politely refused. She sat up very straight and looked out at the water. I felt Aunt Betsy glancing at her awkwardly, studying her closely and then quickly looking away.

"Listen to all that screaming down there," said Grandma, pointing down to the beach. "Josephine is certainly enjoying herself with those kids. Vicky and Shirley really like Jo."

"Yeah," said Uncle Jim, "do you think Jo can corrupt them in an afternoon?"

"Hush," said Grandma.

330

"Well, it's almost the end of summer," said Aunt Betsy. "Every child has to let loose one last time. I used to hate the last week of vacation."

"Now, Elizabeth, don't prevaricate!" said Uncle Jim. "You told me you loved school. Remember? Remember how you were always begging your mama to have the teachers over to dinner?"

"She wasn't like you, Jim," said Grandma. "The teachers didn't like you much. You argued with them."

"I argued with old Celie Bell Sikkema about predestination," said Uncle Jim. "Somebody had to set her straight."

Behind us, my father waddled along with three chairs crashing and bouncing on his hip. He reached the blanket and planted them on flat ground and made us sit in them. He took Phuong's hand, sitting close to her.

"Well, how are you doing today?" Grandma asked Phuong, as if she had just arrived.

"I feel better, thank you," said Phuong.

"I didn't know you'd been feeling poorly," said Aunt Betsy. "Is that why we haven't seen much of you? Davey, you should have told us."

"I better now," said Phuong.

"No more seizures?" said Grandma. "Is that right, Davey?"

"No seizures," said Davey. "Maybe the Lord has healed her." Phuong nodded.

"She certainly looks lovely today." Grandma looked down sadly, or I thought she did, at her own culottes, her blue, spider-veined calves curving down to skinny ankles, bony toes.

"Why don't you read to us, Mother?" Aunt Betsy asked. "We love to hear you read on a sunny day at the lake. Did you bring us anything?"

Grandma reached into her bag and took out a book by Corrie ten Boom, the Christian Dutch woman who hid Jews in a secret room in her house during World War II. Aunt Betsy cried out with pleasure and the rest of us prepared to listen quietly. While Grandma began to read in a bold voice, Aunt Jo returned from the beach alone. She fell into a chair and fanned herself. Grandma put her book away.

"Thought you weren't going to get in the sun anymore, Jo," said Uncle Jim. "You're burned. Look at yourself."

331

"Oh, I was having too much fun down there to worry about my skin," she said. "I actually like your children, Jim. I actually do."

"Mother was reading to us," said Aunt Betsy.

"Oh, well, go on then, Mama," said Aunt Jo. "I won't stop you."

"You'll be critical," said Grandma.

"I won't," said Aunt Jo. "I'll be asleep."

We listened a little longer, while Aunt Jo slept and Aunt Betsy embroidered away at a piece of white cloth on a round wooden frame. Finally, Grandma put her book down again and leaned back for a nap under her hat. Phuong took her Bible out of a plastic sack and opened it on her lap. I started to fall asleep myself. I heard Aunt Betsy singing softly next to me in a birdlike soprano:

> The love of God is greater far
> Than tongue or pen can ever tell,
> It goes beyond the highest star
> And reaches to the lowest hell.
> The guilty pair bowed down with care
> God gave his Son to win.
> His erring child he reconciled
> And pardoned from his sin.
>
> Oh love of God, how rich and pure!
> How measureless and strong!
> It shall forevermore endure—
> The saints' and angels' song.

I barely heard her over the screams of the children and the rustling trees. But soon Father joined her and they sang the second verse more heartily:

> When years of time shall pass away
> And earthly thrones and kingdoms fall, . . .
> It shall forevermore endure—
> The saints' and angels' song.

"How do you like that hymn, Jim?" asked Grandma, stirring from her nap as the grill popped and fizzled loudly. Maybe she hadn't slept at all. "Does it make you a little uncomfortable to hear those words?"

"Not at all," said Jim. "Not at all. Why should it?"

"Well, they're a trifle Baptist for one thing. It's an emotional song."

"I'm not against emotions, Mother," said Uncle Jim. "I experience them almost every day."

"But you don't really believe that God's love reaches down to the lowest hell, do you Jim? You would tell us that God only loves the elect."

"The point is," said Uncle Jim, "that the infinite nature of God's love isn't compromised at all."

"Compromised by what now?"

"By the fact that he created hell."

Grandma frowned. "Well, it seems to me that—"

"Why do you try to blame me for these doctrines?" said Uncle Jim. "The dominie believes the same things. So does Davey, if you drag it out of him."

Father nodded and smiled. "I speak softly and carry a big tulip."

"I just can't make sense of it all," said Grandma. "I realize that you educated men know a lot more than I do, but I can't figure it out. Why would God create some folks just to send them to hell? Not even try to save them. That seems wasteful."

"These are mysteries," said Aunt Betsy. "We can't really understand these things."

"There's no mystery," said Uncle Jim. "It's very clear in the Scripture. God creates some folks as 'vessels of wrath fitted for destruction.' He uses them for his purposes and then he destroys them to demonstrate his own holiness."

"And why doesn't he love those folks?" said Grandma. "Why didn't he die for them?"

"It's a mystery," said Aunt Betsy.

My father smiled.

"Because," said Uncle Jim, pointing a spatula at Grandma, "because God has to use the destruction of the wicked to bring the elect into his kingdom. Listen. It's just like football. Wouldn't it be nice if a receiver always made it to the end zone without being tackled? If nobody ever sacked the quarterback? Wouldn't that be nice? No, it would be dull. That's why we make rules, and even if they seem unreasonable, they make the game interesting. Otherwise it's not even football. Well, in this world, God has some rules of his own, and he has to play by them or else—listen, Mama—or else this would be a different world and we wouldn't be here discussing it, anyway. So it's beside the point why God did it this way. He did it this way."

"I don't understand football," said Grandma. "Davey, what do you think?"

"Sometimes," said Father, "I wish God hadn't given me a mind to think about it. But I have to say that it comforts me to think of God loving us first, wooing us, drawing us along every step of the way."

"It's a mystery," said Aunt Betsy.

"There's no mystery," said Uncle Jim. He lifted the grill rack and squirted the charcoals with more lighter fluid.

"Now Jim!" said Aunt Betsy. "I know you, Jim! You think you know what you're doing, but you don't—"

Frruuummmmmmm! Smoke shot up in a tube and spilled over like root beer foam. When I looked up, the trees were liquid and shivering. Over our heads stretched a membrane of heat. Grandma grabbed up Zachary and tried to shield him. Jim laughed, unscathed. My father laughed, too.

"Jim, you need help there?" offered Father.

"No. I told Nate he could help when he's tired of swimming. Thought I'd better teach my only nephew the manly art of grilling."

"Manly!" said my grandmother. "Just don't sear Nathan's hair off. Not that he couldn't use a haircut. And you, too, Davey. You're looking like an old brown collie."

"Betsy," said Uncle Jim, "go get those kids. Tell them we'll eat in about fifteen minutes."

"Yes, dear," said Aunt Betsy. She went off down the beach and returned with Victoria and Shirley.

"Where's Nate?" asked Uncle Jim. "He's going to help me with this grill."

"I don't know," said Aunt Betsy. "He wasn't in the water."

334

Uncle Jim shrugged. "He must have taken off into the woods."

"The woods?" Grandma stood up and looked across the beach into the woods. "Why would that boy have gone off in the woods?"

"Better not to ask some of these questions," said Aunt Jo. "That's what I've learned."

"Now, don't worry," said Uncle Jim, "he's a big boy."

Grandma huffed and walked away to look for him, her hands swinging in front of her. Phuong, too, stood up and looked around, worried. Aunt Jo continued to act unconcerned. Within minutes, Nathan did appear on his own and said sheepishly that he'd been in the restroom all this time, reading a magazine.

"Well, now where is Mother?" Uncle Jim asked. "This burns me up. Can you imagine anything more ridiculous than Mother walking off by herself in the woods?"

"She'll be back any minute," said Father. "Don't you start worrying now."

"And I've got these steaks all ready. Let's go ahead and eat. I'm hungry."

"Me, too," said Nathan.

So we all took plates and lined up in front of Uncle Jim, who dropped a heavy steak on each plate, after which Aunt Betsy spooned out hot beans and cold potatoes for us. We ate in peace, looking down on the bright strip of beach beneath us. Father made jokes. Uncle Jim could not relax. He put down his plate at last and looked out at the beach for any sign of Grandma.

"Why don't you go after her, dear?" suggested Aunt Betsy.

"Because there's nothing sillier than that," he said. "She'll come back two minutes after I'm gone."

"But you're worried about her and you're just going to keep worrying, so just go on. It'll make you feel better." It was rare for Aunt Betsy to talk like this. We looked at her admiringly, but Uncle Jim would not give in.

"I can't leave this grill," he said, "and anyway, I'm not worried about her. To tell the truth, I'm frustrated with her foolishness. She's getting too old to go out tramping around by herself. One day she'll learn her lesson."

"I see her coming up now," said Aunt Jo. "Look over there, toward that big clump of trees. Look, Jim, don't you feel like a worrying fool? I'm going to tell her you were acting like a fussy old maid worrying over her like that."

"Don't get me steamed," he said. "I'm already burning up over this fire. Davey, you take the grill for a minute, would you?"

"Sure," said Father.

Uncle Jim walked off in the direction of the restrooms. When Grandma reached us, her face was red from walking.

"There's only one steak on the grill," said Father. "And it's all gristle."

"Don't apologize," Grandma said, "that's all I deserve for my foolishness, walking around the woods in circles. And now where is Jim gone? Did he go off looking for me?"

"Indeed he did not," replied Father. "He is in the men's room."

Grandma took her plate, looking a little downcast. She settled herself in her chair under the full sun and admired Aunt Betsy's handwork. A few minutes later, Uncle Jim returned. For the next half hour we all sat together with messy plates in our laps—all of us except Shirley, Victoria, and Nathan, who sat on some rocks nearby, eating quietly. Our conversation was as clear and uneventful as the blue water on the horizon.

Still, how could I help but wonder about Victoria? She sat just a few feet away from me in her modest blue bathing suit. Down her freckled back ran streams of clear water, dripping from her thick hair, which was already dry at the crown. She crawled over to Shirley and they discussed business of their own in low voices. Aunt Betsy called out, "Why don't you girls come over here and share your conversation with the rest of us?" And Grandma said, "Yes, let's fellowship as a family for a while." But the sisters just nodded and held their places on the rock. As Nathan stole sideways glances at them, I stared and thought about the musical. What would Victoria do? How would she get to the show?

After lunch, the girls slept in the sun. Nathan and I climbed down the hill to swim with Aunt Betsy. "Remember!" called Grandma. "Wait thirty minutes before you go in over your head!" Aunt Betsy laughed. "We'll remember, Mother. Stop worrying and rest yourself."

The water was clean and cool. I sat in the shallows and let my legs float up, plump and pale against the dark sand like slices of pear. After a while, my father came down and shouted, "Rain clouds gathering! Let's pack up!"

We pulled our things together and left. The rain felt good on our skin as we climbed into the hot cars, following the same seating order as before. Aunt Betsy and Grandma waved from the wagon. Father took the Dart onto the highway first, but Uncle Jim followed close behind. On the first open stretch, he raced ahead. Soon, we couldn't even see them.

"Dangerous," Father said, and he laughed.

Later that day, Vicky drifted calmly through the house, like afternoon drifting into evening. I watched her float from the television to the kitchen, back to the television, to the front porch, and finally to her room, smiling down on me as she climbed the stairs. "This is the best day of my life," she said. I went and looked at the calendar in the kitchen, where I had circled today's date in red.

"I guess somebody's glad it's our last day here," said Uncle Jim, looking at it over my shoulder.

"I'm certainly not," said Grandma. "I'm just heartbroken." She pounded the chicken breasts ferociously and wiped her eyes on her apron.

When dinner was ready, Grandma asked Aunt Betsy to call upstairs for the girls. "Girls!" called my aunt sweetly. "Get washed up. We're almost ready to eat."

Grandma sighed. "Now what else is there to do? I need Vicky. I need her to fold the napkins that special way she does. Neat little triangles."

"Vicky!" called Aunt Betsy. "Hurry up."

Grandma searched for the cotton napkins in the high cabinet over the refrigerator. Stepping up on a chair, she reached in and said, "Now what? What's this here?" And she pulled out the beautiful dish that Phuong had bought to replace the broken one.

"Well, look at this lovely thing," she said. "Where in the world did it come from? Betsy? Did you bring this?"

"I didn't. You must have bought it somewhere, Mother, and forgotten."

"I suppose I did. It's a real treasure. I'm always forgetting things. It worries me."

"Oh, it even happens to me," said Aunt Betsy. "It's a magnesium deficiency."

I wondered whether I should tell Grandma about the dish. Phuong had asked me not to. As I was thinking, Shirley stomped into the room alone, with an envelope in her hand. Her face was puffy and red.

"Shirley, dear, have you been crying?" said Aunt Betsy.

"It's just sunburn," Shirley said gloomily. She handed the envelope to her mother and left again quickly, without another word.

Aunt Betsy opened the envelope and slowly read the letter inside. She grimaced and put her hand to her head. "Oh, Mother," she said.

"What is it?" Grandma asked. "What is it?"

"Something horrible. Jim is going to be furious."

"Tell me now." Grandma wiped her hands off and grabbed for the letter. "Don't keep me in suspense."

"It's our Vicky, Mama. Here, you read the letter."

Grandma held the note high up in the light of the kitchen window, almost over her head. She squinted at it, reading again and again. "An actress!" she cried at last. "She wants to become an actress! Someone has led that girl astray. She's just like Jo."

Aunt Betsy clenched her teeth. "Jim will have to go looking for her. I'm afraid to tell him, Mother."

"Well, I'll tell him," said Grandma. "I'm not afraid of Jim. This is partly his fault she's run away, the way he talks so hard to these girls."

"Don't go yet," said Aunt Betsy. "Don't tell him yet, Mother. Let's try to think of a way out of this first."

"I know," said Grandma. "We'll ask Davey." She held the letter ahead of her and rushed out to the porch, where my father sat with Phuong. Aunt Betsy stayed close on Grandma's heels, whimpering and looking out for Uncle Jim. I followed too and hung back.

"Storm clouds on the horizon again," said Father, as he saw them coming.

"This is no joke," said Grandma. "I've got something serious to tell you."

"I wasn't joking." Father pointed southwest to a black cloud shaped like an iron kettle, drifting toward us, ready to bash Uncle Jim over the head. Grandma handed Father the letter and he read it calmly.

Father stared at the letter. "Where's Jim?"

"He's in the bathtub," whispered Aunt Betsy, with a wince.

"All right," said Father. "Soon as he gets out, he and I are going to go looking for her."

I stepped forward and looked back at Grandma and Aunt Betsy. "I want to go, too."

"Well, certainly not," said Grandma. "Absolutely not."

"I can help them," I said. "I know where she is."

Grandma stared at me. "And where is she, child?"

I licked my lips. "She's with Bernie Grunstra. She's at his theater."

"What?" Her jaw dropped. "So it's Bernie Grunstra behind this! I just knew it. I've told you girls to stay away from him."

"Please don't fuss at her now," begged Aunt Betsy. "Let her go if she knows where my little Vicky is." She looked at my father. "Why don't you hurry on, now, and get her. Let's not even tell Jim about it if we don't have to."

"He'll be pretty mad if he finds out," said Father.

"Just go," she said. "It'll upset him so much. I don't want to upset him, Davey."

Father looked as though he wanted to tell a joke but figured this wasn't the time. He nodded again. "All right," he said, "then I'll go myself. But I'd like to pray about it first."

Father prayed aloud. He said something about the Lord knowing best where Victoria was at this moment, protecting her just like the little sparrow that falls. After saying "Amen," he got up and immediately headed for the car, taking Phuong by the hand. I followed behind.

"Now, why does Phuong need to go?" asked Grandma.

"I just feel there should be a woman with me," Father said. "Why don't you ladies go talk to Shirley? It seems to me she might be in on this, too."

Grandma nodded reluctantly and waved us away. As we climbed

into the car and pulled onto the road, I saw Uncle Jim step out onto the porch and frown after us.

"Carolyn," said Father, "are we really going to Bernie's theater?"

"No," I said. "Just take the Powhatan Bridge, and I can point the way on from there. I can't tell you the road names, but I'll know the way when I get there."

"All right," Father said, shifting in his seat. "We'll take the Powhatan Bridge. I hate that bridge."

"I'm sorry," I said quietly. "I'm sorry you have to do this."

Phuong held her hands up to keep her hair from lashing her face. We drove across the Powhatan Bridge, Father, Phuong, and I. Did Phuong know what had happened here? She kept her eyes straight ahead on the road. The ruts sang under our tires like sirens. Far below us, the water seethed silently. Father looked over at me and said, "Carolyn, did I ever tell you how I met my wife?"

"Not really, sir," I said, wondering which wife he referred to. My mind was on my mother.

"Well, how we first got to talking anyway." He started to laugh. "We were at the refugee camp, both working there, and I thought that this poor little Vietnamese girl hardly knew a word of English. My Vietnamese isn't so good, so, when I spoke to her I did lots of motions like this—" He motioned wildly in the air. "Yep, I'm making a fool of myself motioning away and she speaks only Vietnamese to me all this time, acting like a scared little rabbit. Well, there was this dog that hung around the camp, stealing food and carrying off shoes and clothes. And one day I go out into a field on my own to put up a clothesline and I hear this woman shouting at the dog, 'Come back, you dog! Come back with my shoe!' I turned around to see Phuong standing in the middle of the field in her bathrobe and bare feet. She didn't know anyone was watching. It was the first English I heard her speak. That's a woman for you. They've got deception in the blood."

"I have not decept you," said Phuong. "I like hear you speak bad Vietnamese."

He laughed again.

I led them all the way to the theater without any of us mentioning Victoria. It was early evening and the parking lot already overflowed with cars. Father took us into a front lot, not the one used by the cast. I couldn't see Ginger's car from here, though I tried. Older people climbed in and out of cars everywhere, ladies with heavy rouge and small black purses on chains. The Dela Fox Biddle looked more stately with all these people around and the tall fountains whishing in their brick bowls. For the first time the marquee announced:

Broadway's Henry Harrison
in
Lady Don't Laugh
Fridays, Saturdays 8 P.M., Sundays matinee
Call 458-TICK

"Well, Carolyn," said my father, "this is a very impressive theater. Don't tell me Bernie Grunstra has anything to do with this."

"He doesn't," I said.

"Who does, then?" He cocked his head around and stared at me.

"I can find Victoria," I said. "You all wait here in the car."

"Hurry then, Carolyn. I'm hungry."

"Yes, sir," I said. "I'll hurry."

I didn't go into the lobby, as it was only a few minutes until show time and I had no tickets to get past the doors. Instead I walked around to the back, tried a side door, and found it locked. I climbed through some shrubbery and knocked on the window of the dressing rooms. A dancer finally came to the window. She smiled and signaled that she would meet me at the back. While I waited for her at the door, I watched people stream in from the most remote parking lots. They smelled like soap and perfume. There were other scents in the air, August parking lot scents—hot tar, cigarette ash, and the breezy sweetness of flowers in planters. The black kettle cloud had followed us all the way from Dutch Falls. It was about to storm.

At last the door swung open. The dancer smiled, recognizing me. "Did you come back to wish us luck?"

"There's no such thing as luck," I said.

She shook her head and swung back toward her dressing room. I headed for the green room. Dancers ran by me with rouge on their

341

cheekbones, red stripes like slap marks. Their rhinestone jackets glittered gold and black. Their black satin bell-bottoms hugged their taut thighs and swished down to the floor. They were shouting to each other. "Twenty minutes!" "Where's my eye pencil?" "You don't need it."

I looked around warily for Ginger. If I came near her I would head the other way, knowing that she had read my letter by now and wondering what she had thought of it, or if she had laughed as she read, "You are truly my best friend in the whole world."

I thought she must be deep in the building somewhere, probably doing a last-minute warm-up with Henry and Myra. But just at that moment I saw Henry himself, rushing to the water fountain. In costume, Henry looked almost normal. He wore a suit and tie—except for the rouge, he could have been someone like my Uncle Jim, maybe a lawyer. Henry bent over the fountain, hugging it against his shoulders like a basketball. Standing close by in the shadows, I felt the heat coming off his back.

Suddenly, I heard a noise behind me. Henry turned and looked up. His eyes caught something. He glanced down at me and away, out a window. I whirled around. There was no one there now. Henry walked off quickly into a dark hall, toward the art exhibit. It must have been Ginger, I thought suddenly. She ran away because she didn't want me to see her. She was avoiding me. I went quietly into the hall a few yards behind Henry and watched until he turned a corner. Then I ran and watched him again. He went into a stairwell. The door sighed and closed behind him. I walked a little closer, stopped, and started to turn back.

A couple of female dancers were behind me in the hall. They giggled sharply and pointed at the exit sign.

"Did you find him?" called another voice around the corner.

"Down here."

"Oh, great. Out here in the dark? Who's he with?" Dianne appeared. She marched forward in my direction and I saw that she wore a long black dress and a tall hair bow. Her face was like a melting candle, sinking under the red light of the exit sign. She brushed past me and pushed open the door. I moved closer.

"You!" she said to someone inside, with the light on her melting face.

I thought she must be addressing Ginger. She hated Ginger, she mistrusted Henry, and now at last she had discovered them together. Surely Ginger would stand up to her. Surely an answer would come back fast and hard. But no one said anything in the stairwell. The dancers walked past me and stared through the door, their hands over their mouths. I edged forward with my back against the wall, keeping in a shadow. I wanted to see without being seen.

"Hey, wait," said one of the dancers, speaking to me. It was a girl I had played cards with. "Where do you think you're going?"

"Get her out of here!" yelled Dianne, suddenly seeing me. She put her hand out to push me away, but it was too late. I had already seen Henry Harrison in the dense light. Just behind him sat Mary Burrows.

Dianne yanked me aside and hit me hard on the lower back. I yelled out in pain. "Get out of here!" she screamed. "Everybody get out!"

I stepped back. Henry and Mary came into the hall.

"Dianne!" yelled someone back in the atrium. "Dianne! Al's looking for you. Ten minutes till curtain."

Dianne wheezed and shook her head like a horse. "No, sorry, I'm going home."

"Aw, come on, honey," said Henry sweetly, "we were just talking. Mary and I were just talking. You're overreacting."

"No, I'm not!" Dianne screamed. "I know what you do behind my back. I saw you two together."

"Come on, Dianne—"

"Henry, what is she talking about?" Mary asked innocently. "What's between you and Dianne?"

Henry ignored her. "I never did a thing, Dianne, honey. Mary was coming on to me and I was just telling her how I have absolutely no attraction for her. Come on, calm down."

"What?" yelled Mary.

"Oh, I knew you liked her," said Dianne. "I could tell." She burst into tears. "Why her? Why? She's not even beautiful." Dianne fell sideways against a wall and sobbed. The dancers nearby stared at Henry for an explanation.

"Jealous," he mouthed, and he made a "crazy" sign and shrugged his shoulders. Mary stood up and whizzed past me into the darkness of the hall.

"Go get Al," said a dancer. But Al was already running our way. He shouted before he reached us. "What is the problem here? What is your problem, Dianne? We've got ten minutes till curtain; what is the problem?"

Dianne cried and shook. Henry shrugged his shoulders.

"Everybody get to your places," said Al fiercely to the rest of us. "Get to your places. I'm dealing with this."

The dancers ran ahead of me down the hall. I went slowly. I passed the green room and came to the door of the stage, which stood wide open. The lights were up, the set ready. There were shadows moving behind the backdrop, but the stage itself stood abandoned. Where was everyone?

Someone on the tech crew was whistling in the hall behind me. I moved through the stage door, out of sight, and walked up the steps to the wings. I looked around. Here at stage left was a dark corner where a girl could sit and not be seen, looking out from behind a huge sheet of plywood. It seemed to me that I had a right to be here. So I sat, intending to stay for just a minute or so. On the other side of the curtain the audience fidgeted, sneezed, shushed, clicked, zipped. The piano lid snapped shut. Papers rustled. A moment later the violins took in a long breath and breathed out again in bursts. The audience gradually hushed. Then all at once the full orchestra embraced the stage. I put my hands up to my face and sat stiff against the wall, looking straight up through the busy catwalks and the high, stiff folds of the curtains.

Soon there were quiet footsteps on the stairs. Al came up, and behind him Henry, Ginger, and Vicky, the last two arm in arm. They came into the wings silently and moved past me without seeing me. Henry crossed to the other side of the stage. Al looked around anxiously. Dianne wasn't with them.

"Well, here we go," Al said nervously, as the orchestra crescendoed. He turned around and snapped to Henry, "Break a leg. Maybe I'll break it for you. Is the crew ready? Where's the crew? I don't see the crew."

"They're all here, Al," said Ginger. "Don't panic. It'll be all right."

"Yeah, without Dianne, well."

"We know what to do."

"Yeah, just get to your places."

"Don't worry. You should pray, Al. Pray to God that the show goes right without Dianne. It'll relax you."

"Stupid preacher's wife," Al mumbled.

Ginger laughed in a bold voice because the music was loud and high. She took Vicky by the hand and they stepped onto the stage. They exchanged a look, a smile, a kiss on the cheek. They took their positions and stood in the bright watery calm of the stage, poised and still for a long half second. Their smooth skin caught the golden light and held it. They had color but no depth. They were full of beauty without shadows. Victoria was blue-eyed and serene. Her face was my grandmother's face but without the hard edge that measured the world by its evil. There she stood with Ginger, shadowless, while I curled up completely in the shadows.

Henry made an O.K. sign. They waved back. He rubbed his hands together. On Henry's side of the stage stood men from the tech crew with their arms up, their hands on the curtain levers. Al licked his lips and looked around again. The orchestra stopped. We could hear whispers in the audience. An awesome pause followed, and then Al's signal. He raised his right arm sharply and held it in the air like Moses commanding the waters of the Red Sea. The levers went down. The curtain rose. The first polite thunder of applause cracked rickety packety smash against the concave ceiling and stopped. I could not see the faces in the theater from where I sat, only light pouring across a black corner of the ceiling like a waterfall, and a maelstrom of dust spinning in it. When Ginger lifted her voice to speak her first lines, I suddenly felt jubilant. Her laughter was clear and happy. I wanted to step out and wave to her and call "Good luck!"

At stage right, in the corner across from me, Tommy Depew and Mary Burrows whispered heatedly. I couldn't see them very well on account of the props crew diving back and forth to rearrange furniture. They both watched Henry, who was about to walk out on cue. I saw Mary's hand come down quietly but hard on Tommy's cheek.

Then Henry stepped forward and a row of young dancers moved back and I saw Tommy standing alone and mute with his fingers on his cheek, his eyes welling up with tears.

"Look at that," whispered Al to Myra Woods, who stood with him. "Look at the trouble men go through for women."

"What about the trouble women go through for men?" asked Myra. "Think of poor Dianne."

"Oh, yeah, poor Dianne. She might ruin me tonight."

"Think positive, Al."

"I'm trying. At least there's Ginger. She can do no wrong."

At the end of act 1, the applause raced in like rain. It was all for Ginger, who had just sung with the chorus, Calypso style, before she dived over the side of the ship to fake her own death:

Atlantic nights can be romantic,
If your love is not too frantic.
When the ocean sweetly rocks,
Is her stomach in her socks?
When the north winds churn and wail,
Is your true love turning pale?

Oh, tell her to forget the motion,
Just make her dance, ignore the ocean.
And though the boat is soon capsizing,
You will be cap-it-alizing,
For while she's dancing on the ceiling,
Delicious kisses you'll be stealing.

Al beamed as the curtain dropped. He ran to Ginger and caught her and swung her off her feet. The music came up again to hide her scream. "Oh, Al, stop!" Her face was flushed and her eyes bright.

"You're doing it, baby," he said, "You're doing great!"

Henry kissed Vicky, who had been standing very near me for a long time with her hands together properly, also smiling. If I wanted her attention I could have reached out and touched the backs of her knees.

"Take a break, honey," said Ginger. "You did a great job. Go freshen up."

346

Vicky blinked her eyes and nodded. As she moved through the inner curtains, toward the steps, I got up and followed. It was time to talk to her now; I felt it like a wind on my face. I followed her through the bustling corridors into the women's bathroom. The dancers smiled at her as she moved gracefully by, shimmering in a pink chiffon nightgown from scene 2 of the first act. Vicky smiled back and went to a sink to touch up her hair with a curling iron. I stepped after her. Did Vicky ever see, ever hear anything that she didn't want to?

"Victoria?" I asked, stepping up beside her.

She turned quickly. Her hair stayed in place. Her smile fell. "Oh, gosh, you scared me. What are you doing here?"

"I thought the first act went real well," I said. "I thought you did real well."

"Thanks."

"Victoria, my father is waiting for you out in the parking lot."

She frowned. "I guess he'll just have to wait. Tell him I'm real sorry but I'm not coming home."

"Did you really run away from home?"

"That's what it looks like. So I guess I did."

"You're never going back?"

"I don't know, Carrie. Maybe or maybe not. It depends."

"On what?"

"On how the show goes. And it's going real good so far."

"I think my father wants to talk to you. Why don't you go out there right now and talk to him?"

"Carrie—my gosh, I'm wearing a nightgown!"

It was true. She could wear that nightgown onstage in front of hundreds of people, but outside it wouldn't do.

"He might come in and talk to you," I said.

She sighed. "It's no use anybody talking to me because I have made up my mind and I'm not going back. Tell my mother I'll call her soon so she can send me all my clothes."

"Where are you staying?"

"I'll be at Ginger's. But don't you tell them that. You swear you won't tell them?"

I hesitated.

"You swear?" She narrowed her eyes and looked almost like Shirley. I nodded and went back out into the hall. I wandered in different directions through the hallways, wondering where to go, whether to go back to my father and Phuong or try to sneak into the wings again or just sit. As I wandered, the whole backstage rumbled with laughter from the auditorium, the way the earth rumbles with motion that we never feel.

19

ore than an hour had gone by since I left my father in the parking lot. How could he help me here among these show people? Entering a theater, didn't one twirl out from the good people of Dutch Falls like a diver into the sea? This was a sinner's world. This was not the world of the Reformed, and really, I didn't believe that a man like my father could even reach this world, backstage in the Dela Fox Biddle. So it was up to me. I would bring Victoria home again, or not bring her, which was almost my preference. But as I sat down in the quiet hall, feeling sorry for myself and thinking what to do next, I heard a deep Dutch voice from another direction. It wasn't my father's voice, or my uncle's, but it was familiar.

I sat up straight. Then I stood and straightened my hair. Someone had directed that voice this way. Other voices crowded around it in a low male murmur. A moment later I watched as Dominie Grunstra, my own Dominie Grunstra, plodded down this very corridor in the direction of the women's dressing room. He wore square-toed, shiny black shoes, white socks that stood out stunningly under his brown plaid slacks, a dull sports coat, and a plaid hat to match his pants. His barrel chest strained the buttons of his shirt. His white chin jumped out over his wrinkled neck. Behind him walked my father, my grandmother, and right on the dominie's heels, Uncle Jim. Uncle Jim vied for position with the dominie, stepping quickly to right and left to move around the big man, only to drop back again at every other step. Three or four young dancers sat in the hall. Not even in the presence of the head teaching elder of the First Reformed Church of Virginia did they interrupt their conversation or move aside. But the dominie glided over them like Christ walking on the water.

"There's Carolyn!" said my grandmother. She had spotted me first, though I stood practically in the dark. "Carolyn, what on earth is going on here?"

"Where is Victoria?" Uncle Jim demanded, looking at me angrily. He still stood behind the dominie. "I want to know right now where Victoria is. You tell me, little miss."

I shrank back and looked down. "I don't know where she is. She's somewhere around here."

"Now—now, Carolyn," Grandma sputtered nervously. She wiped her hands on the side of her purse. "Tell us what Victoria is doing here."

"She's acting in the show," I said.

"Well, that's just ridiculous. How would Victoria know anything about shows?"

"It's Jo's doing," said Uncle Jim. He shook his head and slapped the wall. "Victoria's been spending time with Jo. They must have come here. I should never have allowed that."

"It's not your fault," said Father. "Don't blame Jo either, not until we know."

"At least, son," said the dominie, with a hand on my uncle's shoulder, "at least we know that the child is here. Why don't we send your mother to look for her and you and I can wait here and talk it over? We need to know what to say before we say it, don't we, Jim? Don't you think so?"

"That's right, Jim," said Father. "You need to get control of yourself before you see her."

Uncle Jim sighed in a disgusted way. Grandma stepped forward and put her hand in mine. "Oh, I'm worn out by all this. Will you show me the way, Carolyn? You know the way around here. I just want to go straight to Vicky."

"I really don't know where she is," I said. "I can try to find her, but I don't know for sure."

"Well, go look," said Uncle Jim. "Stop talking about it and go look. Hurry up."

Grandma and I walked around the corner together, holding hands. She gripped my fingers tight. "I couldn't believe it," she said. "I couldn't believe it when Shirley told me where you'd come. I just hate to see you here. Here with all these—all these worldly English people. And Vicky told Shirley you've been coming here for weeks. Why have you lied to me, Carolyn?"

"What did Shirley tell you?" I felt my face redden.

"She told us that Mrs. Jordan is appearing in this show here. Is that right?"

"Well . . . yes, Grandma."

"Oh, dear Lord, I can't believe it. But I should have seen it coming, shouldn't I?"

"Just don't be mad, Grandma."

"I'm only mad at myself."

"Please don't be."

"I should never have let you associate with that woman. The Lord tried to tell me it was all wrong. I only have myself to blame."

"I'll never come again, Oma."

Grandma sighed.

"I think maybe Vicky's in the dressing room," I said. We went by the costume room and pushed through a crowd of salty bodies in front of the green room. I kept my face down, hoping no one would acknowledge me, but I felt the dancers staring. Inside the theater I heard Tommy Depew singing.

"Here it is; this is the women's dressing room," I said to Grandma, as we came to the tall door near the green room. I led her inside, around the corner, past the lockers to the sinks. She stepped over piles of clothes to check the stalls. "Abominable," she said.

"It's messy," I agreed, noticing puddles of makeup in the porcelain sinks. "I've never seen it so messy in here."

"Well, Vicky's not in here," Grandma said quickly, with her hand over her nose. "Let's get right out of here."

We went back to the hall, made a complete circle of the building, and finally returned to Father, Uncle Jim, and Dominie Grunstra. I was horrified to see them huddled in a drinking fountain alcove, praying, while dancers passed back and forth.

351

"And we commend unto thee thy covenant child, our Victoria, for your special grace and provision. In thy gracious name, Amen." The dominie grasped my uncle's hand. Grandma and I stood back. The three men lifted their heads, and just then Henry Harrison breezed by in the hallway. He took a quick look at us and kept going. The curtain had fallen on act 2. Places were being called for act 3. I heard Ginger's name shouted. She must be in these halls somewhere. The dominie blew his nose into a cloth handkerchief from his pocket.

"Can't find Vicky?" Father asked Grandma.

Grandma shook her head. Uncle Jim moaned and put his hand to his head. "Well, we didn't look everywhere," Grandma said hastily. "I expect we should try again. Let me go alone."

"No, Mother," said Uncle Jim firmly. "I'm going. I figure I've calmed down sufficiently to find my own daughter and set this situation straight."

"Wait a little longer, Jim," said Grandma.

"It won't take me long." He walked off quickly in the same direction as Henry Harrison.

"Oh, dear," said Grandma. "I wish we'd found her first. We better follow. Davey?"

"No," said my father. "Jim should handle his own family matters, Mama. Let him go."

"Well, I don't agree at all," she said. "He's hard on that girl. Dominie, he's hard on her. That's what's brought this trouble on us."

"Is that it?" said the dominie.

"Yes, I think that's it," Grandma said. "I think Davey ought to talk to Vicky himself, while Jim calms down."

"Carolyn," said the dominie, turning down to me with a somber face, "I want to ask you, do you know whether my brother Bernie has really had any influence over your cousin? Is he the one who instigated this behavior?"

I shook my head. He put his heavy hands on my shoulders and pressed his jaw against his neck so that his jowls fanned out like feathers. "What about you? Has my brother talked to you? Has he suggested that you become involved in—" The dominie's voice hushed. "—the theater?"

"Do you mean the movie theater?" I asked. "I did go there once." I put my eyes down quickly.

He looked grave. "I'm sorry to hear that, Carolyn. Sometimes my brother promises things to young girls, puts them in with the wrong sort of people. Did he do that to you?"

I shook my head. "No, sir," I said. "I lied. Bernie didn't have anything to do with this."

"'Mr.' Bernie," corrected my grandmother. "And Carolyn, I just don't understand you, child. That you should tell such a lie—"

The dominie breathed a sigh. "Thank the Lord. It was wrong of me to suspect him."

"Places!" came the shout again. "Ginger Jordan, Tommy Depew, places!" A stagehand zipped through the hall, looking from side to side. He stopped, stared at me, and said, "Where's your mother? I'm looking for her everywhere."

My father had been standing quietly to the side, but now I felt his eyes on me. I stammered and said to the man, "I think you must be looking for somebody else. My mother's deceased."

The stagehand gave me a wild look and hurried on. I hadn't even time to glance at my father's face again before there was a laugh behind me. Grandma stared over my head. The dominie looked too and dropped his mouth. I turned again. Right there in the hall, not five feet behind me and walking toward us, was Arnie Hagedoorn with Ginger on his arm. I had only imagined a moment like this. Here they came, one party from Dutch Falls toward another party, and though they glanced our way, and though we saw them so well, they hardly saw us at all. Arnie Hagedoorn looked intently at Ginger like a man trying to dribble a basketball for the first time. Ginger laughed again, stretched up, and gave him a kiss on the mouth, right there in the sight of us all. It was no friendly kiss, either. It was the kind of kiss my grandmother always said was just the tip of the iceberg. If people kissed like that in public, she said, you hated to think what they were doing in private.

"Excuse us, Arnold," said the dominie loudly, and Arnie Hagedoorn looked up and still did not immediately understand. So the dominie said, "Arnold, how is Nancy? How is the baby?" Only then did the head deacon of the F.R.C. of V. react. He stopped in his tracks and curved his back and drew his arms up against his sides. Ginger didn't let go of him. Her eyes flitted back and forth.

"How are you, Arnie?" said the dominie.

There was no running away for Arnie; there were no excuses to be made. My father and Dominie Grunstra faced him—two dominies against a debauched deacon and a wayward pastor's wife. Around the corner, Al screamed Ginger's name, but she didn't let Arnie go.

"Hi, Carla," she said to me. "Hello, Mrs. Grietkirk," she said to Grandma.

Grandma said nothing.

"Hello, Mrs. Jordan," said Father. "Arnie, hello. Have you seen my niece, Victoria? We're looking for her. We're hoping to fetch her home. Her father went after her."

"Davey," said Arnie Hagedoorn. That was all he could say.

"Do you want a ride home, Arnie?" asked Father quietly. "Do you need a ride home?"

"No." Mr. Hagedoorn shook his head.

"Excuse me," said Ginger. "I'm wanted." She laughed, just a little, and then let go of Arnie's arm at last and hurried by us. I thought that my grandmother might jump forward and catch her by the sleeve. Grandma let her pass.

"Mrs. Grietkirk," said the dominie to Grandma in a low voice, "why don't you send young Carolyn out to the car? Let us have a word with Arnie alone."

"I don't want to go out to the car," I said. "I can wait in the bathroom."

"You obey the dominie," said Grandma sharply. "Go out, Carolyn."

"That's right," said Father. "The dominie is making good sense. We all have a lot to talk about."

I didn't want to go. Mr. Hagedoorn cringed in the hall, confused and red. I didn't care about him. What was it that compelled me to stay? Could it be that I saw Ginger slipping away, that I knew I was abandoning her when I should be her champion? I didn't want to go, knowing it was the last time I would leave the Dela Fox Biddle. My grandmother pinched my shoulder and urged me away. Father gave

354

me a stern look. The dominie waited patiently, his eyes on the floor. Well, I would have to go after all. Children could not be champions. And there was no fighting Providence.

It was raining hard in the parking lot as I left through the back door near the art exhibit. Over the fountain, the three flags whipped against their poles. I ran as fast as I could to the car and plunged into the backseat. I had forgotten about Phuong, as everyone always did. Had she been asked to stay outside, or did she prefer to? She lay stretched out in the front street, her eyes closed.

"Oh!" she said, when I slammed the door. Her face dripped with the gray shadows of the rain on the windshield. She sat up straight. "Do they find Vicky?"

"No," I said. "Not yet."

"I am not sleeping. Praying for her."

"Good," I said. "She'll need it when her father gets hold of her." I didn't know what Phuong knew or didn't know—about anything, really. I stretched my legs out and leaned against the cool window. I couldn't think now, not with someone else here. My thoughts were too private. I wanted to run and ask Ginger if it was true. Did she love Arnie Hagedoorn? Would she leave Frank and live with Arnie? What were her plans? What was the truth?

"I can just pray in my mind," Phuong said. "I don't mind to wait, because I pray. I pray about everything."

"Uh huh," I said. I was seeing it all again in my mind.

Phuong sat up and frowned. She cocked her head back in my direction and sighed. "I am a little worry," she said quietly, "to move to Pennsylvania."

"Oh," I said. It wasn't a good time to discuss it. I only wanted to think about Ginger.

"Carolyn," Phuong said, "you don't worry?"

"I don't think so. Why should I worry?"

"I don't know. It's different place. It's cold."

"Dutch people were made for cold weather," I said.

"Tell me about Pennsylvania," she said.

I thought for a moment and shrugged my shoulders. "I stayed in a motel once in Pittsburgh, but it was after dark. I guess I don't know anything about Pennsylvania. But I'm not worried. I think I want to move away now."

She stared away thoughtfully and said in a hopeless voice, "Do Presbyterians baptize the Holy Ghost?"

"No," I said, "I don't think so. Maybe you can find a church that does."

She nodded. "And I miss your grandmother."

"Yeah," was all I could say. I hardly knew what it would be like to be away from Grandma. But when I thought of giving up Ginger—and I would have to, no matter what happened now, whether I stayed in Dutch Falls or went to Pennsylvania or died and went to heaven—what mattered? What mattered at all when you had lost your best friend in the world, the only person worth living for? I was orphaned again. I wanted to cry, but not here in front of Phuong. We dropped down in our seats. The wind gusted against the windows, each gust bringing a small explosion of rain. Then the wind slowed for a while and we waited.

The show ended and the big doors at the front of the theater pushed open with the weight of a crowd. Into the parking lot the crowd surged and filled the rainy darkness, laughing and holding hands as they scrambled to unlock car doors and close umbrellas. Then the cars trailed slowly out of the parking lot bumper to bumper like a string of beads untwining. We watched the whole scene intently and strained to see whether Father might be the next person out of the doors, or Grandma, or Uncle Jim. But they didn't come.

Someone knocked on the window beside me. I hadn't seen anyone come up, and when I looked out I saw only a dark umbrella bouncing against the glass. When it collapsed, there was my Aunt Jo, knocking and staring into the window. I opened the door quickly and she slid in next to me.

"What are you doing here?" I asked.

"What a night," she said. "There are tornadoes around, too."

"Where's Grandma?" I asked.

"Well, how would I know? I left the house right after you and your daddy. I came over here on my own to see Vicky, in case she needed me."

"Vicky's still inside the theater," I said, "and Grandma and Uncle Jim and the dominie are in there, too."

"Your grandma?" Aunt Jo sounded horrified. "What's she doing in there?"

"They found Arnie Hagedoorn in there," I said, as if that explained everything.

"They found Arnie?" Now she lifted her eyebrows and stared at the theater building. "What was Arnie doing in there?"

"He was with Ginger."

She dropped her eyebrows. "I'm not surprised," she said. She put her hand on the door of the car and looked for a moment as if she would go back inside. "No," she said finally. "I figure I'll stay out of this. The dominie's in there, is he?"

"Yes," I said. "He wanted to know if Mr. Bernie was the one who got Vicky into the show."

She smiled and her voice dropped to a whisper. "That's because Bernie Grunstra tried something with me once, when I was about Vicky's age. He told me he wanted to take some pictures of pretty girls, and that if my friends and I would pose for him, we might get a small part in a movie sometime. It sounded fun, so we went to his apartment. But somebody from the church saw us going up there and called Mrs. Grunstra. She was our Sunday school teacher at the time. She shut us all in the bathroom and pulled Bernie out the door of his own apartment by the ear and yelled at him for the whole world to hear. Blah blah blah. And then the elders kicked him out of the church because he wouldn't repent." Aunt Jo started to laugh but looked guiltily at me and stopped. "Mama was afraid what might happen to my reputation after that. She thought I'd never get a good Dutch boy. So she was real happy when I started dating Arnie Hagedoorn!" She slapped the seat and laughed out loud this time. Phuong pulled up against the car door and looked the other way.

"How long did you date Mr. Hagedoorn?" I asked.

"Long enough to be sorry," Aunt Jo said. "Well, I broke up with him. He was always ninety to nothing where women are concerned. Anyway, Grandma didn't want me to marry him for fear my children would inherit his glands."

"I don't like Arnie Hagedoorn," I said. "I don't see what women like about him."

"Oh, he's cute, Carolyn."

"I don't think he's cute. I think he's ugly and I hate him."

"Well, give yourself a few years. When's your grandma coming out, anyway? This wind is making me nervous."

"We've been waiting forever," I said.

Aunt Jo laughed again. "They're probably praying over old Arnie. Praying fire and forgiveness on his head. Serves him right."

When that remark had died in the air we sat stiffly and waited a little longer. At last they came. Father and the dominie ran first from a side door. Uncle Jim followed, holding an umbrella over Grandma and Victoria, who was sobbing. Grandma held her around the arms, as if she could shield her from things that had most likely already happened.

"Oh, great," said my aunt just before they reached us. "I can tell we're going to have a scene. Guess Jim will blame me for all the evil in the world." She opened her door of the car and Grandma, hurrying up, said, "Jo! What are you doing here? Jo's here."

"I'm not surprised she's here," said Uncle Jim. "She goes where trouble goes."

"Did you all know there are tornadoes out tonight?" said Aunt Jo. "It's real bad out here."

"I can't listen to any bad news," said Grandma. "Not right now. Let's hurry home."

"I'll follow you all," said my aunt. "My car's across the lot."

"No, you stay with us," said Grandma. "Let's keep the family together. I need all of you. Let's all take the Dart. Here Jo, make room for your brothers."

"Mama, it won't work," said Father, who still stood in the rain. "We're all too fat."

"Speak for yourself," said Aunt Jo.

"In any case," he said, "you ladies can take the station wagon. Jo, you drive since Mama's out of sorts."

"I am not out of sorts," said Grandma.

358

"You are too," said Aunt Jo, "and anyway I won't be carted home by my mother."

"I don't trust your driving," said Grandma.

"Mama," said Uncle Jim, "I demand that you go to the station wagon now."

"Well, yes, sir," said Grandma bitterly. "I suppose my grown children know best. But I don't trust Jo on the road—I just don't trust her. And I'm already nervous besides."

Grandma and Vicky moved in a huddle to the wagon. Aunt Jo and I followed and Father escorted Phuong. He shut the door and waved. My aunt spent some time adjusting the seat, buckling up and arranging her sweater just right over her back and around her shoulders.

"Hurry up," said Grandma. "Start the car. The men are waiting."

"I have to be comfortable," said my aunt. "Don't hurry me." She smoothed down her hair, looking in the rearview mirror. When she was finished the mirror stayed twisted, so that I could see myself in it. Uncle Jim was at the wheel of the other car. He honked. Aunt Jo honked back. We proceeded together out of the parking lot, into the rain, through an elegant suburban neighborhood. Grandma sat regal and tight-lipped in the front. Victoria sat next to me by the back left window, slumped over and pouting. Phuong sat on the other side of me. Going around curves, we crunched elbows and shoulders. We jounced over a broken cobblestone road, turned a corner, and surged onto the highway that would take us back to Dutch Falls. So many times I had made these turns with Ginger. I looked behind me. I was hoping to see Ginger's car. But maybe she had left with Arnie.

"I know what happened in there, Mama," said Aunt Jo. "I know you saw Arnie with Ginger Jordan."

Grandma didn't answer.

"I guess they finally caught him, didn't they? They'll have to kick him off the board of deacons. They'll have to discipline him. Why don't you answer, Mama?"

Grandma opened her mouth, took a breath, and closed it again. "I'm nervous and upset tonight," she said. "Let's talk about this tomorrow when the children aren't with us."

359

"I don't see why we should hide it from them. They probably know more than we do."

"Why does there have to be so much sin?" cried Grandma suddenly. She held her fists in the air. "I just want to know. The world's coming apart."

Suddenly the air cracked like a great egg and rain rushed down again. Aunt Jo switched on the radio.

"What are you doing?" said Grandma.

"I'm just wondering about the weather. This wind is crazy." The radio hissed and crackled. Aunt Jo switched it off and Grandma switched it on again.

"I believe you're right about the wind," said Grandma in a breathy voice. "Look at those trees bending. Look at the trash blowing across the road. It must have come from someone's house."

"Hold it—leave the dial there, Mama—that's it. Oh! Now why did you turn the dial right when they were giving the weather?"

"I was trying to get it on the right station."

"That was the station, Mama. I told you not to turn it. That was the station. See the red light come on? That indicates the station, Mama. Well, I can't find it now."

"I'm almost sure I heard them say tornado," said Grandma.

"Don't get panicked," said Aunt Jo. "It's probably somewhere else."

"Oh, but the wind looks bad," said Grandma anxiously. "Did they call it a 'watch' or a 'warning'? A warning means that there's been a tornado sighted already."

"Don't say it like I don't know, Mama. Everybody knows that. I didn't hear them say 'warning.' It can't be near here."

"Just look at that wind. I can tell there's a tornado around here. How are you keeping the car on the road?"

Aunt Jo sighed. After a few more minutes of fighting the wind she said, "I think you're right. I'm going to try and signal Jim to stop." She slowed down and unrolled her window. But the wind caterwauled so furiously that even when Jim slowed down ahead, there was no chance of shouting to him. The Dart careened off the road and halted on a sloping stretch of grass. Aunt Jo pulled off next to a big ball of twiggy, leafless bushes. Jim jumped out and ran toward us. His hair stood straight up in the air, stiff, whipped into peaks like egg whites. He stumbled to the window through the mud and my father ran up to Grandma's window.

"What's the matter?" Uncle Jim shouted.

"Do you hear that wind howling?" shouted Grandma to him over Aunt Jo's arms on the wheel. "We think we might have heard a tornado warning on the radio."

Jim rolled his eyes. "I knew I shouldn't have put all you women in the same car."

Shick, boom! A spray of lightning sparks rose and arched in the air about ten yards away. Uncle Jim's knees buckled and he fell right in the mud.

"Thank the Lord!" said Aunt Jo. "He heard my silent prayer!"

"This is God trying to tell us all something," said Grandma.

"Come on," said Jim, picking himself up, "let's get going. Sooner we get home, sooner we're warm and dry."

"Mama," said Father, "you want to ride with us?"

"Yes!" said Grandma eagerly.

"No, I'll drive them, Davey," said Uncle Jim. "We have to think of the girls, too. You go on with the dominie. We'll see you back at home."

Aunt Jo snorted and protested. "I can drive as well as you can, Jim. You know it's true. I've been driving all over the country."

"I won't relax until a man is driving," shouted Grandma. "Please move over, Josephine, and let your brother drive."

Uncle Jim backed in to the driver's seat triumphantly, bottom first. Jo slid angrily to the middle of the seat and sat with her arms crossed and her chin out. At first Jim tried to adjust the seat to make room for his knees.

"Hurry!" insisted Grandma. "Let's go! Forget about that!"

Uncle Jim pulled up his knees and put his feet on the pedals and looked as though he were driving a tricycle. The car drooped on his side. Soon our wheels cavumped onto the highway again. We followed the Dart, tearing through the rough air. Phuong and I looked out to see the dark sky rolling up like a cream horn just above the streetlights. I imagined the wagon rising in the air and surfing along the rain.

"Oh, let's pray," shouted Grandma. "Let's just pray that we make it home!"

Was it only my imagination that the car slowed then, that my uncle gunned the motor just to keep us crawling forward against an unyielding column of air? I felt the front wheels lift, then set down again.

"Jim, listen to that!" yelled Aunt Jo. "It doesn't sound right."

Jim listened for a moment. Then he shouted, "Out of the car! Everybody out of the car and into the ditch!" The Dart kept going, but Uncle Jim threw on the brakes of the wagon and stopped in the middle of the road. We rushed out, with our ears popping and the sky rolling, into the grass. There was no ditch.

"Lord, why is there never a ditch when you need one?" shouted Aunt Jo.

"How about a culvert?" shouted Grandma.

"What's a culvert? What is that?"

"Hit the dirt!" cried Uncle Jim.

We dropped flat on the ground and put our hands over our ears. The sky shrieked, the clouds coiled down, branches flew over our heads spinning in the air like the spokes of wheels. The wagon lifted its nose and bounded on its back bumper like a rearing horse. We groped for each other and pressed our arms into cloth, flesh, hair, and bone. Aunt Jo had me by the ankle. Grandma gripped me around the waist and held Victoria under the shoulder blades.

Phuong screamed, "Help! God, help!" She lay alone, face down in the mud. Uncle Jim grabbed her tight and crouched on top of her, his arms wrapped around her waist, her hands in his. He looked straight up into the sky, cast his eyes around, looked over all of us. He said something, but I couldn't hear. The roar numbed my ears. I could barely hear the slow snap of big trees not fifty yards away.

"Oh, pray!" I thought. "Just pray!" But though I could say, "Lord, oh, Lord, save us, please!" it wasn't enough. The wind was strong. What prayer could break the back of a tornado? What whispered words could turn aside the energy of a mighty whirlwind? We clutched the weeds, we dug our fingers like shallow roots into the soil, and braced to be torn away from the earth. We expected any moment to be kites, soaring above the landscapes, miles high. Our eyes were full of terror and empty space. But we held each other by the arms and hands and around the waists, and Phuong twitched between my uncle's armpits like a fish in a bucket. I knew that she was having a seizure, but no one could go to her now. She might bite her tongue off, or even swallow it, and we could do nothing. "Oh, Lord, save us!"

When the worst was at last over, we lay perfectly still, even Phuong. The sky flashed in every direction. The ground rumbled. The rain was warm and dense, falling in sheets. We shivered, unable to speak.

I heard Phuong mumbling underneath Uncle Jim. He rolled off of her immediately and set her up on her knees, with her forehead touching the soaked ground. Then he squatted next to Grandma with his head in his hands. While Phuong kept mumbling, Grandma whimpered, "I thought we would all be killed! I thought we would all be killed!"

"What's she doing?" asked Uncle Jim, pointing at Phuong. "She's crazy. She's having a breakdown."

"I think she's all right," I said.

"Oh, yes, she's all right," said Grandma. "But I think I'm having a heart attack." I put my arms around Grandma and patted her back.

"You don't look so good," said Aunt Jo to Uncle Jim.

"I guess I feel about as good as I look," he said.

"That was something else."

"It sure was. I don't think we can drive the car, either. Looks like the front tires are both flat and one of the rims is bent. Hopefully Davey will come back for us."

"Oh, Davey!" said Grandma, and she began to cry. "And the dominie. I hope they're all right."

We stood up from the mud together, bleary-eyed and frightened. Aunt Jo helped Phuong to her feet and I helped Grandma. Victoria struggled on her own.

"We're near the bridge," said Uncle Jim. "It can't be more than a half mile."

At least that was some consolation, to be so near Dutch Falls. Grandma leaned on me and we started to trek together down the shoulder of the road, around curves, past acre after acre of dense woods, until the trees thinned and the rain blew straight and heavy in our faces with the river smell on it. We reached the river and looked across to a dark row of houses, which we could see only in flashes of lightning.

"We can call from over there," said Uncle Jim. "Just another little bit, Mama. It won't take long."

"I'm having trouble," said Grandma. "I think I might be about to die."

"Hush now," said Aunt Jo. "Don't be morbid."

"It isn't like me," said Grandma. "But I'm having trouble."

Uncle Jim and Aunt Jo looked at each other. We crossed the bridge on foot. Phuong limped against me. Not a car came by, from either direction. The Appomattox below us was a vast, fleeced blacktop. The wind howled over the concrete handrails, threatening to tear us away from the bridge. We felt safer when we had finally touched solid ground on the other side of the river.

"It'll take forever if we stay on the main road," said Aunt Jo.

"That's right," said Uncle Jim. "Let's look for a footpath near the bank. There used to be such a thing. Remember how we fished here, before it was polluted?"

"I do remember," said Jo. "Mama? You doing all right?"

"I'm holding up," said Grandma weakly. She swayed with each step. "I hope Jim knows what he's talking about. I don't recall you all fishing here."

"That's because we weren't supposed to," said Uncle Jim. "Arnie talked us into it. He even talked Davey into it. He could talk anybody into anything, that Arnie." He glanced at my aunt.

"Let's not start on that now," said Aunt Jo.

"Yes, let's please drop it," said Grandma. "I just want to find a place to sit down and rest. Maybe Davey will come back for us any minute."

The footpath was trashy and rugged and sometimes disappeared altogether in brambles. We rested on the bank for a good while, so that in the end it took us an hour to reach the edge of the woods and arrive at the subdivision we had seen from the other side. The houses turned out to be only wood skeletons floating on mud, with lumber and insulation stacked in their raw brown driveways. The storm had torn some of them apart. Segments of plasterboard lay scattered in the street like playing cards. This was just like the neighborhood I had

364

visited with Annajane, where her uncle had seen Arnie Hagedoorn visiting a strange woman, and where he had found a woman's slip. Now I thought that the slip must have belonged to Ginger.

"Great," said Aunt Jo. "This was some idea. Nobody home here."

"Don't complain," said Uncle Jim. "Think."

"I think we better keep walking, if Mama can stand it."

"I'll survive," said Grandma. "Let me just rest again."

Victoria suddenly burst into tears. "Oh, Grandma! This is all my fault!"

"Oh, please," said Aunt Jo. "Not now. I can't take it."

Uncle Jim slowed and fell back in order to put his arm around Vicky. She cried furiously. My grandmother, too, tried to comfort her. We rested again. Then, because of the grief and commotion, we walked slowly down the sludgy streets, taking another half hour to reach the older English subdivisions where people actually lived. The windows were dark. Up and down the blocks, people stood outside surveying the damage with flashlights and car lights. Trees lay across the road. Branches and sticks and pine brooms cluttered the yards.

"Ma'am?" my aunt called to an elderly woman standing in her drive-way. "Could you help us? We're stranded and can't get home."

"Well, I live with my son," said the woman in a timid way. "I don't know what I can do for you."

"Is your phone working? Can we call home?"

"You could try, honey. Now, I don't know if it's working because I ain't tried to call nobody. My son's gone out looking at all the power lines that's down, because he works for the electric company."

"Well, I'll try," said Aunt Jo. "Thank you, ma'am." And she hustled onto the porch and into the house, leaving the rest of us in the yard. A pair of headlights flashed on in the next-door driveway and suddenly we stood in full, brilliant light with mist curling behind us. Grandma's face shone stark white.

"Did y'all hear there was a tornado?" asked the woman on the porch. As she spoke, she caught our faces in the light and stared mainly at Phuong, who stood pale and bent over behind me. Grandma stepped out of the glare and went closer to the porch.

"We were out in it," Grandma said. "It was the most terrible thing. I can't even tell you."

"I listened on the radio and there's a woman saying it wiped her house clean away, over in colored town."

"How did she have a phone to call on then?" asked Uncle Jim.

"I guess she had to call from a neighbor's," said the woman. "That's what she must have done."

"Takes all kinds," said Uncle Jim in a grumpy voice. "If my house was blown away, I don't think I'd go running to call a radio station."

"I wouldn't doubt anything at this point," said Grandma. "It was just terrible. I didn't know wind could blow so hard."

"I didn't either," said the woman. And she stared at Phuong again.

When my aunt came from the house, she gave us a somber look. "I can't get through," she said. "They're saying on the radio that a lot of trees and lines are down. Nobody's driving anywhere right now. So I guess Davey won't be coming for us."

"We'll walk it," said Uncle Jim. "It's only—what—four miles?"

"Mama can't do it," Aunt Jo said.

"I can," said Grandma. "I'm having trouble, but I've prayed and the Lord has helped me."

"Well, you can't go with us," declared Aunt Jo. "I think you should wait here with the girls while Jim and I walk back to the house."

Grandma put her hand over her heart. "But I'm as worried as you all are. I'm as worried about Betsy and Nathan and Shirley as you are. And Davey, too. I'm so concerned about my Davey."

"Ma'am?" Aunt Jo asked the woman on the porch, "would you allow my mother and my nieces to stay here for a while? My brother and I want to go home and check on the rest of the family."

"I told you I'd like to come," said Grandma.

"I guess they can stay," the woman said slowly. She looked around and pointed at the steps. "They can all sit here on the porch. I don't think my son will mind about it."

"Can I please go with you?" I asked Aunt Jo. "I don't want to just sit. I'd rather walk."

"Grandma needs you here, Carolyn," said my aunt.

"But Victoria's with her," I said. "Phuong's with her, too. They know how to take care of her." I glanced at Phuong for reassurance. She wasn't paying attention. She stood looking out at the dark horizon. Grandma and Victoria had already gone to find seats on the porch.

"Let's go, Jo," said Uncle Jim. "Quicker there, quicker back to get Mama."

"Should we let Carolyn come then?" asked my aunt.

"I don't care if she comes or not. Let's go."

The three of us walked steadily through the light rain past rows of English houses and groves of dark crab apple and plum trees. The clouds broke for a moment and we saw the moon, slipping down like a shiny dime in a slot. We picked our way over scattered shingles and bricks.

"Did you see how that woman back there was behaving?" asked Uncle Jim.

"How do you mean?" Aunt Jo asked.

"Just rude. She didn't even offer Mama a chair or a drink."

"I guess she doesn't like Dutch folks," said my aunt.

"I guess we know that's not it," he said. "Well, it's Davey's problem who he marries, not mine."

"Hush up, Jim. Don't you have any sense?" My aunt sniffed. We passed the neighborhood of Arnie Hagedoorn's unfinished house and I said, "Down there is where the Hagedoorns are building."

Aunt Jo looked curious. She lifted her head and studied the scene. Snarled plywood and jagged pine beams cluttered the streets. Everywhere there were pieces of houses mangled by the storm.

We passed through the Black neighborhoods, at the center of which a large group of people watched a broken power line convulse on the sidewalk. The damage here was great. Giant old trees rested stiffly across the road. An apartment building had lost its roof, someone said, just a block out of our way. We didn't turn off to see. Uncle Jim was anxious to get home. But as we finally reached Church Street, just a half mile from our house, we heard fire trucks. We followed them in the opposite direction, half running. We smelled burning wood. There was a glow in the sky.

"Oh, no," said my aunt. "It must be a big house, or a store. How terrible."

"Lightning," my uncle said. "With this wind, a fire could get going pretty good inside a wood building, even in the rain."

We kept running further into town, and then our steps slowed. We had reached Church Street. Why did it take us so long to see, to believe? We looked at the fire and the sky and we looked carefully down to the ground, as though we were tracing directional lines on a map. How could it be? Was this the meeting of horizontal and vertical, the absolute intersection of God's will and our own? We ran again, toward the fire and the crowd ahead of us, until we had no doubts. A great silhouette bent against the flames. Could that crooked silhouette be the First Reformed Church of Virginia? The beloved building, the house of God? Now we saw her windows like red mouths crying out to us.

"Lord," said my aunt hoarsely.

My uncle was already rolling up his sleeves. He gnashed his teeth as he lumbered away from us, across the church parking lot through a large circle of Dutchmen that surrounded the church like a hedge. On the other side he joined the firemen and deacons. My aunt began to cry.

"You go over and stand with the Ten Kates," she said. "I don't want to be responsible for you right now. Go on, Carolyn."

The Ten Kates stood on the opposite corner of Church Street with a half a dozen other Dutch families. Not even Annajane noticed me as I walked up quickly and turned to watch the fire. Behind Annajane, Mrs. Ten Kate tried to comfort her husband, who sat hunched over in his wheelchair with his face in his hands.

"Can I stand with you?" I asked.

"Doyle," Mrs. Ten Kate said, "Doyle, Carrie Grietkirk is with us now."

"Where is her father?" said Mr. Ten Kate. "Where is he? We can't find the dominie. One of the dominies should be here!"

Annajane stepped up close to me, so close that I thought she would hold my hand. Now and then as lightning glowed heavy in distant clouds you could catch a glimpse of the whole scene. Every Dutch person in town, I thought, and many of the English, had gathered at this place. Some of them stood still and watched silently, but most shifted up and down the street, shouting at each other, pointing, announcing that all was lost. They were red, yellow, blue raincoats, a field of tulips bending and swaying. They were actors at an early rehearsal, crashing through the first wild scenes. They were the children of Israel, roving over the wide, dry desert looking for a lost cloud. They were a universe, trying to reach order from chaos.

Suddenly, I saw my father. "There he is," I said to the Ten Kates, as if it could really help. "There's my father. He's here now, with the dominie."

"You run to your family then," said Mrs. Ten Kate. "That's what you should do, Carolyn."

My father stood in front of old Mrs. Hagedoorn's house a block down. I ran instantly to him and he hugged me and said, "Carolyn, am I ever glad to see you. Oh, this is a terrible thing. Just terrible."

"We got caught in the tornado," I said. "And the car's broken down. We had to walk here from across the bridge."

He squeezed my arms and frowned. "Is your grandma O.K.?"

"She's O.K." I told him how we left Grandma and the others at an English lady's house while we walked back to Dutch Falls. I didn't tell him about Phuong's seizure. He looked relieved. "Praise the Lord they're all right," he said. "I had to leave the car back a ways, the roads were so bad. I'll send somebody after them as soon as the roads are clear. Listen now, Carolyn, you tell them I have to go help over at Lumpkin Street. You tell everybody at home that I'll be back just as soon as I can."

"Can I stay here for a while and watch?" I asked.

"Don't get in anybody's way, Carolyn. Keep with the Ten Kates." He shook the dominie's hand and left quickly.

I turned to go back to the Ten Kates and the dominie said morosely, "Take a last look at our dear church, young lady. Part of it was built by old Janz DeGroot himself. I really thought it would be here when our Lord came back."

369

*I*t would have taken a spectacular miracle to save our church, the kind in which God undoes history like a woman ripping out a crooked seam and joins it again, finely, so that to the eyes of the observer the world looks smooth and pristine, a new garment. But there was no miracle, and midnight struck now on the clock of Mt. Sinai Baptist nearby. Mr. Ten Kate had all but cried himself to sleep. His crushed face was invisible in the folds of his raincoat hood, which Annajane had lifted for him time and again to keep the last light rain from puckering over his bald head. Mrs. Ten Kate, normally the flighty one in the family, stood straight and alert, watching the firemen cut down the last crumbs of fiery plaster and drown them furiously in arcs of white spray. We saw the landscape clearly in the engine floodlights. Nothing remained of our church but two blackened rock walls and a great, gray, ash-filled hole where the once mighty fellowship hall had sprawled underground, steaming with coffee and *oliebollen.*

"I guess it's time we should go," said Mrs. Ten Kate at last. She looked bleakly at the dark sky behind us. Taking hold of the wheelchair, she began to turn her husband.

"No," he said, "I don't want to leave my church."

"You need to rest, Doyle."

"I don't want to leave. I want to stay with her."

"Doyle," said his wife, "do you want the girls and me walking alone in the dark? The streetlights are off. Do you want us to leave you here and walk home alone?"

He shook his head.

"Well, then you'll have to come with us."

She wheeled him around and dropped the chair over the edge of the sidewalk with a thunk. He swung from side to side and steadied himself, moaning. Annajane reached for his hand.

"Wait a minute," I said. "I should tell my aunt and uncle that I'm leaving."

"Hurry, then," said Mrs. Ten Kate. "I want to get Doyle home to bed."

I left them and ran through the crowd to find Uncle Jim, dirty and grim, carting singed hymnbooks to a pile on the sidewalk.

"I'm going home with the Ten Kates," I said. "Is that all right, Uncle Jim?"

He shook his head. "Right now I couldn't care less, Carolyn. Do what you feel is right."

I was afraid to say anything more, but I remembered my father's message. "Well," I said, "I have one more thing to tell you."

"What is it?"

"My father came by."

"Oh, he did?"

"Yes, sir. He came by and said to tell everyone at home that he was going over to Lumpkin Street to help. He'll be back later."

Uncle Jim nodded down at me and wiped his face. His eyes searched out mine now. "Lumpkin Street? He came by to tell you he was going to Lumpkin Street?"

"Yes, sir."

"I guess he told you that the colored people over on Lumpkin Street needed him more than his own church tonight?"

I stammered as I answered. "He didn't say anything like that."

Uncle Jim spit across a pile of ashes. "Oh, you go on home. Make sure someone has fetched your grandma. I don't want her with those English all night."

"Yes, sir."

"Tell your father if you see him that we could have used him here."

"Yes, sir."

The Ten Kates had kept going without me, slowly, and now I caught up with them and we walked together for the last and quietest stretch of my long journey home from the Dela Fox Biddle. A few people, mostly elderly English, stood on their porches and called out sadly to know whether we had seen the fire and whether the church had really burned to the ground. They felt sorry for us, they said. They would pray for us. Most of the Dutch houses sat silent. People were yet to come home from the fire, or else they had lost hope earlier and gone to bed. I noticed little tornado damage here compared to elsewhere, but the Ten Kates hadn't seen the Black neighborhoods or the riverside neighborhoods, and they declared every broken branch in a Dutch driveway a great loss. Mrs. Ten Kate began to cry at last, over an upturned rose bed.

"Didn't you notice that before, Mama?" asked Annajane. "I saw it when we were running to the church."

"I was only thinking about the church then," said Mrs. Ten Kate. "Look at all the gardens, Anna."

"How can you cry over flowers? They'll grow again next year."

"I don't know why I'm crying, Anna. Don't expect me to be reasonable now. Those roses were so tender, they remind me of you." And she began to cry again.

When we came to our street, I looked eagerly at my own house. An upstairs shutter lay on the grass near the porch steps. Thick branches hung from the trees. But I saw no other damage.

"Carolyn," said Mrs. Ten Kate, "you're welcome to spend the night at our house. We don't have electricity, but we have good lanterns. It would be nice for Anna. I'd give you a good breakfast."

"Thank you, Mrs. Ten Kate," I said. "But I want to see my family."

"Are you sure they're home?" Annajane asked. "The house is so dark."

"They may not be home yet," I said. "But I'm sure someone will come soon."

"Don't linger alone in a dark house," said Mrs. Ten Kate. "You can always come back to us if you're alone. It might ease your grandma's mind to think you're with us."

"Yes, ma'am," I said, "but she'll want me home."

Mrs. Ten Kate sighed. "You tell your grandma I'll call first thing in the morning to check on her. You hear?"

"Yes, ma'am."

"This has been a terrible, terrible night. We shall never forget it. I think you girls will remember this night till your dying days, if you remember anything."

"Yes, ma'am," I said.

"Good night, Carolyn."

"Good night."

Mrs. Ten Kate lifted her broad hand into the dark air. She waved and pushed her drooping husband across the street. Annajane lagged behind momentarily.

"Are you all right?" I asked. I could barely see her.

She nodded and looked over her shoulder at her mother. "It was strange tonight, Carrie. I thought I would feel so bad, but I didn't. I wanted to."

"You mean you didn't feel bad about the fire?" I said.

"No, I didn't. Did you? Do you feel bad?"

I shrugged my shoulders. "I don't know. I think I did."

"I guess that's my first confession to you, Carolyn." Annajane hugged her arms and put one foot out to follow her mother.

"I'll call you tomorrow," I said.

"I wonder what they'll do about the school. I'll be over at the high school this year, anyway. But what about you? With the fire, I wonder if you'll have to go to public school this year."

"Maybe so."

"I don't think you'd like public school. I wish I could be there to help, but I'll be over in the high school."

"That's O.K.," I said. "It'll all work out." I decided not to mention anything about Pennsylvania, not now.

She frowned. "Well, I'll see you later, Carolyn."

"Good-bye, Annajane."

I watched her walk into the deep shadows and I felt a surge of love for her. She was, after all, my last, best friend in Dutch Falls. When she had disappeared I climbed the steps of my own porch, found the front door open though I had expected it to be locked, and entered the house quietly. The living room sat black and empty, but I heard soft voices in the kitchen. I went and found Aunt Jo, Nathan, Shirley, and Aunt Betsy sitting around the kitchen table. At the center of the table a small red candle burned, throwing off a disgustingly sweet smell, a leftover Christmas scent. The red light flickered under Aunt Betsy's nose, around the big bones of her eye sockets, and over the gently wrinkled skin on her hands.

"It's just Carolyn," Aunt Jo said.

Aunt Betsy sighed. "I heard her at the door and hoped she was Jim."

"I came home with the Ten Kates," I said. "Uncle Jim stayed behind." I sat down at the table and folded my hands like the others.

"She got to see the fire," said Shirley bitterly. "She's been there all night. Why couldn't we go?" No one answered her. Shirley bent over, with her head on her hands, and let out a long, hard breath.

"Is the fire out yet?" Nathan asked me, more placidly.

"Yes," I said. "There's nothing left."

Aunt Betsy clucked and shook her head.

"Did anyone fetch Grandma?" I asked.

"There's no one to fetch Grandma," said Aunt Jo sadly. "Nobody here has a car. What about your father? Has anyone seen him?"

I gave them the message that I had given Uncle Jim. Aunt Jo glanced up at the clock and put her cheek against her fist.

"Such a night," said Aunt Betsy. "Why don't we send these children to bed. It's almost one thirty."

"I'm not sleepy," said Shirley. "I'm not a child, either."

"I'm sleepy," said Nathan. "Can I go to bed?"

"Please do," said Aunt Jo. "I feel like it myself, but I guess I better wait for Mama."

"I can wait, Jo," said Aunt Betsy. "You all go on and Shirley and I will just wait. We can pray together."

"Never mind," said Shirley. "I'd rather sleep."

"Do you know," said Aunt Betsy, "I'm sure Mother will say that this happened because of the sin in our lives?"

"Oh, please, Betsy." Aunt Jo grimaced. "Don't you say it."

"I'm sorry, Jo, but I believe it's right. I believe it is." Aunt Betsy stared up at us. In the flickering light of the candle, she looked like a stuffed doll. Her fair freckled cheeks crowded out her upper lip and pressed in on her nose. "I know for instance that Jim and I have a lot of unconfessed sin. I guess we've just put off dealing with it, because it's not fun to deal with your sin. But I think I'd like to start tonight by thinking what it is that God might be telling me."

"What are you saying?" asked Aunt Jo. "Are you telling me that God brought a tornado and a fire on all these people just to point out the sins of one little woman?"

"Well, God doesn't reason the way we do."

"I should hope not!" Aunt Jo looked tired and annoyed. She got up from her chair and we followed, all but Aunt Betsy, who waved good night to us and put her head down. Shirley fetched a flashlight from the tool drawer. We passed through the family room and onto the staircase with the smooth yellow light bouncing ahead of us. Aunt Jo and Nathan kept going, toward the basement stairs.

"You won't be able to see anything down there," Shirley called to them. "You want me to go down with you and shine the flashlight around?"

"Good night!" Aunt Jo called back. "We'll find our own way." She disappeared ahead of Nathan into the pitch black, her loose hair swishing back and forth over her shoulders like a curtain. Shirley and I parted at the second floor. I found my way easily in the dark, thanks to the window at the end of the hall and the clearing sky outside. I sat down at last by my own window in my own room, without changing into a nightgown. My clothes were stiff with rain-thinned mud. I intended to stay awake all night and watch for my grandmother and my father to come home. I thought of what Aunt Betsy had said, that it was all our fault, that it was our sin that had caused all of this. Yes, Grandma probably would say such a thing.

And as for me. Who had sinned worse than I had? I had obeyed Ginger rather than God. I had wished for her to commit adultery. I had lied to my grandmother. I had put my cousin in the way of corrupt theatrical people. I had lied to the Holy Spirit, promising to do good things that I was unwilling to do.

I opened my window and the breeze felt cool on my skin. It was a sky-clearing wind. It gusted up and rushed into my eyes and stung them. I sat for a long time, more than an hour, and then I began to feel overcome, like the disciples who slept while Jesus watched and prayed. I put my head against the frame of the window and closed my eyes. It was a long time again before I sat up and wiped my face. I thought I heard movement nearby, papers rattling. The noise came from outside, no doubt from the window next to mine. So Phuong must have come back while I was asleep. Grandma and Vicky would be back, too, then. Maybe my father had gone to get them at last.

Still without changing my clothes, I lay down on my bed. I should be able to sleep now, knowing everyone, or nearly everyone, was home. But it was hard to sleep again. I lay there thinking. Then I heard a knock at the door. It startled me.

"Carolyn?" came a soft voice, muffled by the heavy door. I got up and opened the door slowly, thinking it might be Grandma coming to check on me. Instead I found Phuong standing with the stinking red candle in her hand. She wore a robe that Grandma had given her. She looked at me. At first it was just a blank look, and then her face changed and I saw that she was sad and tired.

"May I come in?" she asked.

I moved aside. "Well, so how did you get home?" I asked casually. "We were all worried about you. I was waiting up."

"The English man have bring us home," she said.

"How is my grandmother?"

"Oh," Phuong moaned, "so terrible, so sad about the church."

I looked through my bedroom door before I closed it, down the shadowy hall at the steps. I should go downstairs to Grandma.

"May I talk to you?" Phuong asked.

I paused for a moment, thinking, and then said, "Yes."

We sat down on my twin beds, facing each other, I with my hands under my thighs.

"I am very worry," she said. "I want to talk to you."

"O.K." I waited for her to start. I could only think that a lecture was coming about my disobedience and lack of respect. It was ultimately my fault that we had been at the theater tonight, that we had all nearly lost our lives. Surely she realized all of that by now.

She settled back on the bed, against the wall, her arms folded. Her feet stuck up in the air, silhouetted against the candlelight like little dark fans. "I don't mind to talk to you," she said, "because you with me on the night I am baptize in the Holy Ghost. Do you remember?"

"Of course."

"I have to tell the story of my first husband that night, that was a Communist. I have tell about the village where we live and the way the people were kill and torture. My husband friends set fire to the village when we go. You remember my story?"

"Yes."

She nodded and breathed. "Do you want to know about your father?"

"My father was there?"

"Yes," she whispered. She watched me for a second.

"What did he have to do with it?"

"Do you want me to tell the story?"

"Yes."

She lowered her eyelids. "One night in the war I was sleeping, and it was the monsoons season. The rains has come down and very hard. So my husband has meeting with these party leaders in the other house. I know they was definitely coming home drunk later, so I stay awake afraid. I hear the dogs outside. When I hear the dogs, I was afraid of a villager might try to running away and be shot. There is always a young man or a young woman who want to run away to go to the American camp, so I was going outside to see the individual and telling him to stay, because it is so danger. Although I was worry, too.

"It was very dark and hard to see. My feet were sinking down in the mud. I yell. Nobody answer at first. And then I have hear a man call in English, 'Can you help us?' At first it scare me so much I have wanted to run away, but the man call, 'Please, for God's sake, help us.' When I have go to see, I seen your father have kneeling over a very wounded man on the ground. I pretended I don't understand the English, but your father have told me how that they have a jeep accident and this man was a driver. Could not walk because his legs was paralyze.

"I did not think I can take them into the village. I know my husband will find them and kill them. For two day I have bring them water and rice and bandages, and after two day the wounded man have die. We have try to bury him at night, but some of the village girls discovers us and runs to tell my husband. I was afraid. I want to run away, but I did not."

"Because of your mother-in-law?" I asked.

She hesitated, and then nodded. "Yes, but also—" She put the candle on my nightstand, then moved up on the bed and put her arms around her bare knees. "—because I have the daughter, and she was only four years old. My little daughter, I don't tell you about her before because you think I bring the bad luck to you like I doing to her. I am afraid if I leave her to my husband, what happen to her, so I have run home to get her, take her with me. Your father not understand, and he have try to come to the house. I mean he have follow me. But my husband is there, and when I see my husband I afraid I say that the Americans is outside trying to get me, to rape me, and my husband run out shooting the gun. I have even tell my husband, 'I kill one American, and now you can kill two Americans.' My husband believes me, and I am not seeing your father again.

"But two week later the soldier have come to clean up the Vietcong in the area. There is a big fire, in which the Communists have start. My husband have die in the fire, and when the village burn I run away with my daughter to the mountain and leave my mother-in-law; God forgives me. Cam Vien and I have go to another small village, where the Catholics can keep out the Vietcong all the time. And I lie about myself of course. If nobody have found I was Vietcong, I could be kill. But my daughter, my poor Cam Vien, she die of dysentery there. See what bad luck I bring her?

"After the war," she said, without changing her expression, "I just want to die. Everybody I love has die. I think I have kill Cam Vien, it my fault, because I bring her to this village where she get the dysentery. But the Catholics have arrange for me to go to refugee camp in Guam. First happy, but it was so bad there. Worse than the Vietcong. I was just wanting to go out of this terrible camp, because the children always stealing and the women have been beating and rape— but at least I have hear about Jesus there from the missionary. Praise Jesus. I afraid to leave the missionary, because of what they do for me.

378

I have not been baptize yet with the Holy Ghost, but I feeled so good about Jesus and about the missionary.

"So then one day, I was surprise. I have seen your father's picture, to preach in the camp! I go to hear him. And hear from a missionary that your father has negotiate with Vietcong to leave my village and five other, to protect the people who still lives there, to protect the good people from being all kill. He almost dies to do this good thing, because he have go himself to meet Vietcong, and they have the Christian. He was capture and torture for five days. But he pray and the Vietcong have change mind to leave the six village."

"Is that how he got his medal?" I asked.

"Yes," she said. "He get medal because he save many life, Vietnamese and American. When I see him again we both have feeled like good friend after all, everything. But I was embarrass to tell him I speak English, so he find that out later, and then we talk and talk. When he was going, I feeled so bad. I was thinking he is my only friend. And nobody ever leave the refugee camp anyway, so I was thinking I never be happy again, I just live in the camp forever.

"A year go by. It a really terrible year for Vietnamese in camps. Some of the people who come to the camps have been beating by pirates on the ocean, or they children kill or drown. Most people have lost somebody. Everybody is angry, even the Christian, because nobody have left the camps even after one year. Food was usually bad, and air so smell because of the bad sanitations. There were people who says it was better in North Vietnamese prisons. And I don't make friend with nobody, because I so scare they can find out I was a Communist and kill me. But one time a woman has recognize me. She can remember my husband, because her nephew has growed up in our village. When she has told the camp directors that I am Vietcong, they have question me for three hour about my husband and myself. And they put me in jail for a month, where it stink, with very bad food to eat, and then no food.

"For the most part I was wanting to kill myself, but I remember that I supposed live for Jesus, like the missionary say. Every day I have pray this prayer, 'Jesus, get me out of this camp; I want to die or go to the United States.' The pastor and the Christian nurse have coming to see me to cheer me up, but one day the pastor have telled me he is going away for a while and a replacement to come. I feel so sad. But he has leave and I can't eat anything because I am sick. But one day the new pastor is coming to see me. And praise God it is my one good friend in Vietnam, Chaplain David! Praise Jesus! When David come, he have visited me every day in jail, sometimes three time a day. I have hear that he tries to get me out, but the directors say, 'No, she a Communist. No, she a spy. We going to send her back to Vietnam.' There was many people talking about that the government would send me to Hanoi to get rid of me. I have had no hope at all because I don't believe in Jesus enough."

Phuong looked down at her knees. "One night your father have come to me and sit in the jail for a long time. He have said there is only one way so I can get out of jail. Is for us to marry with each other, so he can get me out of the camp and bring me to America. I was thinking it's a bad idea, since the marriage usually don't work between Vietnamese and American. American soldier always want to marry in love, and I think he don't really want to marry me. He feel grateful to me, but I don't think he love me. But he say he is going home to the United States soon. When he say that, I just have to pray and pray, because I so afraid. I have ask God what is right, if it selfish to marry with this man. I think he don't love me. Maybe don't love him—then I am afraid of pray anymore, because what God might say to me."

She stopped talking. Her eyes opened wide. She nodded and mouthed silent words and I wondered if she would speak in tongues again, or even have a seizure. I waited and finally realized that I would have to say something.

"But, Phuong," I said, "you married my father. When did you fall in love with him?"

She lifted her face. "I have prayed God will show me what to do, and I open my Bible. And I look and the Bible says, 'Get you up this way southward, and go up into the mountain, and see the land, what it is, and the people that dwelleth therein, whether they be strong or weak, few or many.' So I know God is telling me 'go,' and my heart and the Christian say, 'go.' Praise Jesus, yes. Praise Jesus, Carolyn. Praise the good Lord Jesus. You know, then I can see what God is telling me. I can see for so definitely God tell me to marry him. Not is my will, but God's will. I never have felt the will of God like this. So David marry with me in the jail, and the nurse is our witnesses. And so I have go to him, after some time more in this jail. This is how I go here. I don't know why God bring me here. Maybe because I can serve a good husband and serve a good mother-in-law. But I don't want to ask God why he do this, because I wonder why God let me live at all, except for serving. If I remind God how bad I was, I don't want him to take me away."

She put her hands up. Her arms threw dim shadows across the walls, while the candle trembled on the nightstand. "Praise Jesus," she said. "Oh, praise Jesus. Bantalanava. Tra teckle upharsid, bansha da."

"What does it mean when you speak in tongues?" I said. "What are you saying when you speak in tongues?"

"I see things," she said. "I can see you and me, from heaven. Everything else is dark, but the Holy Spirit like this candle. I feel it light on me. God lifting me up. He telling me to lift my arms and talk for him in angel language."

I closed my eyes and moved my lips, but I wasn't lifted up. The walls of my body closed in; my eyelids were like prison doors.

She said quietly, "I have got something else to tell you."

"What is it?" I opened my eyes and stared around at the corners of the ceiling.

She opened her eyes, too, but she still held her hands in the air. "I am going to give birth to baby."

"Oh," I said. "A baby?" But how was it possible? How could it be true? Grandma had said that Phuong was too old. She had said with a sigh, "At least I don't have that to worry about."

Phuong stood up from the bed and stepped toward me. She put her hand on my shoulder. I didn't push her back, but I leaned away into the wall and pressed my hands together.

"You can keep me a secret about baby," she said.

"Why?" I asked.

"I don't want to tell your grandmother."

"Why not?"

"She don't like the baby. She don't like me too much."

381

"Oh, it just takes her a while," I said uncomfortably. "That's because she's Dutch. She holds in her feelings. Just wait."

"But I telling you about the baby because you and I understand. I didn't think to have more children. I know God have give me this child—he forgive me now for bringing the bad luck to Cam Vien. I know, I know you love your grandmother so much. You too old and disobedient for a Vietnamese mother now anyway. I can be a mother for this child."

I smirked and held my hands tight together.

"But we can be friend in Pennsylvania," she said. "I can be a good friend, or like you aunt. Maybe you call me aunt?"

"I don't think people would understand," I said. "They would wonder about my father living with a Vietnamese woman that I called my aunt."

She frowned. There was another long silence and then she said, "Now I have talk, and I am tired, but I can't go to sleep because I worry about your father."

"Don't worry," I said.

She turned and went to the door. "I leave you this candle," she said, and she nodded at me and slipped into the doorway. "So you don't be scare of dark."

"I won't. I'm not scared of the dark." The door closed softly. I wished I had said more. I could have asked her many questions. After a while I blew out the candle and climbed under the light summer covers of my bed, but I didn't sleep that night. I lay awake listening to heavy voices, footsteps on the porch and the sidewalks, car engines. The whole town was afflicted with insomnia.

21

*B*y morning, the power worked, the phones worked, and Dutch Falls began to repair itself in earnest. It was past ten when I went down to the kitchen. I found Aunt Betsy serving Zachary his breakfast. She kissed me.

"Where is everyone?" I asked.

"Your uncle is sleeping, dear. Aunt Jo took your cousins over to Church Street. They wanted to see the devastation." She pronounced the last word in a whisper, as if it were obscene. "I told them they ought to fill their heads with better sights than that, but so it is."

"I want to see, too," I said. "I'll catch up with them." I thought the church might look different in daylight, as things often did. Maybe there was something left of it after all, maybe a seventh grade classroom.

"Don't go anywhere, Carolyn," said Aunt Betsy, again in a whisper. "When your grandmother wakes up, she'll need you."

"I could go see her now," I said.

"No, Carolyn, not now."

"Well, I could run quick to Church Street and come right back."

My aunt put her hands flat on the table and looked up at me harshly. "Carolyn, you've caused enough problems, you and Victoria. I want you to be here when Grandma wakes up."

"And where's my father?" I asked. "Is he in bed, too?"

"Your father should appear soon. You stick around here until Grandma's awake. She'll need all of us."

"Yes, ma'am." I wanted to see the church. I wanted to go with the others.

When Grandma did emerge, just before lunch, I was the only one to meet her. Aunt Betsy had taken a casserole to a family whose garage had been destroyed in the storm. The others hadn't returned. Grandma looked hazily at me as she passed through the family room and padded down the hall to the bathroom in her slippers. Coming back through, she stared at an open window and pointed out to a hummingbird hovering by the remains of a hanging vine. Then she turned on the television and sat. She did not sit in her rocker or knit. She sat bent over next to me on the couch, her white hair dirty and flat, her face gaunt. She rubbed her hands together, closed her eyes and sucked in air, rubbed her hands together again, put them against her nose, opened her eyes again and shut them again. A game show prattled on. I knew that she was praying silently.

"I'm not really feeling so bad as I look," she said finally, with her eyes open. "I know I look terrible."

"That's all right, Oma," I said. "We've all been worried about you."

"Where is your father, Carolyn? Is he asleep?"

"I don't know. Aunt Betsy just said he would appear soon."

"And where is Aunt Betsy?"

"She took a casserole to someone."

"Where are the others?"

I hesitated. "The others went downtown to look."

"Oh. To look at the church. Yes."

"Are you hungry, Grandma?" I asked. "I could get you something."

"You're a good girl," she said. "You are a real blessing to me, Carolyn, to be with me now. I pray for you every morning and every night, you know. I do pray for you. I pray for all my children."

"I know you do, Oma."

"I pray for your father. I pray for Jim. I pray for Jo. I pray for Betsy. I pray for Shirley and Victoria and little Zachary. I pray for Nathan. I pray for the dominie. I pray for the missionaries, one every day. The list just goes on and on. I have prayed all my life. Prayer means so much to me. It means as much as food and drink. And you know it's only prayer that holds Satan back. Can you imagine how the world would be if we stopped praying?"

"I don't know, Oma."

"Awful. It would be a living hell, and you know that I don't use that word lightly. I just don't like to make a great production of my prayers. I don't go on and on for hours. I pray in my little closet, and I make it brief. The Lord appreciates a brief prayer, I think. He already knows what we have need of before we ask, Carolyn. Before we even ask. He's in command of everything. But he wants us to pray."

"Yes, ma'am."

"He knows what you need. You pray to him, Carolyn. He wants to talk to you."

"Yes, ma'am."

"I don't hear you pray enough."

"No, ma'am."

"Something is wrong in our world. What is it?"

"I don't know. Maybe it's that we don't pray enough."

"Well, I'd like to figure it out. I would."

"Yes, Oma."

Suddenly she let out a little cry. I stared at her, until I was sure she wasn't going to do it again. We sat in silence until we heard soft footsteps on the stairs and Phuong entered the family room cautiously, with her head bowed.

"Carolyn," said Grandma. "You did not tell me that Phuong was here."

"I didn't know she was here, Grandma."

Grandma watched without blinking as Phuong sat down in the recliner, Father's chair, and folded her hands over her stomach.

"How are you feeling this morning?" asked Grandma. "Have you recovered from our ordeal?"

Phuong said meekly, "Fine, thank you. How are you?"

"I'm not fine," said Grandma. "I think I would feel better if I got busy. That always helps me. Does it help you?"

"I can make you cup of coffee," said Phuong.

"You don't have to go to trouble just for me," said Grandma. "I should do it myself. I should do my own fetching. Why don't you do something for your husband? Go wake him up and tell him to come to his mother."

Phuong looked ashamed. "He has not come home last night."

The clock ticked on the wall. Grandma looked up at it and raised her eyebrows. "You might bring me that cup of coffee, then. Someone. Either of you. It could be Carolyn."

Phuong nodded and went into the kitchen.

Grandma looked at me and her face tightened. "I'm sorry for the way I've treated her," she said. "I know I'm a hard woman sometimes. I feel I can hardly help it, and I know how she must despise me for it."

"She likes you," I said.

"Do you know that?"

"Yes. She bought you that beautiful dish, Grandma. She wanted to replace the one she broke."

"Phuong bought that dish? Oh my." She was quiet for a moment. "Well, I have good intentions, Carolyn, half the time. I'm under conviction. You don't know the terrible feelings that overcome me. Carolyn—our church!" She began to moan. She leaned down almost into my lap.

"Grandma," I said, "do you want me to read to you from the Bible?"

"Oh, yes, Carolyn, please. Read Grandpa's favorite passage, from Revelation."

"That passage? Are you sure?"

"Of course."

I took a Bible from a bookshelf and began to read to her the terrible prophecies for the seven churches, although I didn't think it was a good idea. I saw her face crease with anguish when we came to the prophecy for the church at Thyatira, the church that had good works, faith, and patience to its credit, but that tolerated the fornication of a woman called Jezebel. Was Grandma thinking of Ginger? Did she realize that God had brought down the church because of my sin? Before I finished reading, the phone rang. "That may be your father," Grandma said, and she hurried stiffly to answer it herself in the kitchen.

"Good morning to you, Sadie. Thank you, yes, I'm feeling all right. How is Doyle?"

While Grandma talked, Phuong brought her the coffee and slipped out to the front porch quietly. I got up and followed. She sat on the

386

porch swing, I on the bench, and we were quiet, listening to the buzz of a chainsaw. What was there to say? We looked out at the library, which had come through the storm just fine, and I wondered where Arnie Hagedoorn was at this very moment. I wondered where Ginger was. I wanted to call her, just to make sure she was O.K. After last night, how could I speak to her again?

"Oh, Carolyn, your father is coming home," said Phuong smiling, looking out into the sunlight. I looked and sure enough he was far down the street, about a hundred yards away, walking in a jaunty way. His shirttail hung out. Phuong stood up and waved. He waved back. I said to Phuong, "I'll go tell Grandma he's home."

"O.K.," she said happily.

I went back inside but stopped to watch my father through the bay window. As he landed on our walkway, as he climbed the short steps of the porch, he smiled and pushed his hair behind his ears. Under one arm he carried a lumpy paper bag, like a sack lunch.

"Hello," he said to Phuong, and kissed her lightly on the cheek. "I'm dirty."

"Grandma," I said loudly. "Grandma, Father's home!"

"Oh, praise the Lord," Grandma said from the other room. "Praise the Lord. Sadie, I have to go; my son just walked in. Yes, I'll tell him. And you take a rest, Sadie. Let Annajane run the bakery; she's a good girl." The phone clattered down and there was a long pause. "Well, where is he, Carrie? I thought you said he was coming."

"He's on the porch."

"Waiting on the porch? Why doesn't he come in? Does he expect me to come out?"

"He's talking to Phuong."

"Well, I guess he does expect me to come out then." Grandma pushed through the swinging door from the kitchen and hurried by me, breathing hard. She stepped out to the porch and I followed her.

"Well, there you are," said Grandma.

"Mama," Father said. He had sat down by his wife. Now he stood up to hug Grandma gingerly. "I'm dirty, Mama. I'm real dirty; be careful."

"It's all right." Grandma hugged him tight. "I knew I couldn't feel right until you were back at home."

"Here," he said, and handed her the paper bag. "Peaches."

"From a colored woman? Are you tired, Davey? You look just exhausted."

"So do you."

"Yes, I'm tired." Grandma sat down across from him. "Will you tell me what you've been doing all night?"

He sat back and stretched. "A little bit of just everything."

"Have you been over there this morning?" she said slowly. Of course she was talking about the church. "Have you seen it, Davey?"

He shook his head and stared down. "I don't even want to go look."

"Jim won't let me go over there."

"And well he shouldn't," said Father. "You don't need to be seeing that. Jim's right." His shoulders rose slightly, and fell. He sighed.

"Oh, tell us a joke," Grandma said. "Why don't you say something funny to make us laugh?"

"I'm a bit tired." He lifted up on his weary legs and bent down to kiss all of us—first Phuong, then my grandmother, and last of all me. He kissed me warmly on the cheek and put his dirty hand on the nape of my neck to pull me up close for a hug against his face. All I could think of then was my father visiting Phuong in the jail at the refugee camp, coming to see her every day. I imagined him sitting on some hard chair or dirt floor, thinking how to get her home, worrying what my grandmother would say or do.

"You are a good man," said Grandma. "I'm proud of you."

"I'm proud of you, too," he said. When he went inside, the mail truck appeared at the curb and the postman hopped out in his blue-gray shorts and navy kneesocks. He was a quiet man with fat knees. On any other day we would just have said "Hello" and grabbed the bundle of bills and letters from him with a wave. But today he seemed a prince among men, just for making it on time amid the clutter on the streets. Grandma nearly hugged him.

"We've just been talking about the terrible fire at our church," she said. "I haven't seen the building yet, Mr. Jenkins. Have you?"

"The Presbyterian church, was it? Yes, ma'am."

"The First Reformed Church of Virginia," Grandma said proudly. "I was married there, and so were my parents. It's all I can think about. My son won't let me go over there. Is it really that terrible?"

"Oh, it was a bad fire, Mrs. Grietkirk."

"Burned right to the ground, is it?"

"Yes, ma'am."

"That's what they say. My older son is very upset about it. I've hardly seen him so upset in my life. I won't rest till I get over there."

"No, ma'am." Mr. Jenkins handed a stack of mail to Grandma and then said, "And here's a letter for the little girl." He smiled and bowed as he passed me a small envelope.

"Thank you," I said. I glanced at the envelope quickly and pressed it down in my lap with my hands over it. It was from Ginger.

"What's that, Carrie?" said Grandma, as Mr. Jenkins walked back to his truck. "Who's it from?"

"I don't know."

"Then open it."

I opened it carefully, in such a way as to prevent her from seeing the return address on the envelope or the signature at the end of the page-long letter. And I read rapidly,

Dear Carrie,

I just read your note. Heavy stuff. I have about a million things to say to you, but no time to say them all. Guess I hafta think what's most important for you to hear. You are twelve years old. I have truly never met a twelve-year-old like you. You are smart, and savvy. You see right through me so much that I'm kinda scared to tell you what's on my heart. Hafta to make sure it's the truth. Most of all, I don't want to hurt you, cause you're someone very, very special to me. You are the daughter I never had, the friend I always wanted when I was your age, when I needed someone to confide in, a shoulder to lean on.

I just thank you, kiddo, for all those wonderful things you say about me. As you know, acting is my forte and not writing. I hate writing letters, so know you are special because of this. Kiddo, you will be part of my memory for the rest of my life. Like I said, you are the daughter I never had. My very best friend when I needed a friend so very

389

badly. You are so young, and just as there are places you will go where I can't come (like boys and dating, parties, dances) there are places I must go where you just can't come, either. I am a grown woman and my life is more complex than you can imagine. Frank and I are not perfect, like your family. We make many mistakes on the incredible journey of life. God knows I have hurt him and I am still hurting him, but I have to find my own way of being happy. And I want him to do the same, even if that means taking a road that I cannot travel with him. Maybe someday we'll be together again. That would be great, because in a crazy way I still love him. But we're some of those people who are better apart. Maybe if I am lucky you will keep acting and we can do some more shows together. There are many things I wish for you. Most of all I wish a lot of love for you. I know I have hurt you, but I wish you the best. No matter what I do, be sure you always know that I love you like my own baby girl. Yule always be special.

Luv ya lots,
Ginger

The postmark was two days old. She must have mailed it right after she got my note. I held the letter in my hands, just staring at it, until Grandma said, "Well, what is it? It must be good."

"I don't really want to talk about it," I said. "Excuse me; I have to go upstairs. I have to go to the bathroom."

I went inside and up the stairs to my room. I sat down immediately at my desk to write my reply. I took a pen in my hand quickly, but then I wrote nothing. Nothing. I had already told her everything! And still I felt that I had to say something else. I would never speak to Ginger like this again, as a child, as a best friend of hers. How could the half of me that worshiped her ever be united with the other half? How could I be a Dutch girl and also Ginger's girl? I couldn't. I could not be both, because the two halves were opposites. They could only meet like warm air and cool air, forever stirring up storms. So there was a choice to be made, and I felt the choice before me this day more than ever before. What would I choose? I would choose to be Dutch, a child of the First Reformed Church of Virginia, a daughter of a dominie. I would declare myself. I would force the terrible words out, only half believing them. I would choose against my friend.

390

Dear Ginger,

I don't know where you are right now or what you are doing. I have been praying about you since last night that God would take care of you. That was an awful storm. We were nearly killed and could not get back to Dutch Falls until late. Then our church burned down (as you may have heard). That church meant a lot to us. We will never be the same.

First of all, I am very happy that you say I am like a daughter to you. You are the greatest person I have ever known and I will never forget our times together, though they can never be quite the same again, since I cannot be in the theater, though I really want to be. Even if my family would let me, we will be moving to Pennsylvania soon and it will be impossible. I will miss you more than you can ever know. I am sorry that I doubted your love for me.

I know you will say I am in love with Frank when I say what I am about to say, but I am not. I do love him, as a Christian. He is handsome, too, but he will always be your husband in God's eyes. I am sorry but I truly believe that. I just hope you will not ruin your soul by what you are doing. Once you told me that you are really a Christian. I have often wondered who really became a Christian first, you or Frank. My guess is it was you, because you always do things first. You have helped many people because of your testimony.

Are you still a Christian? Then please don't marry Mr. Hagedoorn, because that is simply going against God's will in every way. I have been thinking a lot about Mr. Hagedoorn. I think that God may have punished our church because I told you to fall in love with him. I know I don't always follow God's will myself, but I know that you will be very unhappy if you do not follow it, because someday he will definitely make you follow it.

My aunt thinks that God sent the storm to punish us. I don't know if my sins have been punished, but at least I know that I should not have told you to fall in love with Mr. Hagedoorn. I will always pray for you. I guess I'm more serious now because after the storm I feel just grateful to be alive. You don't have to answer this unless you really want to.

Love,
Carla

I went downstairs with the letter in my pocket. I didn't want to put it in the mail, since this was Saturday and my letter would only sit for a whole day at the post office and then, who knew what would happen? Who knew if Ginger would leave Dutch Falls forever before Monday arrived? I wanted her to see the letter soon, read it, and know the worst about me. I decided to take it to her house myself, leave it in the door, and run away. At least I could see the house, maybe even her car, one last time. I thought I would ask Annajane to walk with me. It was a long walk. Even without stopping for lunch, we might not be back till supper.

"Grandma," I said, finding her and Phuong still talking on the porch, "I want to walk to Ginger's house to deliver this." Finally I could be truthful. I held up my letter in its envelope.

She looked sadly at me and considered. "There may still be hazards on the roads, Carolyn. Why don't you just run and catch the mailman?"

"But I want her to get it today. I don't want to waste any time."

"I just don't want you walking over there alone."

"Grandma, I've got to go. I've really got to go today. Please."

"Carolyn," she said soberly, "sit down."

I sat down across from her.

"I can't allow you to spend any more time at or near that woman's house," she said slowly. "You understand that, surely, after everything that has happened. You have to let this friendship go. Mrs. Jordan is a worldly woman, trapped in the web of the world."

"But Grandma," I said softly, "this doesn't have anything to do with Mr. Hagedoorn."

"Don't even mention that name to me. I want to strike last evening from my memory."

"This is a good-bye letter for Ginger, that's all."

"She already told you good-bye in her own way last night. There's no more to be said."

"Grandma, I have more to say. Please, this is a letter I have to send. God wants me to send it."

She smiled and shook her head. I stood up and moved back inside. I let the door slam shut behind me.

"Oh, me," I heard Grandma saying.

Phuong said, "She love Mrs. Jordan like a mother."

"Like a mother. If you could only have known her poor mother."

My mouth was dry. I poured myself a glass of water and went and sat down on the rocker in front of the television. "Dear God," I said, "let me go to Ginger's one last time. I only want to be your witness. I want to tell her not to sin anymore, before it's too late. Please." Soon I fell asleep with my head against a soft pillow on the rocker. God gave me no dream. I dreamed of nothing in particular. When I woke up, my neck was stiff, my ear was hot. I opened my eyes and turned to find my father sitting on the couch in his bathrobe, holding a sheet of white paper in his hands.

"Oh, I'm sorry," he said guiltily. "I didn't mean to be reading this, Carrie. It was lying on the kitchen table and I thought it was for me or Grandma." He held it out to me. I was mortified. I leaned forward and snatched it away from him, ripped it to shreds, and ran to throw it in the trash. He followed me.

"Don't throw it away," he said. "I think it's a very nice letter."

"Nobody was supposed to read that," I said. "Don't say anything to me about it. I can't stand to think that you read it. It makes me sick. Don't you ever say anything about it!"

"I thought it was very nice," he said, gesturing at the trash can, where it lay in curls like a pile of apple peelings. "You showed a lot of concern for your friend. A lot of Christian concern."

"I don't feel like much of a Christian," I said, my eyes down. "I feel stupid. She'll hate me."

"No, Carrie," he said, and he held his hand out again and I shied away. "Don't be embarrassed. There's nothing for you to be embarrassed about."

"I bet you think I should never see Ginger again," I said. "You think she's a bad woman."

Father just stared at me, half smiling. "I think we should pray for her. God has his eye on her, Carrie, and he's going to bring her down hard one day. Nobody can resist God forever."

"People are always saying things like that." In my heart I thought that if anyone had the will to resist God, it was Ginger. But I wasn't sure. "Can I take my letter to her today?"

"It's in the trash, Carolyn."

"I could write it over. I could still take it."

"That might be pretty hard, considering everything. Considering Arnie and all. Carolyn, you don't know how her husband might be feeling right now. Think of him. What if you ran into him? What would you say?"

It was the first time I had really thought about Frank, though I had mentioned him in the letter. I didn't know what I would say to him, but that didn't change my mind. I wanted to take my letter to Ginger. "Can I take it to her?" I said. "Can I walk over with Annajane? I just want her to see it right away."

Father hugged me. When I was pressed against him, the white terrycloth of his robe smelled like a bandage. "I guess I could jog it over for you," he said. "You think for a while and decide if that's what you really want."

I thought for a second and said, "All right, that would be O.K."

"It'll take me a while to get over there and get back. You'll have to care for your grandma."

"O.K., I can do that. Can I go now?"

"I love you, Carolyn."

"O.K. Please let me go now."

Father let me go. I sat down and quickly copied the letter again at the kitchen table while he made himself a sandwich. He put the letter in his pocket and went upstairs to dress. A little while later he took off down the street with a promise to Grandma that he would be back late that afternoon. Although he didn't mention what he was going to do, it didn't seem to matter. Grandma trusted him. Anything my father chose to do was all right with her. And when he did come back a few hours later, he only smiled and nodded to me. I didn't ask him any questions, either.

That night Grandma sat in her chair in front of the T.V. and rocked and talked mournfully about the church. Aunt Betsy joined in. Uncle Jim stared ahead and said nothing, even when a team of Clydesdales clopped across the T.V. screen and disappeared behind a big bottle of

Budweiser. Nathan did a crossword puzzle. On the floor lay Shirley and Victoria, looking miserable and bored. Vicky already knew that Walter Pinkney had been called back to replace her in the musical. Shirley sighed and slept for a while and at last sneaked away upstairs, possibly to call Billy De Ruiter for the last time, since the station wagon had been fixed during the afternoon and she would be swept back to Charlottesville after church the next day.

For more than an hour, Aunt Jo read silently in the La-Z-Boy with her big bare feet up in the air, splayed north and south. Now and then, Father teased her and she threw back impatient answers—"Leave me alone, Davey; I'm not in the mood tonight . . . just like a man. . . . What makes you so cheerful . . . can't you see I'm reading?" Then, as Grandma and Uncle Jim talked about the church, Father said seriously, "Maybe when we rebuild the church we should change our game plan."

"How's that?" asked Aunt Jo.

"Well, instead of building another Dutch church for Dutch people, maybe we should build a church, just a plain old church, and make it a place where everybody's welcome. Even Yankees." He punched Aunt Jo in the foot.

"Are you joking now or serious, David?" asked Grandma.

"Well, I'm mostly serious. We could have Black and White folks, Baptists and Presbyterians, everybody who wants to come."

"Nobody would come to a church like that," said Uncle Jim. "People look for a church that offers important distinctives. There's nothing wrong with distinctives." He coughed.

"No, Davey's right," Grandma said. "I think we need a more evangelistic focus in the new church. I'm always telling them over there that we need to bring in the unchurched. Let's start with those English folks by the river."

Phuong sat at Grandma's feet, nodding, ready in the next minute to wind yarn or fetch coffee or warm milk. She looked tired. Knowing everything I knew about Phuong—about the terrible years in which she had endured hunger, beatings, rape, confinement, and even the death of her child, all to come and sit and wind a skein of peacock blue yarn threaded with gold—how could I think that I had anything to fear or anything to regret? I went to sleep that night imagining her in faraway places, staging the tragedies of her life in the theater of my mind.

The next morning was Sunday, and the all-important news came down to us through the women's telephone prayer chain: We would worship with the Baptists. I was thrilled. I practiced singing the Baptist hymns that Grandma had taught me—"In the Garden," "The Old Rugged Cross," "Jesus Saves."

"What have you got to be so happy about?" asked Shirley.

"I don't know," I said, smiling. "Maybe it's because you all are going home."

An hour later, I sat by my father at Mt. Sinai Baptist Church and watched a preacher push a girl under water behind the choir loft.

"I wish I could have been baptized that way," I whispered to Father.

"You were just a baby," he said. "You would have been drowned."

I thought, "Maybe in Pennsylvania—maybe in Pennsylvania I could become a Baptist, or a Pentecostal, or anything I want to be."

But we never did go to Pennsylvania. I spent the rest of my childhood in Dutch Falls, peacefully, in a church built upon the ashes of the old and pastored by my own father. Dominie Grunstra decided that he was too tired and infirm to undertake the construction of a new church, and so he retired, at last providing my father with his call. The new church was full of the old faces, but Father preached about bringing in the Black folks and the English folks, and one Sunday we had a river baptism for some of the previously unchurched, five young English women who wanted to be immersed rather than sprinkled.

I did not see Ginger or Arnie Hagedoorn again, except four years later as I lingered with Grandma and Aunt Betsy at the white marble gravestone of old Mrs. Hagedoorn—and then there was a wide lawn between Ginger and me, not to mention Nancy Talsma Hagedoorn who stood at the center of things with her son, Arnie Jack. I was afraid to seek them out, and so I let them go. But Ginger was still beautiful, and the sky was brilliant green through my sunglasses. I remembered everything.

Aunt Jo and Nathan came to live with us. Aunt Jo attended church, joined the choir, and became a good friend of Mr. Bob Ferring, trading quiet jokes with him after services in the organ room. Sometimes she wept at prayer meeting—was it because she loved Mr. Ferring? If so, it came to nothing, for eventually he moved away, to live with his own elderly parents up North. Grandma always said that all Aunt Jo needed was the right man. She would find him yet.

And so life proceeded. Annajane had her call to the mission field. I had only the haze of my own personality, the jigsaw of my faith and my questions. I wanted to be a whole Christian. I wanted to be true to God and true to my family, but other desires called me in every direction. I loved myself more than I loved God. I lied and sinned, and after I confessed my sin, I lied and sinned again. Was I one of the elect? Would God continue to reach down and snatch me out of my own wickedness?

It would always be hard to understand God's ways, or even believe in his love, until I dwelt again on the life of Phuong. I thought of her faith. I thought of my father, who had redeemed her from prison, whose love for her seemed to grow all the time. I saw my younger sister as a jewel even in my grandmother's eyes. And then the love of God swept over me, and with a breath of wind I was lifted up for a glance at the entire map of life laid out on the ground before me, the good roads that often merged with the bad, the anguished narrow streets that ultimately bent off toward bridges that brought us at last to heaven. Then I opened my mouth, and I almost spoke in tongues. But the words didn't come, so I sang a hymn instead.

> The love of God is greater far
> Than tongue or pen can ever tell,
> It goes beyond the highest star
> And reaches to the lowest hell.
> The guilty pair bowed down with care
> God gave his Son to win.
> His erring child he reconciled
> And pardoned from his sin.
>
> Oh love of God, how rich and pure!
> How measureless and strong!

It shall forevermore endure—
The saints' and angels' song.

When years of time shall pass away
And earthly thrones and kingdoms fall,
When men who here refuse to pray
On rocks and hills and mountains call,
God's love so sure shall still endure
All measureless and strong,
Redeeming grace to Adam's race—
The saints' and angels' song.

Oh love of God, how rich and pure!
How measureless and strong!
It shall forevermore endure—
The saints' and angels' song.

DATE DUE

JUN 16 2004			